D0954094

NAUTILUS

VONDA N. MCINTYRE

BANTAM BOOKS

NEW YORK   TORONTO
LONDON   SYDNEY   AUCKLAND

NAUTILUS
A Bantam Spectra Book / October 1994

SPECTRA *and the portrayal of a boxed "s" are trademarks of Bantam Books,
a division of Bantam Doubleday Dell Publishing Group, Inc.*

ISBN 0-553-56026-3

Published simultaneously in the United States and Canada

*Bantam Books are published by Bantam Books, a division of Bantam
Doubleday Dell Publishing Group, Inc. Its trademark, consisting
of the words "Bantam Books" and the portrayal of a rooster, is Registered
in U.S. Patent and Trademark Office and in other countries. Marca
Registrada. Bantam Books, 1540 Broadway, New York, New York 10036.*

PRINTED IN THE UNITED STATES OF AMERICA

RAD 0 9 8 7 6 5 4 3 2 1

TO THE GWNN

ACKNOWLEDGMENTS

Many thanks to:

John Chalmers
Suzy McKee Charnas
Howard L. Davidson
Jane E. Hawkins
Andy Hooper
Nancy Horn
T. Jackson King
Ursula K. Le Guin
Debbie Notkin
Kate Schaefer
Carol Severance
Janna Silverstein
Amy Thomson

And to:

Gerard K. O'Neill and the
Space Studies Institute, for
the work on which
Starfarer's campus is based.

One

J.D. Sauvage, the alien contact specialist, waited all alone in the airlock of the *Chi*.

Outside the airlock, the pressure crept upward from zero.

J.D.'s heart pounded. Her metabolic enhancer quivered on the edge of activity. Through J.D.'s link to the *Chi*, the other members of the alien contact department sent their reassurance: Victoria, cool and intense; Satoshi, reserved; Stephen Thomas, excited and uneasy. Zev, the diver, J.D.'s lover, spoke a buoyant word in true speech through her link.

Europa and Androgeos observed in silence. The composure of the alien humans was tinged with amusement.

The air pressure outside the hatch nearly matched the pressure in the lock.

J.D. took a deep breath, calmed the metabolic enhancer, calmed her heartbeat.

This isn't the time for a fight-or-flight response, she said to herself. After all, this isn't the first time I've met an alien being. Nemo was the first.

Sadness touched her. Her friend Nemo, the squid-moth, had died, leaving her the starship *Nautilus*.

This encounter was completely different from her meetings with Nemo.

1

It *is* a first time, J.D. thought. Every new encounter will always be a first time.

She brushed her fingertips across her hair.

You'd need a lot more than a finger-comb to be glamorous, especially in free-fall, she said to herself in a wry tone. Isn't it strange, all the time I've spent thinking about how to meet an alien being, I never thought about how I should look or how I should dress.

She was wearing regular canvas pants from *Starfarer*'s stores, a pair of soft-soled shoes, and a blue cotton shirt. Her fair skin was free of make-up, her blue-gray eyes their natural color. She had done nothing to her short straight brown hair but comb it—she had never found much of anything that she could do with it without going through a lot of fuss.

The pressure equalized.

The *Chi* opened its hatch.

A cool, earthy scent wafted into the airlock from the connecting corridor of the Four Worlds ship. J.D. breathed deep, parting her lips, letting the damp and vital air flow over her tongue. The alien tang excited her. The back of her neck prickled.

Shadows moved in the darkness; the tunnel rippled between the two spacecraft. Light gleamed in the distance. It rolled toward her like a slow storm, carrying a sound of gentle thunder.

J.D. pushed off into the passageway. The tunnel around her began to glow. A cylinder of light surrounded her and moved with her.

Several recording devices, little tiny machines from the *Chi*, followed her into the tunnel. She scooped up one of the little tiny machines and let it cling to her shirt. The LTM would transmit her experiences back to the *Chi*, and through the *Chi* to *Starfarer*. All her colleagues could watch and listen.

The central darkness shrank swiftly.

Accompanied by light, a mass of multicolored, multilimbed fur floated toward her.

J.D. touched the warm, wrinkled tunnel wall and frictioned herself to a stop. The tunnel's light shone between her fingers, outlining her fair skin in pink.

The multicolored mass separated and resolved into four individuals.

Each of the beings had fur of a different color. One was silky black, with black-on-black longitudinal stripes visible only at certain angles. One was Appaloosa-spotted, orange on rust-red. Another was particolored, a riot of hot fluorescent pink, chartreuse, yellow. The fourth, the upside-down one, had longer, cotton-candy fur of a soft mauve, but its lower legs and the end of its tail and the beard of fur on its chin were all cream-colored.

They made J.D. want to smile—they made her want to laugh with joy. But she kept her expression neutral. Collapsing in ecstasy would give a poor impression of her to the mainstream of Civilization.

The representatives' voices filled the passageway with a low, trilling hum. J.D. wished circumstances had allowed her the time, the opportunity, to study their language.

The alien people arched their necks. Their small round ears lifted and swiveled toward her. Their faces were long and pointed, like an otter's, angling sharply up to wide brows over large, limpid eyes.

Like humans, the representatives were bilaterally symmetrical. They had long, graceful, muscular bodies, powerful, sinuous necks, long-faced heads, long mobile tails.

Prehensile, J.D. thought, or almost. Pushing off from the wall, J.D. moved forward again.

The representatives were as large as lions, as lithe as otters.

Each being had six limbs. In zero g, the beings flowed along the tunnel, using all six hands and feet to guide and propel them. The mauve one even used its tail: A serpentine movement touched the tail-tip against one side of the corridor, then the other.

The beings came toward her, each at a different orientation, the mauve one—the one who used its tail—upside down, from J.D.'s point of view. They traveled as if they were enjoying themselves, not only because of the free-fall, not only because of the excitement of meeting an alien, but because they were altogether delighted, and delightful.

Silver threads lay in graceful arcs along the lines of the alien people's bodies. Small polished stones and beads, vials and shells, bells and rattles, braided and tied in patterns into the beings' fur, swung and clicked and rang.

The illumination that moved with J.D. and the illumination that paced the alien people touched and melded.

The representatives' similarities to earthly creatures struck her as far stranger than the differences. She would have to remind herself, continually, that these were alien people. She would have to be even more careful than with Nemo about the assumptions that she made.

"Hello," J.D. said softly.

"Hello," said the mauve being.

J.D. opened her hands and held them before her.

"I represent the starship *Starfarer*, from Earth, and all the people on board. My name is J.D. Sauvage." Her voice was trembling.

The mauve being arched its neck gracefully forward. Fur rippled across its neck and shoulders and chest.

"I help represent the Four Worlds," it said. "I am Quickercatcher. Welcome."

"Thank you."

Quickercatcher moved nearer. J.D. caught its scent, a fragrance of raspberry and citron. It reached toward her, open-handed, with its middle limbs.

J.D. suppressed surprise. Quickercatcher's arms, rather than being the first set of limbs, were the second. Projecting from a second set of shoulder blades, halfway down the back, Quickercatcher's arms reached past the front shoulders, dexterous and rather longer than the front legs and the hind legs.

J.D. placed her palms against Quickercatcher's hands. Quickercatcher's two opposable thumbs gently clasped her wrists. J.D. tried to replicate the gesture, first using a normal grasp, then, when that felt awkward, by using her thumb and her little finger as Quickercatcher used two thumbs.

"I feel your vitality," Quickercatcher said.

"And I feel yours." A vibrating rush surged against J.D.'s fingertips. "And . . . my hands are shaking. Human beings sometimes tremble when they're excited and elated."

Quickercatcher spoke, a low trill that dropped in pitch, and relaxed the grip on J.D.'s wrists.

J.D. drew her hands back. "What did you say?" she asked.

"I said . . ." Quickercatcher's mauve fur caught the light, turning silver-gray and rose, as the being raised its chin then ducked its head, and repeated the trill. The silver strands glistened. "It is not a word, but a sound of understanding."

J.D. tried to replicate it. To her ears, the noise she made sounded similar.

All four beings gazed at her with increased intensity, their small round ears aimed stiffly forward.

"I hope . . . I didn't say something offensive," J.D. said.

"You were understandable." Quickercatcher's purple eyes opened wide, then closed, the lids shutting in a wave from outside to inside. The lower lids and the upper lids each covered half the eye. Then Quickercatcher was looking at her again. "But you spoke with a very heavy accent."

"Our brother will introduce us," the black-on-black being said in a soft, low-pitched voice.

Quickercatcher touched his chin to the back of the

head of his black-furred companion and stroked down to the first shoulder blades.

"This is our sister Longestlooker," Quickercatcher said.

Longestlooker was lithe, muscular, powerful. Her sinewy arms stretched forward. J.D. took her hands. Longestlooker's grip was far stronger and tighter than Quickercatcher's. Longestlooker extended sharp claws that dimpled J.D.'s skin. When Quickercatcher touched her, she had not even realized the beings possessed claws.

She gripped Longestlooker firmly but gently, neither retaliating against the strength nor trying to match it. She kept her expression calm. She gazed, straightforward, into Longestlooker's silver eyes.

"Welcome," Longestlooker said. She blinked slowly, from outside to inside corner, the same way Quickercatcher had.

"Thank you."

"You have a starship of the other ones," Longestlooker said.

"Yes. It was a gift."

J.D. would have told them the story of Nemo, and *Nautilus*, if they had asked, but they did not. Better to say too little than too much, J.D. had decided long ago.

"This is our brother Fasterdigger," Quickercatcher said, touching the Appaloosa-spotted being with the same chin-stroke as before.

Fasterdigger, the burliest of the four, unclasped his hands; they had been folded, fingers interlaced, on top of his back. J.D. steeled herself for the grip, but Fasterdigger's touch was as gentle as a caress, as soft as his honey-gold eyes. J.D. noticed more about the beings' hands: hairless palms, skin the color of the predominant fur, the fur narrowing to delicate tracings along the backs of the fingers.

"Welcome," Fasterdigger said, giving the L a sharp, high trill.

"Thank you."

"And this is our sister Sharphearer," Quickercatcher said, stroking the back of the particolored being's neck. Sharphearer quickly nuzzled Quickercatcher's throat, and turned to J.D.

Sharphearer was delicate and sharp-boned beneath her raucous fur. She placed her frail hands in J.D.'s palms. She had blue eyes, not sapphire-blue like Stephen Thomas, nor gray-blue like J.D., but a clear pure robin's-egg blue, very calm and quiet.

"We will be friends," Sharphearer said.

"I hope so," J.D. said. "That's my sincere wish."

Sharphearer trilled and hummed. "I just said 'hello and welcome,' " she said.

J.D. tried to mimic the sound. The quartet nudged each other and blinked their eyes.

J.D. laughed. "I'm grateful to you for learning one of our languages."

"It would have been difficult for you to learn a language of ours," Quickercatcher said, "since you didn't know we existed."

J.D. smiled. "That's true. During the plans for the deep space expedition, one of the biggest questions was how to communicate, if—when—we met other people."

Quickercatcher made a graceful movement of his head and neck, a shrug and ripple, a figure-eight tracing of his chin.

"Yes, that's often hard," he said. "Sometimes we have to build machines to translate."

"I would have difficulties with a person who spoke by taste," Sharphearer said.

"So would I." J.D. provisionally assigned the figure-eight gesture as one of agreement. She wondered if she could do it herself; she could approximate it, but she would need six or eight more vertebrae to replicate it without a heavy accent.

The quartet all spoke excellent English, as Europa

VONDA N. MCINTYRE

did, idiomatically, with a slight, stiff old-fashionedness.
Though English had not even existed when Civilization
rescued Europa and Androgeos from the destruction of
Crete, the Minoans had observed Earth, from a distance,
for a very long time. But they had retreated to Civilization during the past fifty years, when Earth's technology
might detect them.

"What should I call you?" J.D. asked.

"You may use our names," Quickercatcher said.

"Some people in Civilization use honorifics," Longestlooker added, hard on the heels of Quickercatcher's
words.

"But we don't bother," Sharphearer said.

"I mean—a collective name. What do you call your
species? For instance, I'm a human being. All the people
on board *Starfarer* are human beings." More or less, she
thought, but did not try to complicate things by explaining further.

"We call ourselves . . ." Quickercatcher spoke a hum-
ming moan.

The sound made J.D. shiver. She tried to repeat it.

Quickercatcher and the others reacted with the slow
close of eyes from outer to inner edge.

Amusement, J.D. thought.

"Not too good, huh?"

"Not too bad."

"I appreciate your graciousness," J.D. said. "Does the
word for your people translate into English? Or should
I think of you as 'Citizens of the Four Worlds'?"

"It means . . . 'people,' " Quickercatcher said.

"You will find, in Civilization," Longestlooker said,
"that the word most people use to name themselves is . . .
'people.' "

"Which of you is from which world?" J.D. asked.

"We aren't from all the Four Worlds," Quickercatcher
said. "Only from one."

"Oh," J.D. said, taken aback. "When you said you were

the representatives, I thought you meant one from each world."

They suddenly grabbed each other and clung together, rolling over and around in a riot of color, chattering in quick singing tones. J.D. watched them, bemused, but also wishing she were in the midst of the pack. When finally they separated, they all spoke in quick succession.

"We're all from one—"

"—from one world—"

"—the Largerfarther—"

"How's she to understand 'Largerfarther'?"

"—The larger of the outer pair of living worlds—"

"We're from one world, one family—"

"—one world, one family, we're—"

"—family, we're identical."

"Identical!" J.D. exclaimed.

They settled down as abruptly as they had burst into activity.

"Yes, identical," Quickercatcher said.

"You don't *look* identical!" J.D. said.

"No, of course not, not *now*. You wouldn't want to go through life exactly the way you started out, would you? But when we were born, we were identical."

"You're a clone?"

"I suppose you could say that," Fasterdigger said. "We're identical quadruplets."

"Oh, I see." J.D. thought, Their genetics are different from ours, starting with sex determination.

"What about you?"

"I'm a singleton," J.D. said. "Most humans are." The quartet did not follow up with more questions, and J.D. thought, Of course not, why should they? They've had four thousand years to observe human beings.

But even the quartet might be surprised by J.D.'s parentage. Most people found the complexity confusing. It had not been confusing to J.D.

9

"Are multiple births unusual or common to your people?"

"Most Largerfarthings are twins."

"Many triplets."

"A few quadruplets, like us."

"And you're sisters and brothers. You have two genders, like humans, or more?"

"Two."

"And you start out the same, but differentiate later—or choose which to be?"

"Choose, and change, too," Quickercatcher said.

"Changing back and forth is hard," Fasterdigger said.

Before J.D. could ask more about the Largerfarthings' gender choices, a gentle motion on the tunnel wall caught her attention. She glanced—not up; in free-fall it did not feel like "up"—toward it.

The quartet followed her gaze, their limber necks curving and bending, their ears springing alert.

A being like a giant, double-wide caterpillar crept toward them, flattening itself close to the tunnel surface. Green and gold and brown mottled its undercoat, giving it the look of sun-dappled leaves. Coarse brindled hair, or slender quills, formed a guard coat. As the being moved, clusters of long sharp emerald spines angled up through the fur, then disappeared beneath it.

"It's late!" Quickercatcher exclaimed.

"Late?" J.D. said. "Should we be somewhere—?"

Quickercatcher touched his tail to the tunnel wall and pushed off toward the creature, pressing between Sharphearer and Fasterdigger, who turned and followed.

J.D. pushed off too, following them toward the new being. She longed to touch it, to brush her fingertips across the dappled hair or the tips of the dangerous spines, even at the risk of injury or poisoning. She held back; Europa had cautioned her not to touch anyone without permission or invitation.

Whether this was a person or a creature, a pet or

a worker or a construct like the silver slugs back on *Starfarer*, or an entity for which she had no equivalent, she had no idea. She intended to take no chances.

The creature's body was almost as long as J.D. was tall, wider than her armspan, and the span of her hand deep. Its feet remained concealed beneath the fringe of hair, but it left a faint glistening trail behind it, so J.D. guessed it used suction and moisture to hold fast.

Quickercatcher and Longestlooker hovered over it, pressing close but adroitly avoiding its spines.

"You're late, Late!" Quickercatcher exclaimed.

"As usual," said Longestlooker.

The creature's leading edge lifted from the tunnel surface, arching upward, making small sharp snapping sounds. Its underside was covered with glistening black suckers. The spines bristled out, narrowly missing Quickercatcher, who undulated to stay out of their way.

A warm spot appeared at the back of J.D.'s mind. She opened her link.

"I serve as I'm able," a new voice said inside her mind, traveling through her link. "You might have waited."

An opening appeared, a vertical slit beneath the fur and running between the first few rows of feet. Within it lay rows of small sharp emerald teeth, arrayed on a band of flesh. The band flexed; the being flattened itself to the tunnel again, hiding its underside, its feet, its teeth.

"Is this any way to behave toward our client?" Quickercatcher's voice echoed in J.D.'s ears and through her link as well.

"If we'd waited for you," Fasterdigger said, "J.D. would have had to travel the whole passageway by herself."

"I wouldn't have minded," J.D. said, speaking aloud and sending the same message out over her link. She did not know if the new being could hear her, so she replied in the same medium as it had spoken.

"It would have been rude," Quickercatcher said.

11

Sharphearer nosed Quickercatcher roughly. "As you are being to our colleague. Leave Late alone."

"Would you introduce me?" J.D. asked. "And why do you call me your client?"

"This is Late, from the Smallerfarther," Longestlooker said. "The Representative's representative. Late, this is J.D. Sauvage from Earth."

J.D. smiled. The quartet had made several jokes that she was in danger of not recognizing, of taking too seriously. "Late" was the quartet's name for the dappled being. Late: the English word, the English meaning, not an alien homonym. They teased him about his tardiness; they teased him by calling him a Representative's representative. She hoped he had a good sense of humor.

"How do you do," she said, again speaking through her link.

"I am as well as possible, after so much activity," Late said. "Kind of you to ask. And you?"

"Exhilarated," J.D. said. "The Smallerfarther—that's the twin of the Largerfarther? You're all from the outer companion worlds?"

Quickercatcher's head traced a figure eight. "Exactly. Largerfarther is ours, Smallerfarther is Late's."

"Largernearer and Smallernearer are the inner twin worlds," Sharphearer said.

"Their people never leave them," Longestlooker said. "But they send greetings, and invite you to visit."

"What are they like, the people from the worlds nearer your sun? Why don't they ever leave? How did they join Civilization without star travel?"

"They have it," Longestlooker said, "in a manner of speaking."

"All living worlds are unique," Quickercatcher said. "The nearer worlds . . . are more unusual than most."

"You'll see," Longestlooker said. "There's time. Come with us into the ship."

"We just *got* here," Late's voice said inside J.D.'s mind.

"*You* just got here," Longestlooker replied.

"We came all the way out here just to turn around and go back? I need to rest. Let's stay here and talk for a while."

"What you need is a promotion," Longestlooker said.

"Don't tease," Sharphearer said. "Come along, Late, I'll help you."

"Be careful!" Longestlooker said, sharply, aloud.

"I'll not hurt you." The tall thin emerald spines folded close along his back. He let himself loose with quick snapping pops of his sucker-feet.

"Are Late's spines poisonous?" J.D. asked, glad she had restrained herself from touching the Smallerfarther inhabitant.

"Not to you," Quickercatcher said.

Sharphearer edged close to the tunnel wall. Late undulated sideways and curled the front edge of his body over Sharphearer's second shoulders. His body floated above her back like a thick, heavy cape.

"Late's poison is like any chemical from a separate evolution," Quickercatcher said. "You're either immune to it, or it kills you."

"Unless you're allergic," Fasterdigger said. "Another question entirely. Unusual but possible."

"The spines are poisonous to us," Longestlooker said.

Never mind the poison spines; J.D. wondered if she would have the nerve to let Late come quite that close to her skin with those wicked teeth.

J.D. glided through the tunnel, now and then pushing off, traveling in a series of long zigzags from one side to the other, now and then turning like a diver to see behind her.

The quartet followed, three grouped together, moving around and between each other in a dancing pattern. Heedless of the sharp spines and the poison, Sharphearer floated near them with Late flowing along afterward, covering all of Sharphearer's long lithe body except the chartreuse tip of her tail.

13

The band of illumination traveled with them, following them to the Four Worlds ship.

In the center of the *Chi*'s observers' circle, the holographic image of J.D.'s LTM transmission displayed her progress toward the Four Worlds spaceship.

Outside the transparent walls of the observers' circle, the huge Four Worlds spaceship loomed close. The great alien spaceship filled Victoria Fraser MacKenzie's view with a bright confusion of detail. The connecting tunnel stretched between the spaceship's flank and the *Chi*'s hatch. Victoria had watched it grow, seeking its bearings by feel like the trunk of an elephant, until it reached the *Chi*.

Useful technology, Victoria thought. A sensible way to join different types of spacecraft. Europa's boat fitted itself to *Starfarer* like this, and even Nemo's web grew a tunnel. We'll have to work on building something similar.

Glimmers of light reflected into the observers' circle, flickering like sunshine through water.

The asymmetrical Four Worlds ship dwarfed *Starfarer*'s explorer craft. The *Chi* was designed for short trips, for landing on new planets, while the alien ship would never touch any world. It bristled with a concatenation of organic and mechanical elements.

"It looks like it's been repaired and refitted and retrofitted," Victoria said. "It looks old."

"It is," Europa said. "It isn't as old as my starship, of course."

Europa's starship, like J.D.'s *Nautilus*, was a remnant of the unknown, extinct alien species known only as the other ones. Interstellar civilization could build starships, ordinary starships, like *Starfarer*. But no one in Civilization could reproduce the starships of the other ones. No one knew how to build a starship around a singularity, a quantum black hole. The squidmoths had taken over the starships of the other ones long before Civilization existed. Civilization salvaged the rare ship abandoned by the squidmoths, and constantly sought the origin of the other ones.

Right now, *Nautilus* formed the gravitational center of a small and complicated constellation of spacecraft. *Starfarer* orbited *Nautilus;* the *Chi* had traveled from *Starfarer* to the approaching Four Worlds ship. Europa's terraformed starship, a living planetoid with islands and oceans, paced *Nautilus* and *Starfarer*. Europa had left it at a distance so its mass would not perturb *Starfarer*'s orbit too severely.

"The Four Worlds ship is several generations old," Europa said. "No need to build a new ship for an advance in design or an improved function."

"Some worlds change their ships with the fashion— but that requires great wealth," Androgeos said.

The rounded surfaces of the Four Worlds ship bristled with transceivers, antennas, sensors. Unlike the *Chi*, it had no windows and no ports.

"I wish you'd gone with J.D.," Victoria said to Europa. "To introduce her."

"That would be bad manners," Europa said. "It would be insulting to my friends."

"What if something goes wrong?" Satoshi said.

"Four Worlds people are sophisticated. J.D. cannot offend them."

Europa's voice was aristocratic, her tone cool. The elegant Minoan had no reason to be nervous; she had been living among alien people for nearly four thousand years.

"Your job is to help us," Victoria said. "Or so you told us."

"I *am* helping you," Europa replied. "I know how things are done, and the job of alien contact specialist belongs to J.D."

"She isn't going to act like a bumpkin!" Zev said, springing to his friend's defense.

"Good," Europa replied drily.

"She was the first ordinary human to live with my family," Zev said. "She was wonderful. Even my cousins like her, and they're hard to please."

The cousins of divers were orcas. Killer whales.

"She'd be safer in a spacesuit," Stephen Thomas Gregory said.

"Then she *would* look a bumpkin," Europa said. "She would insult the representatives, and embarrass me. Humans and the Four Worlds *cannot* exchange pathogens—"

"We know that," Victoria said mildly.

"—and the representatives would think you feared they might wage deliberate biological warfare."

"We might fear that they'd brought us another bacterial gift," Stephen Thomas said with asperity. "The way you did."

Europa remained composed as she replied to the geneticist's accusation.

"You must get over being angry at me for—what was the word you used? Supercharging, I do like that—for supercharging *Starfarer*'s bacteria. After all, you aren't mad at Zev for turning you into a diver."

"That was an accident," Zev said.

"I know it, Zev, young ichthyocentaur," Europa said.

"Just understand," Satoshi Lono said. "It's hard for us to trust you now."

"I did what I did deliberately—" Europa said.

"Without asking us," Stephen Thomas said. "Without telling us."

"—so you're angry. You shouldn't be. You're too clever. You shouldn't have figured out what I did so quickly."

"J.D.'s almost at the end of the tunnel," Zev said, his attention on the LTM transmission.

16

"Everything would have been all right," Androgeos said impatiently, "if you'd all gone back to Earth without knowing about the changed bacteria."

"*If* we get back to Earth," Satoshi said, "they probably won't let us land!"

"They must," Europa said. "You cannot join Civilization without the protection of the supercharged bacteria. If I hadn't inoculated your ecosystem, the Four Worlds wouldn't be meeting you now. They wouldn't take the risk of their free-living bacteria taking up residence in *Starfarer*'s—"

"She's there!" Zev said.

As the tunnel's end approached, J.D. quickly touched the *Chi*'s computer through her link.

Victoria waited, her link wide open.

"Are the LTMs coming through okay?" J.D. asked.

"Sound and pictures, all there."

"Great. Thanks, Victoria." Like most people, Victoria did not often use her link for direct communication. J.D. was getting used to the sensation of having voices in her mind, but she understood why other people preferred to avoid the experience.

I think I'd better learn to like it, she said to herself.

Zev sent a wordless message of support and love. J.D. reciprocated. Smiling, she thought, I do like that.

While her link was wide open, the alien knowledge surface of *Nautilus* beckoned her toward the starship's heart. It tempted her, as it always did. But she could not give it time or attention now. She touched it just long enough to be sure it was as she left it, to be sure Esther Klein and Nikolai Cherenkov were safe there.

Kolya replied through Arachne, *Starfarer*'s control computer, but Esther opened her own link and spoke directly to J.D.

"We're fine," she said. "Let us house-sit, don't worry."

J.D. could feel the smile behind the young pilot's words.

"Thanks," she said. She let the connection fade. It had existed for all of three or four seconds.

The passageway opened out into the Four Worlds ship, into soft light and bright color. J.D. took up her momentum against the wall by using her arms and legs as springs. She hovered in a floating stop, uncertain.

The quartet gathered behind her. Late slipped free of Sharphearer's back and glided along with them, undulating slowly, looking in profile like a giant furry inchworm.

J.D. entered a wide, circular chamber. Four Worlds people filled it, waiting for her, dozens of them, an anarchy of colors, their speech a shower of trills and hums. The quartet pushed forward around J.D. The room was full of Largerfarthings like the quartet; Smallerfarthings, people like Late, carpeted its inner surface. Small bright creatures flitted through the chambers, like sparrows. Each had two sets of wings, one set of central feet.

Among the Largerfarthings, a larger, darker shape moved and flowed.

Like the exterior of the ship, the interior was a mix of organic and mechanical elements, the surface soft and rumpled, light shining from round, precise fixtures. Where Smallerfarthings did not cover the wall, the surface held clusters and patterns of small objects tucked into its folds.

The room smelled of damp earth, and electricity, and perfume. The tantalizing sweet sharp fragrance of the quartet concentrated in the meeting room.

Bright-furred Largerfarthings floated in small groups. Now and then groups exchanged members, or an individual switched from one group to another. They watched J.D. with their great shining eyes, their hands folded atop their backs or their arms stretched forward and crossed just above the forelimbs. Some held hands with each other; some stroked each other with their chins and throats. They gave the impression of serenity and joy, amusement and anticipation.

Longestlooker trilled to the waiting group.

"This is J.D. Sauvage, from Earth," Quickercatcher said in English.

Quickercatcher's people responded with a quavering murmur, a few attempts at English, and several fluent exclamations of "Welcome!" The people from Smallerfarther raised their front edges from the inner surface of the room, each exposing a glistening radula of rows of sharp teeth. Late crept along the wall and joined the soft patchwork of the other Smallerfarthings. When J.D. glanced back a moment later she could not tell which of the beings was their representative. The Smallerfarthings' dappled patterns all differed, but much more subtly than the fur of Quickercatcher's kind. Silver threads glimmered among the dapples and the spines.

A fashion? J.D. wondered.

"We all welcome you," Quickercatcher said.

"Thank you," J.D. said. Her voice shook slightly with excitement and eager apprehension. She drew a deep breath and steadied herself. "I'm glad to meet you all. I'm glad to meet Earth's neighbors."

A massive Largerfarthing floated forward. If the Largerfarthings had been horses, this one would be a Percheron—a Percheron with long bright yellow fur.

"This is Carefulspeaker," Quickercatcher said. "We all chose him to represent our community, and he accepted."

Carefulspeaker balanced a stoppered amphora between his hands. He kept up a deliberate motion by swimming with his front and rear limbs, and stopped by back-paddling.

"The inhabitants of Largerfarther and Smallerfarther offer you a gift." Carefulspeaker gazed steadily at her. His eyes were brilliant gold, like molten precious metal. He drew his hands away from the gift.

The amphora drifted between them. Graceful, delicate handles arched out from its shoulders, like fan-shaped wings.

J.D. hesitated. You may accept one gift, Europa had said. I do not know what it will be, but my friends will not harm you. You may show good manners by sharing the gift with them.

Europa and Androgeos had objectives that did not entirely coincide with the goals of the deep space expedition. But Europa had every reason to hope J.D. would make a good impression with the Four Worlds.

J.D. put her hands around the amphora, accepting the gift. The cool, damp earthenware fit her hands strangely. It was wide in one dimension and narrow in the other. It curved abruptly in at the bottom to form a cutback ridge. J.D. imagined herself with three central fingers and a thumb on each side of her palm. The top thumb and the fingers would pinch rather than grab; the lower thumb would support. She slid her little finger around the bulge and pressed it against the ridge. It still felt strange, but steadier.

The Largerfarther inhabitants watched her expectantly.

J.D. moved the jar. Liquid shifted inside it, not splashing as it would in a gravity field, but rolling from side to side. She held the jar still with her left hand and removed the stopper with her right. Like the amphora, the stopper and the opening were wider in one direction than the other. The opening came to an edge rather than a lip. Inside, the liquid continued to move.

A transparent, colorless globule protruded from the neck of the amphora, then burst free and hung quivering in the air. J.D. stoppered the bottle. Beside her, Quickercatcher made the figure-eight head motion of agreement and approval.

The liquid globule might be perfume. It might be an

alien artform. For all J.D. knew for certain, it might be rocket fuel.

J.D. bent toward the globule. It had no smell, no color.

She touched it with her lips, kissed it, drank it.

Cool, pure water flowed into her mouth. She swallowed it.

A few drops floated free. One of the four-winged creatures flitted past, scooping water into its mouth.

Carefulspeaker motioned his approval, and so did the rest of the Largerfarthings. The Smallerfarthings did not perceptibly change the way they moved. If they had expressions, J.D. could not yet distinguish them.

J.D.'s link made her aware of the apprehension of her colleagues back on board the *Chi,* but they were less frightened than when Nemo offered her decorative food.

They must be getting used to my taking risks, she thought. Getting used to seeing me do my job.

With Nemo, she had known the offering was food. Here, she had been guessing. Thanks to Nemo, it was an educated guess.

"Thank you," she said to the representatives. "Will you share the gift with me?"

"Yes," Quickercatcher said. "Welcome to the Four Worlds."

She opened the amphora and drew it toward her. The water flowed out of the amphora's mouth, kept behind by its inertia. A swirling stream of water broke into vibrating, rotating bubbles.

Several of the Smallerfarthings loosed their hold on the wall and undulated into the group, swimming like rectangular manta rays. J.D. thought the one who came nearest to her was Late. To drink, he approached a globule, curled back the front edge of his body, revealed open mouth, radula, and sharp teeth, then reversed the curve and bent around the water.

A few droplets splashed free when his sharp teeth

burst the bubble into his mouth. Another of the bat-birds swooped by for its share.

In a moment, the water was gone and the representatives clustered around J.D. Again, she glimpsed the unfamiliar, elusive shape. It appeared and disappeared between the other people. J.D. could not get a clear idea what it looked like.

It can't be a representative of the Nearer worlds, J.D. thought, because Quickercatcher said no one from the Nearers ever left the surface. Is it another sentient being? Does one of the Four Worlds have several sentient species? Is this another form of the kind of people I've already met?

Or maybe it's a pet, J.D. thought, and smiled to herself.

"I brought you a guest gift, too," she said. "It's a copy of a performance by a talented artist. It's called 'Discovering the Fossils.' "

The LTM on J.D.'s shoulder projected a hologram in response to her request. It appeared and expanded. The Four Worlds people moved aside to make a space for it.

In the image, a river ran through a canyon on the inner, living surface of *Starfarer*'s cylinder. Crimson Ng, the sculptor and performance artist, walked at the river's edge. She strode along the beach, her gaze intent on the canyon wall.

An anomalous line of stone appeared, pale against the dark volcanic gray. It thickened, widening to one handsbreadth, two. The paleness took on a definite color, a rosy, sandy pink.

Crimson looked across the river. There, too, on the opposite riverbank, the pink stone streaked the lava. The river's creation had carved away volcanic moon rock, and part of the unexpected sedimentary layer within it.

Crimson touched the pale streak of rock on her side of the river. Her fingers with their dirty broken nails were as gentle as a caress. An analysis appeared at the edge of the hologram. Ancient moon rock, a lava flow a billion years old, lay below the strange pink layer. Another lava flow lay above it, the second flow older than the first. More confusion of the provenance: The rock lay upside-down compared to its orientation on the moon.

The two ancient flows sandwiched the anomalous, impossible layer of sandstone.

More information appeared at the edge of the display: Tests, analyses, sonar tracings, potassium-argon dating of the volcanic flows, all evidence that the anomalous layer could not have originated naturally on the moon.

Crimson slid her rock hammer out of the loop on the leg of her pants. She stuck its claw into a crack and pried gently. A chunk of stone fell away into her hand.

A dark sharp shape thrust from it, the shape of a tooth, a fang.

The hologram faded.

"Very moving," Carefulspeaker said, "to observe discovery."

"Crimson is a talented performer," J.D. replied. "A talented artist."

A buzz of amusement—J.D. chose to perceive the reaction as amusement, and hoped she was right—passed through the crowd.

"Thank you," Longestlooker said. "Will it be possible to view the site in person?"

"I'm sure Crimson would be pleased to have a live audience," J.D. said.

One of the Smallerfarthings—Late, J.D. wondered?—magic-carpeted its way to Quickercatcher. J.D. caught part of the transmission with her link, but it was not in English.

"I will finish the introductions here," Quickercatcher said to Late, "and then we'll take J.D. to meet Smaller-farther's Representative."

"But isn't Late—" J.D. had misunderstood. She had taken the quartet's description of Late, "the Representative's representative," as teasing. But they meant it literally.

Relieved that she had not made a visible misstep, she concentrated on the introductions. She had trouble keeping everyone straight. Yet she began to detect differences in the Smallerfarthings' brindled pelts. She tried to remember everyone's name, but as backup she kept the information at the other end of her link. If she needed a reminder she could get it quickly, without going into a noticeable fugue.

"This is Swiftseer," Quickercatcher said, introducing J.D. to a Largerfarthing with a silky gray coat. "She's been interested in human beings for a long time."

J.D. clasped hands with Swiftseer. A fringe of beads, threaded into the Largerfarthing's long gray wrist fur, brushed softly against J.D.'s fingers.

In the background, the mysterious shape darted forward. It accelerated faster than one could easily swim in air. It must have pushed off from something . . . except that it was in the middle of the circular room.

"I'm very happy to meet you—oh!"

The shape pressed through Swiftseer's gray-dappled shoulder. Halfway out, it stopped. Swiftseer cocked her head but took no offense at being swum through.

An image! J.D. thought. Just like something Arachne would project.

"And here is the Representative of Largernearer," Quickercatcher said, indicating the image.

"How do you do?" J.D. said. The image had startled her badly, and the sight of it sticking halfway out of another person's body made her uncomfortable, but no one else reacted to this odd sight.

I guess it isn't rude to overlap image and reality, here, the way it is back on *Starfarer*, J.D. thought. On the other hand, the images Arachne projects usually stay in one place. They're easier to avoid.

The being flipped its heavy, sinuous body, came free,

and brought itself to the level of J.D.'s nose. It was dark and sleek, striped with four fins that stretched the length of its body. Eyes surrounded its central toothed mouth in an irregular circle.

The image swelled.

Its head expanded. Its body moved back and away. The air thickened, darkened; most of the being's body disappeared into murky depths. J.D. started and caught her breath. The effect was of falling at a terrifying speed till a small, distant shape became a close, enormous one.

The perception of motion stopped; the being stopped expanding.

J.D. found herself floating among insubstantial shadows, drifting in the dimness of deep turbid water. Largernearer's representative loomed before her; the illusion concealed the meeting room and all the other people in it.

J.D. could not accurately estimate the representative's size, but it was larger than the one blue whale she had ever met. Its iridescent blue-black body stretched back, turning to shadow the color of the water.

Unlike a blue whale, a peaceful baleen filter-feeder of plankton and krill, this being possessed a circle of huge shiny black teeth. The being floated before J.D., very still, its mouth expanding, contracting. The teeth unfolded from their closed position, opening like jackknives, like snake fangs, to line the mouth. Each tooth was a sharp spike half J.D.'s height.

The irregular scattering of eyes focused on J.D.

J.D. shivered. The illusion of being underwater was so real that she could imagine herself swimming, buoyed against gravity yet aware of "up" and "down." Far overhead, the surface of the sea rippled and sparkled in the light of 61 Cygni.

Pull yourself together! J.D. said to herself. It's an *image.* It might be any size, in reality, the size of a dolphin rather than a blue whale . . . or an island. Maybe it's just trying to impress me—or scare me—rather than showing me its true size.

J.D. spoke, greeting the representative in true speech, the language she had learned from Zev and his family of orcas and divers.

The illusion of being underwater shattered: Sound in air felt altogether different from sound in water. Whatever the visual image, J.D. *was* still surrounded by air.

The huge whale-eel lay before her, still as a coiled spring, eyes wide, its mouth partly open. It sucked in water, tasting the scents around it. Silt and tiny swimming creatures and large many-eyed fishes moved with the water, into the whale-eel's mouth. The teeth sliced the fishes into pieces. With the next inhalation of water, the fishes disappeared, leaving only shreds of flesh.

The whale-eel responded to J.D.'s true speech greeting. Its voice surrounded her, reaching through her to her bones.

"Quickercatcher!" J.D. said.

Quickercatcher moved closer, at first ghostly in the image of murky water, then clearer. He hovered at J.D.'s side.

"Tell me what I'm hearing, please," J.D. said.

Quickercatcher repeated part of the trill that had surrounded her.

"That's a name-sound," Quickercatcher said. "It means . . . music with many sources. 'Orchestra.' She welcomes you."

"Is this her real size?"

"No. She's much bigger."

"No wonder Orchestra's people never leave their world. It would need some spaceship, to take them. Please tell her I'm . . . impressed to meet her."

Another song surrounded J.D. She glanced at Quickercatcher, questioning.

"Orchestra asks if she may communicate with you directly."

"Of course."

"Welcome, Sauvage Earth," Orchestra said through J.D.'s link.

I guess that's better than Earth Sauvage, J.D. thought.

"Thank you, Orchestra Largernearer," she said.

"We could build a starship, if we wished," Orchestra said. "We joined Civilization by proving it."

"By building it?"

"By proving we could if we chose." Orchestra emitted a high, skirling hum. A narrow column of water spun into existence before J.D. The column dragged a swarm of many-eyed guppies into its bottom end, twirled them around, and ejected them from its top. The hum faded; the water-devil dissipated.

"We have the capacity to manipulate matter," Orchestra said. "And we have auxiliary animals."

"And the hands of friends." Quickercatcher stretched his hands out and flexed his fingers, his double opposable thumbs. "We came to know Orchestra's people by the messages they wrote across the surface of their world. Now, they grow antennas and radiotelescopes on their seas. Their astronomy was always far in advance of ours."

Several of Orchestra's huge slate-gray eyes turned completely black for an instant. The gray eyes, with their long horizontal pupils, returned. A blink? J.D. wondered. Orchestra had no eyelids. Her eyes had rolled backwards, vanishing into the eye socket, then forward into view again.

"We joined Civilization by helping each other," Orchestra said. "By sharing our knowledge and our abilities. Civilization accepted us all by accepting one of us. Even though my people prefer to remain in the sea."

J.D. wished she were really swimming with Orchestra, in Largernearer's sea.

She thought: Wait a second! Wait *several* seconds! Orchestra *can't* be talking to me in real time. If she were, there'd be a perceptible delay in her replies.

"Are you an AI?" J.D. asked the image. "An artificial intelligence?"

"Yes, of course," Orchestra said. "I represent the real person, Orchestra, on Largernearer. She reviews our conversation as it reaches her. She will make corrections to my statements, if she sees fit."

Several of Orchestra's eyes—different eyes than before—rolled back, then reappeared.

"She does not often correct me," Orchestra said, in a voice J.D. perceived as being tinged with pride.

"You represent her admirably," J.D. said.

"Thank you."

Orchestra's image shrank suddenly. The underwater illusion vanished. J.D. sank back in the air, startled by the abrupt change. Orchestra's smaller self swam forward till she was nose to nose with J.D. All the Largerfarthings in the meeting room drifted in an open sphere around them, making soft trilling sounds and motions of amusement and agreement; the Smallerfarthings, on the other hand, clung to the walls and moved with unusual agitation, curling their leading edges outward.

"We've been waiting for Earth's people for a long time," Orchestra said. "You've had a difficult journey. We thank you for persevering, and we welcome you."

A dappled Smallerfarthing gradually detached itself from the wall, undulated slowly toward J.D. and Orchestra and Quickercatcher, and came to a stop at J.D.'s elbow.

"Quickercatcher," Late said, "the Representative is waking up. We should . . . hurry."

The last word came into J.D.'s mind as a frightened whisper.

Two

An organic tunnel, soft and warm as mole-skin, led deeper into the Four Worlds ship. Small carvings and sculptures and bangles and growing plants nestled against the rumpled wall. The ornaments gleamed in the diffuse, low light. When J.D. paused to look at them, Quickercatcher urged her along.

"We shouldn't tarry," he said.

Sharphearer carried Late, whose body flowed like a cape. With each undulation, the stiff emerald spines rose above his dappled coat, then disappeared beneath it.

Longestlooker glanced over the small procession. Fasterdigger lifted the guest-water flask from where it balanced on his back, behind his head.

"I have it."

"Good," Longestlooker said.

"Guest water is purest and sweetest," Quickercatcher said.

"It was very pure," J.D. said agreeably, seeing no need to mention that to human beings, pure water tastes flat.

"It has to be," Quickercatcher said. "Otherwise we might lose people, and that would not be a good beginning." Quickercatcher's eyes closed slowly from outer to inner corner.

"True," J.D. said. "But I ate decorative food with Nemo, and I'm still here."

"Who is Nemo?"

"The friend who willed *Nautilus* to me—who gave me the starship of the other ones," J.D. said.

"A squidmoth! Do they have names?"

"Not exactly." She could see, in her memory of the knowledge surface that controlled *Nautilus*, the multidimensional contour that represented Nemo's person. Another squidmoth would recognize the shape as one of its own. "But Nemo took a name to make things easier for me."

"And you ate its food?"

"Yes."

Quickercatcher's jaws opened, then snapped shut sharply.

"It was delicious," J.D. said.

"But no one ever knows what a squidmoth might do," Quickercatcher said. "Are human beings generally foolhardy? Europa isn't."

"We can be," J.D. said. "We aren't all as wise as Europa."

Quickercatcher considered her comment.

"I'd like to talk to the squidmoth who lives in your system," J.D. said. "If there is one. I'd like to ask it some questions. If you wouldn't consider me *too* foolhardy."

"There is one, but it never welcomes anyone—"

"It left us, brother," Sharphearer said. "It left right after *Starfarer* got here."

"Perhaps it knew you wanted to ask it questions," Longestlooker said.

J.D. had hoped for the squidmoth's help and friendship.

She said to herself, disappointed, Maybe it was too much to hope for another friendship like Nemo's.

"I hope *you* won't disappear," J.D. said, trying to maintain her sense of humor, "when I start asking you questions."

Quickercatcher blinked, amethyst eyes narrowing

from the outer corners in, then opening wide. His goatee bristled out.

"We have many answers to give. As well as some questions of our own."

J.D. wished she could take the liberty of stroking Quickercatcher's mauve fur. She wondered if it would be soft or rough, cool or warm.

"Why does it make me so happy to be near you?" She looked away quickly, startled to have put her thoughts into words. "I mean . . ."

"We're welcoming you, after all," Quickercatcher said. "That's some reason for happiness, I hope."

"Yes, but it's more . . . I was happy meeting Nemo, and we became friends. But this is different."

"What about Europa and Androgeos?" Quickercatcher said. "Weren't you happy meeting them?"

J.D. hesitated.

"I was shocked speechless," she said. "I couldn't believe aliens could look so much like humans. I'd've been less surprised if the grass stood up and started talking to me. Then, when I found out they *were* humans . . ."

"Most new candidates for Civilization are glad to have an escort of their own species."

"It isn't that I wasn't glad." Her reactions to Europa had been—and still were—too complex to sum up in a few words. Europa was too complex to sum up in a few words. "It was that I expected . . . alienness. I'd prepared myself for alienness."

"Plenty of time for that," Quickercatcher said. "We're alien to you, Late is, Orchestra is. And others . . . We are not even particularly unusual."

"How do you decide *that?*"

"Patterns. Some patterns are more common than others. Your pattern, my pattern, are common. Late's pattern is ubiquitous. Orchestra's pattern is common, but the achievements of her species are unusual. Underwater beings seldom bother with starship technology. They aim their abilities inward."

"What about the people on the fourth world?"

"Ah," Quickercatcher said in a respectful tone. "Smallernearer is . . . unique. We will tell you about Smallernearer when we have time and quiet."

J.D. would have pushed, if she had thought Quickercatcher was evading her question. But she found she had no trouble taking the comment, and the promise, at face value. Smallernearer was something to savor, something to discover with time. She left it as a warm spot of anticipation, and willingly changed the subject.

"How many species are there in Civilization?"

"That's impossible—"

"Sentient species?" Longestlooker asked.

"Yes, sorry," J.D. said. "Sentient species is what I meant."

"That's also impossible to say," Fasterdigger said cheerfully.

"But why—how?" J.D. stumbled over her question, wanting to ask about Civilization's organization, its size, its age, all at once. "Don't you keep track?"

"Your world," Quickercatcher said. "Your Earth. When Civilization withdrew from your star system, it had many political entities. What about now? It's organized? It has a single government?"

"It has several," J.D. said. "They cooperate. Some of them. Sometimes."

Fasterdigger and Longestlooker snuffled, then nuzzled each others' throats as they floated side by side.

"Is what I said so surprising?" J.D. asked.

"Star travel usually springs from a world's cooperation," Longestlooker said.

"But not always," Late said in his usual lugubrious tone. "J.D.'s Earth is nothing unique."

"Not in its governments," Longestlooker agreed. "In Civilization, we cooperate. But we have no empire, no

32

hegemony, not even a republic. Alliances evaporate quickly. The distances are long. Travel is the only means of communication. The cosmic string extends when your time to join Civilization has come, and it withdraws from violence or aggression."

"Until now," Late said. "The cosmic string withdrew from you at Tau Ceti. Now *Starfarer* has entered our system—yet the cosmic string remains. It's unique, to gain a pardon so quickly."

That answered my next question, J.D. said to herself. Now I know how much Europa told them about *Starfarer*'s journey. She told them about the nuclear missile that came through transition with us. She told them what happened at the first star system we entered. She told them—if they didn't already calculate it for themselves—that the cosmic string withdrew from Earth, leaving our solar system empty and cut off. They know *Starfarer* can enter transition and return to Earth . . . but it would be a one-way trip, until—unless—the cosmic string comes back to Earth, too.

"Do you believe we have been pardoned?" J.D. asked.

"Perhaps," Longestlooker said. "We'll know for sure if the string no longer withdraws from you. If it returns to your solar system."

"We feared you might have to return to Earth," Longestlooker said.

"But we might be able to invite you into Civilization, now, after all!" Quickercatcher said.

"Whoever controls the cosmic string—they must have realized we were caught up in a horrible misunderstanding, a dispute," J.D. said. "*Starfarer* isn't armed."

"The string control has some discretion," Sharphearer said.

"But not this much," Quickercatcher said. "Never before."

"The string aside, disputes within a star system don't preclude joining Civilization," Longestlooker said. "It's when a species tries to transport the dispute to other people—"

"That's what I mean! I think the missile was only meant to scare us. I'm *certain* it wasn't meant to detonate."

Other people on board *Starfarer* thought otherwise, but no one would know the truth till they went home. Perhaps no one would *ever* know the truth. All J.D. knew for sure was that every time she thought of the cloud of radioactive debris they had left floating in the Tau Ceti system, she blushed with embarrassment and humiliation.

"That wasn't how it was supposed to be," she said. "You watched Earth till fifty years ago, till you were afraid we'd notice you were there. So you know how violent humans *can* be—"

"Europa and Androgeos are from a peaceable culture," Longestlooker said. "That's why we chose them to rescue. But their successors . . ." She snapped her jaws.

"We were nervous to meet you," Fasterdigger said softly.

"But you have behaved very gently," said Sharphearer.

"Thank you. We're doing our best to change. We don't always succeed. But we did agree that *Starfarer* shouldn't be armed."

The walls grew more and more rumpled, thicker and more wrinkled. The passageway narrowed; the tucked-in ornaments thinned out, then disappeared.

The passageway ended in silver-gray dusk touched with bright glints of colored light.

J.D. touched the spongy wall, bringing herself to a stop.

An oblate room opened before her. Great spikes of ebony, amethyst, and turquoise erupted from organic swellings on the wall, then speared inward to support a central mass of herringbone bristles several meters across. The mass grew along each spike, coating part of each long semiprecious crystal with a woolly sleeve.

"Is he awake?" Longestlooker spoke quietly, staring at the central shape. It was featureless except for the tweedy pattern of soft tan and warm brown.

Late released himself from Sharphearer's back. He flicked his edge against the wall, snapping himself forward with uncharacteristic speed and animation.

"Please begin," Late said. "I'll relay."

"Representative," Longestlooker said. "This is J.D. Sauvage, from Earth. J.D., this is the Representative from Smallerfarther."

Late echoed Longestlooker's words, in English, through J.D.'s link. The effect of hearing the words out loud and, a moment later, in her mind, disoriented her.

"How do you do," she said.

As far as she could tell, the Representative made no response at all.

Fasterdigger handed J.D. the amphora and nudged her arm with his soft nose.

"I'd like to share the guest gift with you," J.D. said to the Representative.

Late's voice traveled into her mind. "That is acceptable."

"Put the water on the turquoise," Quickercatcher whispered.

J.D. pushed off gently from the edge of the passageway.

She floated forward and drifted to a halt near the Representative's turquoise support. The Representative had not moved. If he breathed, his breath was too shallow to see.

J.D. unstoppered the amphora, drew it back so the last drops of guest water flowed into the air, and waved the globules onto the turquoise support. The water clung to the semiprecious stone, flowed onto its mottled surface, and migrated along the veins in the turquoise toward the tweedy fur.

"I'm happy to meet you," J.D. said.

The far end of each semiprecious spike split into fibers, crystalline strands, that disappeared into the wall-swelling. It was as if the Representative had legs that grew from their tips. More spikes glittered from the dimness at the back of the Representative's chamber, green and blue and pure clear white light refracting into rainbows.

What a strange being, she thought. But Quicker-catcher said the pattern of this species is ubiquitous!

Late's echo of J.D.'s words appeared in her mind a split second after she said them. The effect was even more discomforting than hearing Longestlooker's words echoed. J.D. paused, then forged ahead.

"I hope Earth and the Four Worlds will have a long and friendly relationship."

Again, her words echoed in her mind. She opened her link wider, hoping, but failing, to detect the translation.

If Late can talk to the Representative in ordinary English, she thought, why can't I speak to him? If Late is doing a simultaneous translation, then why don't I hear . . . whatever his people use for language?

"When will you give Civilization your algorithm?" The shout—Late's voice amplified and resonating—burst through her link.

The powerful transmission dizzied her. At her elbow, Quickercatcher flinched.

J.D.'s surroundings spun. She closed her eyes a moment, shutting out the multicolored pinwheel of gleaming, glowing spokes. When she opened her eyes again, the visual hallucination faded. The Representative's bracing structure splayed across the chamber, solid and unmoving.

J.D. blew out her breath. Victoria's new, faster algorithm for interstellar navigation could be remarkably valuable to Civilization. Europa had made it plain that the algorithm was an important resource for Earth, not to be squandered.

"Who said anything about giving?" J.D. said.

Behind her, Longestlooker snapped her jaws, but Quickercatcher made a sound J.D. took to be more amusement than offense.

"Uniqueness results in esteem."

"What does esteem get us?"

"We want to inspect your fossils. Images are not acceptable."

J.D. negotiated the abrupt change of subject. "Crimson Ng would be happy to show you her sculpture. You're welcome to visit *Starfarer* and see her work. We'd be honored by your presence."

Late fluttered his edge, scooping himself backward. The last drops of guest water vanished beneath the edge of the Representative's herringbone bristles.

Does the Representative disbelieve me, too? J.D. wondered. Will he make himself believe the fossils are real? No one else accepts that they're an art project. Why should he be any different? Does it even matter what I say?

"The reception is over," Late said in his own voice.

The quartet withdrew. Sharphearer grabbed Late by one corner and pulled him awkwardly away.

J.D. followed.

In silence, they drifted down the corridor. Longestlooker and Fasterdigger floated into a bend and pushed off with both hind feet. Pulled off balance by Late, Sharphearer bounced softly from one wall and twisted to orient herself. She hoisted Late onto her back. Late clung fast. Quickercatcher spiraled his tail like a spring and pushed off against the wall.

Shaking hard, J.D. caught herself against the squashy

corridor surface. Instead of following her hosts, she let herself bump gently against the sides of the passage.

Ten meters farther on, Quickercatcher noticed that J.D. had stopped. He scrambled to turn, to rejoin her. The rest of the quartet followed.

"Come along, J.D.," Quickercatcher said. "What's the matter?"

"Would you—"

She paused to swallow, to lick her lips. Her mouth was dry and her stomach had tumbled somewhere beyond her feet. She wished the amphora still contained guest water.

"Quickercatcher, what *happened* back there? Late, can you explain—?"

Quickercatcher moved very close. Warm fur tickled J.D.'s hand. She breathed fast and deep, nearly sobbing. Quickercatcher ducked against her shoulder, nudging her hard.

"Is this all right?" he asked.

She quivered at the touch of smooth fur, powerful muscles.

"Yes," she said. "Yes, please."

Quickercatcher's touch eased some of her tension and quieted her shivering.

"The elderlargers of Late's people tend to be abrupt," Quickercatcher said. "We forget how peremptory they sound at first."

At first? J.D. said to herself. That exchange would *always* sound peremptory.

"That was no conversation," J.D. said. "That was a series of demands."

Quickercatcher's eyes closed slowly, outer corners to inner corners.

"And you acquitted yourself well to them."

"The algorithm isn't mine to give," J.D. said. "It belongs to Victoria Fraser MacKenzie. She allows *Starfarer* to use it to navigate through transition. Just like Crimson

Ng allows us to watch her performance and appreciate her sculptures."

Longestlooker's jaw snapped shut quickly, sharply. "It all belongs to human people," Longestlooker said.

Fasterdigger added, "Any human should be able to give it."

"Is that how it works with you?" J.D. asked. "Not with us."

"How can you withhold achievements?" Sharphearer asked.

Longestlooker said, "We might build on them faster."

"Faster than primitive Earth science?"

"She didn't say that!" Quickercatcher said.

"We should cooperate," said Fasterdigger.

"You didn't answer my question," J.D. said. "So far, the only person I've met in Civilization who's answered my questions has been Nemo."

At J.D.'s reference to the squidmoth, Longestlooker snuffled in surprise. Quickercatcher raised his chin, whiskers bristling, hesitated, then slowly lowered his head to gaze at J.D.

"I'd like to stop meeting people for a while," J.D. said. "I'd like to talk about what's happened so far."

"It's just that the Representative can't waste his motion," Late said. "He has to conserve it for essential occasions."

Offended, J.D. scowled at him.

"That didn't come out quite the way Late meant it," Quickercatcher said.

"It's their physiology," Sharphearer said.

"Biologically determined rudeness?" J.D. said sarcastically.

"He was extremely generous to you," Longestlooker said.

"We've known Late for quite a long time," Quickercatcher said.

"This is the first time we've ever met his master," Longestlooker said.

"We've encountered other elderlargers, of course," Sharphearer said, with such sincere reassurance that J.D. wondered why it made any difference.

"This is the first time the Representative has spoken with us," Fasterdigger said.

"He didn't exactly speak to *us*," Quickercatcher said, amused, eyes closed halfway.

Sharphearer said, "Nor we to him."

Quickercatcher added, "Only to J.D."

"True," said Longestlooker.

"Could someone please explain to me what's going on?" J.D. said plaintively.

"Come along," Longestlooker said.

"We'll go to the resting nest," Quickercatcher said.

J.D. wished the Four Worlds enclosed ship had windows, ports, or open spaces. Only the ornaments tucked into the spongy surface of the ship's tunnels provided any variation in the wrinkled gray-green walls. Whenever she tried to pause to look at one of the tiny dioramas, Quickercatcher urged her onward.

The quartet took her along twisting, narrowing branch passageways until she was thoroughly lost. Finally they reached an offshoot that dead-ended in a large, oblong pouch.

Terraces, ledges, and fissures furrowed the inner wall. Fabric rumpled over some of the surfaces; bare stone formed others. In the indirect light, the glow of green and purple velvet set off the gleam of faceted garnet, chalcedony, and obsidian. Here, too, figures and decorations had been tucked into the wall covering.

J.D. drifted past a ledge covered with frilly red lace. She brushed her hand across it. It possessed the delicate irregularity and complexity of a living thing. She thought it might be vegetation: a succulent, or a fungus? Suddenly she remembered Europa's caution, not to touch anyone without permission or invitation. She snatched back her hand and glanced at Quickercatcher, but her host showed no alarm.

How am I supposed to tell what's an "anyone" and what's an "anything"? J.D. wondered. For all I know that red stuff could be the intelligent equivalent of lichen.

Late unlatched himself from Sharphearer's back and fluttered like a sea creature, coming to rest against the red lace. The spines along the edges of his body extended and dipped gracefully into the foliage, securing him like pins. As he moved forward, the spines withdrew, advanced, and plunged, like narrow oars. From beneath him came a soft crunching noise. Bare swaths of stone, the width of Late's mouth, cut through other expanses of the red lace. Late was grazing on the vegetation that grew on the stone.

The alien equivalent of lichen, J.D. said to herself. But not intelligent. I think. I hope. I guess I got away with screwing up, this time.

Over J.D.'s head, Quickercatcher slid sinuously into a nook in the wall and nestled into the soft loose material that filled it.

"Come here with us," Quickercatcher said.

"We'll rest and talk," Longestlooker said.

"J.D., do you want water plain?" Sharphearer asked. "Or water with simple sugars? Would you like ethyl alcohol? Europa likes the alcohol, she says it kicks."

"I don't doubt it," J.D. said, amused, tempted to try it just to see if Europa really did drink absolute alcohol. "Just water for now, Sharphearer, thank you." She was touched that they had gone to the trouble of preparing refreshments compatible with her biochemistry.

Interesting that both the alien species she had met had offered her intoxicants. She had enjoyed Nemo's decorative food. Her mouth still watered when she remembered its evanescent taste, its delicate high.

41

She acknowledged the inconsistency of using Nemo's intoxicant, while preferring not to drink alcohol.

Quickercatcher wriggled around in the zero-gravity nest, making a place for J.D. She slid into the folds. It was like getting into a bed made with sheets of warm velvet. With all her clothes on. She brushed her fingertips against the fabric, turning the nap from soft leaf green to bright emerald. She smoothed it back to leaf green.

Quickercatcher nudged her arm with a friendly push. Longestlooker slid in on J.D.'s other side, and Fasterdigger dove between them, with a slick flip to reappear head first. Sharphearer joined them, balancing a spherical bowl between hands and nape and shoulder blades. She also batted a water-filled globule through the air with quick touches of her nose and knees, as if it were a soccer ball.

Sharphearer tapped the globule toward J.D. J.D. caught it out of the air. It yielded between her fingers. Water crawled and bumped inside it.

J.D. touched a lump on its side. A long flexible spout extruded. She sipped the cool liquid. Like the guest water, it tasted pure and flat.

Sharphearer raised the bowl, ducked her head beneath it, brought it forward and down to her chest, and offered it to the other members of the quartet. Dark granules of coarse sand and fine gravel filled it. Here and there, against the side of the transparent bowl, the gravel spun in small vortexes.

J.D. watched, fascinated, as Longestlooker reached out of the nest and past her front shoulders, slid the globe's cap aside, thrust one hand inside before sand could float from the opening, and sifted through the globe's contents. Her hand produced a cascade of rapid peeping noises from the globe.

"Ah, got one." With a dexterous reverse of the routine, Longestlooker snatched a bright rounded shape from the globe, covered the opening, and passed the bowl to Fasterdigger, who repeated the procedure.

"What is it?" J.D. asked. "Can I look at it more closely?"

Longestlooker showed J.D. the fluttering handful. A creature like a baby bird translated through a funhouse mirror struggled between two thumbs. Several delicate webbed feet grew out of its fuzzy, iridescent red feathers. They beat against the air, against Longestlooker's fingers, scrabbling for sand to swim through. The creature's four-pronged beak opened and closed rapidly, and its chirping rose in pitch. Its bright blue eyes blinked.

Fasterdigger pulled another birdlet out of the bowl. As Quickercatcher slipped one hand into the globe, Fasterdigger freed the creature he had caught. It tumbled in the air like a feathered Ping-Pong ball.

"Is it a pet?" J.D. asked.

Fasterdigger snapped it out of the air with one bite.

"It's food," Fasterdigger said, crunching it.

A few bits of shiny red down spun in faint air currents. Sharphearer plucked the puffy feathers out of zero g and twisted them into her shoulder fur.

"You shouldn't eat them," Quickercatcher said to J.D. "You'd have difficulty digesting them. Our biochemistry is similar to yours, but we use a different set of amino acids."

J.D. felt queasy. She hoped she would not find herself committing bushushiro. Throwing up during dinner would not impress her hosts. Though the birdlet was hardly as strange as the food she had eaten while visiting Nemo, she had no wish to sample it.

Why is that? she wondered. I didn't have any trouble eating a live animal that looked like an insect. Why should I balk at a live chick?

"It burrows," Longestlooker said.

"In the sand back home," Quickercatcher said, pulling one out of the globe. Frantic peeping ended, mid-crescendo, with Quickercatcher's contented crunch.

"This kind is a delicacy," said Sharphearer.

"What do you call them?"

Longestlooker trilled and clicked. J.D. tried to mimic the sound.

"Sometimes we haven't time to dig for fresh food, out here on the ship," Longestlooker said.

"Then we have to eat preserved stuff," Quickercatcher said with distaste.

Sharphearer's lips drew back, revealing sharp teeth. "As I'll have to do," she said, "if my siblings don't hold the grower for me."

"You eat this one," Longestlooker said to Sharphearer fondly. "I'll get another." Longestlooker fed a birdlet to Sharphearer, who plucked it delicately and coyly from Longestlooker's fingers and munched it, blithely heedless of the peeping cries.

The shrill sound was beginning to get on J.D.'s nerves.

The Largerfarthings ate with their mouths open. A birdlet's foot, its webs clutching at the air, floated away. Sharphearer snapped it up and swallowed it.

Sharphearer joined her siblings in the nest, curving around behind J.D., resting her head on Quickercatcher's shoulder, curling her tail around Longestlooker's throat.

The quartet passed the gravel-filled sphere back and forth, one holding the grower while another reached in, sifted through the contents, and plucked out a snack, sometimes eating it, sometimes feeding it to one of the others, sometimes letting it free and biting it out of the air.

J.D. breathed deeply and slowly until her stomach felt more settled.

Maybe it's those little blue eyes, she thought.

On board the *Chi,* Victoria floated against her couch, loosely secured by her safety straps. Several holographic images hovered in the center of the observers' circle. In the most prominent, J.D. rested with the quartet in their nest. One of her LTMs had clambered onto the wall of the chamber to transmit the scene.

Victoria sighed with relief when J.D. handed Longest-looker the birdlet. The LTM gave an all too detailed image of the little creature.

Victoria grimaced. "It's like biting the head off your Easter chick."

Her partner Satoshi chuckled. "I thought J.D. might eat one," he said.

"She wouldn't be so foolish!" Europa said. The elegant, exquisite alien human frowned. "Would she?" In zero g, her hair's silver-dressed black curls bobbed softly in random directions, like loose springs.

"Probably not," Victoria said. "But J.D. isn't as predictable as you might think."

"If she ate it, would it hurt her?" Satoshi asked.

"It would upset her stomach rather badly."

"She handled the question of the algorithm well," Androgeos said.

"Hmm." Victoria was noncommittal.

"I thought you *wanted* us to give you the algorithm," Satoshi said.

In the holographic projection, J.D. and the quartet rested together in companionable silence. J.D. dozed with her head against Quickercatcher's shoulder.

"I want you to give it to us," Androgeos said. "Not to give it away freely. Europa and I know how to distribute it so it will benefit Civilization—and Earth."

"I've told you I'd consider it," Victoria said. "But I'd rather not discuss it right now."

In the holographic image, Sharphearer idly untwisted several beads and bangles from her fur, tucked them into a fold of the wall, regarded them critically, and changed the position of the bangle imperceptibly. She added one of the bits of scarlet down, traced a small figure-eight of agreement with her nose, then folded her hands beneath her chin, snuggled into the nest, and closed her eyes.

"What's Sharphearer doing?" Satoshi asked.

"Hm?" Europa said.

Instead of watching the holographic projection, Europa was staring through the transparent wall of the observers' chamber. Androgeos was watching the auxiliary projection from the LTM in the connecting corridor, where nothing at all had happened since J.D. left.

"There, on the wall."

"I didn't notice," Europa said.

Satoshi closed his eyes to go into a momentary communications fugue. In response, the LTM observing J.D. turned its attention more closely to Sharphearer's creation. The image zoomed.

"Don't!" Androgeos said.

The zoom stopped.

"Why not?"

"It's . . . private," Androgeos said. "It wouldn't mean anything to you."

"Is it a religious ceremony?" Victoria asked.

"The Largerfarthings have no religion," Europa said. "I've tried to explain religion to them. They don't understand it."

"It is a ritual," Androgeos said. "But it's one you don't have, so I can't explain it."

"Will Sharphearer be upset if J.D. asks her about it?" Victoria said, concerned. "She might, eh? Why didn't you warn her?"

"I . . . didn't think of it," Europa said. "It's very private and I'm accustomed to not noticing it."

"Is J.D. in any danger?" Zev asked. The diver ran his webbed hand nervously through his white-blond hair.

"Certainly not!" Androgeos said. "The Largerfarthings wouldn't hurt anyone—at least they wouldn't hurt a guest."

"A breach of etiquette won't be a fatal error," Europa

said. She sighed. "Ah, Victoria, I've waited so long, prepared so long, for these encounters, but everything that's happened has been unpredictable. You have left me . . . off balance."

"We'd've liked things to go more smoothly, too," Victoria said. She could not bring herself to apologize to Europa—the alien humans owed Victoria an apology or two themselves—but she did feel a pang of sympathy.

Victoria stretched in her couch, arching her back, pressing her shoulders and heels against her couch and her hips against the safety strap, trying to achieve some feeling of resistance in zero g.

She was impatient to meet the Four Worlds representatives herself. She hoped J.D. would invite them to *Starfarer* when their nap ended.

A faint shadow fell across Victoria's face. She glanced up.

Beyond the circle of observers' couches, Stephen Thomas floated free near the ceiling of the chamber. Notably, and uncharacteristically, quiet, Victoria's second partner drifted against a backdrop of space and stars. His body and arms and legs were relaxed into the partly flexed position most natural to weightlessness. Starlight turned his delicate gold pelt into a translucent shining outline, and glowed amber through the new webs between his fingers. He had braided his blond hair roughly at the back of his head; escaped tendrils floated around his face. He wore running shorts and a loose silk t-shirt. Heavier clothes had become uncomfortable for him, since he started to grow fur.

His skin's getting so dark, Victoria thought. He's darker than I am, now. And redder. Mahogany, like Zev. What a pretty color . . . he's more beautiful than ever. I'm glad his eyes are still blue. I think I wouldn't mind, too much, if his hair changed, but Stephen Thomas without those sapphire eyes . . . that would be hard to bear.

The changing virus had transformed him from an

ordinary human being—not so ordinary, Victoria thought
fondly—into a diver. All the divers she had ever seen had
dark skin, fair hair, and dark eyes. That was Zev's coloring.
Zev said some divers had dark hair and a few had blue eyes.
He had no idea whether Stephen Thomas's eyes would
turn brown, but he thought it would be good if they did.
Divers lived in the sea—Zev's family had allied itself with
a pod of orcas in Puget Sound—and dark eyes were less
sensitive to bright light reflecting from the water.

It's Zev's fault Stephen Thomas is changing, Victoria
thought with a tinge of bitterness. I'm angry at him for
not knowing the details of how the changes happen, for
putting Stephen Thomas through so much uncertainty
and confusion.

A few days ago, Victoria and Satoshi and Stephen
Thomas had gone skinny-dipping. Remembering what
happened still upset her. Stephen Thomas had discovered, with an unpleasant shock, that his genitals were
changing, that his body was changing to enclose his penis
and his scrotum. It had never occurred to Zev to tell him,
to warn him, because Zev had not known that ordinary
male humans were so different from male divers.

Victoria had not seen Stephen Thomas naked since.
They had not made love. They had not even slept together. For several nights, he had stayed away from the house
he shared with Victoria and Satoshi. Victoria did not even
know where he had gone.

Satoshi thought Stephen Thomas planned to leave
them, but Victoria would not believe it. Their younger
partner, moody under the best circumstances, wanted
time to himself while he was under so much stress. Victoria wished she could help him, but all she could do
was acquiesce to his desire to be left alone.

Feral's death hit him hard, she thought. But maybe
he's getting over it. He doesn't look as sad as he did.
He'll come home soon.

She gazed at Stephen Thomas as he hovered over her

head, outlined by the multicolored tapestry of stars. In a moment of the strange vertigo of zero g, Victoria saw herself falling toward Stephen Thomas, saw him falling toward her—

She blinked to make her eyes refocus.

Across from her, Zev occupied J.D.'s couch. He gazed intently at the transmission from J.D.

No one in the alien contact department would sit in a colleague's regular place, Victoria thought, startled by an observation she had not made before. Maybe we're getting inflexible.

But Zev was not a member of the alien contact department. He should not even be on board the *Chi*, but Victoria did not have the heart to tell him to stay behind on *Starfarer*. He was J.D.'s friend, her lover. He had left his family for the first time in his life to be with her. He missed her desperately when they were apart, and J.D. missed him.

Victoria understood how Zev felt. She missed J.D., too. Their dawn excursion to the beach, several days ago, was the most fun Victoria had had in too long.

"Victoria!"

Europa's voice cut through Victoria's distraction. The alien human frowned at her from her place in an auxiliary couch between J.D.'s place and Stephen Thomas's.

"What is it?" Victoria spoke sharply, too, her sympathy cut away by Europa's imperious manner.

And admit it, Victoria said to herself. You shouldn't be daydreaming about your family, or about J.D., during humanity's first real meeting with Civilization. J.D. might need your advice, or even your backup.

The Minoan frowned briefly, then shrugged. "It isn't important," she said, her tone implying that it was important but that she did not care to repeat the question. Satoshi glanced quizzically across at Europa.

The frown-lines between the alien human's graceful black eyebrows smoothed from her ageless face. Victoria kept expecting to see evidence that Europa was thirty-seven-hundred years old, but found neither deterioration nor infirmity. Europa presented herself as a mature woman of exceptional beauty, with flawless red-brown skin and perfectly arranged black hair dressed with metallic silver threads. Who does her hair? Victoria wondered. Have she and Androgeos spent every Saturday night for four millennia refreshing each other's curls and ringlets?

"How long will you live?" Victoria asked abruptly.

Europa, bemused, started to reply.

"That's rather a personal question, don't you think?" Androgeos said, always ready to be offended or irritated at the modern humans who had so badly disappointed him.

"That's what we're here for, Andro," Satoshi said, in his usual reasonable and matter-of-fact way. "Asking questions is our job."

"Getting Earth accepted into Civilization ought to take precedence," Androgeos said. "If you behave with gratuitous rudeness, that will never happen."

"I think J.D. is doing quite well at being accepted," Victoria said. "Half an hour with the weasel people—"

"The Largerfarthings!" Andro said.

"—and she's in bed with them."

"They're taking a nap," Europa said. "They are crepuscular beings. Their rhythms are different from ours. Don't read more into what's happening than is warranted."

"You must have spent a fair amount of time with them, over the years," Victoria said. "With the Largerfarthings."

"With the quartet, yes, but not on their planet. It's difficult to live on a world where you can't eat the natural food, you can't comfortably breathe the air, speaking the language makes your throat sore—"

"Wait," Victoria said. "Back up. Can't breathe the air? J.D. isn't having any trouble."

Europa made a hissing, rasping sound that made Victoria jump.

"The Four Worlds representatives, I meant to say," Europa said in English instead of the Largerfarthings' language, "have changed themselves to breathe an atmosphere that can sustain humans. Largerfarther's atmosphere has more trace gases. J.D. would find breathing it unpleasant."

"And the Smallerfarthings?" Satoshi asked.

"Their air's quite toxic to us. I visited their world only twice. You can always smell the chemicals, even when the air in your quarters is safe. Largernearer's air is pure and sweet . . . but the world has no land to speak of."

"You didn't answer my question," Victoria said.

"How long will I live? I have no idea."

"How long *can* you live?"

"I suppose I'm immortal. Effectively. I don't age. Repair enzymes—" She implied Civilization's knowledge of human biochemistry with a gesture.

"Are you immune to illness?"

"Yes. I'm susceptible to accidents . . . but even there I have considerable resilience."

"You don't have much to worry about."

"I've been told," Europa said, "that you die when you get bored." She smiled at Victoria; her large, dark eyes shone with delight and amusement. "So far, I'm not the least afflicted by boredom."

"If everybody lives forever, where do all the people go?"

"What people?"

"People's offspring. Immortality—the result would be a permanent accelerating population explosion."

"There's no one answer to your question—it's the wrong question. Everybody *doesn't* live forever. The Largerfarthings seldom use immortality. They prefer a full life, a shorter life, in a family of at least three generations."

"A shorter life of four thousand years!"

"Not at all—where did you get that idea?"

"They rescued you from the eruption of Thera."

"Their people. Their ancestors." She smiled. "Ah, I understand what you thought. Longestlooker and her siblings aren't my mentors. Quite the contrary. I'm their mentor."

"They prepared themselves to meet us," Satoshi said. "But they couldn't be sure we'd arrive during their lifetimes."

"That is true," Europa said. "They are young, relatively speaking. They'll age, and die, at about the same rate as a healthy human being. There's no one system that all worlds follow. Not for longevity, not for *anything*. I keep telling you that. Each species controls its own destiny."

"Within the rules of the cosmic string."

"Yes. But it's *because* of the string that each species can make its own decisions."

"There must be some kind of consensus—"

"Why? Even the Four Worlds, who have been in communication for millennia, all approach the question differently. You'll find examples—successful and unsuccessful—that may help you solve your problems. But Civilization gives perfect answers to very few questions."

She stroked the curl of liquid silver in her hair, twining it around one finger. Victoria turned her attention to J.D.'s transmission, but Stephen Thomas, floating overhead, distracted her. He pushed a stray lock of his hair behind one ear. It slipped free and drifted in front of his eyes. He dragged his fingers through his hair to loose the untidy braid, and twisted the strands into a sloppy knot.

Zev fidgeted in the couch; Satoshi studied the image of the Nearer worlds, transmitted from *Starfarer*'s observatory: Largernearer, Orchestra's ocean-covered planet, and Smallernearer.

Satoshi had immediately pointed Smallernearer out

to his colleagues as the strangest planet in the system, the strangest planet of any system they had visited.

Stephen Thomas kicked off from the ceiling and brushed past Victoria, returning to his place in the observers' circle. Without thinking, she reached toward him, longing to caress his long leg with her fingertips, eager to smooth the gold pelt on his dark thigh. Before she touched him, she snatched back her hand.

How strange, Victoria thought. Stephen Thomas never distracts me when things are going well in our family. When I know that I can touch him, and have him respond with a smile or a kiss or a caress—then I can concentrate on other things. But now, when he's so distant, when I don't know what he's feeling or what he's thinking, or whether he's in pain, when I'm afraid that if I touch him, he'll withdraw, it's all I can do to keep my attention on my work. Or my hands to myself.

She squeezed her eyes shut and tensed her arms and legs and back; she clenched her fists.

The family *has* to take second place, just for now, she told herself. For all of us.

She said to herself, I *can't* make my partners take third place. What am I going to do, so I don't hurt J.D.?

She felt pulled in all directions by the whirlpool of events.

Damn! she thought. Stephen Thomas didn't *have* to decide to go through with the changes. But even if he'd stayed the same, he'd still be mourning Feral. If I've let my family fall to third in my attention, Stephen Thomas has let it fall to fourth or fifth.

A quarter of the way around the observers' circle, Satoshi gazed through the images and watched Stephen Thomas. His strong square face was grave. He was taking the changes in their younger partner very hard. Victoria found Stephen Thomas even sexier than before, if that was possible. The differences excited her. But Satoshi . . .

Satoshi dropped his gaze, then stared deliberately at his hologram of the eerie dark disk of Smallernearer.

He'll get used to what's happened, Victoria told herself. Won't he?

The awakening of the quartet roused J.D. from a doze.

I meant just to rest and observe, she thought. But it's so warm, so comfortable . . .

Sharphearer nuzzled Longestlooker's ear, making soft snuffling noises. She groomed the fur at her sister's throat with one hand, claws extended, leaving comb-marks in Longestlooker's pelt. Longestlooker pressed sideways, leaning into the pressure. Quickercatcher nudged J.D. Taking a chance, J.D. stroked her host's bright fur. Quickercatcher began a low, musical hum. Fasterdigger scratched Quickercatcher along the spine, between the first and second sets of shoulder blades.

"What happened to the silver threads in your fur?" J.D. asked.

Quickercatcher flicked the forefingers of his left hand rapidly across the nest bedding.

A multitude of thin silver strands wriggled over the edge of the nest and onto the back of Quickercatcher's hand. The silver worms crept into the fur of his wrist and disappeared. As J.D. watched, fascinated and dismayed, the worms reappeared in their usual places, slithering out through the fur of his shoulders to sketch the suggestion of a decorative collar.

J.D. forced herself not to move, not to shudder, not to shove herself out of the resting nest and brush frantically at her clothes. She imagined the worms had crawled up under her pants legs—

She set her jaw.

It's no creepier than the artificial lung, she told herself firmly. It's no worse than eating the birdlets.

"Are they—" She cleared her throat, disguising her

54

question. She had almost asked about parasites. "What are they?"

On her other side, Longestlooker scratched in a different rhythm, and another set of worms glided from the nest and into her shiny black fur.

Maybe Sharphearer and Fasterdigger will take theirs back, too, J.D. thought. Soon. Then I won't have to worry that some of those things are crawling on *me*.

"They're my biters," Quickercatcher said. "My mutualists."

"What do they do?"

"They keep my fur clean. And the bedding." Quickercatcher teased one loose and wrapped it around his finger, where it clung. "See? It has those long biting jaws, it can eat crawly things, and also hold on tight to my fur when I'm carrying it around."

J.D. felt queasy, though the solution made perfect sense for a person with a heavy coat.

How long would it take, every day, to wash your hair and comb it and dry it, if you had as much fur as Quickercatcher?

"And if there are any dangerous parasites around," Fasterdigger said, "the biters kill them."

The Largerfarthings' mutualists functioned like Nemo's attendants. The attendants had not bothered J.D. at all. She had thought them fascinating and beautiful.

Why do the mutualists faze me? she wondered. She answered her own question: Nemo was so different, and the Largerfarthings are so similar. This is one of those times I have to remind myself that we're aliens to each other.

Quickercatcher teased the biter, loosening it from his finger.

"Would you like some?" Sharphearer asked.

"No," J.D. said. "I don't think so. Thank you."

"J.D. couldn't use ours." Quickercatcher guided the

biter into his fur. "They wouldn't like living on her, and they couldn't eat anything in her environment."

"Europa might give you some of hers," Fasterdigger said.

"I'm sure she would," Sharphearer said. She flicked her fingers lightly against the resting nest. Her biters crawled out and rejoined her.

All along, J.D. thought, I've been thinking that the silver in Europa's hair moves like something alive. It was a prettier image when it was metaphorical.

"I'll think about asking her," J.D. said, to be polite.

"You said you have questions for us," Longestlooker said.

"So many I hardly know where to start." J.D. was glad to change the subject. "Why did you call human beings your clients?"

All four members of the quartet answered her question at once.

"Because we're your sponsors—"

"—We first explored your system—"

"—As far as we know, we're the first. The first from Civilization."

"If the Fighters had ever visited Earth, they probably would have changed it—"

"Destroyed it!" said Sharphearer.

"So much that human people would never have evolved."

"Who are the Fighters?" J.D. asked.

"We've found the remains of civilizations, old ones—"

"—the remains of people who destroyed each other, people who tried to take over living worlds."

"But it never worked!" Sharphearer said.

Quickercatcher agreed. "Star travelers wiped out tribespeople. But the Fighters died. They couldn't thrive on their conquests."

"They withdrew," Longestlooker said.

"Leaving ruined worlds," Sharphearer said sadly.

"How much uniqueness was lost," Fasterdigger said in the same tone.

"But you survived," J.D. said. "Civilization exists!"

"Before Civilization existed, the cosmic string withdrew."

"From everywhere— Every living world that we know of."

"We found records . . . The isolation lasted a long time."

"When it ended, new intelligences had arisen on worlds that would have been destroyed."

"The people of the Four Worlds," Sharphearer said.

"And the people from Earth," said Fasterdigger.

"And many other people," Longestlooker said.

Quickercatcher's nose described a figure-eight of agreement. "If the Fighters survived, we've never met them. Only their ruins. And . . ."

J.D. waited.

"A few stars . . . should possess amenable worlds. We should be able to visit them."

"But they're empty of cosmic string, so even if we could reach them, we could never return."

J.D. realized what Quickercatcher was explaining. "You think Fighters live there. Permanently isolated."

Quickercatcher hesitated.

"Tell me, Quickercatcher," J.D. said.

"Open your link. Just a little."

J.D. complied, for a split second—

An endless shriek, inarticulate and low-pitched, insinuated itself into her mind. If it contained words, she could not understand them, but the meaning pierced her to the center.

The upper harmonics cried of isolation, of exile and loneliness, begging forgiveness and compassion.

But the lower harmonics reverberated with a dirge of hatred, enmity, and threat.

—J.D. cried out and snapped her link shut, just as Quickercatcher cut off the transmission. She wrapped herself in fetal position, fighting to steady her rapid, shallow breathing.

"J.D., J.D., I *said* just a little bit—" Quickercatcher rubbed against her, soft fur sliding on her cheek and neck, urging her to relax her body from its distress.

Without thinking, J.D. flung her arms around Quickercatcher, hugging herself to the powerful body, the comforting fur. Quickercatcher's warm nose snuffled at her hair. His front feet hooked over her shoulders; his arms wrapped around her waist. The sensation was so strange that J.D. came back to herself. She drew away, scrubbing her eyes on her sleeve. Quickercatcher released her, watching with concern.

"I—I thought I did open the link only a little," J.D. said, embarrassed. "I enhanced it a few days ago, so I could communicate with Nemo, with the knowledge surface—with Nemo's starship. My starship. I'm not used to it yet." She drew a deep breath. "I'm all right now. That sound . . . was it a sound? What *was* it?"

"It is an electronic transmission from a system that should have hospitable worlds."

"Do you know anything about its people?" she asked.

"We don't even know for sure that people are sending the transmission."

"No one has ever translated it," Longestlooker said.

"If it carries within it the means for its own translation," Quickercatcher said, "we aren't clever enough to figure it out."

"It felt . . . It felt real," J.D. said. "It felt like it came from someone crying to get out. But I think I'd be too afraid of the person to help him." She shivered, remembering the low, angry harmonics.

"We have a similar reaction to it," said Sharphearer.

"As far as we know," Fasterdigger said, "no one has ever tried to respond to the transmission."

"What many of us believe," Longestlooker said, "is that those isolated systems *do* harbor sentient beings."

"The beings who chose to destroy other people for their own gain," said Sharphearer.

"The Fighters," said Fasterdigger. "They're cut off."

Quickercatcher made a figure-eight of agreement. "Maybe the string, and whatever controls it, will never reach out to them again."

J.D. thought of being isolated forever, trapped in one small spot . . . a star system would feel very small to people who had visited other systems, who knew that other worlds existed but lay forever out of their reach.

"You can't be sure . . . maybe it's just an artifact of the star. A magnetic field and a stellar wind . . ."

"Perhaps," Quickercatcher said doubtfully.

"A banshee," J.D. said, trying to smile.

"Banshee?" Quickercatcher jerked his chin upwards, then ducked his head.

"We don't know that word." Longestlooker sounded surprised.

"A mythical being. Outside your house, at night, it cries. Like the wind screaming through the trees."

"Like the wind," Quickercatcher said. "Yes."

"That describes what we hear very well," Sharphearer said.

"A banshee," said Fasterdigger.

"You're lucky that the Fighters never visited Earth," Quickercatcher said.

"We think," Longestlooker said, "that the other ones controlled the cosmic string."

"Set it up to guard us from the Fighters!" Sharphearer said.

"But it's far too restrictive," Longestlooker said. "We don't need to be protected so much anymore."

Quickercatcher said, "So if we can learn more about the other ones—"

"—how they controlled access to transition."

"By looking at *Starfarer*'s fossils—"

"The fossils are performance art," J.D. said.

Longestlooker's eyes closed in amusement, while at the same time she traced a figure-eight of agreement.

"Your joke about the fossils is funny." Longestlooker's tone was agreeable, even condescending. "It's good to joke about serious things."

J.D. did not know what to say. Gerald Hemminge, the assistant chancellor of *Starfarer*'s campus, wanted her to lie about the fossils, the sculptures, but she could not bring herself to do so.

It probably doesn't matter, J.D. thought. Whatever I say, no one in Civilization will believe the fossils are fakes. Crimson is right. Everybody *wants* to believe they're real.

"We will have to come to some arrangement over the fossils," Quickercatcher said.

"But they have nothing to do with your question," Longestlooker said.

"If the fossils mean the other ones visited Earth," Fasterdigger said, "that was a long long time ago."

"Before Earth had human people," said Sharphearer.

"So we were the first to visit human people," Longestlooker said, looping the explanation back to the beginning of its long and irregular path.

Late stopped grazing. The spines on his back stiffened and raised.

"You should know," he said, "that by 'we,' my friends mean all of us, all the Four Worlds. Their people, and mine, and Largernearer's . . ." Late's voice trailed off.

"What about Smallernearer's inhabitants?" J.D. asked.

"There is only one."

J.D. gave Late a questioning glance.

"Look."

In the center of the resting room, an image glowed into existence: the Nearers, eerily like Earth and the Moon. Atmosphere, clouds, and water covered Largernearer's surface with a gauze of blue and white. From

Starfarer's position, the disk of Largernearer was half full. Smallernearer's surface was barren, nearly dark, a uniform silver gray.

But that was impossible. It *had* to be in the same phase as Largernearer.

"Can I look at Smallernearer more closely?" J.D. asked.

At her request, the image enlarged.

Smallernearer contained no craters, no volcanic plains. Its featureless surface was the uniform color of ash.

Where 61 Cygni illuminated it, it glowed a soft gray, with very little albedo. It was a shadow against the stars.

"It supports life?" she said. "A being inhabits it?"

"You see that it's strange," Quickercatcher said with approval.

"Satoshi noticed it was strange. I didn't realize how strange."

The image expanded.

The featureless surface looked as unpromising for the evolution of life as the surface of Earth's moon. And yet J.D. knew from Satoshi's observations that the world was a major source of electronic transmissions.

"Do they—does it—live underground?" Perhaps the inhabitant was like Nemo, living a solitary life in interior chambers, the only being on its planet. "Is it a squidmoth?"

"Certainly not," Longestlooker said.

J.D. had learned to expect that curt, dismissive tone when anyone from Civilization discussed the squidmoths.

"Then where is it? What is it?"

The image expanded again, and the point of view dropped closer to the surface of the small world.

The image folded itself around J.D., reaching from the center of the chamber to the wall. She found herself surrounded by a nearly invisible mist, a frail network of branching hair-thin fibers. It was so fine that she could see through it for hundreds of meters.

"This *is* it," Quickercatcher said.

"It's an aerogel!" Victoria whispered in the back of J.D.'s mind. "Its density is just this side of vacuum. It's a substance that doesn't occur spontaneously—we thought."

Once Victoria had named it, J.D. remembered reading about the material. Unpromising as a substrate for intelligence.

And then she thought, It's a network—a web. If it's made of something that conducts electricity, or light . . .

She saw—or imagined she saw—a flicker of illumination in the far distance, nearly obscured by the gauzy substance.

"How did it evolve?" J.D. asked. "How did it form?"

"An excellent question," Longestlooker said. "The Smallernearer doesn't know. It has no memories for the first several million years of its existence."

"We think the other ones might have made it," Quickercatcher said. "Invented it, created it, given it life, allowed it the time to become aware."

"But we have no proof," Longestlooker said.

"No one's ever found another being like it," said Fasterdigger. "Or any antecedents."

"Can't you investigate?" J.D. asked. "Search for remnants of the other ones?" She grinned; she could not help it. "For fossils?"

"Smallernearer says no evidence of the other ones remains."

"Are you sure?" J.D. asked.

The quartet fell silent. Sharphearer nuzzled the underside of Longestlooker's chin, pushing her head deep against her neck, till Sharphearer's eyes were covered and her ears fluttered against the side of Longestlooker's jaw.

Quickercatcher scratched roughly with one hand beneath one forward leg. Scratching his armpit? J.D. wondered. His legpit?

"What's the matter?" J.D. asked.

"You know, of course . . ." Longestlooker said carefully, "like you, we are transmitting this meeting. To all the Four Worlds. To Smallernearer."

And I just called the Smallernearer a liar, or as good as, J.D. thought.

She struggled to control her instant, furious blush. She was good at other forms of biocontrol: suppressing her fertility, directing her metabolic enhancer with the touch of a thought, adapting to her expanded link within a few days. But she always blushed furiously whenever she was embarrassed.

"I'm sorry," she said, quickly. "I apologize. I didn't— I only wondered if you had helped look."

"Where would we land?" Longestlooker asked.

The image of Smallernearer receded rapidly, leaving J.D. giddy. When the dizziness faded, Smallernearer, the planet, covered with the Smallernearer, its inhabitant, spun before her. No point on the surface of the small world was free of the kilometers-deep layer of wispy aerogel.

A spark of light raced across the surface of the world, following a complex and recursive path.

"No one has ever landed there," Quickercatcher said.

"Not since the beginning of Civilization," Longestlooker said gravely.

"If anyone did land," Quickercatcher said, "the damage would be terrible."

"We can't visit Smallernearer," Sharphearer said sadly.

"Can you visit *Starfarer*?" J.D. asked. "Will you? Would you like to?"

Longestlooker spiraled out of the resting nest.

"You've visited us. We'll visit you, if you like."

Three

J.D. followed the quartet through the tangled tunnels of the Four Worlds ship, letting them guide her through the maze. They passed hundreds of tiny dioramas tucked into the walls. J.D. still had not had the chance to inspect one closely. Now and again a colorful bat-bird winged past.

At the entrance to the connecting tunnel, Smallerfarthings and Largerfarthings waited to see them off, bringing with them baggage and equipment and food, all the supplies their colleagues would need while visiting *Starfarer,* an alien ship.

In the connecting tunnel, J.D. led the way toward the *Chi,* feeling like the leader of a caravan on the silk road. The contents of the Farthings' baggage, no matter how ordinary to them, would be as strange and wonderful as any cargo of rare spices.

Victoria unfastened the safety straps of her couch and let herself float free in the observers' circle.

"Let's go," she said eagerly. "Let's go meet the Four Worlds people."

"And their parasites," Satoshi said. He grimaced. "Ugh."

"Their *mutualists,*" Europa said. "Not parasites at all."

"Whatever you say," Satoshi said.

Zev pushed off to the ceiling and rebounded to the doorway. Satoshi floated to Victoria's side. Europa and Androgeos joined them; Stephen Thomas followed last.

"Are those things in your hair really alive?" Zev asked Europa.

"Yes, young ichthyocentaur."

"I'm not part fish," Zev said. "And I'm not that young!"

Europa smiled. "You are to me."

Stephen Thomas's hair came loose again. He gathered it up at the back of his neck and shoved the tangled strands down the neck of his t-shirt. The soft loose fabric would not hold it. It came loose again and drifted in front of his eyes.

"Fuck it!" he said angrily. "Is there a pair of scissors on board?"

"Don't cut your hair!" Victoria stopped, embarrassed by the strength of her outburst.

"Take this, Stephen Thomas," Europa said. She drew one of the silver worms from her hair.

"What the hell for?"

She teased it around her finger. It wrapped snugly, searching with its biting end for something to grasp.

"To hold back your hair. You'll break Victoria's heart if you cut it, and your fussing is driving me crazy."

Stephen Thomas looked at the silver worm.

"Do they disturb you as much as they do Satoshi?"

He shrugged. "Interesting critter."

She drew the worm across the nape of his neck. The worm coiled around his hair, keeping it in place. The biter clamped its jaws onto a few strands of hair.

"That's better," Europa said.

"How do I get it out?"

"Tease it, stroke it. It will relax."

Stephen Thomas fingered the thin silver strand.

"Do you want it, or not?" Europa asked.

"Yeah, I guess so," Stephen Thomas said. "Thanks."

Victoria wondered how it would feel to tease the silver worm out of Stephen Thomas's hair. But Satoshi looked ill.

The airlock clanged. Victoria forgot the silver worm.

The Farthings and all their baggage piled into the *Chi*'s airlock, crowding the small chamber. J.D. edged in after them. Late floated from Sharphearer's back, his spines undulating out of his coat and beneath his fur, scarily close. J.D. believed that his poison would not harm her. But she also believed those long sharp spines could give a painful jab.

"Goodbye," J.D. said to the Farthings who had accompanied them down the connecting tunnel. "I'm sure we'll meet again soon."

The hatch closed, sealing off the *Chi* from the Four Worlds ship.

Orchestra, the artificial intelligence from Largernearer, popped into view.

"May I go with you?"

"Of course," J.D. said.

Outside, the connector tunnel released itself from the *Chi*. Light streamed through the port. The *Chi* hummed faintly, its steering jets gentling it away from the Four Worlds ship. It powered toward *Starfarer*.

The inner airlock hatch opened. J.D. ushered her companions into the explorer craft.

Europa and Androgeos joined the quartet and embraced them, one by one and all together. The trills and hums of the Largerfarthings' language shimmered in the air.

Zev met J.D., grabbed her hands as he sailed past, and drew her into a slow spin. Diplomatic restraint was foreign to him, and J.D. was glad of it. He pulled himself closer to her. The speed of their spin increased. J.D. hugged him, laughing. The quartet watched, tangled together in a similar conglomerate. Longestlooker's low trilling hum tickled the lower ranges of J.D.'s hearing.

She touched the wall to slow the spin. Zev slid his hands down her arms, hooking his fingertips with hers till they were barely touching, rotating very slowly. Finally he let her go. He caught himself against the wall and used up his momentum with his legs. He hovered, smiling, watching, fascinated by the quartet.

J.D. hugged Victoria, but instead of an embrace she received a brief, cool touch of Victoria's cheek to hers. She drew back, startled, thinking, I stepped over a line, I *know* Victoria's more proper in public than Zev is. Of course, almost anyone is more proper in public than Zev is.

Like J.D., Zev missed the casual, continual physical contact among the divers and the orcas of his family.

Regaining her composure, a composure Victoria had never lost, J.D. introduced the other members of the alien contact department.

Victoria offered her hands to Longestlooker. The two touched. Longestlooker raised her chin and ducked her nose thoughtfully.

"I'm honored to meet you," Longestlooker said. "It's rare, and wonderful, when new members bring a unique contribution to Civilization."

"I hope Earth will be allowed to join Civilization," Victoria said evenly, "so we can all share our work."

"We all anticipate a favorable result," Longestlooker said. "And we're anxious to appreciate what you've done."

"And use it," Stephen Thomas said.

J.D. flinched, but Victoria's lips twitched in a quick smile.

"Yes." Longestlooker closed her eyes slowly from outer corners to inner. "We have our practical side."

"Perhaps you're wise to wait," Quickercatcher said.

"We want to proceed on a basis of trust and goodwill," Sharphearer said.

"We'd like to proceed as members of Civilization," Satoshi said. "That won't be till our solar system regains its access to the cosmic string. Till we can come and go freely from our home."

Quickercatcher made a figure-eight of agreement.

Esther Klein bounded over the craters of *Nautilus*, moving easily in the low gravity. Soon the bright orange top of the excursion tent rose above the starship's curving horizon.

The tent was a windowed elongated orange dome with an airlock projection, like half a giant squash. Liftoff scars and bootprints scuffed the dust around it, marring the pristine surface. In a million years, J.D. was the first being to visit Nemo.

Esther lengthened her stride. She would be glad to get back. She bounced completely over one big crater. She was tired and hungry. Before leaving the expedition tent, she had watched J.D.'s first encounter with the Four Worlds. She was rapt, like everyone else on the expedition.

But *Nautilus* fascinated her. As soon as the quartet cuddled down with J.D., Esther had hurried outside to explore *Nautilus*. Now she was hurrying back, to watch the Four Worlds' first encounter with *Starfarer*.

Starfarer's sail rose over the horizon.

The spin of *Nautilus* and *Starfarer*'s orbital motion brought the enormous sail, the gossamer lines, and the double cylinders of the starship into view.

The stellar sail lay edge-on to 61 Cygni. Iphigenie Dupre, the sailmaster, wanted to be sure the push of the stellar wind did not conflict with the gravitational attraction of *Nautilus*. To avoid the stress of furling the sail, she oriented it to cut the wind instead of catching it.

Reflected light illuminated the silver sail, turning it into an immense mirror. On its surface, a reflection of

Nautilus shimmered behind the minuscule reflection of *Starfarer*'s double cylinders.

Esther watched, awed, as the starship rose farther above the horizon and passed overhead. The mirrored images crossed the surface of the sail, then disappeared, as the sail's angle to her changed. For a few minutes the sail reflected stars. Then it was directly overhead, edge-on to her as well as to 61 Cygni, visible only as a silver streak.

She raised one hand toward the starship.

"Doing okay?" A disembodied voice spoke to her through her suit radio.

Esther smiled.

"Yes," she said, replying to Infinity Mendez through the personal channel. "Watching the sights. I didn't think anyone would see me wave."

"I've got your transmissions running," Infinity said. "Quite a change, from when J.D. was there. Before Nemo died."

"Yeah."

When Nemo was alive, the planetoid teemed with Nemo's attendants, strange creatures that draped the caverns with iridescent silk, created the air, maintained the complex network that was either an ecosystem or Nemo's body, depending on the observer's point of view.

"How about you?" Esther asked.

"Okay so far," he said. "I miss your help. And Kolya's. And I plain miss you."

"Thanks, Kenny," she said. "Me too."

When Infinity Kenjiro Yanagihara y Mendoza had joined the deep space expedition, he decided to stop being Kenny Yanagihara and start being Infinity Mendez. No one ever called him Kenny anymore. Except Esther, once in a while, for old times' sake . . .

It surprised him; he took a moment to reply.

"See you soon," he said.

"I hope."

As *Starfarer* dropped toward the horizon, the edge of 61 Cygni flared above the rough edge of a crater. Esther's faceplate darkened against the light.

She reached the tent, entered the airlock, and waited for the pressure to equalize. The interior door opened. Esther stepped through it, unfastening her helmet and pulling it off over her short curly hair.

"Hi, I'm back, you should see—Oh."

Holographic images filled the main room of the tent, nearly hiding Kolya.

Awfully crowded in here, Esther thought, considering that Kolya always describes himself as a hermit.

Some of the images moved aside. Beyond them, Kolya Cherenkov sprawled in one of the air-tube chairs, all lanky limbs and angles.

He raised one hand in greeting. His smile deepened the lines at the corners of his dark eyes and made his striped eyebrows look even bushier than usual.

The largest image had not moved. It sat before Kolya, bringing the real-time presence of Griffith into the tent.

"Sorry," Esther said to Kolya. "Didn't mean to interrupt."

"You're welcome to join us."

"That's okay. I've got some work to do."

Esther disliked Griffith. He was in the employ of the people who had tried to disrupt the deep space expedition. She believed that if he ever got the chance to make *Starfarer* return to Earth, he would take it.

She tried to avoid him, but that was tough. Esther had volunteered to help Infinity, and so had Kolya. They worked together frequently. Griffith tagged around after Kolya all the time.

I can understand admiring Kolya, Esther thought. Join the club, Griffith. But don't act like a puppy dog.

Esther wished she had entered the tent in silence. Then Griffith would not even know she had returned. Now she had to make an appearance in the transmission area, or be directly rude. She considered rudeness, but decided not to make Kolya uncomfortable.

"Hello, Griffith," she said.

"Yeah," he replied, and went right back to his conversation with Kolya. "There's no sign that the Four Worlds ship is staging an invasion," he said. "I *don't* like the idea of letting them on board *Starfarer*. If they try to take *Nautilus* . . . I'm keeping a lookout, don't worry."

Disgusted, Esther left the focus of the tent's transmission spot.

So much for being civil, she thought. Why do I even try? And he's so damned paranoid . . . On the other hand, if we all didn't feel a little paranoid about *Nautilus*, Kolya and I wouldn't be standing in for J.D. in the first place.

She stripped off the rest of her suit and sat down to clean it. She was tired, but she was too pissed off to sleep. She felt sticky and she wanted a shower, but if she had to go outside in a hurry she wanted her suit clean even more.

"I doubt the Four Worlds will be so inhospitable as to invade *Nautilus*, Petrovich," Kolya said. "They would risk their representatives, besides."

"That's a small price to pay for a starship," Griffith said. "Anyway I'm going to keep watch."

What the hell for? Esther wondered. *Starfarer*'s unarmed—unless Griffith sneaked some ordnance on board, and I wouldn't put it past him, in which case we're in even more trouble. We could use *Nautilus* as a great big wrecking ball, but . . . what a waste.

"Thank you for your vigilance," Kolya said to Griffith, sounding perfectly serious. "I'll speak with you later."

Griffith's image faded from the center of the room, clearing some space. Esther felt relieved.

I try to be civil to him because I'm scared of him, she admitted to herself. Because he *is* scary, when he lets that undercurrent of danger show, when he isn't making himself invisible.

Usually he acted as if Esther and everybody else on board *Starfarer* was invisible too, not worth bothering about, no threat. Except Kolya, of course.

Maybe, Esther thought, I ought to ignore him and let myself *be* invisible.

She wondered what it would be like to go through life like that, ignoring everyone who could not be of direct use or direct threat, pretending to be of no interest to anyone. She did not think she would like it much.

So far she had avoided any direct disputes with Griffith. She had been in her share of scuffles, even a few real fights. She had always been able to take care of herself. But she had never been in a physical confrontation with someone who had serious training. Griffith did not brag, did not show off, did not even mention his background. But Esther had no intention of testing him.

"I apologize for his rudeness," Kolya said.

Kolya smelled of stale tobacco. She had not seen him smoke since they had come to *Nautilus*. An open flame was not a particularly safe thing to have in an expedition tent, with hard vacuum a few layers of fabric away.

Esther applied a trickle of lubricant to one of her spacesuit's stress points. After she had tested the range of motion, she shrugged.

"You're not responsible for Griffith's behavior," she said. "No reason for you to apologize."

She wondered what Kolya was doing about his nicotine addiction. Not smoking made him sick. Cigarette smoke made Esther sick; stale smoke was even worse.

"But I *am* responsible for his presence," Kolya said.

Esther chuckled. Infinity Mendez had told her about finding Griffith trapped in an emergency pouch, where Kolya had left him.

"Ah," Kolya said. "You know what happened. I wasn't sure if you'd heard the story."

"Infinity probably would have kept his mouth shut, if Griffith hadn't threatened him about talking to anybody. Infinity's a lot more stubborn than most people think, and prouder. Griffith's not too smart, I think."

"He's as smart as any of us. Maybe not Victoria, or Miensaem. But as smart as the rest of us. He has a different viewpoint. And conflicting loyalties."

"He's a spy!"

"A guerrilla accountant," Kolya said.

Esther laughed. "Guerrilla *accountant?*"

"He says he is an accountant."

"And you believe him?"

"I believe . . . what he tells me. I might not be so quick to accept what he told anyone else."

The deep lines in Kolya's face, and his brindled hair, fascinated Esther. She wanted to ask him if they were the result of living in space for so many years. She respected and admired him. There was hardly a pilot in space who did not admire Cosmonaut Cherenkov.

"Why do you call Griffith 'Petrovich'?" she asked instead.

"An old custom from my homeland," Kolya said. "The custom has probably disappeared as thoroughly as the country."

Esther wished she had not said anything; she had brought up a subject far more painful than the effects of solar radiation on hair follicles.

"The Mideast Sweep banned the Russian language when they took over," Kolya said. "Perhaps no one uses patronymics anymore. I call Griffith by his patronymic, he calls me by mine. By chance, they're the same."

"Why not call him by his given name?"

"He doesn't like it."

"What is it?"

"You'll have to ask him that."

Provoked, she touched Arachne and asked for information. She got nothing back but the passenger list of an incoming transport that she herself had flown. It recorded only his initials, his job—his cover—with the General Accounting Office.

Griffith was not a member of the deep space expedition, so his résumé was not on file. He was on board now by mistake, along with two United States senators and the niece of the U.S. president, carried away when *Starfarer* fled the order to turn it into an orbiting weapons platform. And fled the military carrier sent to enforce the order.

"We owe him some respect, my friend," Kolya said.

"Respect! He was spying on us. He—"

"He would have sacrificed himself to try to help us."

"How do you know that?"

"Because I wouldn't let him. That's why he was in the survival pouch. I put him there to keep him from throwing himself out the airlock."

"Why?"

"Why did I stop him?" Kolya asked, startled.

"No—why did you have to?"

"He thought the carrier might end its pursuit. He thought it would stop chasing us to rescue him." Kolya hesitated. "I feared it would not do so."

"You were probably right," Esther said curtly. She knew most of the people on the carrier; many had been her friends, until they ordered her not to disembark from *Starfarer* with her transport full of people. They had fired the nuclear missile. Only Kolya and J.D.'s actions had kept the missile from destroying *Starfarer*.

Esther still felt embarrassed and guilty about obeying the order not to undock.

"The expedition has reason to be suspicious of him," Kolya said. "And he's certainly alienated enough of its members. Florrie, for instance, and Stephen Thomas, not to mention you and Infinity. He's not a hero in wolf's clothing. But like most people, he has heroic potential."

"Why would he want to help the expedition? He tried to destroy it!"

"As I said . . . conflicting loyalties."

"He did it for you." It was the only reason that made any sense.

"He tried," Kolya said, troubled.

"Then he's not a complete bonehead—*somebody* got through to him."

"I wish that was true," Kolya said. "I wish he had heard me out, and considered, and decided I was right. Instead, he divined what I wanted—what he thought I wanted—and he tried to make it occur."

Esther shrugged. "What's the difference?"

"A great deal, to him and to me. Perhaps not so much to *Starfarer*." Kolya sighed.

Esther hung up her suit.

"In any event, I'm sorry he was rude to you. I think perhaps he was not brought up very well—"

She shrugged again. "I don't care what he thinks about me."

"—and he is, of course, furiously jealous."

Esther frowned. "Jealous? Of what? Of *me*?"

"Of your being here. On *Nautilus*."

"He could've come, if he wanted." She flung her hands up, spreading her arms wide. "I only came because J.D. asked me to. I wanted to see *Nautilus*, sure—what pilot wouldn't?"

"Very few. I couldn't resist."

"But it's not like either of us can fly it. There's not even much left to see, since Nemo died. Nothing but a few curled-up shells from the attendants."

"And the core."

"Yeah. Only I'm not a physicist. *Or* an engineer. I can't take the center apart and figure out how it works and put another one together. And I don't much feel like getting irradiated."

"There is that."

"So there's no reason for me to be here. Or you."

"Someone must be here."

"A couple of warm bodies. So Civilization can't claim it's abandoned. Salvage it. Take it away from J.D."

"Not much satisfaction to my friend Petrovich."

"I'd be a lot more use back on *Starfarer*. Working with Infinity. God forbid any of the faculty should get their hands dirty."

"They would if he asked. They helped you get the artificials back to work."

"This is supposed to be a community—he shouldn't have to ask." She snorted in frustration. "I suppose I'll have to read them the riot act. That's what it took last time."

"The point is," Kolya said, "that J.D. asked you. She didn't ask Griffith."

"He's not a member of the expedition," she said. "He—"

She stopped, realizing the contradiction before Kolya voiced it.

He drew his eyebrows together in a quizzical glance.

"Neither are you," he said.

"I know, I know, I don't know why I said that. But it's *different*—"

"Neither am I." He knitted his eyebrows in a thoughtful look. "It occurs to me, J.D. may have chosen you, and me, for exactly that reason."

"Because we're *not* members of the expedition?"

"Because we have no contractual obligation to *Starfarer*. No matter. She trusts you. She does not trust Petrovich. So he is jealous."

"It isn't *my* fault—!"

"But that is the explanation."

"He's a scary guy, Kolya."

"I suppose he has that effect," Kolya said reluctantly.

"Not to you," Esther said. She realized what it meant, that Kolya had forced Griffith into the survival pouch.

She saw Kolya anew, not as the legendary cosmonaut turned starfaring hermit, but as the former guerrilla fighter who had bested a similarly trained man less than half his age.

"He's scary, but you're not," she said, with wonder. "Why aren't you scary?"

"Because I'm not dangerous."

"You could be."

"Not to anyone on the expedition. Except perhaps the person who killed Feral."

"Yeah," Esther said. "Me too. I've had some pretty awful dreams about what I'd like to do to Chancellor Blades."

"The evidence points in his direction, but nothing is proven," Kolya said.

"It's proven enough for me."

"Nothing is that simple," Kolya said. "He has not had his say."

"He had a chance to defend himself."

"I'm glad he refused," Kolya said. "What would have happened if Iphigenie had made him admit he was guilty?"

"Beats me," Esther said, recalling Jenny Dupre's first mob, recalling how close she herself had been to joining it. "He's lucky he's got the silver slugs to hide behind. He's lucky that Infinity thought of making him stay in his house."

She shivered. The chancellor's house was blocked up and cut off, isolated by the silver slugs. It was dark, and silent. The chancellor was too dangerous to allow back into Arachne, even if *Starfarer*'s control computer would have him. The evidence J.D. and Stephen Thomas had discovered was enough for Arachne; the computer had immunized itself against the chancellor's neural pattern.

The evidence proved that the chancellor had crashed Arachne twice. Feral had died during the second crash.

Maybe Blades had not hunted him down and killed him; maybe his death had been an accident. Blades was still responsible. The chancellor lived in darkness, and loneliness. But for Feral, the darkness and loneliness would last forever.

Kolya patted Esther gently, awkwardly, on the shoulder. She flinched, and he jerked his hand away.

"I—"

"It's okay," Esther said quickly. She took his hand and squeezed his long bony fingers. The smell of smoke was pungent, unpleasant. "You startled me, that's all."

"Ah." He let his hand fall; Esther released him. Her exertions were catching up with her; she yawned.

"I'd really like to grab a catnap," Esther said. "Just until the *Chi* gets home."

They both glanced at the small hologram being transmitted from the *Chi* as it approached *Starfarer*.

"I'll call you when it's time," Kolya said.

"Or if anything happens."

"Yes."

"Thanks." She had her link set to nudge her, but she appreciated Kolya's consideration.

Soundproofed fabric walls segmented the tent into several cubicles. Esther was glad of a place to herself. She kicked off her pants and pulled off her sweaty t-shirt. Feeling drained, she slipped into her sleeping bag and hugged it around her.

Being in the exploration tent made her appreciate *Starfarer*, where she could sleep in a bed, with sheets, and open all the windows and doze in the sweet cool breeze, the birdsongs, the scent of rain showers.

Not to mention blizzards and floods, she reminded herself. That was the trade-off for a dynamic weather system.

The tent felt stuffy, the air flat.

Esther stretched and closed her eyes.

She could not sleep.

She had been startled by Kolya's comforting touch. He did not often touch people. But more than that, she had been startled by the pure sexual desire that radiated across her skin when she felt his hand on her shoulder.

He was attractive. She had always thought so, even when he was a distant, elusive, larger-than-life myth. She had not been prepared for the strength of her reaction.

Lousy timing, Esther thought. Back on *Starfarer*, it crossed my mind once or twice to see how he'd react to a pass. Even after I found out about the cigarettes. I don't know how he'd react to a pass, and I don't know how I'd react to kissing a smoker. Too much was happening, anyway.

Now we're stuck here on *Nautilus* until . . . who knows? If I proposition Kolya now—if he's even interested—talk about a cliché. Two people working alone, and all one of them can think about is sex.

Half my friends would fall apart laughing. If anything happened, the other half would never speak to me again from jealousy.

I'd probably never live it down.

The *Chi* decelerated as it approached *Starfarer*.

The explorer craft docked easily against the axis of *Starfarer*'s campus cylinder. The *Chi* settled; the hatch connected; variations in pressure equalized.

The hatch opened.

J.D. and Quickercatcher paused at the entryway. It was as crowded here as it had been in the reception room of the Four Worlds ship. Nearly everyone on board the starship floated in the waiting room, anxious to meet the alien people of the Four Worlds.

Quickercatcher ducked his head and brushed the side of his neck against J.D.'s arm, a nervous and endearing gesture. *Starfarer*'s people sighed with a collective intake of breath, and an exhalation.

Another first time, J.D. thought. The first time anyone except alien contact has been able to meet an alien being. Except, of course, anyone could go out on *Starfarer*'s surface and meet Nemo's offspring. Not many have.

Then she thought, Can you meet a being who isn't born yet? Or is "born" even the right terminology to use about the squidmoth egg?

Had her colleagues accepted Civilization's assessment, that the squidmoths were not worth any bother? Androgeos thought the squidmoth nest should be pried off *Starfarer* and jettisoned. J.D. avoided drawing attention to the nest, afraid others would agree with the Minoan.

Gerald Hemminge, the Acting Chancellor, floated forward to greet the Four Worlds people. He was, as always, well turned out, wearing a dark suit, linen shirt, leather shoes with a high polish. The impeccable white linen set off his dark skin and hair, his golden brown eyes.

How can he always wear linen without getting wrinkled? J.D. wondered. Gerald's clothes were impractical in zero gravity, but he did look elegant.

"I'm Gerald Hemminge, the acting chancellor of the deep space expedition," he said to Quickercatcher. "Welcome to *Starfarer*."

"Thank you," Quickercatcher said.

J.D. and Quickercatcher floated into the waiting room. Victoria followed with Longestlooker, Satoshi and Stephen Thomas and Zev with Fasterdigger and Orchestra's artificial intelligence, Androgeos beside Sharphearer and Late. Europa watched from the entryway, like an apprehensive chaperone.

The members of the alien contact department spread out behind J.D. and Quickercatcher. The rest of the faculty and staff of *Starfarer* hovered in an irregular array behind Gerald and the two United States senators.

Late rode Sharphearer's back like the caparison of a show horse. His rear edge fluttered; his spines glistened.

Just behind Gerald, Senator Ruth Orazio carried a ceramic vase, a strangely curved container with a twisting, interconnecting handle and spout. The shape formed the three-dimensional projection of a four-dimensional object, a closed form possessing a single surface, its interior contained by, yet connected to, the exterior. The Klein bottle's graceful pattern of glazes accentuated its strangeness.

"We offer you a guest gift of water," Gerald said.

Ruth Orazio touched off from the wall at her feet. She moved forward, offering the bottle. William Derjaguin moved beside her.

J.D. felt uncomfortable. The two senators were not members of the expedition. At best they were unwilling passengers, at worst hijacking victims.

The senators had every right to watch the welcome, to attend the meeting. How could they resist? But they were acting as major participants. J.D. thought it was inappropriate. She glanced toward Victoria. Victoria's shocked expression left very little to the imagination.

"This is too much," Quickercatcher said. "You have already reciprocated our guest gift."

Ruth Orazio froze. J.D. had a quick sharp shock of apprehension, of something gone wrong. But Longestlooker scooted up beside her and spoke without the edginess that so often colored her voice.

"It is all right, brother," she said to Quickercatcher. "We accept the gift in the spirit of its giving."

J.D. still felt the introduction had gone awry, but Ruth smiled and opened the vase. In a neat maneuver, she spun it. A globule of water popped from the spout in its side.

Quickercatcher hesitated, glanced at Longestlooker, then stretched his long muscular neck and snapped the globule between his sharp teeth. A few bright drops glistened in the fur of his muzzle.

"The water is very pure," he said formally.

Orazio handed the Klein bottle to Derjaguin. He spun it, releasing another blob of guest water.

The quartet drank some of the water. Late rose and captured a sphere of water, balanced it against his teeth and his radula, and broke it into his mouth. Orchestra swam through a loose spray of droplets. Longestlooker accepted the bottle and freed the water left in it for everyone to drink.

Gerald introduced the Four Worlds representatives to the faculty and staff and to the images of Esther Klein and Nikolai Petrovich Cherenkov, projected from the surface of *Nautilus*. J.D. shared her colleagues' reactions, reexperiencing delight and amazement, curiosity and trepidation.

Gerald introduced Longestlooker to Professor Thanthavong, who was losing her usual equanimity; she pressed her sleeve against her eyes to stop tears of elation.

"Professor Thanthavong is a Nobel laureate. That's our greatest scientific honor. She developed a way of combating viruses, and she stopped a terrible plague."

Longestlooker raised her chin, then ducked her head, and made the soft trilling purr of pleasure.

"We of the Four Worlds have great respect for scholars," she said.

"I never dared believe I'd see this day, meet someone from another world—I'm honored."

"We are honored, too," Longestlooker said.

When Florrie Brown was introduced, she took Longestlooker's powerful hand and enclosed it between her palms, her fingers shaky and frail. Longestlooker gazed at Florrie and closed her eyes from outer to inner corners in friendly amusement. In the meantime Quickercatcher hovered near them, inspecting Florrie's three long braids with interest. Florrie was the only human in the room whose hair was as flamboyant as Quickercatcher's fur: one braid pink, one green, the third natural white, all three plaited with beads and bells.

Longestlooker gracefully extricated her hand from Florrie's, and moved on. When J.D. glanced back, Quickercatcher and Florrie Brown were trading hair ornaments.

The representatives moved among *Starfarer*'s faculty and staff and guests: Orazio and Derjaguin. Iphigenie Dupre the sailmaster and Chandra the sensory artist. Avvaiyar Prakesh the astronomer and Infinity Mendez the gardener. All the graduate students, including Mitch and Lehua and Bay who worked for Stephen Thomas, and Fox who was in Satoshi's department. Griffith, who in a moment of uncharacteristic straightforwardness had recently described himself as a guerrilla accountant. Esther and Kolya back on board *Nautilus*, who welcomed Orchestra's virtual presence with their own.

Drifting at the edge of the crowd, J.D. enjoyed watching the encounters. Stephen Thomas floated nearby, withdrawn and distracted. J.D. was worried about him.

Gerald Hemminge moved free of the crowd clustered around the Largerfarthings. He gave Stephen Thomas a disdainful glance.

"I must say this, Stephen Thomas," he said. "Don't you ever think of dressing adequately—let alone properly— for any occasion?"

Stephen Thomas looked through him, then brought his attention to Gerald with an angry snap of his head.

"Fuck off, Gerald."

He kicked off hard with both feet, flew over the edge of the crowd of his colleagues, and arrowed out the waiting-room door.

Gerald watched him go, grimaced with disbelief and distaste, then turned to J.D.

"Quite a successful meeting, I'd say."

"It was until a minute ago," J.D. said, but Gerald ignored the implication.

"And do you think," Gerald said, "that they'll agree to return with us to Earth?"

"No, Gerald," she said. "Why do we keep having this conversation?"

"For one thing, because Nemo would have agreed if he—she—if it hadn't been entering metamorphosis."

"You can't keep asking members of Civilization to strand themselves in our solar system."

"We have no choice. We have to prove aliens exist."

"Why are you so anxious to go home?" J.D. asked. "If we're patient, the string might return to our system."

"It's selfish of you to stand in the way—"

"I don't think I'm alone—"

"—just because of *Nautilus*."

J.D. frowned. "What does *Nautilus* have to do with anything?"

Gerald glanced at her quizzically. "You'll have to turn it over to EarthSpace, of course," he said.

She stared at him, shocked. "What—?"

"It's in your contract," he said.

"*Nautilus* was a gift."

"Come now, J.D."

Gerald's upper-class condescension made her grit her teeth.

"You know perfectly well," he said, "that as an EarthSpace representative, you aren't permitted to accept valuable gifts. It would be a conflict of interest."

Nautilus is *mine*, she thought desperately. She could not think of anything to say.

"And here's Crimson Ng," Gerald said heartily. "At last!" He pushed off from the wall and floated toward the artist, leaving J.D. without a backward glance.

Orchestra's AI vanished from one side of the room and reappeared directly before Crimson, who started with surprise. All four members of the quartet arrowed toward her, and even Late stirred himself to rise up and watch her with animated interest.

"You're the archaeologist—" Longestlooker said.

"—who found the fossils—" Quickercatcher said.

"—that Androgeos showed us!" said Sharphearer and Fasterdigger at the same time.

"Are there any more?"

"Your analysis is impressive!"

"Is the physical provenance preserved?"

They all spoke at once. Crimson, flustered but pleased, spread her hands. She had dirt beneath her nails.

"You can see the dig. After the floodwater recedes. If there's anything left of the site. Maybe tomorrow."

"The fossils were damaged?" Late asked, stricken.

"We're lucky to find them at all!" Crimson said. "We dug them off the *moon*, you know."

Gerald moved between Crimson and the quartet, bluff and hearty, smoothing over the possibility that the flood had washed out the site.

"I'm sure the fossils are safe," he said. "Let's go see you settled in. It's traditional on *Starfarer* to give a party for newcomers. That will be this evening. Tomorrow's soon enough for serious matters . . . such as the fossils."

He wanted Civilization to believe in the fossils. J.D. did not see any way of persuading Crimson to admit the fossils were fakes. Not since the sculptures had fooled Androgeos and Europa. J.D. sighed.

Late clamped himself against Sharphearer's back, quivery with disappointment, but Longestlooker reacted with patient amusement.

"Come with me," Gerald said, "and I'll show you where you'll be staying. The artificials will bring your baggage along later."

The Four Worlds representatives followed Gerald from the waiting room and into *Starfarer* proper.

Soon J.D. and her colleagues in alien contact were the only expedition members left behind.

"I don't *believe*—" Victoria said. She stopped, and blew out her breath, and smiled sadly at the others. "I suppose I should get used to the way Gerald gravitates toward power, eh?"

Before anyone could reply, Europa left the *Chi*'s hatchway and joined them.

"It went rather well," Europa said. "Despite the extra gift. You should be proud of your colleagues. Proud of yourselves."

"Proud, and superfluous," J.D. said.

"I'm not ready to step out of this picture," Satoshi said.

"I have to," J.D. said. "You have other work to do. My job is to open the door, then stand out of the way."

She tried to keep her voice cheerful, matter-of-fact, job-well-done. But she felt sad.

She left the waiting room last, following her colleagues and the alien humans and *Starfarer*'s faculty and staff and the ambassadors from the 61 Cygni system. The Farthings had left without giving her a backward glance. Not even Quickercatcher had looked to see if she was coming.

The members of the alien contact team straggled apart. Victoria moved through zero g, floating easily along the corridor. Zev and Satoshi had gone ahead; J.D. and Victoria were alone.

J.D. caught up to Victoria.

"Victoria," she said hesitantly, "if I was presumptuous—when I hugged you—I'm sorry. I won't—"

Victoria touched J.D.'s wrist, her fingers strong and gentle and cool.

"Don't apologize. Please. I . . . I was afraid to hug you back."

"Why? I don't . . ."

"I enjoyed our time together so much. I think about it, I find myself planning when we'll have a chance to be together again. But . . ."

Her partners don't want her to, J.D. thought, her spirits sinking. Did I misjudge their relationship that badly? She felt herself blushing.

"Is it Satoshi and Stephen Thomas?" she asked.

"It is, in a way." Victoria sighed. "But not in a way that has anything to do with you! Not directly."

"I don't understand."

"You've probably noticed . . . some strain."

"Some," J.D. said, thinking, that's putting it mildly.

"Everything is so complicated. Satoshi and Stephen Thomas and I, we have things to work out together." She hesitated, then said sadly, "If we can."

"Do you think . . ."

"It isn't that I don't want to be with you—it's that I feel fragmented . . . I feel like Satoshi and Stephen Thomas and I are desperately hanging on to each other by our fingernails." She hesitated. "Oh, I'm so sorry, I love you, I don't want to hurt you—I wish I'd never led you on!"

J.D. managed a smile. "The leading on was mutual."

They reached the border between the stationary axis of *Starfarer* and the rotating campus cylinder. They crossed the boundary; microgravity gave a faint perception of "up" and "down." The radial acceleration here, several levels down from the axis, was strong enough to create a perceptible sensation of gravity. The gravity increased as they continued downward.

"After you and your partners work things out," J.D. said, and let the unfinished sentence hang in the air.

"Would you let me start over? Could you?"

J.D. brushed her fingertips gently against Victoria's cheek.

The corridor opened out onto the hillside sloping from *Starfarer*'s axis to its living surface, the hill that formed the end cap of the starship's cylinder. Here they could walk, instead of bouncing and gliding. J.D. paused to regain her equilibrium on solid ground, after so many hours in weightlessness.

All around the conical hillside, switchback trails led downward to the floor of *Starfarer*. The cylinder stretched away into the distance. Hills and streams and rivers, groves of young trees and fields, paths and gardens covered the starship's inner surface. At the campus's far side, fog obscured the ring-shaped sea.

A little way down the hill, at the first switchback turn, Satoshi and Zev waited with Europa and Androgeos. Stephen Thomas was nowhere in sight.

At the bottom of the trail leading down from J.D.'s position, Sharphearer's bright fur stood out in the group of Largerfarthings. A number of *Starfarer*'s faculty were still following the Four Worlds people, but Gerald and the senators were monopolizing the visitors' attention. Gerald joined the faculty members, spoke seriously for a few moments, then left the group behind and hurried after the representatives.

The faculty members began to disperse.

Victoria whistled softly in surprise. "Gerald's got more nerve than brains," she said. "I wouldn't want to be the one to shoo that group away. He shooed Professor Thanthavong!"

J.D. knew how they all felt, as the group broke up and straggled toward home or work, most accompanied by Arachne's holographic projection of the Farthings.

J.D. reminded herself that her part of this meeting was over. She and Victoria joined the others at the switchback turn. Zev slid his warm webbed hand around J.D.'s fingers.

"I think I'll go back to *Nautilus*," J.D. said to Victoria. "Kolya and Esther must be getting bored out there all alone."

"*You'll* be all alone," Victoria said, protesting.

"I'll be okay," J.D. said.

"You won't be all alone," Zev said. "I'll go with you."

J.D. squeezed Zev's hand gratefully.

"I wish I could talk to Alzena," J.D. said. The head of the ecology department had fled from *Starfarer*, seeking sanctuary from Earth and from her family. Europa had taken her in.

J.D. glanced at Europa, beseeching. "Won't you ask Alzena if she'll help terraform *Nautilus*?"

"Don't you care how fragile she is?" Androgeos said angrily. "She's beginning to regain her equanimity. To find some happiness. She doesn't wrap herself up in a shroud anymore—"

Europa put one hand gently on his wrist. He fell silent, but glowered at J.D., at Victoria.

He's trying to protect Alzena, J.D. thought with surprise. His reaction eased her perception of the arrogant younger Minoan into a new, more sympathetic, shape.

"Give her more time," Europa said. "She thought of herself as dead, you must let her think of herself as alive again. Reborn." She smiled. "Haven't you thought to ask me for help?"

"Yes," J.D. said. "But . . . I'm afraid to owe you a debt."

Europa's voice held sadness. "I can't blame you for making that decision. I can only blame myself."

"You don't have time to go back to your squidmoth ship," Androgeos said.

"All I have is time!" J.D. exclaimed. "Why are you trying to keep me away from *Nautilus*?"

Suspicion crept into J.D.'s reaction. Europa and Androgeos knew how to exploit the great value of *Nautilus*. But J.D. was not prepared to give it up. Not to EarthSpace, not to Europa, not to Civilization. Especially knowing that Civilization's method of controlling the massive little starships required destroying the knowledge surface. Even if J.D. never found out how to use the knowledge surface to its whole potential, it was all she had left of Nemo.

"We won't prevent you from returning to your ship,"
Europa said. "But first you have another task."

"What's that?"

"The Nearer Worlds, of course," Europa said. "A visit
to the Nearer Worlds."

Four

J.D. closed her eyes and opened herself into her expanded link. The rest of the world disappeared. Within Arachne's web, Esther acknowledged that she and Kolya were safe within the expedition tent, prepared for *Nautilus* to move.

J.D. passed beyond Arachne; she touched the knowledge surface of *Nautilus*.

In response to J.D.'s thought, her starship pressed itself into a new course. Moving it was as easy as walking. *Nautilus* curved toward Largernearer, gently, gently, so its gravity drew *Starfarer* with it.

J.D. opened her eyes to blank darkness. Startled, she squeezed her eyes shut, withdrew herself from her link, and looked around again. The world and her body returned.

She stood up, shaky, taking herself back from the dissociation of the link. The knowledge surface exhilarated her, yet saddened her because of Nemo's absence.

Nemo was gone, but one of Nemo's offspring remained, clinging to the side of *Starfarer*'s wild cylinder.

It was past time to pay the young being a visit.

Senator Ruth Orazio walked beside Sharphearer, who paced easily along despite carrying the Representative's representative. Senator William Derjaguin, known to his colleagues as Jag, walked uneasily beside Quickercatcher, while Gerald Hemminge shepherded Longestlooker and Fasterdigger.

Sharphearer squinted in the bright light of *Starfarer*'s sun tube. She opened a tiny pouch tied into her fur and drew out a gauzy, bright yellow scarf that contrasted violently with her multicolored coat. She placed it on top of her head so its edge shielded her eyes. Several of her mutualists twined around the corners of the scarf to hold it in place. Fasterdigger, too, shielded his eyes with a sheer scarf, while Quickercatcher combed his thick fur forward to shade his eyes and Longestlooker laced her fingers together against her forehead.

Europa and Androgeos rejoined them, and the group set off across the meadow at the bottom of the hill. The beads and knick-knacks braided into Sharphearer's fluorescent fur clicked in rhythm to the Largerfarthing's steps. Several of Europa's meerkats scampered out of the bushes to accompany them.

Sharphearer and her siblings were as tall as Ruth, who was of medium height. When they stretched their long necks upward they reached two meters high. When they rose on their hind legs, as they sometimes did, they were much taller than a human being, and quite imposing.

Ruth glanced sideways. She met Sharphearer's equally sidelong gaze. Behind the flutter of yellow gauze that shaded her large, shining eyes, Sharphearer blinked, slowly, in friendly amusement.

Like spray from a cold shower, a shock rushed through the senator.

I'm walking with an alien, she thought. *Two* aliens. The alien contact department did their job; now it's my responsibility to forge a relationship between our governments. *All* the governments.

It was easy to overlook Late, but he represented an equal member of the delegation. Ruth had too much experience to offend any participant. She had seen delicate negotiations fail because an arrogant envoy offended an assistant or a secretary, somehow never having noticed that assistants and secretaries ran the world.

Late lay draped over Sharphearer's back like a horse blanket, his front edge resting just behind Sharphearer's arms. One of Europa's meerkats rode with them, perching on Sharphearer's front shoulders. It balanced itself by clutching at Sharphearer's neck with its front paws.

Ruth and Sharphearer led the way into *Starfarer*'s only real forest. The pleasant approach to the American Embassy in Denny Hill wound along cool shade-dappled paths. On the rest of campus, two-meter saplings or tall fast-growing bamboo covered the hillsides. The embassy architect had insisted on landscaping with well-grown trees, imported at some expense from one of the older O'Neill colonies.

The forest ended. The diplomatic group paused at the edge of the glade.

The imposing facade of the embassy, a cliff of natural-looking stone, loomed above them. Above the treetops, the stone gave way to irregular streaks of glass, the outside window walls of the embassy proper. Rimrock capped the embassy design.

Twisted sideways by *Starfarer*'s spin, a waterfall coursed down the cliff. At each step, the water picked up speed and weight. At the top, it billowed down in slow rainbow spray and settled like a cloud. It flowed like a silk curtain from the first pool to the second. It spilled out of the second pool and crashed down the cliff. With a sound like kettledrums, water cascaded and splashed into a final deep basin.

Longestlooker arched her neck and flared her nostrils. From beneath the shade of her long hands, she gazed at the waterfall.

"The effect satisfies me," she said quietly.

"Thank you." Ruth wondered where on the scale of compliment the comment fell, and wished Gerald had not been so eager to cut the representatives of Civilization loose from the alien contact specialist.

The lowest pool flowed into a stream that passed beneath a rustic bridge of heavy logs. The recent floods had left the logs sodden, but the massive bridge remained steady beneath the footsteps of three pairs of shoes, a pair of sandals, one set of bare human feet, and the catlike pads of the four Largerfarthings. On the other side, the path led to the embassy's front door.

The group entered the cool foyer. Sharphearer petted and poked her mutualists until they released her sunshade. The Largerfarthing delicately pushed the gauze back into its tiny pouch. The material folded into almost nothing.

Ruth felt elated and exhausted and vaguely ill. Excitement had kept her awake since J.D. met the quartet. Even Jag Derjaguin reacted to meeting the interstellar civilization—worlds with government, culture, trade, not passive observers like the squidmoth Nemo. Jag looked amazed and bemused. Once in a while, an expression of pure disbelief passed over his face. Ruth kept expecting him to pinch himself.

"Here's the elevator." Everyone piled inside. Ruth did not feel up to climbing stairs today.

She glanced at her Senate colleague, with whom she had had so many vehement arguments about the space program. Jag grimaced and raised his eyebrows in a self-deprecating, you-were-right expression. Ruth smiled at him, in sympathy rather than triumph. She appreciated his grace. His opposition to the deep space expedition had been proven wrong: completely, intensely wrong.

Ruth found herself pressed against the polished wooden wall by Fasterdigger, the most massive of the Largerfarthings. He gazed at her, direct and friendly and intense, arms stretched forward, elbows resting on front shoulders, hands pillowing chin. Both his thumbs curved beneath his chin, while his three central fingers lay against his cheeks. His nails were orange, the same color as the spots of his fur. Ruth wondered if he painted them, or if they grew that color naturally. The silver mutualists glittered against his brown background fur.

The elevator powered upward. Ruth closed her eyes and clenched her teeth against the strange feeling of a moving elevator inside a spinning cylinder: the perception of gravity slid from beneath her feet to behind her.

The Largerfarthings trilled with delight at the sensation.

"Is this an entertainment?" Sharphearer asked.

"Only a function of vector interaction," Gerald Hemminge said. "It will stop in a moment."

Ruth slitted her eyes open. Fasterdigger was still watching her. Mutualists decorated his forearms and his jowl hair. One thread twined through a delicately carved jade bead. Locks of his hair braided and knotted around mysterious pouches and vials.

The sweet spiciness of his scent made Ruth dizzy.

The elevator stopped. Gravity returned to its proper place. Ruth plunged into the wide hallway.

"We'll put you here in the VIP suite." She hurried toward the doors and flung them open. She felt better with more space around her. Breathing deeply, she entered the suite and crossed the flagstone floor.

The suite was spacious and bright. Comfortable couches and chairs clustered on thick silk rugs. The central room flowed across several levels. An irregular streak of window glass followed the stepwise pattern. The glass formed the suite's outside wall and stretched across seaward Denny Hill, facing the length of *Starfarer*.

The forest undulated over foothills, then gave way to meadows. Overhead, at the axis of the cylinder, the sun tube streaked away in a bright line of light. Streams and lakes decorated a landscape green with spring grass, marked here and there with the muddy wash of the snow-melt flood. To either side the land curved upward, as if Denny Hill lay at the head of a huge, deep valley, a valley whose sides closed together far overhead. The cylinder stretched to the blue and gray and purple distance of the sea, a ring of water pierced by the sun tube.

The aliens, the alien humans, and Gerald and Jag paused in the wide double doorway of the suite. The meerkats scampered in and rushed around, exploring.

"I've not visited your Embassy since it's been finished," Gerald said. "It's very impressive."

"Please make yourselves at home." Ruth gestured to mirror-image spiral staircases, one at each end of the wide room. "The suite has four bedrooms upstairs and four on this level. This is the sitting room. We have plenty of office space, if you need it."

She did not mention that the office space was empty because the United States had recalled its diplomatic staff before *Starfarer* left the solar system.

"And let us know what we can do to make you comfortable."

Ruth hesitated, waiting for some sign from the representatives of Civilization that the accommodations were acceptable or out of the question. She had decided to offer each individual from the Four Worlds a separate room. She had no idea how to ask about their sleeping arrangements.

Gerald strode to the window. "A magnificent view— you Yanks always do things on the grand scale."

"Thank you," Ruth said, and thought, I'm repeating myself.

The administration building, where Gerald normally spent most of his time, had a similar view. Ruth smiled to herself. She was as uncertain of where Gerald's comment fell on the compliment scale as she had been of Longestlooker's.

Maybe I should have angled for some diplomatic time at the Court of St. James, she thought ruefully.

She had always specialized in the space program; she got along fine with scientists and engineers.

The group of Four Worlds representatives entered the big sitting room. When the quartet walked, the decorations and bells and beads in their fur clicked and jingled.

Europa's sandals squeaked, but Androgeos walked silently, barefoot. He curled his toes against the warm stone tiles.

"Just like home," he said.

"J.D. mentioned the warmth of your starship's ground—" Ruth said.

"I meant at Knossos," he said. "We used to warm the floors at Knossos."

Sharphearer flopped onto her belly and looked over her shoulder at Late. The Smallerfarthing lifted his anterior edge, suckers extended, quivering. After a silent communication with Sharphearer, Late slid from the Largerfarthing's back to the floor. He spread himself across the stone. Except for the faint ripple of his breathing, he lay perfectly still and silent.

"What's he doing?" Ruth asked.

"Appreciating your artwork." Sharphearer rose gracefully to her feet.

The room held only a few of the paintings it had been designed to display. None of the art glass had been shipped into orbit. Ruth regretted all over again her government's withdrawing its support for the deep space expedition.

"Which pieces does he like?" Jag asked.

"The floor."

"Eh—?"

"He can explain," Europa said, "if you communicate

directly. It's hard to describe. He can help you perceive what he experiences. Imagine the sun on your skin, tracing patterns—but we humans aren't physiologically fitted to experience it firsthand."

"I'll settle for an inadequate description," Jag said. He stood in the doorway, apart from the group.

Is he scared? Ruth thought. I've never seen him scared, not about anything.

Ruth gingerly opened her link and listened. Europa explained about heat gradients and thermodynamic patterns. Ruth felt in her mind the sensations that Late perceived as art. It did not affect her as art; the faint mental prickles of the heat flow tracings made her edgy and uncomfortable.

Ruth let her link close.

We should have brought the alien contact department with us, she thought. J.D. didn't deserve a brush-off: "You've done your job, now we'll take over." She might not understand why the floor is a work of art—or maybe she would—but she'd ask gracefully about sleeping arrangements for two kinds of aliens. I don't even know whether to put Europa and Andro together.

"Can you cover the windows?" Europa asked.

Ruth touched Arachne. The windows darkened and polarized. The white slash of the sun tube dimmed and blued; colors faded across *Starfarer*'s hills and lakes and meadows.

"I mean manually," Europa said pointedly, "as you will not allow us access to your computer."

"The backup is voice activated," Ruth said. "I'm sure we can teach it to respond to all of you."

"This is much better," Quickercatcher said. He moved sinuously forward into the center of the room.

"We live our lives at dawn and dusk," Longestlooker said. "Your living space is so *bright*—"

"And hard." Sharphearer extended her claws and tapped them on the floor.

Fasterdigger added, "Do you have any nest material?"

"The bedrooms are . . . er . . . softer," Ruth said. "The rooms for sleeping. They have pillows and blankets and—"

Sharphearer and Fasterdigger each swarmed up a spiral of stairs. Sharphearer's serpentine body curved up the nearer stairs. Fasterdigger, stockier and more muscular, rang the twin staircase with his footfalls.

"Are they tired?" Gerald asked Europa.

"It's rest time," Europa said, which did not exactly answer the question.

Pillows rained from one staircase. A moment later, bright blankets tumbled down the other. A white feather-bed fell with a soft thump, and two purple sheets fluttered after it. One of the sheets draped onto the railing.

Sharphearer loped headfirst down the stairs, balancing pillows on her back. As she passed the sheet, she grabbed it with her free hand and dragged it after her. On the other staircase, Fasterdigger thundered down the treads, festooned with the upstairs rooms' blankets.

"The other soft things are too big to move by myself," he said.

Quickercatcher joined Fasterdigger and helped him carry the blankets and pillows to the center of the room. They pulled cushions off the sofas and piled the bedding on top of the cushions. Longestlooker settled on the carpet to oversee the nest construction. Absently, she freed three glass baubles from her fur, added a silky tuft of scarlet fuzz, and unfastened a tiny earthenware vial.

"The mattresses aren't meant to be moved," Ruth said. "They're to sleep on. While they're on the bedsteads. Wouldn't you . . . like to try that?"

"We're always willing to try new things." Longestlooker arranged the miniatures on the corner of the coffee table.

"Oh, no, sister," Fasterdigger said, "there isn't room for every person."

"Not on those little platforms," Sharphearer said.

"We'll put a place right," Quickercatcher said.

"Some other nap, we'll try your way," Longestlooker said kindly to Ruth. Without looking at her minute shrine, she opened the vial, poured out a drop of liquid, stoppered the vial again, and tied it back into her fur.

"There's room if each person sleeps on a different bed," Ruth said.

The three glass ornaments nestled in a bed of scarlet down. A sharp smoky scent rose from the arrangement. Once it was finished, Longestlooker paid it no more attention.

Quickercatcher smoothed his hands down the sides of his neck, sleeking his soft cotton-candy fur.

"That wouldn't be very comfortable," he said. "All spread out?"

"We do want you to be comfortable." Jag's tone was dry.

Fasterdigger piled more blankets on top of the pillows and sofa cushions. Late luxuriated in art appreciation.

"This will do," Longestlooker said "Though it's rather sparse."

"It'll be fun," Fasterdigger said.

"Like a camp-out, the way Zev described," Quickercatcher said.

"In the wild," said Longestlooker in response to Ruth's quizzical glance.

"Zev probably had something a little rougher in mind," Ruth said. "I hope you can swim."

Quickercatcher snuffled sharply. "I sink," he said. "My fur is so long. Will we have to swim?"

"That'd be my first thought, if Zev was involved," Ruth said.

"You don't have to do anything you don't want to," Jag said.

"Good," Longestlooker said.

"I think," Gerald said, "that you'd do better to let an adult expedition member show you around. I'll arrange a tour."

"We would like to see the fossils," Longestlooker said.

"Certainly," Gerald said heartily. "We'll arrange it with Crimson Ng as soon as possible."

Sharphearer loped in with more bedding balanced precariously on her back. She tossed it onto the heap, kicked her hind feet like a young horse, and leaped onto the tumble.

"Look here!" Gerald said. "Have you left any beds for Androgeos and Europa?"

Sharphearer poked her nose out of the blankets and gazed at Gerald.

"Can't they stay with us?" she asked, stricken.

"Of course we'll stay with you," Europa said. "The chancellor and the senators aren't familiar with our customs."

"They are," Jag said, "unusual."

"Perhaps to you," Europa said. "Where Andro and I come from, the members of my household would sleep with me. It was companionable, and I was responsible for them. What better way to insure their well-being?"

"We have different outlooks," Jag said easily. "I'd consider the propriety of the situation."

"We do have different outlooks." Europa smiled. "In Knossos, the head of the household protected vulnerable members—and promoted good matches for those who wished them."

Jag coughed to cover his startled, uncomfortable laughter.

Androgeos joined Sharphearer in the pile of bedding; he leaned against the Largerfarthing, one arm over her forward shoulders. They bent their heads together; Sharphearer twisted one of Andro's thick glossy ringlets around her long pointed finger, then pressed her

101

nose beneath his chin. Andro tickled Sharphearer's frizzy goatee.

Longestlooker blinked, rose, and joined Sharphearer and Androgeos.

"Travel disarranges one's rhythms so badly," she said, curling around a pillow. One of the meerkats pattered over to the nest and burrowed under a blanket.

"I'll leave you to your rest," Gerald said.

"You're welcome to join us."

"It's been a long morning, perhaps you're tired too," Fasterdigger said.

"No, thank you, I never sleep in the middle of the day, and I have a great deal of work to do," Gerald said. "Senators, a moment of your time?"

"Certainly," Jag said.

Ruth smiled. This is irresistible, she thought.

"It *has* been a long morning," she said. "Thank you, Longestlooker, I will join you. Mr. Hemminge, I'll be glad to talk to you later. It isn't critical?"

"Urgent," Gerald said. "But . . . no. Not critical."

As he and Jag left, Jag glanced back at her. His disbelief shaded into disapproval. Ruth barely kept from laughing.

A little embarrassed, Ruth sat on the edge of the nest. Quickercatcher paused before her.

"May I sleep beside you?" Quickercatcher asked.

"Yes, I'd like that."

Quickercatcher curled sinuously behind her and settled himself. Ruth cautiously leaned against the Largerfarthing, between his forward shoulders and his central shoulders. His sweet spicy scent no longer struck her with cloying strength. Quickercatcher's soft fur brushed the back of her neck. The Largerfarthing clasped Ruth's hand. His inner and outer thumbs circled her palm. The bare bright skin was very warm. Nearby, Europa settled down beside Longestlooker, who laid her head in Europa's lap and closed her eyes. The alien human unbraided a lock of the Largerfarthing's hair, unstrung the decorations from it, and gently separated the curled strands.

Outside the resting nest, Fasterdigger tickled Late's front edge with his sharp-clawed toes.

"Late, Late, wake up, it's time to go to sleep."

Late's back rippled, exposing his poison spines. Fasterdigger snuffled sharply and pivoted away. The Largerfarthing leaped into the nest, landing lightly for such a massive creature. He sprawled between Longestlooker and Sharphearer and rested his head on Androgeos's muscular thigh.

"What did Late say?" Ruth asked.

"He is appreciating the artwork, and does not care to be disturbed."

"You shouldn't have teased him about being asleep," Sharphearer said.

Longestlooker let out her breath in a long sigh and fell asleep. Her breathing trilled softly, a musical purr.

Quickercatcher laid his head on his neat front feet and closed his eyes. His hand slipped from Ruth's grasp.

Exhausted but not sleepy, Ruth let herself relax. She entered the same state she used when she had to pull all-nighters back home, when she had to shepherd an important bill or develop a last-minute legislative strategy. With a few minutes' rest, she could gather herself for a long stretch of work.

Back home, she thought.

A pang of homesickness, loneliness, grabbed her by surprise. Tears filled her eyes and her throat clenched, hot and tight.

Oh, god, I miss Dan, she thought.

She and her partner had a commuter relationship. Ruth went home to Bellingham when she could; he visited her in D.C. When Congress was in session, they saw each other only a couple of times each month.

But they spoke together every day, projecting their

103

VONDA N. MCINTYRE

images cross-country. They joked that they had perfected making out on the phone. Once in a while they used VR techniques to be together, but usually they did not even need to.

She had not spoken to him since he saw her off at the space plane. She had planned to call him at just about the time that *Starfarer*, its communications cut by the military carrier's interference, had plunged into transition.

During their last few minutes alone, risk spiced the sudden burst of desire between them. A minor risk. They had thought.

Everything's going to be all right, Ruth said fiercely to herself. It's got to be all right.

The smoky scent of Longestlooker's shrine hung heavy in the air.

A silver thread probed from Quickercatcher's soft mauve shoulder.

The mutualist twined across Quickercatcher's fur. It touched Ruth's arm. Ruth recoiled. The biter writhed away, snapping its clawed jaws, shaking its eyeless head.

A rush of nausea surged in Ruth's throat. She lunged out of the nest and ran to the bathroom. She barely made it to the sink before she threw up.

Her stomach finally emptied itself. The taste of bile burned hot and sour. Ruth turned on the faucet and let the water run, rinsing the sink. She washed out her mouth, drinking straight from the tap. She splashed clean cool water on her face. She felt hot and weak.

"Let me help."

Europa came into the bathroom and closed the door.

Ruth grabbed a towel and wiped her mouth. "I'm all right."

"Of course you are. That doesn't mean you don't need a bit of help."

Ruth froze.

"I don't—"

"It's perfectly obvious." Europa chuckled. "My dear child."

"No one's called me 'child' in a good long time," Ruth said, masking fright with annoyance.

"You're all children, to me," Europa said easily. "Even Andro . . . especially Andro. You're all my responsibility."

"I'll be responsible for myself, thanks all the same."

"I'm concerned. If you stay in Civilization for long, this could present a serious problem."

"It's nobody else's business."

"It's bad manners to reproduce in a star system not your own."

"Then I'll be rude!" Ruth snapped.

"It isn't that easy."

"Is anything? Is anything easy, or simple, or straightforward—in your Civilization?"

"Very little."

"What happens?" Ruth asked in a conciliatory tone. "When someone's rude?"

"That depends."

"Doesn't everything?"

Europa smiled. "You're beginning to understand."

"This is *serious!*"

"Yes. I didn't mean to make light of the situation. The most common reaction to unacceptable behavior is economic sanction."

Ruth shrugged. "We aren't exactly anyone's trading partner."

"But you are," Europa said. "Through my efforts. If you have your baby in the Four Worlds system, the people will be shocked and embarrassed. Earth is, after all, their first client."

"We never asked to be their client!"

"Do you want to join Civilization or don't you? You cannot, without being someone's client."

"Will they do anything beside being shocked and embarrassed?"

"The Largernearlings will boycott Earth's work. The

Largerfarthings will shun you. The Smallerfarthings will fine you. The Smallernearer is indifferent."

"This is crazy," Ruth said.

"Without it, the population—"

"Listen to me, Europa! Back on Earth, government coercion and social pressure and ignorance and compulsory pregnancy and forced abortion and even family bullying never worked to balance the population."

"I know that," Europa said. "I feared . . . but you did bring yourselves under control. I've wondered how."

"I'll tell you what worked. Giving control to individuals worked. Giving us—you, me—the power to decide yes, it's time for a child, or no, the time isn't right. Women died to get that power. No one gets pregnant anymore unless she *wants* to! Nothing the Four Worlds can do will force me to—"

"Dear child, I had no such thought!"

"You *said*—"

"I *meant*—*Starfarer* would have to take you to your own system. Home." Her expression changed from one of reassurance to one of consternation. "They *would* do that—would they not?"

"And be stranded?" Ruth said. "I . . . I don't know. The people on *Starfarer* agreed it wasn't to be a colony ship. They agreed not to have children during the expedition. But I—"

"You weren't meant to come along."

"No. I wasn't meant to be pregnant, either. I wasn't, when I got to the spaceport. Then—" She blushed furiously. "We've been trying for so damned long, we never thought—"

Ruth burst into tears. Europa came to her and enfolded her.

Ruth cried. Europa murmured to her in a strange, melodic language. The embrace of her wiry arms was remarkably comforting.

"Don't tell," Ruth said.

"Shh, shh," the alien human said. "We'll think of something."

"It probably won't matter." A long dark wave of grief and depression washed over her. "I miscarried—"

"Shh! Shh, don't think such a thing." She rocked Ruth back and forth.

Finally Ruth stopped crying. Europa wiped her face with a cool damp towel and led her back into the darkened sitting room. She bedded her down next to Quickercatcher and tucked a blanket around her.

I shouldn't let her do this, Ruth thought. I don't need to be pampered, this is pathetic. I should get up and go find out what Gerald Hemminge thought was so important . . .

Quickercatcher shifted gently in his sleep to make a space for her, and nuzzled her beneath the chin. Europa patted her hand.

"Shh, shh."

With Quickercatcher's fur soft and comforting against her, Ruth fell sound asleep.

Esther Klein entered a hexagonal underground chamber deep beneath the surface of the starship *Nautilus*.

Esther flashed her light around, tracing the rock shapes. Three pointed archways alternated with three round archways. The pointed arches led into large alcoves; the round archways opened into tunnels. She had come in through one of the tunnels. She thought she recognized where she was.

Entering one of the alcoves, she rubbed her glove against the pitted stone of the back wall. The rock crumbled. A chunk fell away. Esther jumped back as steam clouded out from the wall. Water exploded into vapor on exposure to hard vacuum. Most dissipated; some scattered to the floor as ice crystals that glittered for a moment, then sublimated. Water continued to seep from the wall and vaporize, a strange spring. Slowly the surface crusted over.

This is where Satoshi saw Nemo's air being made, Esther said to herself. I'm sure of it. There's nothing left of the critters who produced the atmosphere except a few hairs, a few scales. They must have processed the water to make air. Hydrolysis, maybe an enzymatic reaction . . .

While Nemo was still alive, the silken inner tunnels had held oxygen, nitrogen, traces of hydrocarbons. When the squidmoth died and the tunnels disintegrated, the air escaped. J.D. planned to terraform the planetoid she had named *Nautilus*. Eventually it would be a tiny world in itself, like Europa's ship, with lakes and streams, forests and fields. First it would need an atmosphere and water. If *Nautilus* contained a large deposit of water, that would solve several of J.D.'s problems at once.

Esther sent an LTM out to explore and probe. She put the broken chunk of rock in her sample pouch.

I wonder, Esther thought, if J.D.'s going to need a backup pilot . . .

She had no idea how to move the starship. Only J.D. knew. Maybe she would be willing to teach someone else.

Let's see, she thought. I spent five years doing space construction. Piloting transports, eight. I'll never fly another EarthSpace transport. Even if they'd let me work for them—damned if I want to. But this little starship needs some work. So . . . how does mining oxygen or transporting water grab you, Klein?

Esther wished she had a spaceship. But the alien contact department needed the *Chi*, and Esther's transport had never been designed to land or lift off, only to dock with other spacecraft.

I *could* land the transport here, she thought. And get off again. I'm sure. Nearly sure. The gravity's low enough. But the transport would get pretty beat up if I tried.

She still wished she had a ship.

Esther laughed to herself. You're *on* a ship, the neatest starship you'll ever see.

She climbed toward the surface. *Nautilus* was dark and cold, stripped of Nemo's luminous cables and translucent silk. The tunnel opened into a large, deep crater, one of the pits from which Nemo's offspring had launched their silken balloons.

Esther loped easily up the crater's side. Her boots barely touched the rock before she pushed off again. In five long leaps she reached the surface of the strange little world. The horizon was so close that she could see its curvature.

She paused to gaze into the black sky, the multicolored stars. The constellations nearly matched the familiar patterns of Earth. In interstellar terms, an infinitesimal distance separated 61 Cygni and the sun. The only difference was the small bright spark of Earth's sun. Esther gazed at it for a few minutes, wondering when—if—she would return home.

Here, beyond any atmosphere, more visible stars cluttered the ancient patterns. Esther was used to seeing stars from space, to recognizing familiar patterns against the wash of light of the galaxy. Back home she spent half her life in space. On the deep space expedition, she was . . . what? A fugitive, a stowaway, an inadvertent kidnap victim? Her sympathies were and always had been with the people who would be accused of kidnapping her.

Esther shrugged. She would be in a complicated position when the faculty decided to take *Starfarer* back to Earth. In the meantime, she would do what she could to help the expedition. The consequences be damned.

Bright, hard lights made a spoked wheel of J.D.'s shadow. She hurried through the rough tunnel in *Starfarer*'s thick stone skin. The gravity was higher than on the inner living surface, though still less than one full g.

J.D. glanced at the ceiling, at the harsh artificial glow. Higher above her, deeper inside the starship's second cylinder, lay *Starfarer*'s wild side. J.D.˙had not yet had the chance to explore it, even to visit it. In calmer times, members of the faculty and staff used the uninhabited cylinder as a recreational wilderness, a place to hike and camp and fish. A touch of curiosity to Arachne answered her query: Yes, the ecosystem could support a certain amount of hunting, though no one had yet applied for a permit. Since *Starfarer* had fled Earth before the ecology department established predators, someone would eventually have to hunt to control the herbivore population. J.D. had caught salmon with the divers, but she had never hunted a mammal . . . except when she and Stephen Thomas tracked Chancellor Blades through Arachne's web.

J.D. reached the airlock and put on her spacesuit, comfortable with the equipment but apprehensive about going out onto *Starfarer*'s skin for the first time since the missile attack. Her helmet sealed. She stepped into the elevator and descended to the outside. The airlock pressure fell to zero; the hatch opened. J.D. looked out.

Stars spun beneath her. *Starfarer* loomed above her. At her feet, the inspection web fastened to the lower edge of the elevator shaft. The web stretched all the way around *Starfarer*, a tracery of cables held in place by support struts bristling outward from the cylinder's surface.

Rotation took her over the immense silver canopy of the stellar sail. The stars reappeared, and then the spin plunged J.D. into the shadowed valley between the campus cylinder and the wild side. The campus cylinder, counter-spinning at the same rate so the distant stone surface paced her, gave her a momentary sensation of stillness. Then she burst out over the starfield again. Multicolored points and streamers of light streaked past.

J.D. fastened her lifeline to a safety link and slid one foot cautiously onto the cable of the inspection web.

"It's easier if you don't look down."

Infinity Mendez was waiting for her. J.D. grinned, though he could not see her expression past her gilded faceplate, as she could not see his.

"That's easier said than done," she said.

"True." He balanced easily on the web's tightrope.

"Too bad we're not bats," J.D. said.

"Bats?"

She stretched up and brushed the outer skin of *Starfarer,* the looming stone ceiling.

"We could hang by our feet and swing along."

He chuckled.

"Interesting engineering problem—spacesuit boots for bats."

J.D. laughed.

Infinity spent a lot of time on the outside of *Starfarer* 's skin, especially since the missile attack. He was a staff gardener, but he was also one of the few people on board with space construction experience. Before joining the deep space expedition, he had been on the crew that built the starship.

"Over there, the—" Infinity hesitated. "What should I call it?"

"I don't know," J.D. said. "I thought of them as eggs. Egg cases." She reached back to *Nautilus* and touched Nemo's knowledge surface, but she could not translate her perception of Nemo's offspring into ordinary English words. She could not even translate it into something she could hold in her own mind. Trying made her as giddy as looking at the stars beneath her feet. She drew away.

"This egg hasn't even hatched, but it's growing already," Infinity said. "That isn't any egg I ever ran into."

"No. We'll have to talk to a taxonomist . . . or ask Nemo's child what it wants to be called."

"Can you talk to it?" he asked, surprised.

"I don't know that, either." She sighed. "I wish there was another squidmoth to ask. I *know* the information is all in Nemo's knowledge surface, somewhere, but I can't get it out in a way I can understand it. I don't know what to do. I don't know whether to try to be a parent, or . . ." She shrugged unhappily.

"Let's ask Nemo's kid," Infinity said.

They crossed the strands of the inspection web. Now and then they passed silver slugs, upside-down, flattened to hold themselves fast, performing the constant maintenance that *Starfarer* required. They often worked in pairs: A lithoclast, its color a smooth solid silver, eating away at weakened adhesive rock foam and preparing cracks to be filled; a lithoblast, patterned with moiré rainbows, spewing out new rock foam to re-anchor the moonrock and fill the cracks.

J.D. picked her way across the inspection web. Her safety line followed in its track. She traversed the curve of the wild cylinder's flank. The cylinder's spin pushed her down toward the stars.

61 Cygni shone below, bright and familiar in its similarity to the sun. It fell to *Starfarer*'s horizon and disappeared. J.D. and Infinity plunged into night, and into the valley between the two cylinders.

Infinity ducked under a cluster of large silver slugs.

"Here," he said softly.

Beyond the slugs, a gluey pseudopod hugged *Starfarer*'s side.

It was the color of skim milk, blue-white and translucent, nothing like the iridescent silk that Nemo had produced. J.D. touched it gently.

The gelatinous living plasma cringed away from the contact. The blue-white skin flattened against *Starfarer*. The skin stuck to the rock, turning dry and papery.

J.D. caught her breath with dismay.

"Touchy critter," Infinity said.

"I wish I hadn't done that," J.D. said. "I thought it would be like Nemo." Nemo, a solitary creature, had enjoyed the presence of another being, sought out J.D.'s touch, rippled and purred in response to Zev's petting.

"Maybe when it grows up."

They followed the pseudopod toward the egg nest's center. Above them, it widened and joined others. Like the arms of a starfish, the projections led inward to a central bulge. The organism's appendages spread from it asymmetrically, stretching wide along the circumference of *Starfarer*, gripping tight against the centrifugal force, extending for a shorter distance parallel to the starship's axis.

"It's big," J.D. said. "Bigger than what you could see of Nemo. Without the structure."

Beneath the taut surface of the skin, soft swellings pressed out, then receded. Now and again a sharper shape outlined itself, and disappeared again.

J.D. let her helmet project *Starfarer*'s interior image of Nemo's offspring. Sensors saturated the hull of the starship; they outlined the extent of the larva's penetration. It had dug a pit two meters deep for its body; its arms tendrilled deeper.

"It's living on rock and starlight," J.D. said. "Is it dangerous? Risky to the cylinder?"

"A breach in the hull is dangerous," Infinity said. "How big is it going to get?"

"I'm afraid I have no idea."

Infinity folded his arms and stared up at the squidmoth larva. J.D. was glad she could not see his expression.

He helped build the ship, she thought. *It must hurt him to see it damaged like this. But he doesn't act scared . . .*

That gave her hope.

"It's using water," Infinity said. He sent her a magnification of part of the sensor report. Several of the pseudopods twined around one of *Starfarer*'s water mains. Microscopic tendrils penetrated the pipe.

"When did this happen?"

"Last couple hours."

"How much is it using?"

"Not enough to make much difference—"

"That's good," J.D. said.

"—yet."

"Oh."

"Don't suppose you know how much it will need."

"I'm afraid not."

"Listen, this is going to spook people. It's spooking me."

"Yes," she said. "I don't blame you. Maybe . . . I can persuade it to move."

She was glad she had left the LTMs behind. She had looked forward to the respite, to spending a few hours out of range of recorders. Now privacy was more than a moment's indulgence. Maybe the LTMs' absence would give her time to figure out what to do.

She leaned against a support of the inspection web and gazed up into the center of Nemo's last offspring.

"I was so glad when I saw that one of Nemo's egg cases had come along with us through transition," she said. "But now I wish it had stayed behind at Sirius. Where it'd be safe."

"Sirius is an empty system now," Infinity said. "Whatever—whoever—we left behind, they're stuck there. Who knows for how long?"

J.D. sighed. Nemo's children were stranded, because of *Starfarer*.

The cosmic string moved in and out of star systems in obedience to rules that Civilization had learned through experience and observation and error. The cosmic string had receded from Sirius because *Starfarer*, tainted by the missile blast, had entered the system. The string would return, J.D. hoped, now that *Starfarer* had left. She had no idea how long the return would take . . . but squidmoths lived for a million years.

"That crater Nemo lived in," Infinity said. "If this guy hollows out something that size, it'll go all the way through the wild side's skin."

"I'll try to find out."

Infinity's gilded faceplate obscured his expression, but the language of his body was skeptical.

"Is there an 'it' inside there to communicate with?"

"Good question."

She touched Nemo's knowledge surface, searching for information on squidmoth ontology. But she skidded off the smooth shiny curves.

"Damn," she muttered. "I can't find *anything* I want to know."

As soon as she said it, she had to admit it was not true. A great deal remained accessible to her on the knowledge surface, particularly the ability to control *Nautilus*.

But she wished the surface would tell her how old a squidmoth had to be before it reached the age of reason. A few days? A few centuries? Older than all human civilization?

She wished she knew if it could listen to her, or if it would react to the touch of communication the way it had reacted to the touch of her hand.

Take it easy, J.D. said to herself. The larva is bathed in electromagnetic energy. Heat and light, gamma waves and cosmic rays. It isn't going to disintegrate at the touch of a new radio frequency.

She extended her attention through her link, speaking to Nemo's offspring as she had spoken to Nemo. But Nemo had been an ancient, aware being. For all she knew, Nemo's offspring was mostly a mass of undifferentiated cells.

"Hello," she said through her link. "Hello, I'm a friend of your adult parent. Can you hear me?"

She waited.

115

J.D. gazed up at the baby squidmoth till her neck cricked. She backed away a few steps. Leaning against a suspension strut, she rubbed her cramped muscles. A massage through a spacesuit was completely unsatisfying.

She sat on the inspection web beneath the pulsing mass of Nemo's egg case. Infinity sat nearby, watching, waiting, interested and patient.

Fifteen minutes passed. The cables of the inspection web pressed uncomfortably against J.D.'s leg.

If she let her gaze stray from the baby squidmoth, the stars spinning beneath her feet and the change from light to darkness and back made her dizzy. She remembered what it had been like out here during transition, with the strange substance of another universe gathering around her like curious fog.

She sent out another tentative query. Again she found no reply.

Gingerly, she widened her link to its limit.

Her surroundings disappeared and her perception of her body vanished. Even her perception of time faded.

A tendril of curiosity touched her welcoming link. J.D. gasped—but held herself back from snatching at Nemo's offspring.

The baby squidmoth touched the knowledge surface. It slid along its sharp, multidimensional edge, seeking . . . something.

Is it looking for its parent? J.D. wondered. But that's impossible, that doesn't make sense, because when a squidmoth reproduces, it doesn't live to be a parent.

The baby squidmoth scampered along J.D.'s knowledge surface. J.D. followed it, curious, hoping it might teach her more about Nemo's strange memory. It possessed all of its parents' memories, so Nemo's surface should be familiar to it. Nemo's offspring sank farther into the surface than J.D. had ever penetrated. She watched, hoping to discover new techniques.

The baby squidmoth slid up one multidimensional curve and spun down a slope. Here the edges and surfaces were smooth and clean, polished by long use. In the distance, the jagged new peaks of Victoria's transition algorithm rose like spires, like minarets, like ice castles.

They were new; they were different from anything the baby squidmoth possessed. Nemo had supplied it with all the knowledge of the squidmoths, but Victoria had given the algorithm to J.D. after Nemo died.

The algorithm's unfamiliar pinnacles drew the baby squidmoth. It swerved its attention and streaked toward the algorithm.

"Oh, shit!" J.D. exclaimed.

If the baby squidmoth acquired the algorithm, *Starfarer* would lose Earth's one advantage over Civilization.

J.D. withdrew her link to *Nautilus*. The knowledge surface collapsed.

Nemo's offspring convulsed in protest and confusion. J.D. sent soothing words, words of apology—

"No! No! No!" the squidmoth baby shrieked.

The cry reverberated in J.D.'s brain. Her link dissolved. Her vision returned. Above her, the squidmoth egg case shuddered. Rainbow patterns pinwheeled beneath its skin.

J.D. staggered mentally, jumped to her feet, and stumbled physically. Her legs had fallen asleep.

She slipped. She tumbled off the inspection web, flailing wildly. She missed catching the wire. Her body plunged into space. The stars streaked past her. They whirled. Her safety line caught her with a sharp snap and jerked her to a stop. It pulled her head and body up, and tore the stars out of her sight. *Starfarer* spun, dragging J.D. along with it.

"It's okay," Infinity said. "Just relax, it's okay, you're safe."

J.D. felt like she had been thrown off a moving mountain. She hung beneath the inspection web, her taut lifeline crooked against one of the longitudinal strands. The spin of the cylinder pulled her along. Blood rushed into her feet. Her legs prickled painfully.

At least I'm not head down, J.D. thought.

The line's attachment oriented her so she could climb back to the web. Infinity knelt above her and gave her a hand.

She grabbed his wrist. With his help, she swung one leg over the web and clambered to safety. Her suit pulled her sweat away and cleared her faceplate. Her metabolic enhancer pounded; her body emitted the scent of effort and alarm.

"You're okay?"

"I'm okay," she said. "Embarrassed."

"Don't be," he said. "Everybody falls off at least once, their first few times out." She could hear the humor behind the gold shadow of his faceplate. "Your very first time—you did better than most."

She smiled back at him. "Thanks." Her first time out, she and Kolya had freed the nuclear missile from its crater in the side of *Starfarer*.

"What happened?"

"It was heading toward Victoria's algorithm." J.D. sighed sadly. "I was afraid to let it have the work. I scared it, I think."

She cautiously opened her link and offered the squidmoth a thought of comfort.

"No! No! No!" the squidmoth baby cried. "Give me, give me, give me!"

J.D. pulled back, her mind echoing.

"Want! Want! Want!"

"The terrible twos," Infinity said wryly.

"Huh?"

"Kids. You know."

"I've never spent much time around kids," J.D. said.

"They go through a 'no' phase. If you think this is bad, wait till it hits adolescence."

The egg case writhed, flexing and twisting, bulging downward.

"Let's get out from under it," Infinity said.

They backed off apprehensively.

"Nemo was so gentle," J.D. said.

"Yeah . . ." Infinity said. "Except the time the LTMs bothered the attendants . . ."

"That's true," J.D. admitted.

"And the pool Stephen Thomas saw, with the critters fighting in it. And everything that happened after Nemo died."

"Okay," J.D. said. "I mean, you're right. But, to me . . . I just wish I hadn't scared its offspring." She gestured upward. "I wish squidmoths had names. It's hard to think of it as 'it.' "

Nemo had taken a name, suggested by Zev, for J.D.'s convenience or for its own amusement.

"Too bad Captain Nemo didn't have any kids," Infinity said.

J.D. grinned. "That would be a natural, wouldn't it?"

The pulsing of the egg case continued. It set up a rhythmic wave from one edge to the other. A moment later, a second pulse began, at right angles to the first. The surface of the egg case resonated violently like a wind-whipped sail.

In the back of her mind, J.D. still heard the squidmoth baby's desperate demands.

"We'd better go," J.D. said. "It would be alone under normal circumstances. Out in the wild. Maybe I gave it too much stimulation."

"It's growing again," Infinity said.

J.D.'s helmet showed her what Infinity had found. Beneath *Starfarer*'s skin, the egg-case tendrils probed deeper, dissolving moon rock and rock foam, enlarging into the water conduit. Water drained into it, pushed by the spin to the squidmoth baby. Above J.D. on the surface of the wild cylinder, the edges of the egg case spread.

Silver slugs retreated nervously from the perimeter, obeying their orders not to touch the egg case, fighting the instinct that drove them to repair faults in the cylinder's surface.

"I don't know if they'll hold off indefinitely," Infinity said. "They—"

"They've got to!" J.D. said.

"But if the squidmoth breaches the cylinder—"

"It won't!" she said.

Infinity hesitated.

He won't question me anymore, J.D. thought desperately. He doesn't like arguing, he doesn't like conflict . . .

"Are you sure?" he asked.

"No," J.D. whispered.

Five

The newest results of Victoria's transition algorithm created themselves. Victoria spun the glimmering representation.

Victoria was upset at Stephen Thomas for disappearing without a word. She had hoped work would take the edge off her anger. But her thoughts kept returning to her youngest partner.

He always says what he thinks, she told herself. Why can't he tell me, straight out, that he wants to leave us? Then maybe we'd have a chance. Maybe it isn't too late.

She sighed.

The algorithm evolved and solidified. It mapped a path through transition from 61 Cygni back to Earth. And it confirmed what she had hoped not to see. The solar system, Earth's system, remained "empty:" empty of the cosmic string that had visited it and given human beings such a brief access to Civilization.

Starfarer could return home. It could use the cosmic string accessible from 61 Cygni to enter transition; from transition it could travel to an empty system.

What *Starfarer* could never do was leave an empty system. It could not enter transition without access to the cosmic string.

Once back home, the starship would be stranded until—unless—the cosmic string returned.

"May I come in?"

Europa stood at the threshold of Victoria's office. Victoria collapsed the algorithm to a point of light.

"What was that?" Europa said. "It was beautiful."

Victoria gave her a quizzical glance.

"It's the algorithm."

"Ah," Europa said. "You needn't hide it from me. I couldn't steal it, not just by looking at it."

"I can't be sure of that," Victoria said in a friendly tone.

"No . . . I regret you don't trust me."

Victoria gestured, inviting Europa in. The alien human entered and sank down on a rattan chair.

"I'm not a student of the physical sciences," Europa said.

Victoria imagined having a life span of four thousand years. With that much time to study and learn, she would no longer have to be such a specialist. She tried to imagine living four millennia and *not* studying physics, and more math, and—

The idea made an extended life look, to her, like a desert.

"What *do* you study? What do you and Androgeos do, out here all alone? Or are there other humans in Civilization?"

"I'm a student of our sponsors," Europa said, her voice edgily defensive. "Ah, Victoria, we started out so badly. Is there any way for us to begin again?"

"I wish we could," Victoria said. "But . . ."

"Somehow I must persuade you to trust me," Europa said. "How am I to do that?"

"Tell me the truth!" Victoria said. "Even if it's hard. Even if it hurts us. Even if it hurts you."

Europa shifted in the chair. She glanced away from Victoria, her pure black gaze sliding toward the window, her long eyes seductive beneath dark lashes, kohl-lined eyelids. Like Androgeos, she was remarkably beautiful.

The silver strands in her hair gleamed. Now that Victoria knew they were alive, their motion no longer looked liquid, molten, to her. It looked squirmy.

"You look like the goddess," Victoria said softly. "The Minoan goddess, the one with the snakes."

Europa smiled. "We all cultivated that resemblance."

"All Minoan women?"

"All the Lady's interpreters."

In her mind's eye, Victoria could see Europa standing in a temple on a hill above the sea, her breasts bare, a serpent in each hand. She spoke a blessing to the people gathered around her.

"Were you a priestess?"

"That's the nearest idea you have to who I was to the Lady. I spoke for her, I befriended her."

"Was Androgeos a priest?"

"A priest?" Europa said. "You'd look long and far for a priest in Knossos."

"What about the minotaur?"

"The minotaur wasn't a priest," Europa said offhand. "Andro was just . . ."

Europa fell silent for so long that Victoria expected some terrible secret. Or another lie.

" 'Just'?" Victoria asked.

"I've promised to tell the truth," Europa said, "so I will tell you the truth. Andro was . . . a boy. A common boy. He was a servant in my household. He wouldn't like you to know this. He's become very sophisticated and ambitious over the years."

"Not descended from the Pharaohs, after all, eh?" Victoria said gently.

"Oh, yes," Europa said. "We all were. But everyone can't rule. His family had fallen to a lower class. Sometimes, now, his ambition overcomes his sophistication. So does mine, I fear, and I have much less excuse. Then we behave . . . as we did over your algorithm. Over J.D.'s starship. Will you forgive me?"

"I'd like to."

Victoria appreciated Europa's accepting some of the responsibility. She had never quite persuaded herself that Andro, for all his arrogance, decided by himself to try to get the algorithm. Europa must be thirty years older than Androgeos. Thirty years out of nearly four thousand. Yet she was still the eldest, with the responsibilities of the eldest.

"But it's hard," Victoria said. "Earth is your home—how could you try to take something that's so valuable to us?"

"We thought we had no time to explain. We thought *Starfarer*—Earth—would be banished. We panicked."

"You were greedy," Victoria said sadly.

"No!" Europa said. Then, more calmly, "Not for ourselves. The algorithm has enormous potential for Civilization. Faster travel. More systems in reach. Better communication and trade."

The quartet said Civilization had no empire. Victoria wondered if her algorithm would be of benefit, or if it would bring an era of conquest and imperialism.

Maybe the rules of the cosmic string would protect the peace. She hoped so.

"We wanted to take the algorithm *for* Earth, not from it," Europa said. "You would have gotten credit for it, Earth would have gotten credit. Credit you could have used—"

" 'You' in the general sense," Victoria said. "I wouldn't have lived long enough to see the banishment lifted."

"Perhaps not. But our home world, yours and mine, would have returned from exile with admiration and sympathy. And wealth."

"Wealth. Financial wealth?"

"Yes. Of course." Europa smiled.

"I suppose everyone must pay their way," Victoria said. "Have we run up debts already?" She imagined entry taxes, toll charges, fees for services she had not conceived.

"Certainly not," Europa said, offended. "On the contrary. Our world's balance—" She smiled. "Stands on all four legs, as the Largerfarthings would say."

"How?"

"Because Andro and I work toward that end! All the time we observed Earth, we collected its art."

"Its art?" The comment put Victoria off balance.

"Earth's songs and stories. Some two-dimensional pictures." She shrugged. "The quality there was less than one could wish. We gathered what you transmitted. What we could receive from space. We translated it." She chuckled. "You do transmit an appalling amount of junk."

"Maybe," Victoria said, her own defenses rising. "But who's to say what's junk?"

"An excellent point. We made available the work that caught the fancy of Civilization. In some places, Earth's artworks are highly regarded."

"Primitives, eh?" Victoria said.

Europa frowned. "How is the artwork of Minoan culture regarded, in your modern world?"

"I'm not an expert—"

"Few of us are," Europa said dryly.

"—but I think it's admired. I looked it up, after we met you, and I admire it."

"Civilization is no less perceptive," Europa said, her tone severe.

"Are you saying *art* is the currency of Civilization?"

"What else is worth transporting over interstellar distances?" Europa said, completely serious. "Cleaning robots? Furniture? No. People. Information. Unique organic patterns. And the gifts of creativity."

"People?"

"People who wish to see other worlds. Like you. Like me."

"Tourists," Victoria said. "And great art. I'm afraid there'd be some objection to exporting the Mona Lisa— or the Taj Mahal—to 61 Cygni, eh?"

"That's up to you. To the people of Earth. No one will prevent human beings from dispersing our cultural heritage. But you have some protection from outright thievery or counterfeiting, and many other possibilities exist. I increased the worth of what I gathered for Civilization. I never diminished its value back on Earth."

Victoria mulled over what Europa had told her.

"Civilization chose well, when it chose Minoans to represent human beings," Europa said. "We fit in. We ruled the sea and the islands with trade, not with weapons. Our cities needed no fortifications."

She stared at the empty spot where Victoria's algorithm had pirouetted.

"Do you miss Crete?" Victoria asked. "After all this time? Are you lonely? Are you and Androgeos the only humans in Civilization?"

Europa raised her head, ignored Victoria's question, and returned the subject to interstellar trade.

"Don't misunderstand," she said. "Earth can bankrupt itself. Our world could turn itself into a mockery. This has happened. Civilization *will* change Earth. We must choose the changes—or they'll overwhelm us."

"The algorithm can . . . help Earth's position within Civilization," Victoria said.

"Yes. Between your algorithm and J.D.'s starship, human people can join Civilization in a favorable position."

"J.D. will never give up her starship."

"Under no circumstances should she!"

"But Andro tried to claim it—"

"He thought the ship was abandoned. He had no way of knowing J.D. controlled it. Owned it." She sighed. "J.D. is an extraordinary person."

"I agree with you—J.D. is extraordinary. But she'd probably say all she did was offer Nemo courtesy and friendship."

Europa interpreted Victoria's comment, rightly, as criticism of herself and of Civilization.

"The squidmoths have been reclusive as long as anyone can remember," she said. "They never showed any interest in joining Civilization. J.D.'s the first person to succeed in making friends with one." She raised one hand to forestall Victoria's objection. "The first in a long time to try, I admit it." She chuckled. "Perhaps she might be persuaded to do it again."

"That's a cruel thing to say, Europa!"

"Cruel! Why?"

"To get another ship, she'd have to pick another squidmoth who was near metamorphosis."

Europa looked away. Color glowed hot in her dark face.

"You are right, I—"

"Then she'd have to make friends with it . . . and then she'd have to watch it die."

"I am *sorry*, Victoria, I was thoughtless, I overlooked— I apologize."

"It's bad enough that we've all lost one friend recently. J.D. has lost two."

"Please forgive me. It's only that the starships are so very valuable. They obscure one's critical facilities."

"But you already have one. All your own, only two people—"

"And several thousand other Earth species, some of them otherwise extinct."

"All the more reason not to covet *Nautilus*. It doesn't even have air anymore."

Europa shrugged off the barrenness of *Nautilus*. "A triviality. Each member of Civilization takes on the obligation of supplying a starship—temporarily— to its clients. In order to invite other people into the community."

"I'm not following you."

"My ship, my small world, is on loan from the Four Worlds."

127

Victoria wished she still was not following Europa.

"On loan. You have to give it back. When? Why didn't you say so before?"

Europa hesitated so long that Victoria feared she was about to go back to equivocating.

"Europa?"

"So many answers, to such a simple question. I didn't tell you because it shouldn't have made a difference. If you were banished, the Four Worlds would allow me to keep the ship." She smiled faintly. "With, perhaps, some grumbling. We have been waiting for you for a *long* time."

"And if we'd been accepted?"

"I would have given my ship back to my benefactors. Returned to Earth to act as liaison. Eventually I suppose I would have retired, to Earth or to Tau Ceti II. I had not anticipated . . . how difficult I would find returning the starship to the Four Worlds. It's my home."

"But they can't do anything with it—the Farther worlds both have different atmospheres and the Nearer worlds wouldn't have any use for it!"

"The ecosystem would be replaced. As it was for me, when they gave me the ship. The larger animals, the rarer creatures and plants, they have a niche on Tau Ceti II."

"But we aren't banished," Victoria said, "and we aren't accepted."

"True."

Victoria thought, Europa is about to lose her home— and her freedom. But she doesn't know how and she doesn't know when. And it's our fault.

"What will happen to you?" Victoria asked.

"I don't know," Europa said, so softly Victoria almost could not hear her. Her black eyes were very bright. "I don't know."

Crimson Ng breathed the river's cool deep scent. The water flowed green and quiet in its channel, bubbling into soft white rapids over a tumble of boulders.

The weather of *Starfarer* had stabilized; no one yet knew how precarious the balance might be. The starship had to stop moving from one type of star to another. It had chased the alien humans from Tau Ceti to Sirius to 61 Cygni. It was Sirius that caused most of the trouble. *Starfarer* had never been designed to spend time around a star like Sirius, a star so different from the sun. In trying to compensate for the campus's heat wave, Arachne had created a blizzard.

The snow had melted, saturating the ground. Crimson's waterproof boots sank into cold mud and left deep footprints. She leaned over the edge of the steep bank. Ten meters below, the river had crept back to its channel, exposing its rocky beach. From above, Crimson could not tell how much damage the flood had caused.

During the flood, the river had roiled just below where she was standing now. Its force had pushed boulders along the channel; the rolling rocks thundered. In front of Europa and Gerald and the others, Crimson had feigned detachment. But late last night she had returned to the riverbank. She had stood in the faint starlight reflected by the light tubes. In a fury, she flung cold wet stones into the center of the river.

She felt calmer now, in daylight, still nervous about what she would find on the river beach, but not so nearly in danger of losing control.

Crimson took a deep breath, jumped to her feet, and scrambled down the steep trail in the cliff.

Even between the walls of the river canyon the light was bright; all *Starfarer*'s illumination came from straight overhead. When she dug at the fossil site, she put up a canopy when she wanted shade. The canopy poles had been washed away without a trace; at a river bend, downstream, a branch trailed a bit of tattered blue canvas.

The trail was half as wide as it had been the last time she visited the site. The flood had broken the edges and washed out a long stride of the pathway. Crimson jumped over it, scraped against the wall to catch herself on the other side, and continued to the edge of the water.

The river growled softly. Its contours had changed; it felt strange, and new. A jagged rock cut the surface, catching the flow and spraying it into a fountain. Crimson let the fine droplets fall across her face and shoulders. The scent of icy water and ozone-charged air surrounded her.

She walked down the beach. She had been afraid it would be scoured down to the original unworked moon rock, but the river had only rearranged the gravel and sand and carefully rounded rocks.

At her site, she stopped.

Some of the anomalous stratum had been washed away, but not nearly as much as she had feared. Some of the surrounding volcanic layers had fractured, above and below, and left the shelf of sedimentary stone projecting outward. Fossils rose in organic shapes from the water-sculpted surface. Crimson touched the flow of mineralized bone, recreating the motions of her hands as she had formed the contours.

A scatter of pebbles rattled down the path and across the beach.

Gerald Hemminge, *Starfarer*'s assistant chancellor—acting chancellor, he called himself, since Chancellor Blades's banishment—stood above her on the riverbank.

He said nothing, but stepped down onto the trail and made his way toward her with precise, sure steps. A good deal taller than Crimson, he strode easily over the broken spot in the path.

Crimson scowled at her fossils. She did not want to talk to Gerald about them. She disliked his condescending courtesy.

"Hullo, Crimson," he said.

"Gerald."

"The site took some damage, I see."

"Some."

"Can you repair it?"

"Repair it?"

"Fix it. Put the fossils back. Replace the ones that washed away."

"Salt the site?" She asked. "Very bad technique."

"Look here," Gerald said. "I admire your ability to keep up your act. Performance art is very fashionable. But we must talk *seriously*."

"I'm always serious," Crimson said.

"Your art project—your fossil bed—is a major factor in our being allowed to remain in Civilization. It intrigues Europa."

Crimson had been amazed and delighted when the alien humans stole one of her fossils. Europa was amused by Gerald's transparent efforts to persuade her that the site was an art project. Europa had dated the fossilized bone and returned to *Starfarer*, anxious to investigate.

When Gerald realized it made a difference to Europa that the fossils were real, he had quickly changed his tune.

"Yes," Crimson said. "She'll be glad it didn't all wash away."

"You haven't excavated any more—have you? You promised Europa—"

"I didn't promise her anything!" Crimson said. "She ordered me not to dig the site alone—"

"And you'll follow her order," Gerald said.

"—And I'm not turning it over to any amateur! This is an important site."

"Why must you always be so bloody *contrary?*"

"I'm not," she said.

His lack of any sense of humor was a constant source of wonder to her, but all too often she let him provoke her past teasing to anger.

"We must come to an arrangement," Gerald said. "We must maintain the fiction that the fossils are real."

"What fiction?" Crimson asked.

Gerald smiled. "Good. Then we're agreed."

"I don't think," Crimson said, "that we're agreed on much of anything."

She walked away from him, down the river beach.

Arrogant prig, she thought. Wonder how he'd like it if I told him how to do his job? I could tell him to let Androgeos be the chancellor.

Gerald's irritation bored into her back. After a length of angry silence, he tramped up the trail, kicking shards of stone down onto the beach.

She was glad he had gone. His new enthusiasm for her performance made her perversely uncertain that she should continue it.

Crimson focused her attention on the shore.

Within a few minutes, she had forgotten Gerald. She searched the beach pebbles for fossil-bearing shards. She did not hope to find very much; the rest of the deposit was probably at the bottom of the river.

Maybe Infinity Mendez will let me borrow a silver slug to look along the channel, she thought. The slugs must be finished fixing the place where the missile crashed. They've even made a pretty good start at rebuilding the genetics department. And Esther has some of the inside artificials back with their brains regrown already. They'll be able to take over some of the slug work . . .

A shadow darkened the river canyon, filling it with a sudden coolness. The river's icy green changed to a threatening gray. Crimson glanced up, scared for a moment. The cloud that passed between her and the sun tube was white and puffy. She relaxed again. Neither the near-overhead nor the far-overhead clouds were heavy with rain. The river was not in danger of flooding again; the fossils that remained were safe for a while.

Crimson wished Alzena were still on board. Infinity

did the best he could, but as he kept having to point out, he was not an ecologist. He was not an ecosystems analyst. Alzena had designed *Starfarer*'s weather systems. She might be the only person who could tell if the patterns were in danger of being driven to a fatal new balance.

Wait a minute, Crimson thought. Alzena went with Europa. It isn't as if she's dead or anything. She's probably still on board Europa's starship.

The alien human's terraformed planetoid followed *Starfarer* toward the Nearer worlds, keeping its distance so it would not perturb *Starfarer*'s orbit around *Nautilus*, tagging along with Europa like a friendly puppy.

Crimson sent a tentative message out along her link, asking Arachne to broadcast it toward the alien humans' starship. The computer obeyed.

Alzena? Crimson thought into her link. Are you there? Can you hear me? Please talk to me. Please.

She thought she felt a response a few seconds later, a quick shiver of surprise and dismay. But Alzena did not answer.

I guess I can't blame her, Crimson said to herself. If my family told me I had no soul, I might go nuts too.

Crimson stooped to pick up a fragment of anomalous rock, pale against the darker pebbles of worked moon rock. A large sharp tooth projected from the matrix. She recognized the species, a two-meter bipedal carnivore, large-brained and dexterous.

One skeleton of this species lay in the museum, completely excavated except for narrow pillars of stone that held it in place above the matrix that had fossilized it. It had been preserved in a position unlikely to have occurred naturally. The body had been laid out, as in a burial.

Other fossilized bodies lay deeper within the river-bank.

The fossils' stratum of rock contained no tools, no jewelry, no incomprehensible electronics, no midden heap. No proof that the beings had been starfaring aliens. But . . . how else could they have become entombed on the moon, in a layer of rock that could not exist naturally on Earth's satellite? They had died light-years from their unknown home, and they had been buried by their comrades and left behind.

It was too bad, of course, that the automated mass-driver had chewed into the deposit and flung the pieces of stone into space, to be formed into *Starfarer*'s two cylinders. The fossils would have yielded up much more information if they had been discovered in place. But there was no help for it now.

By good luck, the anomalous stratum was still sandwiched between original volcanic flows, cemented to the older flow by the formation of stone from alien sand and clay, to the younger flow by the heat of flowing lava.

Every test dated the sedimentary stratum at two billion years, plus or minus a hundred million.

The excavated skeleton was magnificent in its size and authority and loneliness. Crimson regretted the existence of the other skeletons, but finding only one would have been too perfect.

She put the fang in her pocket and scrambled to the top of the riverbank.

Satoshi sprawled in a couch in the geography theater. One of his three-dimensional analyses hovered above him, the only light in the large domed room. The analysis moved and changed without his attention or control. He had work to do, observations of all of the Four Worlds that he should look at. He had come to the theater to spend a few hours working, before the welcoming party for the Four Worlds representatives. He was not looking forward to the party. He wanted time alone to talk with Victoria and Stephen Thomas. Since Stephen Thomas was not talking, it did not look as if Satoshi would get what he wanted.

I could do some work, but what's the point? he thought. Anything you can figure out, Longestlooker is probably willing to tell you; anything you can think of to ask, the question has already been answered by Civilization.

You don't believe that, Satoshi told himself. So the Four Worlds have had space travel longer than Earth has. So what? They aren't all inherently smarter than human beings, or morally superior. If they were, the other ones would never have instituted the rules of the cosmic string. They never would have isolated the Fighters.

If they were all smarter than us, they wouldn't want Victoria's algorithm so badly.

And they wouldn't think Crimson's fossils were real, instead of an art form.

That thought cheered him, but it also made him think: I'm a lot more depressed than I thought I was.

He idly scanned Europa's planetoid.

J.D.'s going to want *Nautilus* to look like this, he thought. I wonder if it's possible. There's no air, the gravity's so much lower . . .

In a valley near the south pole of Europa's starship, a small, fur-covered elephant wrapped its trunk around the tender tip of a tree branch, stripped off the leaves, and shoved them into its mouth.

In astonishment, Satoshi expanded the focus. The valley contained a whole herd of dwarf mammoths.

When the starship rotated the valley away from him, he explored the records Arachne had made. He found other prehistoric mammals living on Europa's world: three-toed horses, saber-toothed tigers, no-humped camels, a rhinoceros-sized wombat, and of course the aurochs that had chased J.D.

I *shouldn't* be surprised, Satoshi thought. Europa told us her starship sheltered extinct creatures. I guess I had in mind dodos or passenger pigeons, something more recent.

The dwarf mammoth strolled across the meadow. Nearby, exploring a huge clump of grass, a young one came face to face with a giant ground sloth. The baby mammoth leaped sideways, raising its trunk—Satoshi imagined its shrill trumpet of surprise—then hurried after its mother.

Charmed, Satoshi explored the mammoths' valley. He set Arachne to capture more images each time the planetoid rotated to face *Starfarer*. For a little while, his worries dissolved in delight and amazement.

Finally he broke away from the mesmerizing images. He rubbed his face with both hands, blocking off the kaleidoscope of light shining from the images. He rubbed his temples with his thumbs. He longed for the touch of his younger partner's hands on his neck, on his shoulders, on his body, and yet he did not know how he would react if Stephen Thomas sat down beside him at this moment.

Not that it was very likely.

The seat beside him creaked. Satoshi jumped.

Beside him, Crimson Ng jumped, too.

"Sorry—" they both said at once.

"You startled me," Satoshi said.

"Same here," Crimson said. "I thought you heard me."

He shifted to face her. It had been some time since they had talked. Last winter—winter in the campus cylinder—their brief hot fling had surprised them both. Crimson's attachments usually were with women; Satoshi's were usually with people he had known for a while.

I'm glad we're still friends, Satoshi said to himself. But there's an awful lot more distance between us than there was a few months ago.

Crimson stared at her hands. The moving light accentuated, then concealed, the shadows of exhaustion in her face.

"Is something wrong?" Satoshi asked. "Are you okay?"

She sat forward on the theater seat, as nervous as a sparrow. Satoshi was afraid she would jump up and leave. He lifted his hand to touch her, to soothe her or to keep her from going, then thought better of it and let his hand fall again.

She drew in a sudden deep breath and exhaled fast and hard.

"There's lots wrong," Crimson said. "Do you have time to talk?"

"Always," he said.

"It's the fossils."

"I thought it might be."

"The provenance is such a mess, the rock's upside-down, compared to the way it was on the moon. So the younger lava flow is on the bottom, and the older one is on top, with the fossil layer in between . . ."

Satoshi wondered what she was getting at, and whether she would be willing to talk about the fossils as part of a performance rather than as something real.

"No one is going to think *Starfarer* is a natural formation," he said. "Finding the fossils in *Starfarer*'s shell is like finding Archaeopterix in limestone building blocks, or trilobites in a pile of coal in a train. Not much to be learned from the provenance."

"But it's embarrassing," Crimson said, "to tell people we dug through a unique archaeological site without even noticing it was there."

She had more to say; he left a silence open for her words.

"There's plenty of room for questions!" Crimson said. "But nobody's questioning!"

"They want to believe it," Satoshi said.

"I always thought it'd be great if some aliens came

137

along and found the fossils. But now that the alien people have done just what I hoped . . . I'm not so sure."

"You *are* a paleontologist," Satoshi said.

She sighed. "I was." She kicked the back of the seat in front of her, making it rock.

"What are you going to do?"

"I don't *know!*" Fists clenched, Crimson punched the air above her head. She let her arms drop and her fingers open.

Satoshi smiled. The whole time he had known her, her fingernails had never been clean. Ground-in clay outlined them at the cuticle and beneath the short, broken tips. He felt, in memory, the demanding, rough touch of her calloused hands. He shivered. If Crimson noticed, she said nothing.

"I worked so hard on the deposit, it's funny, sometimes when I'm digging the fossils up, I forget I already know what I'll find." She sighed again. "Now Gerald's pushing my version, he thinks it's one of the reasons we're allowed to stay."

"He may have a point."

"Yeah. But it's harder having him on my side than it was to have him call me a liar."

"He did a pretty quick about-face."

"That's what made me reconsider," Crimson said.

Satoshi sat back, reminded of her temper by the edge in her voice.

"He had nothing but contempt for the work—for the whole art department—till he thought the fossils might have some value to Europa. Till he thought he'd be able to manipulate her. And Civilization. And *me.*"

"Have you talked to him about it?"

"He's talked *at* me about it. He ordered me to keep up the performance. Ordered me!"

"Gerald sometimes just doesn't get it." Satoshi tried to keep the annoyance out of his voice. "I thought I got through to him . . ."

"About the fossils?"

"About community and ethical authority," Satoshi said. "After he jumped down Infinity's throat. He thought I was talking about power. Maybe I should have tried Stephen Thomas's method."

"What's that?"

"Punching him out."

"Tempting thought."

"Except it didn't work. Stephen Thomas didn't get what he wanted, and neither one of them got in a solid hit."

"It makes me furious! I won't base my decision on what Gerald wants. Or what he doesn't want."

"What happens when Civilization finds out the whole story?"

"They applaud," she said easily.

"Or throw tomatoes."

Crimson laughed. "That's the risk, when you perform."

"This is serious to them," Satoshi said. "They think the deposit might lead them to the other ones' home world—"

"Not this one!" Crimson said. "This one is from the Fighters."

"Europa's of a mind to prove it's the other ones."

"Uh-uh. The other ones are in a different deposit. I mean, they were. Most of them got washed out in the flood."

"Really? You made another fossil bed?"

"Sure. Didn't Stephen Thomas mention it? He saw it when I was working on it."

"He's had . . . a lot of other things on his mind lately."

"Yeah, I bet, he sure looks different."

Satoshi did not tell her how different. He did not tell her Stephen Thomas had a pelt of fine gold hair, though she might have noticed that herself. He did not tell her that male divers, unlike ordinary human men, had internal genitals.

He did not tell her how much the changes bothered him.

Satoshi pulled his thoughts away from Stephen Thomas.

"One set of alien fossils is an interesting anomaly. Two—that makes the moon an interstellar crossroad. Hard to explain."

"It's a graveyard," she said.

"A graveyard!"

"There's evidence." She shrugged. "Any good paleontologist could come up with a theory. And . . . I was a *very* good paleontologist."

"I know."

"I thought I was so disgusted . . . so disgusted with having to quit my research, so disgusted with the way the world is. I thought I wouldn't mind playing with my subject. But it makes me uneasy."

"Yes," Satoshi said. Like any scientist, he felt profound discomfort at the idea of fabricating evidence.

"But everybody *told* Europa the fossils were fake—"

"Everybody but you."

"—and she didn't believe any of you. She thinks we're keeping secrets. She thinks we're hiding the home world."

"What about the other side of the question?" Satoshi said. "Europa's looking for the other ones. When she finds out your fossils won't lead her to them—no, when she finds out they *can't*—"

"That won't happen," Crimson said. "She'll hit a dead end, but not a hoax. The fossils look authentic. No matter how you test them."

"Except that they're *not* authentic. If Civilization has tests we don't know about—" Satoshi stopped, aware of the contradiction as soon as he spoke.

"But the fossils *already* fooled them," Crimson said.

"Look, it's ordinary physics, ordinary chemistry. Isotope ratios, fission-track dating. So what if Europa belongs to an interstellar Civilization? Our hosts aren't any cleverer than we are. They don't have different physical laws."

Her independent analysis of what Satoshi had been thinking made him feel better, even though he did not yet have enough evidence to be certain it was true.

"After all," Crimson said, "that's why Civilization left us alone till we came looking for them. So we could think of new things. Make discoveries they haven't made. For them to take, if they can get them."

"None of this answers your question. What to do. What to tell them."

"What do you think? What about J.D. and the others?"

"J.D.'s job depends on honesty. She respects your work and she admires it. We all do. But . . . it isn't science."

"It isn't supposed to be!"

Her impatience with him prodded him into an entirely different viewpoint.

"I don't think *you* should tell Europa the fossils are art," he said. "I think you should keep performing. But all the rest of us should keep telling the truth: You're a respected performance artist. Even Gerald should tell the truth, if we can persuade him."

Crimson considered.

"That might work," she said slowly. "That just might work."

"Are you interested in some help with your excavation?"

"Are you volunteering?"

"Not me . . . I'm volunteering our sponsors. Our guests."

Crimson laughed. The laugh transformed her sulky, intense face to luminous beauty.

Satoshi thought, I fell in love with you the first time I ever saw you laugh. But he did not say it aloud.

• • •

Kolya bounded across the surface of *Nautilus*. It felt good to be out of the tent. He had not spent so much time in the company of a single person since before he fled into space. Esther was easy to get along with, a pleasant colleague. He liked her. He liked her very much, but he also liked his privacy.

He found himself thinking about her to a surprising extent. He had begun thinking about her before they came out here together, so his fancies were not just the result of proximity and isolation.

She did not resemble any woman he had ever been with. His tastes ran to tall women, slender women, women of intense, old-fashioned femininity, women who doted on him and flattered him. As a youth—as an astronaut with access to material goods beyond the reach of most Soviet citizens—he had been spoiled. He had taken advantage of the benefits without thinking about them. One of the benefits was the attention of beautiful women.

Esther respected and admired him. He knew that; he was used to the same reaction from other pilots, male and female. There was a big difference, for Kolya, between the respect of a pilot and the admiration of an attractive woman. He could not help feeling confused. Esther did not react to him the way his experience made him expect an attractive woman to react. She did not look the way he expected a sexually attractive woman to look. He could not imagine her wearing make-up; he could not imagine her concealing her matter-of-fact humor beneath blushes and giggles; he could not imagine her in an evening gown.

And yet he was attracted to her.

I have not spent enough time with women since I escaped from Earth, Kolya thought. I have not spent enough time with anyone at all. The world has changed, and I am hopelessly old-fashioned.

I wonder, he said to himself, if an old man can change . . .

Kolya chuckled ruefully. He was still practicing the habits of a young man, assuming he could have anything, or anyone, he wanted. Assuming that if he chose to approach Esther, she would have him.

The assumption had been true from the time he was a youth and during the war that destroyed his homeland. During the war, a man engaged in a romantic and doomed quest could expect certain favors. Especially when he was outside his country, raising support for the quest among people who did not know how romantic— he always used that word with bitter irony—and just how doomed it was.

Whether Kolya could change or not, the times had changed.

If I can change, he wondered, will it do me any good? Besides, what about Infinity?

Kolya had never loved a woman who openly shared herself with more than one man. Openly was better, he had to admit it, but he did not know how he would react to such an arrangement.

Hopelessly old-fashioned, he said to himself again.

Pilots were notoriously promiscuous. When he was a youth he and his compatriots had had all manner of jocular excuses for their behavior. All their excuses came down to one thing. Even in the dangerous days before Miensaem Thanthavong's research, he and his colleagues behaved as they preferred to behave.

He reminded himself that Esther was an equally experienced pilot. He could hardly object if his professional descendants followed his lead.

And he did not necessarily want to object, even if he had any right. Esther—everything about her—aroused him, excited him.

He slowed his long bounding steps, stopped, and looked up into infinite depths, infinite colors. He sat against a chunk of rock as soft as a feather pillow in the low gravity. Alone, he gazed over the sharp curve of the horizon, and out into space.

In the lab, Stephen Thomas stood up and stretched out the kinks. His body shrugged them off easily. Despite everything, physically he felt wonderful. New energy accompanied the changes. He was alert and his perceptions sparkled; he could run around campus plus-spin without getting winded. He was right on the edge of a pleasurable sexual excitement. And he was hungry.

He had shooed the students out of the lab an hour or so ago, sending them to the welcome party for the Four Worlds representatives. He had intended to follow soon, but an idea about squidmoth genetics pulled him back to his work. Just for another few minutes. Now he had begun a new experiment, but he had lost track of the passage of time.

"Shit," he muttered. He would be late; Victoria would be hurt. He was probably at risk of offending the Four Worlds people.

Fuck 'em, he thought. They went off with Gerald without a backward glance.

But he could not bring himself to be angry with them.

He hurried from the lab and loped home. Campus was deserted. The spicy scent of carnations filled the horseshoe-shaped yard of his home. The green drops of new cherries splayed from the branches of the dwarf trees.

The house was dark. Stephen Thomas entered through the front door, brushing his fingers against the arched lintel. The hobbit-door, Victoria called it, and teased him about being elven, too tall for hobbit doors.

The lights brightened, following him down the back hall. He hesitated at the door of Satoshi's room, smiling fondly at the familiar sight of Satoshi's work in progress arranged neatly around his desk, some in projected form, some hard copy. He passed his own room and continued down the hall. He glanced into Victoria's room: neat, Spartan, but with a bed big enough for four people.

The door of the last room along the corridor was open a handsbreadth. The room Merry had never had a chance to see. The room where Feral had stayed. The room where Stephen Thomas had slept, alone, the last time he slept in the partnership's house.

He stood in the doorway for a moment, then retreated to his own room.

The scent of incense had nearly dissipated. He lit a fresh stick, thinking, You don't have time for this, then reminding himself that he was already an hour late. Five more seconds would not make much difference.

He stripped off his shorts and his t-shirt and teased the mutualist out of his hair. It coiled snugly around his wrist. It had adapted to him quickly, and he to it; he used it without thinking about it.

If somebody had told me, he thought, that I'd be wearing a worm in my hair . . .

He dug his tux out of the back of the closet. He liked it but seldom had an excuse to wear it. He had almost left it back on Earth. As he slipped the studs into the shirt to fasten the front, he shrugged his shoulders to smooth his pelt beneath the heavy white silk. The pants were not too uncomfortable. With the changes to his genitals they did not fit quite right. The cummerbund was tight enough to chafe the fine gold hair, but he wore it anyway.

His dress shoes were impossible. His feet had changed too much. He put on the tux jacket, slipped his feet into his everyday sandals, and looked at himself critically in the mirror.

"Maybe I'll start a new fad," he said.

He put on a sapphire earring. On impulse, he uncoiled the mutualist from his wrist and stroked it till it relaxed completely. He held it at his temple till he felt the quick tug of its jaws clamping onto a strand of hair. He smoothed it into the texture of his hair, matching the curve, metallic silver against blond.

No more delay, he thought, and left his room through the French windows that opened into the garden.

Six

The welcoming party for the Four Worlds representatives had begun.

Dance music trembled through the air like the soft evening's breeze. Decorative lights sparkled in pastel strings. A glass flower covered each small bulb, garlanding the cafeteria courtyard. At the edge of the illumination, J.D. hesitated. Zev stopped beside her and squeezed her hand.

"I like the lights," he said.

"Yes." J.D. wondered if someone on board had made them, heated the glass and given it pure glowing colors and spun it into petals, or if someone had whimsically used their allowance to carry decorations from Earth into orbit. Why not? Victoria had brought clothes, and presents for her partners. Stephen Thomas brought French champagne. J.D. had brought coffee beans and chocolate.

Most of which I gave to Europa, J.D. thought. And she hasn't even mentioned it since. If she doesn't like it, I wish she'd give it back.

Gerald Hemminge crossed the center of the courtyard to greet them. He was, as usual, beautifully dressed in a well-tailored suit.

"Why, J.D., I hardly recognized you."

J.D. repressed an urge to smooth her short brown hair, or straighten the long skirt of her blue dress, or tug at the low-cut bodice. For years, she had not had a job that required a dress. She felt rather uncomfortable in this one. It was the only dress she owned.

"Thank you, Gerald," she said drily.

"And here I was convinced that members of alien contact made it a policy to dress down—under all circumstances."

"We've never discussed it," J.D. said.

If she got into a competition of cutting remarks with Gerald, she would lose. She acted, instead, as if the conversation were completely civil.

"You look elegant," she said sincerely. "As always."

Gerald was carrying a ball of white fluff wrapped around a paper cone. He bit into the fluff; a skein of it pulled away and he licked it into his mouth. Half the people at the party were eating the fluff.

"What is that?" J.D. asked. "Is it cotton candy?" She could not recall seeing cotton candy since she was a child. "Where did *Starfarer* get cotton candy?"

"We had to provide something the Farthings could tolerate," Gerald said. "Senator Orazio discovered they have a taste for sucrose."

"But who thought of cotton candy? And how did you make it?"

"I have no idea. The food is Ms. Brown's department."

"Florrie?" J.D. said, startled. Florrie Brown surprised her at every turn. The only trouble was, J.D. never knew if the surprise would be a good one or a bad one.

"Where are the Largerfarthings?" Zev asked. "I promised to teach Sharphearer how to play chess."

"They're in the main cafeteria, eating cotton candy," Gerald said. "Please don't monopolize our guests with games. Everyone will want to talk to them."

"It's up to Sharphearer," Zev said reasonably.

J.D. changed the subject. "Did you get them settled in at the embassy?"

"In a manner of speaking. They, er, redecorated the American VIP suite in a disorderly manner. I believe the senators were rather put out. I can only imagine what the ambassador would have said."

J.D.'s house was too small to house all of *Starfarer*'s visitors. The VIP suite in the American Embassy was one of the few places on campus where they could stay together. Nevertheless, J.D. envied the senators for hosting the Four Worlds representatives.

You'll get over it, she told herself. Your role in this part of the story is finished.

She was already looking forward to the next first contact, on Largernearer.

"It's a shame the administration building was so badly damaged," Gerald said. "Its guest quarters were much more adaptable. We could change the walls and the floor and the temperature and pressure . . ." He shot a glance across the courtyard. "Ah. There is Europa."

Beneath the flower lights, Europa and Senator Orazio spoke quietly together.

"Ruth doesn't look put out," J.D. said.

"Politicians know how to keep their opinions to themselves. How the Farthings felt about having to make the changes is another matter."

"Did Longestlooker say she was satisfied?" J.D. asked.

"Yes," Gerald said grudgingly.

"Then I expect everything's all right. They did adapt themselves to our environment, after all."

"They like it here," Zev said. "I'm going to take them camping."

"Do tell," Gerald said. "Perhaps you'd better plan to put that off, as well as the games—"

"Zev, that sounds like great fun." Delighted that Zev had made such a friendly and strong connection with the quartet, J.D. interrupted Gerald. "A good break, after everything that's happened. When are you going? Can I come with you?"

"As soon as we get back from Largernearer," he said. "I hoped you'd want to come. We're going to the wild side."

He slid his hand around J.D.'s waist and hugged her. She slipped her arm around him and tickled the short fair hair at the back of his neck. He grinned. If they had been alone, he would have kissed the cleft between her breasts. If they had been in the sea, he would not have stopped with her breasts. She wished they were in the sea, naked.

"No doubt they want to snoop in the wild side for more fossils," Gerald said. "Which, I might remind you, will not exist."

J.D. smiled at him. "Gerald—how do you know?"

Vexed, Gerald drew himself up and walked away.

J.D. chuckled. She and Zev strolled across the courtyard.

"He didn't even notice I wore my suit," Zev said. He was wearing the pants and vest of his suit, and a red silk shirt that Stephen Thomas had given him. The silk kept the heavy wool from chafing his pelt so badly. The vivid red set off his mahogany skin and pale hair, and gave his coppery eyes a wild flare.

"No," J.D. said. "But I did."

"What's cotton candy?" Zev asked.

"Sugar, spun to a fluff. It's usually pink. Do you want to try some?"

"Sure."

As they strolled toward the cafeteria, Europa gave Ruth Orazio a brief embrace, then joined J.D. and Zev. She was carrying a cone of cotton candy.

"Are you enjoying the party?" J.D. asked Europa.

"It's very pleasant." The Minoan nibbled at her cotton candy, and a large batt tore away. She pushed the bright white spun sugar into her mouth, then licked her lips and her fingers. "This is very strange food."

"Cotton candy is more entertainment than food," J.D. said.

"Sticky," Europa said. "Awkward. It *is* amusing."

"Can I try some?" Zev asked.

Europa offered the cone to Zev. He pulled off a shred, and handed half to J.D. She let it dissolve on her tongue. It reminded her of Nemo's decorative food, without the kick.

"There's regular food—everyday food—in the cafeteria," J.D. said.

"Is any of it chocolate?" Europa said.

"Let's go look." They crossed the threshold into the main cafeteria, a large diamond-shaped room with two back walls of grown wood, two front walls of diamond-paned glass doors.

"There's Sharphearer," Zev said.

The Largerfarthing was pulling a wad of cotton candy apart into small pieces, rolling them into balls, and popping them into her mouth. She fed one to Late, who lay on a table with his front third arched up. His radula moved back and forth, pulling the candy into his mouth. An organ like a set of combs appeared from either side of the radular opening, and pushed the sticky strands off his teeth.

"I'll go see what she wants to do about camping," Zev said. He grinned. "And chess." He headed across the room toward Sharphearer, while J.D. and Europa continued toward the buffet.

"I tried the coffee," Europa said. "But it doesn't taste like the coffee you gave me." She hesitated. "Perhaps I prepared it wrong, but I liked yours better."

"If you made it the way I told you to, it is better."

The bitter scent of burned coffee hung in the air of the cafeteria.

"It's hard to make good coffee for a lot of people," J.D. said. "You have to keep it hot, and that makes it deteriorate."

Florrie and her crew of volunteers had put on an impressive party feast. A long table held main dishes, casseroles, salads, spaghetti, baked eggs. Food on board *Starfarer* tended toward the vegetarian because the starship carried so few large animals.

"The chocolate would be with the desserts," J.D. said. "We usually eat dessert at the end of a meal, but some people say 'Life is uncertain, eat dessert first.' "

Europa smiled, getting the joke.

"Or," J.D. said, "did you mean you wanted to avoid chocolate?"

"No, I liked it very much. Didn't I tell you?"

"I don't believe you mentioned it."

"Too many things have happened, I was distracted. But I've wanted to taste chocolate for many years." She added, thoughtfully, "You know, J.D., several members of Civilization have evolved a biochemistry compatible with human food. They might be customers for delicacies. Food expensive enough to be worth importing."

"Like chocolate, you mean?"

"And coffee. We shall have to investigate."

J.D. put a spoonful of each of several salads, and some lasagna, and a spinach crepe on her plate, and steered Europa toward the dessert table.

"You'd better be quick, that chocolate cake isn't going to last much longer."

Europa surreptitiously abandoned her cotton candy. She sliced a substantial wedge of cake and rejoined J.D. They had completely different techniques for approaching a buffet. J.D. liked to sample everything. Europa chose what she wanted most, and concentrated on it.

She ate a bite of cake, savoring it.

"Chocolate is mildly psychoactive," J.D. said.

"That's obvious."

"It's full of an alkaloid related to caffeine. Theobromine."

"Food of the gods?" Europa said.

"What? Is that what it means? How did you learn Greek? Is *Minoan* Greek?"

"No, of course not," Europa said. "Earth's electronic transmissions contain very little ancient Greek, it's true. Most of what I know is medical jargon. Enough to decipher 'theobromine.'" She took another bite of cake.

J.D. ate some lasagna. It was rich with ripe tomatoes—someone must be growing them in a greenhouse—and spicy. J.D. wondered if Earth's future economy, like the economy of Europe during the early days of world exploration, would be based on the transport of chocolate, and coffee, and spices.

A long way to go, she thought, for no change at all . . .

Over in one corner, Avvaiyar Prakesh, the head of the astronomy department, twirled twisted paper in spun sugar and handed it out. She gave some to Zev. Sharphearer accepted seconds.

"Don't you want your own cotton candy?" Europa asked.

"No," J.D. said, "sugar doesn't go well with lasagna."

Florrie Brown had adapted a large vat, J.D. supposed it must be a bread-kneader or a vegetable-chopper or some food processor with rotating blades or vanes, to make the cotton candy. J.D. had no idea how to go about spinning sugar; she had only a vague recollection of what the cotton candy machine at the carnival had looked like. She was sure the cotton-candy seller had looked nothing like the tall, exotic, elegant Avvaiyar.

She chuckled.

"What amuses you?" Europa asked.

"I have some books," J.D. said. "Fiction, speculation, stories of the future. In some of them the plot hinges on developing a great scientific breakthrough."

"Convenient," Europa said drily.

"Yes . . . maybe it's different in Civilization, but back on Earth that kind of high-tech development always takes longer and costs more than you think it will. You could

153

never resolve a crisis that way. Not in a few hours or a few days."

"It's the same in Civilization," Europa said. "We make mistakes, too. We take risks, we experiment. If not for the likelihood of failure, it wouldn't be a risk."

"Yes."

"But why were you laughing?"

J.D. gestured toward the makeshift cotton candy machine. "That's our high-tech development."

Europa laughed, a genuine, open laugh.

On the path to the main cafeteria, Stephen Thomas caught up to Mitch, dawdling toward the party.

"Hi, Mitch."

"Hi." Mitch stopped. "You look amazing—where did you get a tux?"

"Brought it with me, I've had it for a long time."

Instead of keeping up, Mitch hung back. Stephen Thomas waited for him.

"Come on, we'll be late."

"We're already late."

"What's wrong?"

"Nothing," Mitch said. "It doesn't matter."

"Did Fox forget your name again?" Stephen Thomas said with sympathy.

"Who cares?" Mitch said angrily.

"Tell me what happened."

"Between her and me? Nothing," Mitch said bitterly. "It's you she—"

"Shit, I swear I never—"

"I *know* it! Everybody knows you don't sleep with students. I know you never led her on. She knows it. No matter what Florrie Brown's telling everybody."

"I never even talked to her till Satoshi and I tried to get her to get on the fucking transport and *go home*."

"She thinks none of the rules apply to Ms. Niece of the President."

154

"Led her on, Jesus Christ."

"Just because she knows you aren't interested," Mitch said miserably, "doesn't mean she cares that I am."

Stephen Thomas wondered if he was going to have to fend her off again. In his life he had met all too many people who got aroused by an unbalanced power dynamic. Maybe Fox was one of them.

"Hey, give her some time," Stephen Thomas said. "Give yourself a chance."

Mitch shrugged.

"Come on, life always looks better at a party."

"Maybe . . ."

They crossed campus through the twilight. Stephen Thomas looked upward. The sun tubes glimmered faintly with reflected starlight. On the other side of the cylinder, far-overhead, lights shining from recessed porches produced gold fans of illumination.

Mitch suddenly chuckled. "Fox sure was mad at Florrie."

"Yeah, well, I don't blame her." I'm not too happy with Florrie myself, Stephen Thomas thought. I thought we were friends . . . but she took the first excuse she had to light into me.

Party music drifted around Stephen Thomas. He wished he had not come. He felt reluctant to see Victoria and Satoshi and, at the same time, lonely for them. He had not talked to them since they returned from the Four Worlds ship. In better times, they would have met at home and come to the party together. Maybe they would have had dinner together. Recently, he had not been coming home for dinner, or for anything else. He had not even been keeping up the pretense that he might come home, by telling them he would be absent once again.

Do they even expect me to tell them anymore? he wondered.

In better times, Merry would have figured out what

was wrong. Merry would have figured out how to make things right.

Stephen Thomas's vision suddenly blurred. He stumbled. He caught himself from falling; Mitch grabbed his arm to steady him and nearly knocked him off balance again.

"You okay?" Mitch asked.

"Yeah. I was just thinking about . . ." He seldom talked about Merry to other people, never to his students.

"What?"

"My family's fourth partner."

"Oh," Mitch said. "I heard—I mean, I knew you were a, a widower—is that what it's called when there's more than two people?"

"I don't know, I guess so."

"I'm sorry," Mitch said awkwardly. "I didn't mean to say something that brought back—"

"It didn't have anything to do with you," Stephen Thomas said. "When you lose somebody . . . that fast, that unexpectedly . . . you get flashbacks. You think, If I'd done one thing, maybe it wouldn't have been a fatal accident. If I'd done something else, maybe it wouldn't have happened at all. You *want* . . . for it never to have happened at all."

"I'm real sorry," Mitch said.

"Yeah. Thanks." Stephen Thomas wanted to stop and curl up in a protected ball until he stopped shaking. He made himself keep on walking toward the party.

Stephen Thomas and Mitch rounded the flank of the hill that housed the main cafeteria. The diamond-shaped building nestled half beneath the hill. A glass-roofed extension, surrounded by a low porch, projected into the flagstone courtyard.

The last time Stephen Thomas had been here, snow and slush had covered the ground. Now spring had returned.

Pastel lights hovered like fireflies; conversation provided a background hum to the music. The courtyard was full, dancers in the center, people in conversation around the edges. Holographic images touched the night in bright patches. J.D. and Zev chatted with Iphigenie Dupre, the sailmaster. The Four Worlds people stood with the senators, watching the dance. Crimson Ng drew strata in the air for Androgeos. On the far side of the courtyard, Infinity Mendez waved toward Esther Klein and Kolya Cherenkov, who attended by image. They waved back. Florrie Brown sat nearby in a rattan chair. Her gaze flicked past Stephen Thomas. He swerved and circled the dance floor in the other direction.

As Infinity Mendez made his way toward Florrie Brown, the elderly woman's gaze followed Stephen Thomas, then rested on Fox. Neither acknowledged her presence. She looked quickly away and pretended to be watching the other dancers.

She had layered her eyelids with make-up of iridescent black, stark against the pallor of her feather-soft skin. Her hair, instead of being plaited with shells and beads, was twisted with shiny blue-black ribbons. As always, she wore black. Her tunic was fringed with tassels of leather and slender chain. Chrome studs gathered the cloth of her leggings into star-shaped pleats. On her boots she wore discreet silver spurs.

Infinity sat on his heels beside her. She took a sip of her beer, and a nibble of her cotton candy—a combination Infinity would not have attempted—then looked at him quizzically.

"Are you speaking to me?" she asked.

"Sure," he said. "Why not?"

"I thought . . . Oh. You weren't at the potluck, maybe you didn't hear about—it doesn't matter."

Infinity had heard, all right. Everybody on campus had heard what happened. The party had ended with Fox spilling beer on Florrie and Stephen Thomas. Or throwing it, depending on who was telling the story. It was too bad. Florrie had been getting to be friends with both of them. She was new here; it was important to make friends in a new place.

Infinity liked Florrie, and he liked Stephen Thomas. He did not know Fox. But he did know better than to get in the middle of fights.

Goes double, seems like, he thought, when one of the folks fighting is related to the president of the United States.

"Something you should know about the way people treat each other here," he said carefully.

She narrowed her bright gaze, suspicious, waiting.

"People get in arguments," Infinity said. "There's no way around it. But everybody does their best not to pick sides afterwards. Nobody says, 'It's them or me.' If we did, pretty soon nobody would be able to talk to anybody. This is a small town."

Florrie twined the pink lock of her hair around one forefinger. Though her knuckles were gnarled with age, her fingernails were carefully shaped, and painted with a shiny dark liquid crystal polish.

"Hm," she said, noncommittal, reacting neither to his advice nor to his gentle implied criticism. Then, as she often did, she changed the subject abruptly. "I never learned to dance like this."

"It's not hard." Infinity had learned how to waltz from Esther, at a welcoming party a few months ago. He would have liked to dance a waltz with her tonight. To be in Kolya's place, dancing light-footed in the faint gravity of *Nautilus*. Esther and Kolya were projecting their image from J.D.'s starship. Out in the garden, their figures flowed and spun.

The dance ended. Couples parted, applauded each other politely, and laughed. The old-fashioned dance, with its old-fashioned manners, was a minor fad on campus.

"I could show you," Infinity said, expecting another slow tune. But a fast, hard beat began, a discordant electronic throb. He shrugged apologetically at Florrie. "Maybe some other time?"

"You're all so staid!" she exclaimed. She jammed her cotton candy cone into her empty beer glass, pushed herself to her feet, grabbed his hand, and dragged him into the courtyard. "This is more like it."

All the stiffness of her body, all her hesitancy, vanished when she moved into the music. She flung herself back and forth, swinging her head, swaying her arms, bumping Infinity deliberately as she passed. The pink and the green and the natural white braid, with their long black ribbons, slapped against her shoulders and her neck. When she spun, the ribbons fluttered past Infinity's face. Florrie's energy cleared the floor around her.

Infinity danced with her, trying to copy what she did without flinging himself against her. He was amazed by the change in her, but not incredulous. He had seen similar transformations in other elderly people. Florrie combined the freedom of her dance with the compulsive carelessness of a much younger person.

The discordant music crescendoed, then faded. Florrie danced past the music's end, stopped abruptly, and sank in upon herself. Her presence and her size diminished. She clutched at Infinity's arm, leaning on him heavily. He led her to her seat. She was breathing hard . . . but so was he. She sat down, stiffly, and caught her breath.

A slower piece of music began. The dance floor filled quickly.

"Oh," Florrie said in a quivery sigh, "I haven't done that for so long. I used to dance all the time, I used to hit that floor—" She smiled, her eyes half closed, remembering. Infinity got the feeling that she meant the description literally. Florrie glanced at him through her

159

coquettish dark-painted eyelids. "But I haven't pounded for fifty years. I gave it up for my—never mind which birthday."

"The hot tub helps, when you've gotten a pounding." Infinity thought of the elderly martial artists he had known, training hard and smoothly, hobbling off the mat. The older students were not the only ones who headed straight for shower and deep bath.

"That would be pleasant," she said. "Will you come too?"

"Sure," Infinity said. "Sure. I'd like that."

"Maybe when we're done," Florrie said, "all those professors will be done monopolizing the guests. Maybe ordinary people can talk to them, then." She gestured sharply toward the cafeteria, where the Largerfarthings stood in a colorful cluster, surrounded by faculty and administrators. "I made the cotton candy," she said. "I wanted to tint it blue, but the dye wouldn't be good for them."

Infinity offered his arm; Florrie took it, and they strolled into the darkness.

In the shadows beyond the party, Griffith watched Infinity Mendez and Florrie Brown dance with abandon and leave together, without even talking to the aliens.

That's about what I'd expect, Griffith thought contemptuously.

He felt suddenly jealous of their friendship, jealous of the fun they were having. He considered them the least important members of the expedition—Mendez was staff, Brown, a recruit to Grandparents in Space. Neither held much status, yet between them they had caused him more trouble than all the rest of the deep space expedition combined.

Mendez was a chronic thorn in Griffith's side. He might humiliate Griffith at any moment by telling everyone about rescuing him from the emergency pouch. And Brown—Griffith had been effectively invisible till she started ranting that he was a narc. Griffith had not even known what a narc was. Not that it mattered. What mattered was the attention.

On a whim, he crossed the grass and stopped beside Senator Orazio. At first, she did not notice him.

Maybe I'm invisible again, Griffith thought.

She turned toward him.

"Good evening, Mr. Griffith."

"Want to dance?"

"Yes," Ruth said. "I think I would."

He was a stolid, unimaginative dancer. Ruth noticed a few guarded glances from the people around her.

I shouldn't be surprised at their suspicion, she thought. Maybe I was *Starfarer*'s best defender in the Senate, but now I'm dancing with a spy. Maybe Mr. Griffith hopes my good karma will rub off on him.

"Senator—"

"Call me Ruth," she said. "Under the circumstances, formality is silly. People call you Griff?"

His back went rigid under her hand. "How did you know that?"

"They don't send us out completely unprepared," she said.

"Then you know who I am—you *know* I didn't crash Arachne! Why didn't you say anything?"

"Because you're still being Mr. Griffith, the invisible accountant from the General Accounting Office—"

"I *am* an accountant, dammit."

"—and you weren't in danger."

"Forget it. Look. You've got to help me get this starship back to Earth."

"Do I?"

"There isn't any reason to stay longer! They've proved what they came out here to prove. Don't you want to go home? You've got a position, a lover—"

"They don't send you out unprepared, either, I see," Ruth said sharply.

"And the quicker we go back, the quicker you can prove you were right all along."

Griffith's sources of information could not know just how much she did want to go home. Yet she had supported the deep space expedition. It would break everyone's heart, especially J.D.'s, to return to Earth now. Once *Starfarer* and *Nautilus* entered the solar system, they would be stranded until the cosmic string came back. In a hundred years. Or five hundred.

It occurred to her that *Nautilus* and *Starfarer* did not have to return together. J.D. could take her alien starship and go wherever she wanted. Supplies would be a problem, until she could terraform it. But she could do it.

And, Ruth thought, she will, if she thinks the government is going to be hard-nosed about her keeping *Nautilus*. Why couldn't Jag keep his mouth shut?

"Why are you asking me for help?" Ruth asked Griffith.

"Because I didn't want to ask Senator Derjaguin to dance."

"People would have thought you were his spy, that's true," Ruth said.

"That isn't quite what I meant . . . but you're right."

"So now everyone's confused. You think you've made them wonder if they can trust me after all."

"Maybe I think I've made them wonder if they can trust me."

"It's beside the point," Ruth said. "I don't have any authority to tell them to go back home. Even if I weren't more or less a hostage."

"Some hostage," he said. "As for authority—who *does* have any, in this bunch of anarchists? You have as much as anybody."

"Then I'm inclined to give Victoria and her colleagues more time." As much as I can bear, she thought.

Griffith stopped, a few bars before the waltz ended. As

the other dancers took one final turn, parted, laughed, applauded, Griffith pulled back from Ruth.

"Thanks for the dance," he said. He walked away, his expression as bland and gray as usual. It was impossible to tell whether he was disappointed or furious.

Or, Ruth wondered, glad?

He strode directly through the image of Esther Klein. Esther, and Kolya Cherenkov too, noticed his rudeness; Esther stepped back as if she, rather than her projection, were standing in his way.

Within the expedition tent on board *Nautilus*, Esther glared at Griffith's retreating image. It faded out as he left the circle of Arachne's attention.

"Hell with him," Esther muttered.

The holographic image of the party swirled around her. People danced and talked and laughed. All the way back on *Starfarer*, J.D. directed *Nautilus*. *Nautilus*, with *Starfarer* in orbit around it, travelled toward Larger-nearer, and Esther was only a passenger.

The passivity frustrated her.

"Let's go exploring," she said. "All the way to the center. To the power plant." She was neither an engineer nor a physicist; she had no hope of solving the mysteries of the other ones' starships. But she wanted to see the center, the trap for the quantum black hole.

"We don't have the proper equipment," Kolya said. "Or proper shielding."

Restless, Esther strode to the window. Walking in such low gravity felt awkward.

She propped her hands against the wall on either side of the window. It was nothing more than a transparent patch in the plastic wall, no sill, no frame.

"Esther."

She looked over her shoulder. Kolya stood close behind her.

"Would you give me another dance?"

The music spun around them slow, rhythmic, three-

163

quarter time. Another Waltz. The Blue Danube. A close dance.

"I—" She hesitated only a moment. "Of course."

She had to reach up to put her hand on his shoulder, and he was too tall to put his arm around her waist. His hand rested on her shoulder blade. He could easily have picked her up in the low gravity, brought her to his level, and twirled and dandled her like a little girl. For a moment Esther feared he might. To her relief, he did not.

They danced.

Esther giggled. "It wouldn't be so awkward if I were leading."

"True." He smiled down at her, and switched his hand to her shoulder. She slid her arm around his waist. They danced more comfortably.

"Richard Strauss is spinning in his grave," Kolya said.

"So's my grandmother," Esther said. "She made me go to dance classes when I was a kid."

"You dance well."

"I hated it," Esther said. "I guess the partner makes a difference."

They danced, passing among the other holograms as if they were solid and real. Esther touched the tent's computer, faded the images to half intensity, and lowered the lights.

She liked dancing with Kolya. Tentatively, she let her cheek rest against his chest.

He no longer smelled like stale tobacco. And he did not reek with the sour odor that afflicted him when he tried to give up nicotine.

"You don't—" Esther cut off her exclamation. Good grief, what great manners, she thought. I almost told a friend I was surprised he didn't stink!

Kolya smiled down at her. "No smoke!" he said. "I cured some of the tobacco Petrovich found for me. I'm still trying to quit, but in the meantime I can chew it instead of smoking it."

Esther could not imagine eating the stuff; but, then, she could not imagine inhaling it, either.

They spun. Esther's feet left the floor. She tensed, then realized that Kolya, too, had risen into the air. They touched down. Each time they whirled, they levitated for half a turn.

The music ended. They stopped, and moved into a spot free of images, and held each other's hands a moment.

"Thanks," Esther said. Her heart was pounding. It's only a dance, she told herself. One waltz.

"You're most welcome," Kolya said quietly.

She drew her hands from Kolya's; he let her go. She hesitated. Flustered, she returned to the window and stared outside. The change in course had no effect on the angular momentum of the planetoid. It still spun. Esther watched a rapid dawn, sharp-edged shadows creeping back to their sources like a dark receding tide.

She put her hands flat on the window plastic and rested her forehead between them.

"There's time," Kolya said. "Plenty of time to discover *Nautilus*'s secrets. No need to put yourself in danger."

The protective tone in his voice verged on condescension. It startled her. It annoyed her. It scared her, and that was worst of all.

She snapped a command to Arachne and stopped transmitting their image back to the party.

She turned around and leaned against the wall, folding her arms across her chest. She gazed at Kolya belligerently; he looked back at her quizzically.

"There's lots of good reasons to put yourself in danger," she said. "As you well know."

"I thought I did, years ago . . ."

"You went out after the missile."

165

His bushy eyebrows bristled as he frowned at her. "Esther, what does that have to do with anything? What is the matter?"

She turned away again. Outside, nothing had changed. The surface of *Nautilus* was gray and empty, the horizon very close, space near and black. *Starfarer* was on the other side of *Nautilus*, but rotation would soon bring it into view.

"Sometimes I think . . . my whole life . . . is a fake."

"What are you talking about?"

"Courage."

"Is it the transport?" Kolya asked.

Esther shuddered involuntarily. She remembered the draining fear of trying to decide what to do.

"It is, I think," Kolya said.

"I should have undocked!" she said. "No matter what they told me, I should have known *Starfarer* would go straight into transition."

"You did what you thought best at the time."

"Following orders!" Esther said with disgust. "I was just fucking following orders. I can't *believe* I did that."

"It's all right," he said. "It worked out. Most of the people who were on the transport would rather have remained on *Starfarer* anyway. They're all delighted . . ." He hesitated. "Perhaps 'delighted' isn't the proper word." His voice held a smile.

"It doesn't matter!" Esther cried. "The results don't matter! I should have done what I thought was right, whether it was to stay with *Starfarer* or undock like I planned. *That* doesn't matter. What matters is I did what they told me to, I didn't even question—" She shouted an inarticulate sound of anger and disgust. "I could even pretend I did what I did on purpose. But *I'd* know—!"

He touched her shoulder.

Esther forced herself not to fling herself around and into Kolya's arms.

Every time he comes near me, she thought wildly, I start thinking in clichés. Next I know, I'll dream about him running toward me through a field of flowers!

She strangled the laugh that bubbled out of her.

"Did you have any reason to oppose your superiors before?"

"I knew nobody agreed with anybody else about what *Starfarer* should do. I should have thought—I should have planned—"

Kolya chuckled.

"What's so damned funny?"

"Members of our profession aren't renowned for our foresight."

"No," she said, even more bitterly. "We're *supposed* to think on our feet!"

"You made a mistake," he said quietly. "In your own eyes it was a serious mistake. Can you learn from it and put it aside? Or will you let it drive you crazy?"

"Beats the hell out of me," Esther said angrily.

J.D. and Zev joined Victoria and Satoshi at the edge of the dance floor.

"You look wonderful," J.D. said to the partners. Victoria wore the gold scarf and vest and the black silk skirt she had brought back from Earth on her last trip. Satoshi wore slacks and a honey-colored suede shirt. J.D. had never seen him in anything but faded cargo pants and a tank top.

"You do, too," Victoria said. "Zev, that shirt is very flattering."

She pressed her cheek to Zev's. J.D. stood back, unwilling to settle for a cool, formal embrace.

"A party's always a good excuse to dress up," Victoria said.

"I don't get much practice at it," J.D. said.

"Stephen Thomas is here," Satoshi said.

Across the courtyard, Stephen Thomas stood bathed

in decorative light. The pastel colors dappled the smooth black of his tuxedo.

His hair curled loose around his face, the mutualist a silver highlight. He wore a sapphire earring the same color as his eyes. His dark skin and his blue eyes gave him an ethereal appearance. He looked like the hero of a romantic spy movie.

Stephen Thomas let his gaze pass over his partners as if he did not see them.

It's dark over there, Stephen Thomas thought. I *might* not have seen them. His heart twisted with desire and fear and love.

"I must say, Stephen Thomas." Gerald Hemminge stopped beside him. "I'm amazed by this appropriate behavior. You look quite splendid."

"I thought this was a formal party." Stephen Thomas waited for Gerald's usual verbal needle. He expected the assistant chancellor to find something to complain about. A compliment put him off balance.

"The sandals are an . . . interesting . . . touch."

"I didn't have much choice of footwear," Stephen Thomas said. He flexed his toes. His claws scratched against the leather.

Gerald stared at Stephen Thomas's feet longer than idle curiosity required.

The music paused; the first few notes of a waltz began.

"May I have this dance?" Fox appeared between the two men. Stephen Thomas searched for a way to turn her down without hurting her feelings, again, not to mention Mitch's feelings.

"Yes," Gerald said. "Certainly."

Fox glanced at Stephen Thomas, her eyes cold.

Her expression was friendlier when she glanced at Mitch. "Hi," she said offhand.

"Hello," Mitch whispered.

Gerald took Fox in his arms and swept her to the center of the courtyard.

They danced. Other couples joined them. Gerald and Fox were the best dancers, Gerald the veteran of a thousand university fund-raisers, Fox the product of a three-generation political dynasty.

Forlornly, Mitch sighed. "What chance do I have, if it's Gerald Hemminge she's interested in?"

"Fuck it, Mitch," Stephen Thomas said, annoyed as much by his fur, rubbed the wrong way beneath his cummerbund, as by his student's attitude. "They're only dancing. Maybe she'll ask you next. If she doesn't, you ask her."

"She'd turn me down."

"Shoot yourself in the foot, why don't you?"

"What do *you* know about it?" Mitch snapped. "Nobody ever turns *you* down! You get whatever— whoever—" He caught himself. "Look, I'm sorry, I didn't mean—"

"Maybe I don't know how you feel," Stephen Thomas said. The muscles in his jaw were so tight that his voice came out angry and hard. "And maybe I do. But you *asked*—I figured you wanted an *answer*."

Mitch started to apologize again. Too aggravated to listen, Stephen Thomas stalked off along the edge of the courtyard. He wanted to dance. He wanted to dance with Victoria and Satoshi. He wanted to take off his tuxedo, which had always been comfortable before he grew the damned pelt, and dance naked in the grass with his partners.

But I'm afraid, he thought. I'm afraid they'll turn me down. Christ in a conga line, I'm worse than Mitch.

Mitch started after Stephen Thomas, but when Stephen Thomas disappeared into the darkness, he decided he had better wait to talk to him until they had both had a chance to cool off.

He overreacted, Mitch thought. How *could* he know how I feel, I bet nobody in his life has ever turned me down.

Mitch wandered back toward the dance floor, to torture himself for a while longer by watching Fox dance with Chancellor Gerald Hemminge.

I'm going to have to apologize to Stephen Thomas, Mitch realized. No matter whether I was wrong or he was, I'm going to have to apologize. He's my adviser, after all. Maybe he doesn't have life or death power over me, but he sure has it over my career.

Fox and Gerald waltzed past. They looked wonderful together. Even the disparity in their dress, Gerald businesslike, Fox casual, gave them a dashing and adventurous presence.

Mitch waited through two dances, before his nerve coincided with a moment when Fox was free. He hurried to her as she flung herself into a rock-foam chair, flushed with the last fast dance.

"Would you dance with me?"

"Oh, gosh, Mitch," she said. "My dance card's pretty full, I was going to sit this one out—Oh, okay."

She grinned, jumped up, grabbed his hand, and pulled him onto the dance floor. His pulse raced, as it did every time—every rare time—that Fox spoke to him, noticed him, even looked at him. They danced, winding around each other, sliding and twisting to the music. Mitch wished they were four-footed like the Largerfarthings, that they could dance, close together, like the quartet.

When the music stopped, Fox wiped the sweat from her forehead, raked her hair back with her fingers, and grinned again.

"See you," she said in that dismissive offhand way she had.

"Wait— Dance with me again?"

He caught up to her, slipping through the crowd, sweat cooling on his face.

"Nope, I asked Gerald for the next one."

"Is that a good idea?"

He was still following her; he nearly bumped into her when she stopped short.

"What's that supposed to mean?"

"Just—it's kind of dangerous, don't you think?"

"Gerald? Dangerous?" She laughed. "He's a pussycat."

"But there's a big power differential—"

"You sound like the illustrious Dr. Gregory," Fox said, disgusted.

"But he's right. It's awkward. When one person has a lot of power and the other doesn't."

"So who am I supposed to be friends with?" she snapped. "Who am I supposed to talk to? Who am I supposed to *sleep* with?"

Mitch tried to say, Me, I want you to sleep with me, I want you to love me the way I love you.

"God, I can't believe the bullshit," Fox said. "There's not supposed to be a hierarchy, so nobody admits one exists."

Confused, Mitch shook his head—a mistake; the interaction of the ship's rotation with his inner ears dizzied him.

And Fox was not finished yet.

"Maybe I get to talk to Professor Thanthavong? Will a Nobel laureate do? Or maybe I can make friends with Androgeos. Is a four-thousand-year-old grandson of the Pharaohs appropriate? Hey, I have it—you think I ought to sneak past the silver slugs and screw the chancellor!"

"What—? What are you talking about?" He felt as dizzy and confused as if he had shaken his head again.

"Mitch." She glared at him. "Stephen Thomas turned me down because he's a professor and I'm a student. Big hairy deal. Maybe he's right—for ordinary students. But *my* fucking *uncle* is the fucking *president*. Everybody pretends it doesn't count, but it does, and it'll count for a hell of a lot more when we get home."

Mitch spread his hands, speechless.

She stared at him with incredulous realization.

"You honest to god didn't think of that, did you?"

"No—I mean, I didn't want you to—"

"It never occurred to you that *I'm* the one who could be dangerous."

"No," he said.

"You're unbelievable." She laughed. Then she was gone, except for a drift of her voice, "Unbelievable!"

The last time she had disappeared into the darkness, he had followed her; he had comforted her. This time, he slunk away in the other direction.

J.D. saw Stephen Thomas at the far side of the dance floor, talking to one of his graduate students, talking to Gerald.

He'll have to come over here soon, she thought, he'll *have* to come give his regards to the Farthings. It would be rude if he didn't.

But then Fox walked over to him, and walked away with Gerald, and a moment later Stephen Thomas disappeared into the shadows.

J.D. sighed. She did not blame him for wanting to avoid Fox, but she had hoped that somehow, in the magic of the evening, he and his partners might find some common ground.

Nearby, the quartet clustered together at the edge of the dance floor, chatting with Professor Thanthavong and Lehua Aki. Longestlooker, at the center of the conversation, absently arranged beads in the crack between two flagstones.

Late rested flat on a rock-foam table. For most of the evening faculty members had surrounded him, talking to him by communications fugue, their eyes half closed. But the ebb and flow of the party had left him briefly alone. J.D. strolled over and opened her link.

"Are you enjoying the party?" she asked.

"Oh, yes."

"Do you have parties, in the Four Worlds?"

"Parties, and feasts, and ceremonies, great ceremonies."

"Do you have dances?"

"The Largerfarthings dance. I do not dance."

"You . . . are very conservative with your energy," J.D. said to Late.

"Yes," Late said. "Of course."

"Why?"

"Because of my physiology."

"Are you sick? Does moving hurt you?"

"Not hurt, exactly . . . injure."

"I don't understand."

"Moving is injurious."

"Just moving?" J.D. was taken aback.

"Yes."

"How long does it take you to heal?" she asked with sympathy.

"Forever. Never. I don't heal," Late said simply. "The damage builds up. When it builds up too much, I'll die."

"That's terrible!" J.D. exclaimed. "It's so strange!"

"How, terrible? How, strange?" Late quivered against the table, rippling from side to side and back and forth. "Oh, no, you made me laugh . . . Your world must have changed a great deal since Europa and Androgeos left it."

"It has changed," J.D. said, wondering if the subject of the conversation had changed as well. "In what particular way must it have changed?"

"Many of the creatures we took away—for their starship—have a structure, a life path, similar to that of my people. Changing the structure—it's very difficult."

J.D. touched Arachne with a question; the computer replied with an answer. To J.D.'s surprise, Late was right. An enormous number of creatures from Earth, mostly insects, lived and died in the same way.

"Things haven't changed that much." Now she understood more clearly why Quickercatcher had said Late's style of living was ubiquitous. "I never knew before now, about your particular kind of metabolism. I . . . I'm sorry if I teased you."

"You didn't. Not very much. I'm used to it, the quartet is impossible."

"But it's cruel. To joke about life and death."

"No, J.D., what better things to joke about?"

"Can't you—change your metabolism?"

"If my people can, that isn't for someone of my class to know."

"I thought there weren't any secrets in Civilization."

"How in this phase," Late said, in a tone of astonishment and amusement, "did you ever get that idea?"

"I know you keep secrets from us," J.D. said in a level tone. "I thought you didn't keep them from each other."

"We all keep all sorts of secrets. Less between the Four Worlds, I suppose, but secrets nonetheless."

"How can ordinary medical knowledge be secret?"

"We have no medical tradition," Late said.

"Because you don't heal," J.D. said.

"Yes."

"Aren't you allowed to know anything about your own metabolism?"

"I know some things, surely, but mine is not necessarily the same as that of my superiors." Late hesitated. "You disapprove."

"I'm . . . disappointed. That you have to balance so much against the length of your life."

"Our society functions well this way. Our elders are great diplomats and scholars and artists of . . . hmmmm, it's like painting, like the frescoes Europa likes so much. Except the pigments reflect frequencies in the infra-red."

"Heat painting," J.D. suggested.

"Close enough. Heat painting. Thinking does not damage us."

"That means, I suppose," J.D. said, "that the Representative is either a scholar or an artist."

Late hesitated.

"Not a good joke?" J.D. asked.

"He *is* a great diplomat," Late said. "I am not transmitting, not flattering him. I'm telling you the truth."

"I believe you," she said. She did believe him, within his own frame of reference. "But after the way he treated me, it's hard for me to understand."

"Someday he will prove it," Late said, "and that will be a wonderful day for our line. Then we'll have a ceremony, a festival, the like of which no one has ever seen. You must come to it, and celebrate with us."

J.D. touched her fingertips to Late's dappled fur.

"I'd like that," she said. "I'll look forward to it very much."

Professor Thanthavong strolled over to them, her pure expression transcendently happy. She smiled at J.D.

"Representative Late," she said, "I wonder if you can tell me . . ."

J.D. tried to focus on the conversation. The professor asked Late questions about alien genetic systems. Late protested that he was a diplomat's assistant, and knew little of science.

J.D.'s attention wandered to the quartet.

Fasterdigger fed bits of cotton candy to Longestlooker. Quickercatcher's long-furred tail twitched and spiraled with the music and he watched the dancing curiously. He had bits of white sugar on his whiskers. A silver mustache of mutualists formed on his muzzle; the sugar soon disappeared. Sharphearer rose on her hind legs to see across the crowd. Standing like that, she was well over two meters tall, taller than any of the humans. For all her frail grace, she was an imposing being.

She dropped to all fours and nudged Longestlooker beneath the jaw, bending her neck sinuously to reach her sister's soft throat. Longestlooker closed her eyes from

175

outer corners to inner corners, and trilled a few words of the Largerfarthings' language. All together, the quartet paced out onto the dance floor. Surprised, pleased, even apprehensive, the other people made room for them.

Longestlooker started the dance, swaying gently forward and back, raising her arms and moving her hands. Quickercatcher twined his fingers in hers and joined the swaying. Sharphearer grasped Quickercatcher's other hand; Fasterdigger completed the circle between Quickercatcher and Sharphearer. All four swayed, eyes half closed, blinking languorously.

Longestlooker surged forward. The circle broke. Her siblings followed her. She curvetted and leaped, turned and twisted. Her body was remarkably limber. She bounded over Quickercatcher, slipped beneath Fasterdigger, slid past Sharphearer. As she passed them they followed her again, their beads and decorations clicking and chiming, their claws tapping on the dance floor. They braided themselves together, improvising to the unfamiliar music. Their sweet scent, intensified by their exertion, wafted through the air. They trilled in harmony.

The music ended. They fell to the floor in a delighted heap of color, trilling, softly howling, panting for breath.

J.D. burst out with spontaneous applause. Zev joined her, and in a moment nearly everyone clapped and cheered. Longestlooker raised her head, looking around with her sharp, intense gaze.

J.D. hurried toward her. "Longestlooker, that was wonderful, I never saw anyone dance like the quartet."

The Largerfarthings rose together, stretched, gathered around her.

"We'll have to invent dances for Farthings and human people together," Quickercatcher said.

Seven

The path led along the bank of the river, then across a bridge. Stephen Thomas sat on the bridge's edge, staring down into the gentle ripples. At dawn, fog rose from the water, swirling above the current. As the sun tube brightened, the air warmed and the fog dissipated

Maybe I'll go for a swim, Stephen Thomas thought. Zev was right, it does make me feel better.

He wished all his problems could be solved by going for a swim.

After leaving the party, he had spent all night in his lab. He was unwilling to go home till he felt he could face his partners with equanimity. He could have gone back to the guest house, and slept in the room Feral had used as an office. But the room had lost any feeling of Feral's presence.

His vision sparkled at the edges with exhaustion. He doubted he would be able to go to sleep till he could take a look at the results of the new experiment. He hoped it would give him evidence that the dendritic molecules were the chemicals of squidmoth inheritance.

He yawned and stretched, glad of the fresh air and bright light. They would refresh him before he went back to the lab.

Last time he had crossed this bridge, it had been

covered with rushing water. He had run through the current, splashing, exhilarated by the newness of his body, elated by his mastery of it, driven by his anger at Europa and Androgeos and their secret supercharged bacteria, appalled at what he had discovered lurking through Arachne.

He still did not know exactly what it was. Chancellor Blades was cut off from Arachne, his neural node withered and resorbed. But something, something dangerous, remained.

He touched the web tentatively. All his recent interactions with it had been superficial and wary, and he had found nothing. Nothing dangerous, nothing to confirm his experience. No proof. If his suspicions were true, his surveillance had warned off the anomalous presence.

The river flowed peacefully. It had receded to its normal level.

Stephen Thomas stared upstream, letting himself dissolve in the transparent ripples, opening himself to Arachne's web. He offered the web his trust and his innocence.

He waited. He wandered, but there was a direction to his wandering. He found himself in sight of Feral's guest node. No longer sustained by Feral's attention, it had begun to dim and contract from disuse. The files of Feral's work would remain, unchanged, mummified in the archives.

Stephen Thomas could find no echo of the presence that had stalked him during transition. Arachne denied that such a presence could exist, or, if it existed, that it could pass unnoticed through the web.

Maybe not now, Stephen Thomas thought, keeping the idea to himself. But when Arachne's resources are all focused in one direction, getting *Starfarer* into transition . . . that would make an opening for anything to get through.

"Stephen Thomas!"

He drew himself from the web and made his eyes

focus on distant spots of riotous color. He had stared unseeing into the river gorge for several minutes, forgetting to close his eyes while he linked himself with Arachne. His eyes felt dry and scratchy. He blinked rapidly.

At the fossil site, upstream around the next bend, Crimson directed the first interspecies archaeological dig. Stephen Thomas corrected himself: the first interstellar interspecies performance art, complete with sculpted fossils and an intricately designed provenance.

Quickercatcher cantered down the beach toward Stephen Thomas. The Largerfarthings were as graceful in gravity as in free-fall. Quickercatcher folded his arms loosely on his back and ran on his front and rear legs, his long body moving sinuously. The decorations braided into his fur bounced against his neck and sides. Small soft sparks glittered around him, like fireworks in fog, but Stephen Thomas refused to see the Largerfarthing's aura; it faded away.

Stephen Thomas waved to Quickercatcher. He reacted to the Largerfarthings the same way J.D. did, the same way most of the people on board reacted. He loved them without reason.

What is it about these folks? Stephen Thomas wondered.

"I found a tooth, come see!" Quickercatcher looped around, ran back the way he had come, and disappeared beyond the river bend.

If the Largerfarthings had changed themselves to be able to breath Earth's air, to be able to exist in an alien environment, then they might have changed themselves to be appealing to human beings. Stephen Thomas tried to shrug away the idea. He did not want to be manipulated for Civilization's plan. He wanted to like the Largerfarthings for themselves. He *did* like them for themselves, no matter what the reason.

Stephen Thomas left the bridge, climbed down the

steep trail, walked along the river beach, and followed
Quickercatcher to Crimson's stage.

Quickercatcher's mauve fur stood out against the dark
rock of the river channel. Longestlooker and Fasterdigger
blended in, but Quickercatcher and Sharphearer, with
her piebald fluorescent fur, looked like a party waiting
to happen. The sight of the quartet dissolved the sadness
and confusion Stephen Thomas had been feeling.

They stood in a semicircle around Crimson, who
knelt on the beach brushing layers, grain by grain, from
a slab of rock of no volcanic origin.

Amazing how easy it is to accept Crimson's fossils—
and their ridiculous provenance—as real, he thought.

Even though he knew they were fake, even though he
had seen her with her wheelbarrow full of artwork on the
river beach, he found himself thinking of the fossils as a
billion years old.

Coincidences aside, it was an aesthetically pleasing
story. Granted, some of the provenance of the fossils
had been lost by the original mass-driver excavation.
The alternative was that the fossils would never have
been found, for who in their right mind would look
for fossils on Earth's moon?

Stephen Thomas wondered what the Four Worlds
people would say when fossils from a completely different evolutionary system turned up. Crimson's second
group of creatures, devolved from Nemo, looked even
older and much, much stranger than the remains of the
Fighters.

Once the second site turned up—a second site dug
from Earth's moon, which should not have fossils at
all!—the Four Worlds people would appreciate the performance. They would have to get the joke.

All four members of the quartet, and Androgeos,
stood around the cramped slab watching Crimson prepare the fossil for extraction. She used a dentist's pick
and a soft brush.

Stephen Thomas had never been to a dentist who used a steel pick instead of microbial techniques. He had once asked Crimson where she got dentist's picks, if she bought them from some company that manufactured them specially for paleontologists. She had laughed. When she laughed, when she smiled, Stephen Thomas understood why Satoshi had fallen in love with her. She had told him that even paleontologists do not use dentist's picks. She had found the tools at an antique store, and decided to try antique excavation methods.

The techniques worked. The Largerfarthings were fascinated.

A ruffle of green and gold above the site startled him. He focused on the motion: The Representative's representative hugged the volcanic riverbank. He looked like a mat of lichen, until he arched his back and the spines rose up. His leading edge draped directly over the sandstone. He, too, concentrated on the site excavation.

LTMs perched nearby, recording everything.

One of the Largerfarthings' tiny dioramas stood in a crevice of the riverbank: Several tiny wooden figures danced with a bead, a blade of grass, and a feather.

"There, see?" Quickercatcher pointed at the new fossil. "It was my turn to dig, and I found it."

Crimson glanced up. "Hi," she said. She gave Stephen Thomas a quick smile, and went back to her work.

"Hi, Crimson."

"I prepared the surface," Fasterdigger said proudly, without any hint of jealousy that his sibling, rather than he, had found the fossil.

"And then Crimson digs it out, of course," Longestlooker said.

"The star's prerogative," Stephen Thomas said. "Enjoying the performance?"

Quickercatcher nudged Stephen Thomas's arm with his soft, warm nose.

That's one reason why they look so benign, Stephen

181

Thomas thought. Their noses are more like . . . like a horse's, I guess, covered with fur. Instead of like a dog's, or a lion's. They look less like a carnivore. Despite the teeth.

"You're all so funny," Quickercatcher said. "I *do* like human beings. I've always liked human beings." He glanced fondly at Androgeos, who knelt on the gravel beach in his pleated silken kilt, one arm thrown around Fasterdigger's forward shoulders.

They both watched, rapt, as Crimson brushed gently at the projecting fossil fang.

"Are you finding anything else there?" Androgeos asked.

"The rest of the jaw, I think," Crimson said.

"I mean—artifacts."

"They're all artifacts," Stephen Thomas said. "And Crimson only works in organic forms."

Androgeos ignored him, refusing to listen to the Earth humans' deception.

Crimson sat back on her heels. "Look, look here, Quickercatcher. Let's get an LTM to probe this, I think your fang is still attached to the jawbone."

Quickercatcher snaked forward and arched his neck to look over Crimson's shoulder. An LTM scuttled to the work surface and crouched over it.

An enlarged holographic image appeared nearby. A bit of fang projected. A sound trace outlined the jaw beneath it, with a proposed reconstruction in false color that progressed from blue to red as the probability of its accuracy decreased. The missing bits were mostly blue, with a few tantalizing sections of bright scarlet.

Androgeos and the other Largerfarthings gazed at the image, then craned their necks to see the real fossil tooth. Even Late exerted himself to orient toward the image.

Crimson smiled at Quickercatcher. "This is a good find."

Quickercatcher nuzzled Crimson's shoulder, for all the world like an embarrassed kid. Crimson stroked Quickercatcher's angora fur.

"I imagine," Androgeos said, "a starship, one of the other ones' starships. It's so long abandoned that its inhabitants have died."

Fasterdigger's double-thumbed hand draped over Androgeos's shoulder, now and then twirling a curl of the Minoan's glossy black hair between forethumb and forefinger, or hindthumb and hindfinger. Androgeos's usual sulky look had vanished, to be replaced by curiosity and eagerness.

"Their bodies have turned to stone. The starship crashes on Earth's moon. Molten lava covers it over, and there the remnants wait. For us." He paused in his myth-making.

Shit, Stephen Thomas thought cynically, he just hopes we'll lead him to the other ones. But it's a nice change to see him looking like an ordinary human being with ordinary human feelings, instead of . . .

"Then your mass driver chews it into pieces and flings it into space. It becomes *Starfarer*. Starship, to starship."

When Androgeos demanded Victoria's algorithm, the Minoan had looked like an arrogant demigod, questing and rapacious, concerned only with his own perquisites and desires. More Achaian than the ideas Stephen Thomas had of ancient Minoans. But then, of course, one had to balance the kindly-looking snake goddess with the Labyrinth and the minotaur.

"That isn't how it happened," Crimson said. "There's no evidence of a crash. There's no gravitational anomaly, so where's the starship? The strata aren't disturbed. The bones aren't broken. And I haven't found any of their technology. Nor any inscriptions."

"You will. You must."

"I don't think so." She sighed. "It's too bad. We won't

have suitable markers for them, when we lay them to rest again."

"When you—what?"

"When we go back to Earth. We'll re-inter them, of course. It's the only respectful thing to do."

"You'd do better to leave them in Civilization. Where we can learn more about them."

"Of course that's impossible," Crimson said without hesitating.

"We'll see," Androgeos said, more like his usual self. "On Earth, we learned a long time ago to respect people's remains."

"There's too much to learn from them!"

"Tell that to the folks who grew these fangs." Crimson traced the curve of the fang in the hologram.

"But they're *extinct*."

"Are you sure?" Crimson asked. "Are you certain they are who you think they are?"

She turned to Stephen Thomas. "Want to help?"

"No, thanks," he said. "Some other time."

"You always say that."

He smiled. "I'd rather watch than perform."

Pebbles, falling, clicked across the gravel beach. Stephen Thomas glanced over his shoulder toward the bridge and the footpath. Chandra, the sensory artist, climbed down the trail.

"Hi," Chandra said.

"Haven't seen much of you lately," Crimson said.

She shrugged. "Nothing to do. *Starfarer* is boring."

Stephen Thomas would have laughed at her if he had not known she was desperately serious.

Her eyes were silver-gray, a uniform color over the whole exposed eyeball. Her unfocused gaze was as acute as normal vision, and she could save and store everything she saw. Her face and hands and her bare arms pulsed with gnarled nerve clusters.

The sensory artist sought unique experiences. She

made no secret that she wanted J.D.'s job. She would never get it. She barely got along—barely communicated—with human people. She was open to sensation, but only her own. J.D. had succeeded with Nemo, with the quartet, Stephen Thomas thought, because she was so open to others.

That's probably why she and Feral—

Stephen Thomas cut off the thought. It was too painful.

Sharphearer approached Chandra cautiously. The Largerfarthing passed Stephen Thomas, her ears swiveled forward, her muscles so taut she was walking on tiptoe.

"Who are you?" she asked. "You're different. You're almost as different as Stephen Thomas and Zev."

"I'm more different," Chandra said. "And I can do more things."

She moved forward. She and Sharphearer regarded each other warily.

"Sharphearer, this is Chandra," Stephen Thomas said. "She's an artist, back on Earth."

"I'm famous," Chandra said. "I'm more famous than Crimson."

Crimson sat back on her heels and scrubbed her sweaty forehead with her sleeve.

"Artists are always more famous than scientists," she said.

"It's only fair, though," Longestlooker said reasonably. "Scientists have only to imagine what's already there, and discover it. Artists . . ." Longestlooker's voice took on a note of awe, and she spoke completely without irony. "Artists have to invent what they discover."

Chandra held her hand out to Sharphearer. Sharphearer stretched her long arm past her forward shoulder till her double-thumbed hand rested on Chandra's palm. She placed her fingers on the nerve clusters.

When Sharphearer touched her, Chandra froze. Her

strange eyes widened. The nerve clusters, activating, darkened and pulsed.

Sharphearer gazed into Chandra's strange eyes as if she were recording every detail of Chandra's being as Chandra was recording Sharphearer's. She extended her other arm; her wide hand approached the gnarled nerve cluster on Chandra's forehead. She touched it. Chandra leaned into the pressure, closing her eyes. Her expression relaxed into pleasure and happiness.

Sharphearer trilled, a soft sweet purring growl.

With an incoherent shout, Chandra leaped back out of reach, her eyes wide open, shocked. Sharphearer, startled, leaped two meters backwards. Stephen Thomas jumped out of the way, and even so Sharphearer's powerful tail whipped against his leg.

Chandra stumbled around and fled, scrambling up the rocky path to the top of the river canyon. Stones clattered down and scattered across the river beach, vanishing among the gravel.

Sharphearer stood on tiptoe, all five toes on each foot extended, her ears clasping her skull, and her hair flattened close to her sides. Instead of resembling an electrified powder puff, she looked as sleek and dangerous as Longestlooker.

Crimson, Androgeos, and Sharphearer's siblings clattered toward them. Pebbles scraped together and splashed into the river. Chandra vanished over the riverbank. Stopping beside Stephen Thomas, Crimson frowned after her.

"What did I do wrong?" Sharphearer said.

Stephen Thomas hurried to her, limping. His leg stung.

"What happened?" Longestlooker asked. "Did you frighten her?"

Sharphearer raised her head and lifted her chin. Her goatee fanned out.

"Not on purpose," she said.

"Maybe you shouldn't have touched her without her permission," Androgeos said.

"It's all right," Stephen Thomas said. "You didn't do anything wrong. She wouldn't have held out her hand if she hadn't expected you to touch it."

"It *is* all right," Longestlooker said.

Sharphearer lowered her head and relaxed onto the pads of her feet. Her ears swiveled up and forward. She shook herself. Her particolored Day-Glo fur puffed out again.

"Why did she run away like that?"

"She's an *artist*," Quickercatcher said.

"You probably did something she *liked*," Crimson muttered.

Not hearing what Crimson said, or finding it too alien to respond to, Androgeos and the quartet grouped together, soothing Sharphearer, fluffing her fur. Androgeos was as solicitous and gentle as any of the siblings. Even Late raised his forward edge and wriggled his spines in sympathy.

Crimson stood apart from them. She glanced up the trail, where Chandra had disappeared. Stephen Thomas joined her.

"What did you mean by that?" Stephen Thomas asked.

"She's so damn strange." Crimson shrugged. "Have you used her recordings? She never does anything that's fun or pleasant. It's always uncomfortable, or painful—" She fell silent.

Crimson was right. Chandra's sensory recordings struck him as being morbid. Her walk through the natural cathedral of a Northwest forest ended with the freezing pain of a devil's club thorn. She had gone out into *Starfarer*'s anomalous snowstorm and taken off her clothes; she probably would have died of hypothermia if Satoshi had not found her and brought her inside. Stephen Thomas was still aggravated at her for that

187

escapade, because Satoshi had damn near ended up with hypothermia himself.

Crimson's eyes filled with tears. Stephen Thomas had a brief, uncharitable, inexcusable urge to flee before she started to cry.

"I just thought . . ." Crimson said, "I tried . . . Oh, shit, I'm lonely and—Why would I want to get involved with an *artist?*" She dashed the tears from her eyes and grinned at him sardonically. "And what would a famous artist want with a paleontologist? Dirt under her nails . . ."

"Her loss," Stephen Thomas said.

He smiled sympathetically. He had gotten to know her when she and Satoshi were seeing each other. He liked her. He liked her temper and the way she could get lost in whatever she was doing. Most of all he liked the glow she had brought back to the light of Satoshi's spirit, that had faded when Merry died.

"You did okay with a geographer," he said.

Crimson smiled. "True. It was . . . a surprise. It was nice."

"For Satoshi, too."

"But it was temporary. You take good care of him, huh?"

"I'll do my best," he said. Then, more certainly, "Yes."

On the other side of the fossil dig, Longestlooker stroked Sharphearer's neck one final time. Androgeos held the Largerfarthing behind her forward shoulders. Her calm had returned. The group broke apart and rejoined Crimson and Stephen Thomas.

"Should we go after Chandra?" Longestlooker asked Stephen Thomas and Crimson.

"I don't think that's a great idea," Crimson said. "Give her a chance to simmer down."

"We can keep digging?" Sharphearer said hopefully.

"Sure."

Crimson led them toward the fossil bed. She glanced over her shoulder at Stephen Thomas.

"See you."

He raised one hand in acknowledgment—and quickly folded his fingers into a loose fist when he felt the tension of the swimming webs. Crimson made nothing of the changes in him, but Stephen Thomas still experienced abrupt shocks of alienness.

He climbed the path to the top of the riverbank.

He had planned to go straight to the lab and disappear in his work, but his conversation with Crimson had changed his mind. He and Satoshi and Victoria had to talk. He owed them explanations for the way he had been behaving, for the reasons he was afraid to come home.

And he could not keep his suspicions about why Feral had died to himself anymore. It was too dangerous. He owed his partners a warning.

Victoria lay wakeful in her dim bedroom. Outside, beyond the shadows of the porch, the sun tubes brightened to morning. Satoshi slept soundly, his head pillowed between her shoulder and her breast, one arm flung across her waist. She opened her hand and brushed her fingertips against his smooth black hair.

Victoria clenched her fist and opened it again. Her hand prickled uncomfortably. Her arm had gone to sleep.

If *I* could just go to sleep, she said to herself. She had lain awake all night.

Maybe I should give up, she thought. Get up and go over to my office.

She stayed where she was, with the warmth of Satoshi's body pressed against her.

Light lay like gold on the wild garden beyond the deep front porch. A breeze whispered through the open French doors, carrying the scent of carnations and the tang of the distant sea. Most of Victoria's flowers had wilted and died after the snowstorm; a miniature delta of *Starfarer*'s thin topsoil washed across the path, carried by the snowmelt. The horseshoe-shaped hill that covered the house and enclosed the yard had protected one slope of carnations. Their buds opened like popcorn, releasing their spicy scent.

That was a hopeful sign. No one yet knew how much damage the snowstorm had caused. The campus was littered with broken branches and snow-burned seedlings. In the orange grove, the fruit fell, brown and rotting, and the blossoms shriveled. *Starfarer* would have few oranges this season, and probably none at all next year.

Stephen Thomas appeared at the French doors. He hesitated, backlighted, his face in darkness. Victoria could see only the familiar shape of his body, changed now by the gilt aura of his pelt on his arms and legs.

Stephen Thomas always claimed he could see auras—though he had said recently that he had decided auras were bullshit. Not that he could no longer see them . . . just that he no longer wanted to look.

"Hi," Stephen Thomas said.

"Hi."

"Can I come in?"

"Yes!" she said so quickly he flinched. Out of long habit they both fell silent and glanced at Satoshi, wondering if they had awakened him. He was never at his best when awakened from a deep sleep. Then they exchanged a look of understanding and rueful amusement. They *should* wake Satoshi; it was important for all three of them to talk.

"Of course you can come in," Victoria said, whispering. "Please do. Satoshi, wake up—"

"Wait," Stephen Thomas said. "I want to talk to you for a minute. Then both of you."

He stepped over the threshold. He crossed to her wide bed, and sat at its foot. Victoria untangled herself from Satoshi and joined Stephen Thomas, sitting crosslegged beside him.

"I miss you," Stephen Thomas said.

"I miss you, too. So does Satoshi. You looked so hand-some last night."

"I got tired of Gerald giving me a hard time about my clothes." He smiled wryly. "I thought I'd show him up for a change. I couldn't wear my shoes. Spoiled the effect."

Victoria smiled back. "But why did you leave so soon?"

He did not answer her directly. "All my life," he said. "I thought I'd have fun. I thought I'd have sex. But I thought I'd be alone. I thought nothing would last."

"You can't turn *us* into something like that!"

"I know it! I'm not trying to, I don't want to."

"I don't understand what you *do* want," Victoria said. "If you'd tell me, I'd try to give it to you."

"I never thought I'd feel about anyone the way I feel about our family," Stephen Thomas said.

His dark hands, with their amber webs, lay on his knees. Victoria and Stephen Thomas had been dark and fair; now they were two shades of dark: café au lait, and mahogany.

His body radiated heat that caressed her like warm silk.

When's the last time we touched? she wondered. When we all went down to the sea and tried to make love? He petted me with his swimming webs . . . But then Satoshi and I saw some of the changes Stephen Thomas is going through . . . and he saw some of them for the first time himself.

He had on loose running shorts and a sleeveless silk t-shirt, the same kind of clothes he usually wore. She had not seen him naked since the disastrous encounter in the sea, when the skin of his penis was sloughing off and his genitals were drawing into his body. Victoria shivered at the memory.

At her start, Stephen Thomas jerked his head up and drew away. Victoria took his hand and held it tight.

"No," she said, "no, please, I was just remember-ing . . . Are you—?"

"I'm done changing," Stephen Thomas said. "You saw me in the middle. I'll show you. Later. I was a mess, I didn't know any of that would happen. Neither did Zev. I mean, he knows what diver men are like, but he didn't know what ordinary men are like. He didn't know to warn me."

"Oh, love," Victoria said. "You must have been so uncomfortable."

"I'm okay now. I wish . . ."

"What?"

"You and Satoshi didn't think it was so disgusting."

"Disgusting!" Victoria flung her arms around him. Startled, he fell back onto the bed. She kissed him fiercely, hungrily. He opened his mouth for her tongue, and held her hips when she straddled his thighs. She slid her hand under his shirt, tracing his familiar long hard muscles beneath the soft new pelt. She felt him respond. A powerful current of curiosity increased her excitement. She pulled at the waistband of his shorts, expecting him to move, to raise his hips and help her free him of his clothing.

Instead, he shuddered violently and turned away.

Shocked, Victoria sat back.

"What's— Did I hurt you?"

They parted; she knelt beside him, confused.

"No," he said. "It's just that I'm afraid . . ."

He hesitated.

"We can go slow," Victoria said. "You're— It's your first time in your new body."

She had almost said he was a virgin again, but the idea of Stephen Thomas as a virgin was funny and she did not want him to think she was laughing at him.

"Do you want me to—"

She put her hand on his leg, slid her palm hard up his inner thigh, slipped her fingertips beneath the leg of his shorts.

"This hasn't got anything to do with sex!" Drawing away from her, he sat up and pulled his knees to his chest and wrapped his arms around his legs.

"Oh," Victoria said. "What, then?"

The silver mutualist held his hair back from his face, but one lock had fallen free. Victoria stroked it and smoothed it into place. The silver worm loosened, coiled around the vagrant lock, and tightened.

Victoria let her hand rest on Stephen Thomas's cheek. He shivered. She took her hand away.

"I think we should separate for a while. So you guys will be safe."

"*Safe?* From what? What are you talking about?"

"There's something in Arachne, and it's hunting me."

"What? Nonsense. We've checked the system—"

"It can only come out during transition," Stephen Thomas said. "When Arachne doesn't have any attention to spare."

"That doesn't make sense! Come home, we can work—"

"I *can't* come home," he said stubbornly. "I'm afraid for you."

"That is the stupidest, most transparent, idiotic excuse—" Victoria was furious, hurt, and confused. "If you want to leave us—"

"I don't, dammit, there's nothing I want *less!*"

"—why can't you just *say* so?"

"If I come home, you and Satoshi will be in danger."

"But the last transition was perfect," Victoria said. During *Starfarer*'s first two transitions, Arachne had crashed. Only during the third had everything gone smoothly.

"I *felt* it. It tried to beat my brain to shit."

Her eyelids flickered as she touched Arachne.

"All our connections are intact!" she said. She could not see how any damage could occur to Stephen Thomas's neural node without some damage to Arachne's intricate linkages between the partners.

"I was using Feral's account."

"What in the world could you do with Feral's account?" Feral had been a guest; his access had been hemmed in, limited.

"Pretend to be Feral."

He smiled a plaintively charming smile.

His charm annoyed her sometimes, especially when it made her feel as if she were his older sister instead of his lover. Trying to keep the annoyance from her voice, she made its edge razor-fine.

"Feral! *Why?*"

"To find out what happened to him. Why he died."

"It was an *accident.*"

"Like hell it was. He was murdered, and the murder was premeditated. It just hit the wrong target."

Victoria regretted Feral's death and she felt some responsibility for it. If Feral had done as she had asked, he would never have been in the web when it crashed.

"It would be so much easier if there was a reason," she said. "But there wasn't. We have to accept that."

"I got Feral his account. It was linked to mine. When I went in to find out why the system was crashing, I became a threat. If Blades had stopped me—"

"And J.D."

"And J.D. If he'd stopped us, we wouldn't have been able to prove he caused the crashes."

"But it was Feral who got killed."

"He was in the way."

"What about J.D.?"

"Her node wasn't finished yet. Maybe he couldn't get to her deep enough. Maybe he made a mistake, like he did with me and Feral. Maybe he underestimated her." His laugh was quick and sharp. "She caught up to Blades before I did."

Victoria looked away. She sympathized with Stephen

Thomas. The complicated rationale might ease his grief at his friend's useless death. But she could not accept it if it meant he would leave.

"Victoria, I don't *know* all the answers. But when I was in Arachne pretending to be Feral . . . something tried to kill me."

"Not you—Feral. It must have been an echo—a memory of what happened to Feral. If we wipe his records—"

"No!" Stephen Thomas said angrily. "We can't wipe out his work."

"We can make a back-up."

"If we wipe out his node, we'll never know what's wrong with Arachne."

Victoria blew out her breath in frustration. Stephen Thomas was obsessed by Feral, by Feral's senseless death.

"Love, I liked him, too. But we've got to get on with our lives. Besides, I don't see how this connects with your being afraid to make love with me, eh?"

He looked out the French window, into brilliant daylight. Alzena's songbirds shrilled and cried, confused by the direction of the light.

"I'm afraid if I love you," Stephen Thomas said, "the same thing will happen to you that happened to Feral. I think anybody connected with me is in danger."

"But that's crazy!"

She blurted out her reaction without thinking.

"Crazy?" he shouted. "I'm trying to protect you, and you think I'm *crazy?*"

"Listen to me," Victoria said. "Good god, Stephen Thomas, listen to *yourself!* No one's going to die from fucking you! You didn't even sleep with Feral!"

"But he was *connected* to me. You and me and Satoshi, we're so connected our nodes look like a pile of spaghetti!"

"Nobody's going to die because they love you!" she said.

"What about Merry?"

"What has Merry got to do with any of this?" Victoria cried. Merry had nothing to do with Arachne. Merry had never made it into space.

Her vision blurred. After a year, she still could not think of her elder partner without grief. Her heart skipped, as if it had emptied and clenched on nothingness.

"Merry loved me," Stephen Thomas said. His expression went bleak. Hurt and confusion filled his startling sapphire eyes. "And Merry's dead."

"Merry didn't die from loving you, Merry died because of the damned stupid motorcycle!" Victoria's voice broke and hot tears spilled down her cheeks. She fumbled toward Stephen Thomas, desperate for the comfort of his touch.

"I can't do this anymore!" Stephen Thomas lunged to his feet and stood there trembling, out of her reach, looking down at her, his face set. "Fuck it, I can't!"

He ran through the open window, across the yard, and vanished beyond the gateway.

Victoria cried uncontrollably. Fighting to stop only made it worse.

Satoshi enfolded her in his arms.

"It's okay," he said, his voice gruff with sleep. "It's okay."

"I didn't—"

She hiccupped, and swallowed; she wrapped her arms around him and held him. Her tears pooled up on her cheek where she pressed her face against Satoshi's shoulder; they dribbled down his chest. He leaned his head against her hair and rocked her.

"I didn't mean to wake you up," she said.

"Nonsense," he said.

He was right; it *was* nonsense, like everything that had just happened, like her whole conversation with Stephen Thomas—

"I was already awake," he said.

"Then why—"

"Because he said he wanted to talk to you alone . . . Because you needed to talk . . . Because . . ."

He stopped.

"I don't know," he said miserably.

The trail from the partnership's garden ended at a main footpath, one of the walkways that spiraled around *Starfarer*'s interior.

Stephen Thomas stopped running.

He was baffled. Baffled by Victoria's reaction and baffled by his own. He would be lucky if Victoria ever spoke to him again, or Satoshi either once he found out what had happened.

He was not entirely sure Satoshi had been speaking to him anyway.

Stephen Thomas could not believe what he had just done. He had pushed Victoria away. He had fled instead of comforting her, as he had comforted Victoria and Satoshi since Merry's death.

"All you had to do was hold her, you stupid son of a bitch," Stephen Thomas muttered. "And you couldn't even do that. What the fuck is the *matter* with you?"

He felt flayed, slashed.

Stephen Thomas had created a mental glass wall to protect his consciousness from his emotions. It was all that had kept him from collapsing when Merry died, and again after Feral's murder.

When Victoria started to cry, the glass wall had exploded. Instead of protecting him from his grief and anger, instead of walling him off and allowing him to function, it had shattered around him, causing more damage than it had ever blocked out. Its destruction had opened him to a visceral surge of terrifying anger and resentment. All he could think of— No, he had not thought at all. He had simply fled.

197

The glass wall lay in bright bloody shards at his feet.

He had failed Victoria several times over. Besides being unable to console her about Merry, he had disappointed her—and himself; he ached with need for her touch and Satoshi's. And he had failed to explain what had happened in Arachne. He had been so inarticulate about his fear that Victoria did not believe she was in danger.

Maybe she's right, he thought. Oh, god, it would be so much easier if she were right.

But if he was right and Victoria was wrong, Victoria and Satoshi were in peril.

If he could not persuade his partners of the danger, he would have to protect them another way. But the only way he could think of to safeguard them would take time.

If a psychotic pattern in the computer web was hunting him, and the people most closely connected to him, then he had to break the connections. He had to do it before *Starfarer* entered transition again.

No one knew when that might be. *Starfarer* might remain in the Four Worlds for months. But Stephen Thomas could not risk a delay.

He turned his attention to his neural node. Dendrites, tendrils, spread out from it in all directions, touching other nodes, other neural connections. A tangle of interlaced fibers filled the space between his and Victoria's and Satoshi's nodes. In some places several filaments had lost their identity and merged into one.

Stephen Thomas urged his node to disengage. The pattern resisted him. He persuaded it.

The change began.

Each time a connection separated, it left behind a ghost of itself, like a phantom limb. His node drew away from the reflected presences of his partners.

The distance ached.

• • •

The glass wall was full of cracks and missing pieces. One good blow would shatter it again. But for the moment it would hold.

As long as I don't try to talk to anyone I love, Stephen Thomas said to himself, it will hold.

He set off across campus toward his lab. If he submerged himself in work, he could wipe away the emotional tangle his thoughts kept falling into.

Stephen Thomas had succeeded in growing alien cells retrieved from *Nautilus*. While he was visiting the Four Worlds ship, his students had made a lot of progress. Mitch and Lehua and Bay had perpetuated the cells, harvested them, and done a rough separation of their components. Last night, after the party, Stephen Thomas had begun an analysis of what he believed to be squidmoth genetic material.

He had some ideas about how the molecules coded for biological chemicals. He had been worrying the problem around in his mind. The molecules were roughly spherical, but rough was the operative word. They looked less like beach balls and more like dust mice: rough and fuzzy, loose ends of molecules sticking out all over. The roughness would be the key, the variation that produced thousands of different results from a single type of substrate.

Professor Thanthavong had some other ideas about how squidmoth genetics worked.

And she could be right, Stephen Thomas thought, I could be off on the wrong track entirely. But I don't think so. I think those big molecules are what served Nemo and Nemo's attendants the way DNA serves us.

The dendritic molecule was complicated in appearance but relatively simple in structure. The same could be said for DNA. But DNA was like a string of alphabet beads with only four letters, arranged one by one in three-letter words. The dendritic molecules in the

Nautilus samples resembled a clump of beads strung together with a web of connections, tangles, and loose ends. The ends, he believed, would form the blueprints for biological polymers, the way DNA's sequence created a code.

What baffled him was how to limit the degrees of freedom. DNA was a string, one-dimensional, readable in only one direction. Dendritic molecules presented a surface that was at least two-dimensional, possibly three-dimensional, probably a fractional, fractal dimension.

I'd know more, he thought, if my time hadn't been so damned busted up since we hightailed it out of the solar system . . .

If I hadn't felt so crappy during the changes . . .

If Arachne hadn't crashed . . . Even if the artificial stupids hadn't crashed!

If it hadn't been for all the meetings—god, if I never go to another meeting—!

If Feral hadn't died . . .

Stephen Thomas smiled sadly to himself. The truth was that if Feral were alive, Stephen Thomas would happily fragment his time to hell and gone.

The rubble of the genetics department had been cleared, dissolved away and recycled by the lithoclasts, the silver slugs that were so important to the operation of *Starfarer*. The nuclear missile had struck the outside of the cylinder directly below the genetics department, creating an earthquake inside.

Stephen Thomas brushed his fingertips across the new scar on his forehead. He and Satoshi had been inside the genetics department when the missile hit. They were lucky they had not been crushed.

The new genetics building had begun to grow, but no slugs were crawling on the foundation. The small ones might be out of sight, and even the medium-sized ones could be working behind the bits of wall and the fibrous complex of framework. But the big slugs were the size of rhinoceroses, and they were nowhere to be seen. The rebuilding of the genetics department was on hold.

Maybe Infinity Mendez needs all the slugs on the outside of the cylinders, Stephen Thomas thought. Or maybe they're all off fixing snow damage.

Or guarding Chancellor Blades.

He continued along the trail to the biochemistry department, where *Starfarer*'s geneticists were camping out. Stephen Thomas missed his old office, with its sagging rattan chairs, all his intramural athletic trophies, and enough floor space for a sleeping mat. His temporary cubbyhole was too small to let him stretch out for a nap during all-night lab sessions.

Like the genetics department, the biochem building lay inside one of *Starfarer*'s rolling hills. Stephen Thomas strode into the cool shadow of the main corridor. He added tracks to the other footprints before he realized the old towel at the entrance was for wiping the mud off shoes.

Too late now, he thought. Good god, the place is a mess.

Everybody on board *Starfarer* took the artificial stupids for granted. They kept things clean, they kept things in order. They were practically invisible. He noticed their absence more than their presence. The chancellor had disabled them. Stephen Thomas had seen only a few back in service.

We worked on them hard enough, he thought, grimacing at the memory of the artificials' rotting brains.

A touch to Arachne assured him that the ASes were regrowing their brains as quickly as possible.

Stephen Thomas reached the doorway of his temporary lab. All three of his graduate students, Lehua, Mitch, and Bay, sat around a lab table, staring at a holographic projection.

"Think it's a mistake?" Lehua asked morosely. She wrapped her fingers in her red-gold hair and twisted and tugged at one long lock. The nervous gesture clashed with her usual composure and youthful elegance.

"Maybe it's . . ." Bay's voice fell apprehensively. "Maybe it's contaminated."

"Bullshit," Stephen Thomas said.

All three students started at his voice and looked at him without speaking.

Unsettled, Stephen Thomas joined them.

Lehua gestured toward the display with her free hand.

On the graph, straight, perfect vertical lines marked several high molecular weights.

Biological molecules never gave precise results. The natural variation of goopy, sloppy organic systems smeared the peaks out.

"There's no variation," Bay said.

"It's perfect." Mitch wrapped his gangly long legs around each other and wrapped his arms around his knees.

"But it can't be," Lehua said. Her hair snarled in her fingers.

"The peaks for the squidmoth molecules are as sharp as the calibration beads," Bay said. He pointed out the calibration lines.

"Did Arachne run the data through clean-up for you to look at?" Stephen Thomas felt more apprehensive than he allowed himself to sound.

"Of course not," Lehua said. "That's the first thing we checked."

Jesus, Stephen Thomas thought, maybe I screwed up. Maybe I ran the tests on a handful of calibration beads. It was late. I was tired. I was distracted—everyone was distracted. And none of that's any excuse.

"Okay," Stephen Thomas said, more cheerfully than he felt. "We know one thing about squidmoth genetics."

"And what is that?" Professor Thanthavong said from behind him.

Stephen Thomas faced his boss. "It's neater than ours," he said.

Oh, fuck, she's going to tell me to drop the dendritic molecules, he thought.

"I don't think that's terribly likely," the professor said. "Where have you been? I left you several messages."

"I got . . . involved with something in Arachne."

He recalled, with embarrassment, that he had blurted out to Professor Thanthavong his fears that anyone who loved him was in danger. She had told him to pull himself together. He could not explain to her that he was late because he had been separating his neural node from those of his partners.

"Genetic molecules must have some potential for change," she said. "For evolution. Do you agree?"

"Sure," he said. "But . . ." The trouble was, he could see where she was going and he could not think of a good reply.

"But this polymer—if the sample contains any alien polymer!—is uniform within each class and from cell to cell, from widely distributed samples. It came from a being that spent a million years living beneath cosmic rays, unprotected by a significant depth of atmosphere."

"So it'd have to be tough," Stephen Thomas said.

She looked at him askance. He shut up.

"Let us discuss this in my office," she said gently.

In silence, feeling contentious, he followed her out of the lab and down the hall.

He respected and admired the Nobel laureate as a colleague above all others. She expected a lot of the people in her department, but she made fair demands. And she seldom pulled rank. He had argued with her any number of times, on technical questions, theoretical ones. Sometimes he won the argument, sometimes she did. She had never cut off a discussion this way.

They reached her office and went inside.

"Please sit down."

She took the rattan chair facing him, rather than the place of authority behind her desk. The self-conscious choice made Stephen Thomas even more uneasy.

"What's the matter?" he said. "The dendritic molecules are Nemo's analog of DNA, or they aren't. We'll figure it out. We need some time, we've only started."

"The matter is that I'm concerned about you."

He froze. He did not want to have this discussion. With anyone. Particularly with Professor Thanthavong.

"There's nothing to be concerned about."

She gazed at him in silence.

"I spend as much time here as I can!" he said. "The alien contact department—"

She made a sharp, annoyed sound. "Am I that unreasonable?" she said. "Do I expect you to be in two places at once? To give up your position in alien contact? No."

It was Stephen Thomas's turn to fall silent.

"Were you here all night?" she asked gently.

"Yeah."

"You have a great deal on your mind," she said. "I see you grieving, holding yourself together so hard I can see fingernail scratches in your skin—"

"I'm all right!" he said.

"I would like you to take some time to yourself."

"And I'd like to work!"

"I'm sorry, I can't permit it."

It's all I've got, he said to himself, and barely kept himself from saying it aloud. It's all I've got left . . .

"I'm frightened, Stephen Thomas," she said. "You're obsessed with the dendritic molecules—"

"You wouldn't say that if you agreed with me about them!"

She smiled. "Perhaps not. But it doesn't matter whether I agree with you or not. It doesn't matter to the molecules or to the biological system what

204

either one of us *believes*. All that matters is what's true."

"Yeah," he said.

"You will be right, or I will be right—or possibly we'll both be right or wrong."

"You don't have to be frightened for me," he said. "I appreciate it, but I'm okay."

"I'm not frightened for you," she said.

"You *said*—"

"I'm frightened *of* you."

"You're—what?"

"You are young, you think you're invulnerable. Invulnerable to exhaustion, to change, to grief. You are not. You're in desperate danger of making a serious mistake."

Stephen Thomas sat back in the chair, hurt and astonished. One of Professor Thanthavong's few non-negotiable rules was that of safety. She had spent so much of her career working with dangerous diseases that she would not accept sloppy lab procedure.

She was warning him. If he had already made a mistake that involved contamination, the warning was too late.

"I'm not going to walk in the lab and drop alien cells on somebody's foot!" he said angrily.

"I can give you some slack," she said. "All you want—all I can make you take. Now. *After* something goes wrong— then I cannot give anyone slack."

"Goddammit, you're talking as if I've already fucked up!" Stephen Thomas said.

If he had contaminated the cell preparation, he was finished as Professor Thanthavong's colleague.

"I said nothing of the sort."

"So the alien cell preps look different!" he said desperately. "So what? They're *supposed* to look different. They're *alien!*"

At the same time, he thought—all the while trying to fight off the thought—My life is falling apart around me, my partners probably never want to speak to me again, and I'm jealous of J.D. and Feral. Why shouldn't my technical skills turn completely to shit?

He stood up so fast the rattan chair fell over and bounced.

"You dragged me out of the lab in front of my students—"

"I asked you to meet with me—"

"—and you've decided I'm too stupid to know my own limits—"

"I tried to avoid embarrassing—"

"—and you're afraid to let me test my hypothesis—"

"Your hypothesis—!"

Professor Thanthavong sat back in her chair.

"—because you're afraid I'll be right and you'll be wrong!"

His outburst ended. He glared at the Nobel laureate.

The silence lengthened.

Thanthavong took a deep breath.

"I am very angry," she said quietly. "I think it best that we do not speak for a time."

"Fine with me," Stephen Thomas said. "I have work to do."

"You must find alien contact work to do. You may not work in a laboratory in my department until we have spoken again."

Furious, hurt, and humiliated, Stephen Thomas picked up the rattan chair and set it back on its feet. When it creaked in protest at the pressure he put on it, he snatched his hand away.

He strode stiffly out of the office, out of the building.

Eight

The *Chi* plunged through veils of high cloud toward the surface of Largernearer. It broke through the overcast and sailed above the endless sea, seeking one of the few specks of dry land on the alien world.

J.D. stared down hungrily.

She had walked on the moon of Tau Ceti II. She had visited Europa's terraformed planetoid. She would—she hoped—spend a significant part of the rest of her life aboard her alien starship. Yet she anticipated this landing keenly.

Largernearer is my first natural living alien world, she thought. Another first time.

Always a first time.

Far below the transparent floor of the observers' circle, the blue-black surface of the sea moved leisurely past in slow, massive swells.

A glittery disk appeared in the distance, rising gently as a swell passed beneath it.

Victoria leaned forward in her couch. "It's one of their antennas!"

The disk passed beneath the *Chi*. Victoria spun her couch to keep it in view as long as possible. She pulled up an image of the genetically engineered dish to inspect at her leisure.

"Interesting problem," she said, "keeping it focussed."

The *Chi* flew onward.

"J.D.," Zev said softly, "look."

He pointed off to the left of the *Chi*'s path.

Colors swept toward the horizon, beneath the surface of the water. Trying to make out what she was looking at, J.D. asked the *Chi* for a magnification.

A school of fish? she wondered. An illusion, or a rainbow trick of the light?

The *Chi* brought the view closer.

"Flowers!" J.D. exclaimed.

Rafts of blossoms rode the currents beneath her. For all J.D. knew, the flowers might be creatures, like anemones or coral. She cautioned herself, as she always did, about making assumptions. But the correspondence with flowers was striking. The blooms floating just under the surface were as brightly colored as the flowers in any Earthly garden, azure and vermilion, orange and yellow. Deeper, as the water filtered the light, all the petals appeared blue. Small creatures flicked among them. Larger shapes surged through the deep water between the blooming rafts.

The *Chi* stored the magnified image, fading it out as the flower meadows dropped behind.

Far ahead, like a signal, a mass of stone rose from the sea.

On all of Largernearer, only a dozen islands broke the surface: a dozen volcanic seamounts, enormous gouts of lava bulging upward from the deep sea floor, producing enough new rock to remain above the highest waves. Each was the youngest of a string of peaks, the track of a moving hot spot in the crust of Largernearer. Back on Earth, similar circumstances produced series of volcanoes: active, dormant, and extinct, like the Hawaiian island chain. On Largernearer, only the active volcano remained exposed, for the sea eroded the dormant peaks to deep-water mesas before an archipelago could form.

The island's summit rose high above the ocean. Steam

from an active crater swirled and dissipated. Higher in the atmosphere, clouds formed and tumbled as the island created its own weather systems.

As the island approached, the color of the water changed from depthless dark blue, to azure, to tropical green.

The waves of Largernearer undulated around the planet without anything to slow them. One of the long, slow swells, an ordinary wave on Largernearer, reached the slope of the seamount. The wave's force, slamming into the flank of the seamount, pressed the water into a towering wave. The tsunami peaked, crested, and curled, then broke with a tremendous crash against the side of the mountain.

Sea water hit volcanic vents. Plumes of steam exploded from the slope.

Satoshi whistled softly, in rapt appreciation.

"Christ on a surfboard," Stephen Thomas said. "We're supposed to *land* there?"

The *Chi* passed over the flank of the volcano.

To leeward, a tremendous harbor stretched for kilometers. A dormant, drowned crater held the peaceful water in the half-circle of its broken rim; the active volcano, rising to waveward, sheltered it.

Nothing grew on the raw slopes of the island. Like all the dozen land-points, it was bare lava, isolated and barren.

Largernearer, and all its life, belonged to the sea.

The *Chi* swooped around the natural harbor and soared toward a narrow strip of white beach. Beneath the observers' circle, emerald water shoaled rapidly to pale leaf-green above white sand. Intriguing shapes moved below them, but the *Chi* passed so fast and so low that J.D. could no longer look straight down without feeling dizzy.

The engines thundered. The *Chi* slowed, stopped, hovered. Sand sheeted out around the explorer craft.

The *Chi* settled just above the high-water mark. It bounced roughly, then stilled.

The engines cut. The creak of cooling interrupted the sudden silence.

Zev threw off the safety straps. He took two long strides to the transparent wall and gazed out at the sea, at the gentle waves drawing lines of foam across the beach. The gold light of 61 Cygni haloed his fair hair and his fine pelt, and shone amber through the swimming webs between his fingers.

Stephen Thomas was less anxious to reach the water. He remained in his couch. His hands lay relaxed, fingers spread, on his dark thighs. But his feet tensed, and the new claws extended and scraped against the glass of the floor.

Victoria flinched.

"That sounds like fingernails on a blackboard," she said, keeping her voice light and matter-of-fact.

"I haven't quite got used to having claws yet," Stephen Thomas said.

"Me either," Victoria said, then, in a barely audible voice, "but I'd like to."

Stephen Thomas acted as if he had not heard. In silence, Satoshi gazed out at the barren island.

The undercurrent of tension among her colleagues troubled J.D.

"Let's go outside," she said.

The artificial lung was barely mature. It had been unfrozen and revived for this excursion. It clasped itself to J.D.'s back, warm and familiar but unseasoned. Its extensions fumbled over her shoulders and attached themselves to the vents in her mask.

Zev and Stephen Thomas waited nearby, sleek and gilded in the sunlight. J.D. had decided to wear a bathing suit, Stephen Thomas wore his usual running shorts, and Zev had taken off his clothes. Zev was completely unself-conscious about nakedness.

The island radiated heat against J.D.'s bare feet. Wavelets stroked the serene shore, so gentle they were like a different phenomenon than the huge swells of Largernearer's open sea. A breeze cooled J.D.'s skin and skittered angular sand grains across wrinkled lava.

High above her, the volcano rumbled and steamed. Orchestra had assured them it would not erupt while they were visiting. J.D. wanted to trust her host. But back home, predicting volcanic action remained more art than science.

Nothing moved on the island but the windblown sand and the steam. The slopes were barer than any desert, for Largernearer had no land life. None at all. Its bits of dry land were so small, so isolated and transient, that terrestrial life never had a chance to develop.

But the life in the sea vibrated in J.D.'s perception. She could see it and smell it, and when she dipped her hand in the water, tiny finned creatures squirted away from her. Dark against the sea floor, they turned over, exposed a pale side, and disappeared. She tried to catch one, but they were too fast for her.

In the clear air of Largernearer, J.D. could see past the bright green of the lagoon, between the dark lines of the sheltering crater, out across the dark deep sea.

Victoria joined J.D. at the water's edge and gave her a quick embrace. Victoria was trembling. J.D. squeezed her hand gently. Victoria's fingers were dark and cool and slender within J.D.'s larger, fairer hand.

"Take care," Victoria said.

"I will," J.D. said. "What's wrong? We'll be fine, don't worry."

"I don't know," Victoria said. "This is scarier than the other times. Why is that?"

"It's more like home," J.D. said. "More like home, but stranger."

Victoria smiled.

"Zev and I will take good care of Stephen Thomas," J.D. said.

Victoria's expression went solemn. She squeezed J.D.'s hand.

"I'll just say goodbye to him, eh?"

She let J.D.'s hand go and crossed the beach to join her partners. They spoke softly, inaudibly. Stephen Thomas stood with his back to the *Chi*'s recorders.

J.D. turned away, saving their privacy, focusing her LTMs on the sea. She squinted into the bright water.

As far as she could tell, things were going from bad to worse with the partnership. Direct conflict would be easier than the polite tension, but the problems were too complicated for an open fight. If they fought during the excursion, their conflict would be completely public.

J.D. hoped they could work out their difficulties. She liked Satoshi, she had a terrible crush on Stephen Thomas, and she loved Victoria. She wanted them all to be happy.

In the distance, rising from the depths beyond the mouth of the harbor, another island appeared where no island existed. J.D. caught her breath.

Orchestra rose above the surface, water exploding from the bright-colored summit of her head and back. Waves cascaded down her sides, foaming waterfalls that crashed and echoed all the way to the island.

She waited.

The Representative of the Largernearlings could not approach too closely. She was far too large to enter shallow water.

Zev joined J.D. at the water's edge. His face glowed with eagerness and joy.

"Let's go," he said solemnly.

"Okay." J.D. checked the LTMs clinging to her shoulder strap.

Zev sprinted across the sand and plunged into the water.

"Zev! Wait for the boat! I meant—" She ran after him. He was competent and self-assured in the sea, but he had no way of knowing what he might face on Largernearer.

Europa and Androgeos swim here, J.D. thought. Zev's probably safe. But he shouldn't go out alone. Besides, my lung needs to hydrate . . .

She chuckled and stopped making excuses. She wanted to swim here as much as he did.

She stepped off the barren sand and into the sea. She splashed into the warm, alien water, pulling her mask down over her eyes and nose. Life pulsed against her feet.

She pushed forward into the water, entering slowly. The artificial lung quivered and hydrated, plumping against J.D.'s back, pumping fresh oxygen to her. It needed water, oxygen. It worked with elements and simple molecules, oblivious to complexity and alienness.

J.D. could feel and taste and smell the differences. The sea was less saline than back on Earth, making her less buoyant. Even sounds were different, shriller in the thinner atmosphere. When she ducked her head underwater, the sound there was different, too. She was used to swimming with divers, to being surrounded by the clicks and wails and groans of true speech. Here, she heard the beating of her own heart, the shussh of the waves against the beach. She felt, rather than heard, a low drone of complex harmonics.

Alert for an adverse reaction, she tasted the water. The salt was more dilute and more metallic. The underlying organic tang twisted her tongue with an odd bitterness. She spat out the water. She did not have the taste discrimination of a diver, but she could taste the alienness.

The water contained nothing toxic to humans. Neither Europa nor Androgeos had ever experienced allergic reactions here, but allergies differed from person to person. Over time, J.D. or any of her colleagues might develop a reaction to some alien compound. That was a gamble of protein shapes, chance similarities. But allergic reactions increase in severity over time. With luck, the members of alien contact would have some warning.

Zev cried out in true speech, exultant. J.D. could only perceive part of his comment. Stephen Thomas could probably, by now, hear all the frequencies of true speech. J.D. envied him the ability.

She answered Zev, knowing her accent was flat. He replied, caressing her body with his voice.

The shallow water stretched to the mouth of the lagoon. With the sun hot on her back around the thick wet warmth of the artificial lung, J.D. kicked away from shore.

J.D. swam on the surface, powered on her smooth strong long-distance stroke. Thanks to the artificial lung, she did not need to turn her head to breathe. Zev swam fifty meters ahead of her, delighted by the strangeness and the freedom. The water was very clear. At first the sand beneath her was bare, scoured clean by wave and tide. Gradually, bushy plants with tiny brilliant flowers grew more and more thickly until J.D. swam over an underwater veldt.

Stephen Thomas wore running shorts, but in front of his partners he felt stripped to the skin. Satoshi self-consciously did not let his gaze fall below Stephen Thomas's face. Victoria watched him speculatively, with edgy frankness.

"I didn't expect you to say goodbye to us," she said.

She was still angry and confused. He did not blame her.

"You don't know me as well as you thought," he said, keeping his voice light, without accusation.

"Are you sure you're ready for this?" Satoshi said, gesturing toward the sea, the glass boat. J.D. and Zev splashed into the water.

"No. Have to start sometime."

"Sometime when you have an idea what you'll find!"

"Come on!" Zev called.

"It'll be alien whether it's this sea or *Starfarer*'s." The sea drew his attention, distracting him from his partners.

"Oh, *bullshit*," Satoshi said with intensity.

The profanity startled Stephen Thomas. Behind him, the glass boat slid down the ramp and splashed into the sea. Bright drops of alien salt water fell cool on his skin.

"I'd better go."

"Why did you separate your node?" Victoria asked. "There's a void where it ought to be, I keep falling into it—"

"I had to, I told you. For your own good."

"Dammit—!"

"I've got to go!"

He left them behind, strode across the beach, waded into the blood-warm water, and struck out after J.D. and Zev.

J.D. surfaced and looked back at the beach. Leaving Victoria and Satoshi behind, Stephen Thomas waded into the water, pushed forward, and struck out toward her. He swam noisily. It startled her that he was not a very good swimmer.

Silly, she thought. No reason why he should be. He's only just turned into a diver, he doesn't have Zev's lifetime of practice, or my experience at sea races.

J.D. back-stroked for a few meters, allowing Stephen Thomas to catch up. More important, swimming on her back kept the lung wet and allowed it to absorb more oxygen.

J.D. made a connection to the glass boat. It responded, moving silently forward. J.D. waved to Victoria, who raised one hand and sent a wordless touch of good luck through her link to J.D.'s. She and Satoshi would stay with the *Chi*, taking samples and measurements on the island.

The tide had just turned. The tides on Largernearer were even more complex than the tides of Earth. The world was closer to its star, its companion world bigger than the moon. Until the next high tide, getting the boat back onto the ramp would require moving the *Chi*.

Calling the boat to follow, J.D. flipped and settled into her freestyle stroke. Zev swam beneath her. He grinned, brushed his webbed hand across her body, and dove deeper, arching backwards toward the sea bottom and the flower-bushes.

J.D. would never mistake this alien ocean for home.

A crowd of small creatures, their synchronized motion as jittery as old-fashioned film, glittered through the water where Zev swam. The diver spun among them, fearless and delighted. J.D. dove, scared.

They might be like piranha, she thought. They might attack—how would they know he isn't edible for them?

They surrounded Zev like metallic confetti, passed him, and vanished into the distant blue haze of the clear water.

Seeing J.D.'s distress, Zev joined her and pointed toward the surface. They rose together and broke the surface side by side.

J.D. touched her link.

Orchestra, she said, what predators should we watch out for?

Nothing here will eat you, the whale-eel replied.

No, J.D. said. But they might bite.

You're safe in the lagoon, Orchestra said.

"These aren't dangerous," Zev said. "They hardly have teeth. Look."

He opened his hand.

One of the silver-fins flopped against his hand, held tight with its fins folded by the web between Zev's thumb and forefinger. Its sides moved as if it were breathing.

The silver-fin was prettier from a distance. Up close its mouth gaped wide, surrounded by an irregular circle of shiny blue eyes. The fish had four long sharp fins running down its body. Its tail tapered to a blunt pucker.

Zev regarded the silver-fin. He immersed it in the water. It gulped and clenched, taking water in through its mouth and squirting it out through the anus, trying to jet-propel itself to freedom. Its fins jerked convulsively. Zev held it fast.

Zev ducked underwater. He brought the fish to his face and opened his mouth, letting the water flow across his tongue, tasting and smelling the creature. J.D. touched his shoulder quickly. He surfaced again, seawater splashing from his short pale hair, streaming down his face and neck.

"It smells . . . weird," he said. "There's no word for it, not even in true speech."

"Don't eat it," J.D. said.

"All right. But we ate Nemo's food."

"Nemo invented that food for us," J.D. said.

Stephen Thomas caught up to them. He stopped, trod water beside them, leaned back to duck his head. He caught a few loose strands of his hair at the back of his neck; the mutualist took them in and coiled around them.

Stephen Thomas was breathing heavily. He was a natural athlete, self-possessed and graceful on land, taking everything so easily that some people mistook the ease for languor. But long-distance swimming required a different kind of conditioning.

"That's an ugly little SOB," he said.

He poked at the silver-fin. It struggled and gulped and spit water and the sharp edge of its fin scratched his finger.

"Shit!" Stephen Thomas jerked his hand away and stuck his finger in his mouth.

"Let's see," J.D. said. "How bad is it?"

He let her look at his finger. The blood had already clotted, sealing the cut.

"You're really a diver now," Zev said. "Even your spit." The extra clotting factor in the saliva of divers helped keep them from bleeding into the water. In the sea, even a minor cut could attract sharks.

J.D. let go of Stephen Thomas's hand. She seldom touched him. The people of *Starfarer* had a habit of hugging each other, a habit J.D. was growing to like. But she avoided hugging Stephen Thomas. She was afraid she would hold him an instant too long, remind him of her attraction to him, embarrass them both.

At least he isn't as angry at me as he was when he first found out, J.D. thought. That was so strange . . . If I'd tried to predict how he'd react, I wouldn't have predicted anger. She sighed. And I wouldn't have predicted that he'd like it, either, so at least I was right on one score.

She pulled herself back from her instant's reverie and called the glass boat to them. It glided up silently on its magnetic water-jets, stopped, and settled.

J.D. scrambled onto the swim-step and over the transom. Stephen Thomas and Zev followed. Water dripped onto the deck and drained away. The center of the deck was clear glass, the border roughened slightly so it would not be so slick. A profusion of plants and animals lay below.

J.D. touched the boat through her link and sent it toward Orchestra.

The boat surged forward, plunging through the green lagoon. Beneath them, intriguing shapes flashed away.

The wind cooled J.D.'s wet skin. She put on her light jacket. Still cold, she nudged her metabolic enhancer into higher activity. It rewarded her with a wave of energy and warmth.

Zev lounged on the port seat, using the edge of his hand to groom the salt water from his pelt, showing Stephen Thomas how to do it.

The light of 61 Cygni, so much like the sun's light, leaped off the sea's irregularities. Dazzled, J.D. blinked.

The boat reached the opening of the lagoon, where the old crater wall had broken and flooded the wide caldera. Beyond, the water deepened; the sea floor fell out of sight. The green of the sea below them soon turned midnight blue.

They got their first good real-life view of Orchestra.

"Christ on a mountaintop," Stephen Thomas said softly.

The whale-eel loomed before them, a floating island.

J.D. considered turning on the boat's sonar, but decided using it would be like entering someone's living room and shouting at the top of her lungs. Ambient noise made a fuzzy picture of the world below them: deep, deep water, and the huge sonar shadow of Orchestra. The whale-eel was like an iceberg, mostly underwater. Her intermittent subsonics overwhelmed the image like a blinding blast of light.

"Can you hear that?" J.D. asked.

"Sure," Zev said.

"Yes," Stephen Thomas said at the same time.

"Orchestra's been listening for us," Zev said.

Five hundred meters from the whale-eel, J.D. slowed the glass boat to a crawl.

Orchestra rose higher, very slowly, very gently. Seawater cascaded down her sides. The glass boat pitched in the small fast waves.

Shiny bare skin surrounded Orchestra's huge toothed mouth and each bulging eye, like an iridescent black mask. A field of flowers crowned her, covering her back with a cape of gold and orange. On either side of her back, dorsal fins followed the line of her body.

Horizontal bands of different colors, different textures, encrusted the whale-eel's body. Her flanks were like a hillside ecosystem, with a new niche at each level, within each fold and fissure. Some patches met at a sharp, distinct border, others overlapped and infiltrated each other. Long pale-green fronds in one striation tangled with the wiry blue-green branches that sprouted from the next lower ecological band.

Orchestra in real life was quite different from Orchestra's AI representative. J.D. wondered if the AI represented a different stage of Orchestra's life cycle, or whether the intelligence had chosen its appearance itself, to be distinguishable from its creator.

Orchestra's wake reached them. The glass boat pitched again. Even moving slowly, cautiously, the whale-eel roiled the sea.

Zev stood in the spray and laughed wildly.

"Welcome, Sauvage Earth," Orchestra said through J.D.'s link. "And your friends."

"Thank you, Orchestra Largernearer. This is Zev, and this is Stephen Thomas."

As Zev and Stephen Thomas exchanged greetings with Orchestra, J.D. let her eyelids flicker and connected with her link on a wider band. She tapped into the transmissions of the LTMs and directed their fields of view to close-ups. With each magnification, Orchestra's wilderness became more complex.

What an amazing being, J.D. thought.

Orchestra's body above the water was several kilometers long and at least half a kilometer wide. She carried with her a hundred, a thousand, other species of organisms. The animated ones quivered against her sides, scuttling to hide from the air among fronds and leaves, rocky encrustations and flowers.

"I brought you a guest gift," Orchestra said.

The trilling hum of Orchestra's voice vibrated the glass boat. In response, the sea roiled and dappled. Thousands of finger-sized four-finned creatures leaped above the surface and plopped down again, like rain. They refracted the light like water droplets, creating a rainbow iridescence. Beneath the glass boat, a cloud of their rainbow colors flicked from one side of the boat's bottom to the other, then back again. As J.D. bent to watch them through the window in the center of the deck, wishing she could see them better, several of the creatures leaped over the rail and fell flopping at her feet. She glanced at Orchestra, startled, wondering if the whale-eel had directed or herded the four-fins to her.

Zev picked one up. J.D. grasped another one near the head and smoothed its fins backwards so it would not cut her if the edges were sharp. Stephen Thomas watched.

The four-fin in J.D.'s hand wriggled once, then lay quiet. It was similar to the silver-fin that Zev had caught near shore, but its fins were softer, without edges, and the color of an oil-slick on water. Its sides carried a more vibrant rainbow of color. It was smaller than her little finger.

Stephen Thomas abruptly grabbed one of the four-fins. He wrapped it in his hand and it lay quiet.

"We bred the rainbow-fins for Europa and Androgeos," Orchestra said. "For human people to eat while they visit. I brought them for you."

"That's very thoughtful of you," J.D. said. "Are they eaten raw, or cooked?"

"Europa says they cook well, but their proteins are quite delicate. We designed them to be edible as they are."

"May I eat one now?"

"They are yours to do with as you please."

Stephen Thomas gave J.D. an incredulous look. She had never noticed that he was picky about his food, but this was asking quite a lot of him: to learn to eat like a diver and like an alien contact specialist: a live fish, a live *alien* fish, both at the same time.

"You don't have to," J.D. said softly to Stephen Thomas, keeping her comment back from her link. "Honestly, it's all right. That's why I said 'I.' "

It had taken her a few days with the divers, back on Earth, to get over her squeamishness about eating live fish. Now she was used to it—and she was beginning to wonder if human people were the only folks in Civilization who cooked.

I can imagine what the Four Worlds people are all saying about us, she thought: "They denature their food by putting it in open flame, and they cover themselves with weird stuff called 'clothing.' "

J.D. popped the rainbow-fin into her mouth. She bit it and killed it, she hoped, quickly and painlessly.

Unlike Nemo's decorative food, which dissolved into intoxicating evanescence on her tongue, the rainbow-fin was substantial. Meat and potatoes food instead of Nemo's designer drugs. It tasted like fresh halibut: firm and meaty without any strong flavor of fish or the ocean.

Zev popped a rainbow-fin into his mouth, munched once, and swallowed.

"It's good," he said. "Tastes kind of like chicken."

J.D. almost burst out laughing.

Stephen Thomas looked doubtfully at his flopping rainbow-fin as Zev caught another and ate it contentedly.

"It's very good, Orchestra," Zev said. "Thank you."

"I really asked for this, didn't I?" Stephen Thomas muttered. He opened his hand and bit the rainbow-fin out of his palm before it could flip itself away. His teeth crunched through it and he chewed it.

There's not that much to chew, J.D. thought. The bones were so delicate that they merely provided some texture to the flesh. The skin parted easily between the teeth. With a live fish, it was more aesthetically pleasing to eat it in one or two bites and swallow it quickly.

Stephen Thomas kept chewing. J.D. thought with sympathy about the time she had eaten octopus. She remembered its tart raw-rubber crunchiness in her mouth, the texture of the suckers, the certainty that she would not be able to swallow it without throwing up. Like Stephen Thomas, she had kept chewing and chewing, certain she would gag. She had finally forced herself to swallow.

She had never eaten octopus again. She liked the smart curious critters much better alive in the sea than on a sushi plate.

She handed Stephen Thomas the water bottle. He uncorked it and drank, washing the rainbow-fin down.

"Chicken!" he said after he had wiped his mouth. "Raw chicken, maybe."

"The rainbow-fin was delicious," J.D. said to Orchestra. "We brought you guest gifts, too."

"Human people are thoughtful, Sauvage Earth," Orchestra said.

"And diving people, too," J.D. said. "Zev brought an instrument that his people use to make music. If you like, he'll put it together for you."

"I would like that."

Zev threw the buoyed bundle containing the pieces of the sea harp overboard, then fell backwards off the side of the boat and splashed into the water. Stephen Thomas dove in after him, cleaving the surface with barely a ripple.

A moment later he surfaced and threw his shorts into the boat. They landed with a wet slap. He dove again and disappeared. J.D. picked up the shorts and hung them over the rail where they would dry.

"You're very generous, Sauvage Earth," Orchestra said to J.D. "I observed the guest gift you presented on the Four Worlds ship."

"Did you enjoy Crimson's performance?" J.D. asked.

"It was quite provocative," Orchestra said. "It's moving, to observe discovery. Of course the other ones concern the Farther worlds more than the Nearer worlds. As we never travel, my people have little use for starships, either the ones we design or those the other ones left behind."

"Crimson is very talented," J.D. said. "She invented all the beings as well as sculpting their fossils."

"Yes, of course," Orchestra said, amused.

J.D. sighed to herself. Orchestra, too, believed the story that the fossils were real. Her comment about the other ones would have been a complete non-sequitur in response to a piece of performance art; it only made sense in context of real fossils that might point the way to an extinct civilization.

"Are all you humans such talented performers?"

"I'm not a performer at all," J.D. said.

"I believe your moon is lifeless and waterless," Orchestra said.

"Yes."

"And always has been."

"As far as we know."

"How did the bones become fossilized?"

"Crimson made them," J.D. said. "She put them there."

Orchestra considered. Her eyes blinked, one, then another. The boat bobbed gently in the shelter of the volcano. Another of Largernearer's huge waves hit the far side of the island, and another cloud of steam burst into the air.

"How does Crimson think the fossils got to your moon?" Orchestra asked.

"She thinks—" J.D. stopped, amazed at herself; for a moment she too had spoken of the fossils as if they were real. "She designed it as a burial site. The grave of ancient travelers."

She touched the boat with her link and asked it to play the music she had chosen through the underwater speakers.

"I brought another recording with me," she said. "I chose it because of your name. Would you like to hear what an orchestra does, back on Earth?"

"Certainly."

The first few bars of Beethoven's Ninth Symphony, the introduction which sounds like the instruments still tuning up, floated through the water.

J.D. held her breath. Europa had expressed doubts about this gift. To J.D.'s astonishment, the Minoan had never offered Earth's symphonic music to Civilization. To Europa, music made by a hundred instruments playing simultaneously sounded odd and ugly. J.D. was taking a risk that Orchestra would have a different reaction.

Orchestra drowsed, a mountainous phantom island in the green sea. The whale-eel lay very quiet and still, neither rising nor falling in the water. She pulsed slowly, to draw cooling water into her body. Now and then one or a few of her eyes flicked backwards, disappearing and reappearing, never for long, never all at once. The long fins at the sides of her back stiffened, then relaxed.

J.D. searched Orchestra's body for a land biome. But every creature on Orchestra's back had hidden itself, or closed up, wrapped itself in the fronds of seaweed, covered itself with a foam of bubbles. The sea was their natural habitat.

Stephen Thomas surfaced to breathe. For a moment he rested at the border between air and water. Though Orchestra floated at quite a distance, she loomed above him. Being near her was like being at the foot of a mountain. He let his gaze travel up her side, tracing out the zones of life. He wanted to do what would be the equivalent of tearing threads from another person's clothes, or pulling out strands of hair. He wanted samples of the organisms that covered Orchestra. The glass boat would collect samples of the ocean water, of whatever this world used for plankton and krill. But he planned to get as many different types of organisms as he could.

He teased the silver worm free, caught his hair back with one hand, and let the mutualist twine through it

225

VONDA N. MCINTYRE

again. He floated for a moment, gazing into the clear water.

Above the dark depths, Zev swam with the sea harp.

The symphony J.D. was playing sounded fuzzy. An echo of it bounced from Orchestra's body. The water changed the frequencies. Stephen Thomas would rather have heard it in the air.

The diver called to Stephen Thomas in true speech.

The visual language formed an image in his mind. He could hear the shapes. Stephen Thomas understood what he said: Come hold the vanes.

Stephen Thomas replied in inexperienced true speech, the equivalent of a child's stick-figure drawing.

Stephen Thomas dove and rejoined Zev. The resonating bulb acted as a sea anchor, slowing the sea harp's drift, holding the harp nearly steady above the deeper, faster current. It was a hollow sphere of rock foam, made to Zev's order by a silver slug.

The strangest fish Stephen Thomas had ever seen undulated past him, stranger than any of Nemo's creatures, stranger than anything living around a deep-sea vent back on Earth. The mutated eel-shape had projecting gills, multiple quartets of protuberances all along its length. Each gill opened and closed, snapping tiny teeth.

The multimouthed eel disappeared into the murk of distance and gathering darkness.

Jesus Christ, Stephen Thomas thought. There's thousands of meters of water underneath me, I don't know a fucking thing about what lives in it, I wouldn't know a predator if one swam up and bit off my toe. I'd probably give it a stomachache, but the guys with the big teeth wouldn't know it until too late.

I'm swimming naked in an alien sea.

He started to laugh. He tried to stop, but that only made him laugh harder. He inhaled a mouthful of bitter alien salt water. He kicked for the surface, coughing bubbles from his mouth and nose. He burst out into the air, coughed again, and gasped a breath of the cool bitter alien air. He flopped backwards and floated till the fit of laughter passed.

Zev shot out of the water, splashed down, and swam over to him.

"What happened?" Zev asked.

"Sharks," Stephen Thomas said.

"Sharks!" Zev said quizzically. "Sharks?"

"Yeah, sharks, or whatever the hell passes for sharks around here. Tubular piranha. Garden hoses with teeth. Whatever."

"They're funny?"

"It occurred to me—I'm fucking glad my cock and my balls don't hang out anymore."

Zev regarded him curiously. "You've finished changing," he said.

"Mostly." The last time Zev had seen him naked, he had been caught between ordinary human and diver, his penis raw and sore, his balls aching and constricted, half in and half out of his body. Now, finally, he had completed the external changes, and the new neural pathways responded more naturally every time he used them.

"Now you see why we made ourselves be this way."

"Sharks," Stephen Thomas said.

"Yes. Sharks."

Zev paddled beside him. "Can you extend and retract now?"

Stephen Thomas floated on his back and let his toes break the surface of the water. He contracted small new muscles. Right in front of Zev's face, his shiny sharp claws extended.

"That isn't what I meant." Zev grinned.

"I know." Stephen Thomas let his hips sink. He trod water again.

"There's nothing very big around us right now," Zev said. "Except Orchestra, I mean. She's enough predator to scare me."

Stephen Thomas had not even thought of Orchestra as a predator, but of course she must be, with those teeth.

"All that crap on her back must slow her down," he said. "I wonder what's big enough to feed her, and dumb enough to catch?"

"She probably doesn't chase," Zev said. "She probably gardens her body so she's hidden to her prey. She's made herself look like those islands we passed. Probably some of them were beings like her."

Stephen Thomas had not made the connection, nor had the other members of alien contact. But it made good sense.

"Maybe she even gardens her own food," Zev said.

"On her *body*?"

"Sure. She probably needs to eat a lot."

The idea made Stephen Thomas queasy. He tried to shrug away the feeling. He thought, J.D. wouldn't turn a hair at the thought.

The Representative of Smallerfarther drowsed. He wanted to return to his safe, silent hibernation; he wanted to preserve his body and his time for the future. He was very old. He was vital. He had lived this long by careful preservation, waiting for an opportunity of sufficient magnitude to make exertion worth his while.

He drowsed, and thought, using up his precious minutes. He relived the meeting with the human representative.

Was this his opportunity?

The Representative's representative, his proxy, could not function in his place. Not this time. The proxy had been trained to obey him, to anticipate his wishes, and to act for him in day-to-day matters both trivial and important. But he had not been trained to take advantage of unique opportunities. That ability might come to the proxy's grandchildren, if the Representative deigned to allow it.

The Ode to Joy, the last movement of the Ninth Symphony, exploded to its end. Orchestra opened her eyes.

"Again, please," she said.

The sea harp hovered ten meters below the surface. Its resonating bulb doubled as a float, pumping water in and out to hold the harp steady.

Stephen Thomas was tired. Working underwater was tough. One of the harp's vanes slipped from his hand as he transferred it from its buoy to the resonating bulb. He and Zev plunged after it and caught it before it disappeared into the dark depths.

After the Beethoven symphony finished playing through—the second time—Stephen Thomas unfolded the vanes of the harp to their full length. Slender, dense rock-foam strips slipped one by one into a deep current of warmer, saltier water that flexed like a vein through the body of the sea.

The hum of vibrating stone surrounded Stephen Thomas. A second note, a third, joined the first. The glassy harmonics combined, shivering through him. The vanes cut through the warm current. Each one produced a different note. The ambient music changed and rose and fell, varying with the stroke of the water and the relationship of the vanes.

As Stephen Thomas rose to breathe, the sea harp caressed his skin with its long, deep vibrations. He listened to the soft low music, back-floating so his ears were under water, then raising his head to hear the chords as they refracted into the air and danced and shivered around him.

Another sound touched him, a sharp shock of clicks. He struggled upright.

"What the fuck was that?"

"Orchestra," Zev said. "Looking at what we've done. And listening to it. Both." He said a word in true speech, flat and uninflected in the air. "Looking, listening," he said. "Sending out sound to see what's around. Like a flashlight."

The Four Worlds' sun, 61 Cygni, sank toward Larger-nearer's horizon. The air cooled and the colors of the sea softened.

J.D.'s glass boat bobbed in silky gray light, dwarfed by Orchestra. A ghostly song drifted across the water.

"Zev and Stephen Thomas have finished the sea harp," J.D. said. She told the whale-eel the sea harp's commands: to extend the blades to start it, to retract them to make it fall silent, to engage its motor and move it when it drifted.

The harp sang in the current. Orchestra fell silent while the random tones played.

Stephen Thomas and Zev swam to the boat and climbed in. Stephen Thomas curried most of the water off his body, and pulled on his dry shorts. A breeze blew across the water, flicking bits of spray into the air. Orchestra was so big that her body created its own tiny weather systems, onshore and offshore breezes in the mornings and evenings.

He shivered, but he did not want to put on heavy clothes that would rub his pelt backwards. He smoothed the hair on his thigh. An image flashed: Satoshi touching him in the same place, feeling the fur, freezing in surprise, or dismay, or revulsion. Stephen Thomas let his hand fall to his side.

J.D. watched the whale-eel, her face set with worry.

"Orchestra?" she said.

Through the link, J.D.'s voice sounded as pleasant and as ordinary as it always did. Stephen Thomas wondered again, as he had wondered a hundred times, why she had had the chance to make love with Feral while he had not. He liked J.D. as a friend. Friendship was important to Stephen Thomas; in his life he had had fewer close friends than lovers.

J.D. was willing to throw herself, open and trusting, into the unknown. He admired her for that. But he was envious—admit it, jealous—of her relationship with Feral.

"Orchestra?" J.D. said again. "Are you awake?"

Orchestra's voice replied after a time, faintly, an electronic whisper

"On Earth, do you speak during music?"

"No, it's very rude to the performers—"

"And to the music," Orchestra said.

"I should have told you this first thing," J.D. said. "The sea harp music has no beginning and no end. It isn't a performance. It just *is.*"

Orchestra considered J.D.'s comment. The sea harp vibrated the hull of the glass boat until it sang like a crystal goblet. The music vibrated against the soles of Stephen Thomas's feet. His toes curled, extending his semiretractile claws. His claws shrieked atonally on the deck. He flinched and drew them in again.

He imagined the harp underwater, sending out sound to reflect off everything in range, illuminating objects and creatures and variations in the water, shining beams of music on everything. He wanted to jump back in the water, to listen and learn to see.

The harp's music rose in pitch as the vanes drew into the bulb. At Orchestra's command, the music ended.

"It is charming," the whale-eel said. "I will look forward to listening more later. To talk during pure music . . . I will have to consider that idea."

"Maybe we'd better go back to the island and come talk to you again tomorrow," J.D. said. "It's getting dark."

"I'd prefer you to stay," Orchestra said. "I'm more alert during darkness. I have things to tell you that should be said at night."

Orchestra had been sinking as she listened. She had nearly submerged. Fronds of seaweed spread out tens of meters around her sides. The twilight glistened off the shells and skins of many creatures. Several flashed along the fronds, like liquid sparks. At the edge of the flower crown, where the water rose, the blossoms reopened.

"Thank you for your gifts," Orchestra said. "You've entertained me and you've enlightened me and you've even interested me in the other ones."

Stephen Thomas made himself keep a straight face.

Satoshi, he thought, *you're a fucking genius.*

Tell everyone in Civilization the truth, Satoshi had said. *And they still won't believe it. Because they don't want to.*

Satoshi was the quietest and the most reserved of the partnership, in public and in some ways in private. Some people—not Stephen Thomas—underestimated him. Whenever Stephen Thomas was near his partner, whenever he thought about him, whenever Satoshi touched him, he was excited all over again by Satoshi's intelligence and humor.

I bet I've screwed all that up now, he thought.

Stephen Thomas shivered again. Feeling lonely, he put the thought of his partners, and their brittle conversation back on the beach, out of his mind.

"I would like to tell you the story of the Four Worlds," Orchestra said. "Come closer, swim onto my back. It's warm there, you'll be comfortable."

The last edge of 61 Cygni slipped beneath the horizon, highlighting the green-gray sea with fiery colors. The sunset was so like Earth's that Stephen Thomas felt a quick, startling pang of homesickness.

Everyone he loved—everyone he loved who was still alive—lived on *Starfarer*. Back at Tau Ceti, when it looked

like their only choice was to return to Earth as failures,
Stephen Thomas had voted for staying in the alien system
and starting a new life.

But, he thought, if I never saw Earth again . . . I'd
miss it.

Nine

"Look," J.D. whispered.

She gazed not at the fading sunset but in the opposite direction, where the huge full disk of Smallernearer loomed over Largernearer's horizon.

Smallernearer was larger than Earth's moon. Its face was nearly twice the moon's diameter, the color of tarnished silver, old mother-of-pearl. Beautiful and ghostly, it cast an opalescent radiance across the sea.

J.D. urged the glass boat forward. She approached Orchestra head on, avoiding the loops and whorls of seaweed that flanked the whale-eel with her own private Sargasso.

Orchestra let her body sink. Her seaweed drifted and floated upright from her sides, feathering against her rippling back fins. Flowers grew up her snout, spread into a rolling field between the fins, and stretched toward her distant tail. The blossoms luminesced orange and yellow. Mist collected in the hollow of her back.

One huge eye projected above the water, now and again blinking with its disconcerting backwards snap.

J.D. slipped over the side of the boat. Zev dove in after her. They swam toward the whale-eel through phosphorescent plankton. A glowing arrow of ripples lit each wake.

Zev turned over and looked back at Stephen Thomas.

234

"Come on! Aren't you coming?"

Stephen Thomas vaulted over the boat's rail, cannon-balled into the water, and swam after Zev and J.D.

J.D. approached Orchestra's snout. The seaweed fronds reached upward, tickling her toes and stroking her legs. Here, outside the harbor, the sea was wilder. Echoes of the long planetary swells passed by, creating a pattern of surf against the island of Orchestra's body. On her sheltered side, a bay formed against her flank. On the seaward side, whitecaps piled against her, trailing spumes of spray.

Trying to keep her mind off the huge mouth and the sharp teeth just below her, J.D. wondered if one type of plant and animal grew on the lee side of Orchestra's body, different types on the exposed side. Did the alien, when she was on the surface, habitually place her body in the same orientation to the waves?

"Go onto my back, where you can rest," Orchestra said.

J.D. reached the cleft where Orchestra's back fins swept forward and disappeared against the side of her snout. J.D. touched the whale-eel for the first time.

Orchestra's body radiated heat; J.D. felt the warmth like a pressure through a handsbreadth of water. The warm layer covered a profusion of creatures, plant and animal—or plant *and* animal, or some type of life never found or imagined on Earth—that lived in symbiosis with the whale-eel.

J.D. found a bare spot that she believed was Orchestra's skin. She placed her hand flat on the smooth hot surface.

"Hello, Orchestra Largernearer," she said.

"Hello, Sauvage Earth," Orchestra replied. "And welcome."

J.D. pushed her mask to the top of her head and scrambled up the living gully. A school of scuttling creatures fled beneath slick leaves. She avoided a row of sharp-edged rocky lumps like split geodes. In the hollows of the geodes, whiskery fibers waved slowly, catching the mother-of-pearl light of Smallernearer.

She glanced over her shoulder.

Zev sidestroked past Orchestra's eye, fascinated by the whale-eel, reluctant to leave the sea after so many days away from deep and mysterious water. *Starfarer*'s sea was no more than a pond to him.

The huge eye tracked him.

Stephen Thomas ploughed forward, following J.D. He pushed himself ashore on Orchestra. Phosphorescent water cascaded from his body, drops splashing away like sparks. His pelt captured the light. Sometime between diving off the boat and reaching Orchestra, he had taken off his shorts.

J.D. looked quickly away from him and continued climbing.

As the slope of Orchestra's side eased, the rocky growths petered out. The whale-eel's skin was soft and very warm beneath J.D.'s feet. The small flowers on Orchestra's snout gave way, on her forehead, to blossoms the size of J.D.'s opened hands. The alien bitterness of Largernearer added a strange tang to their sweet fragrance. J.D. wondered how many components of the fragrance evaded her sense of smell. She made sure the LTMs were taking samples of the air.

Zev appeared beside J.D. He slipped his warm webbed hand into hers. They climbed together to Orchestra's crest, and J.D. felt grateful all over again to have him with her. He had left his home, and everything he knew, to join her on board *Starfarer*.

The crest-flowers brushed J.D.'s knees. Orchestra's heat rose around the delicate roots and stems, warming J.D.'s bare feet. On the other side of the low hill of Orchestra's head, fog covered a quiet pond. Water and mist filled the hollow on Orchestra's dorsal surface and blanketed the flowers. Orchestra sank further into the sea. Beyond the rubbery protective ridges of her fins, the ocean climbed her long, underwater flank and pressed itself into a wave. The wave crashed, and spray exploded overhead. A rain of salt water spattered into the quiet flower-filled pond. Rivulets tumbled and splashed down the ridges, forming creeks that fed the flower pool.

If Orchestra submerged, she would draw them all underwater with the whirlpool of her disappearance. Zev could extract oxygen directly from the water, in emergencies, enough to sustain his life if he did not have to exert himself. J.D. had her artificial lung, but it could be torn loose. J.D. wondered if Stephen Thomas had yet developed the ability to breathe underwater.

As J.D. was about to warn their host of their frailties, the being steadied. J.D. waded into the warm pond, pushing through the heavy mat of flowers. Their colors had turned deep black and shining white in the darkness. Heat rose up around J.D., and the warm water steamed. A humid, foggy cloud swirled before her.

"Swim a bit farther," Orchestra said. "Then the water will be deep enough and warm enough to let you rest."

"It isn't quite deep enough to swim," J.D. said. "We'll walk."

The whale-eel's huge body shuddered. J.D. staggered, thrown off balance. The water in the pond rippled and splashed. Loose flower petals spiraled to the surface.

Zev gripped J.D.'s hand. He stood spraddle-legged, joyful and excited.

"Shit!" Stephen Thomas said. "What's going on?"

The shudder subsided. The loose petals sank forlornly, disappearing beneath the blossoms or catching in the cups of the flowers.

"Orchestra? Are you all right?" J.D. spoke hesitantly, ready for another shudder. She trembled with the effects of surprise and fear and an intoxicating surge of energy and adrenaline.

237

"You startled me," the whale-eel said.

"What? How?"

"Walking." Orchestra trembled again. "It's hard to understand. It's hard to think about! You put your body on dry land, you risk yourself to the air."

"It's natural to us."

"But alien to me." The whale-eel quivered, creating only a gentle earthquake. "Frightening, like few other ideas." Her voice carried a tone of pleasurable apprehension.

"Alien horror stories," Stephen Thomas muttered. " 'A Walk on the Beach.' "

"I understand how you feel," Zev said. "My cousins the orcas never go on land, unless one is in despair and decides to die."

"A painful way to die! Your cousins must be courageous—or desperate. I myself plan to die in my flowers, in the deepest water on Largernearer—but not for a long, long time."

"A person after my own heart," Stephen Thomas said.

"I'm sorry if I frightened you," J.D. said.

"A stimulating experience."

For us, too, J.D. thought.

"Please rest now," Orchestra said. "I want to show you something. But I must swim, to clear away the mist. Can your boat follow?"

"It can follow."

J.D. sank into the warm pool, lying on soft, sweet flowers. Fragrant steam beaded on her hair and trickled down her face.

At first nothing happened.

Zev splashed down beside J.D. Stephen Thomas lowered himself into the water nearby and back-floated. His toes stuck up: He flexed them, gazing at the sharp claws that extended and retracted.

Distracted for a moment, J.D. tried not to stare. She knew what a male diver looked like naked. But until today she had not known what Stephen Thomas looked like naked, either before or after the change.

She felt like a curious and ignorant adolescent, pretending she was not looking at him, pretending she was not even interested in the shape of his body, the muscles of his chest and shoulders, his long blond hair held back from his face, curling wildly around his shoulders in the heat, the pelt of fine white-gold fur nearly invisible against his dark skin, the delicate fur growing together in a darker line down the center of his chest, breaking at his navel, continuing down his belly, spreading into a soft mat of hair over the pouch concealing his genitals. Not concealing, exactly, but covering and softly outlining them.

J.D. made a short sharp sound and shook her head in frustration. This was no time to be distracted by anything, especially by Stephen Thomas.

"We've been waiting for you for so long," Orchestra said. "The Four Worlds anticipated our first clients' entrance into Civilization. You were so slow! Europa despaired, I think."

"We did our best," J.D. said. No thanks, she thought, to Civilization.

"You were under such limitations," Orchestra said.

"Why do you say that?"

"Can't you guess?" Stephen Thomas said out loud, not feeding the words through his link. "I can think of plenty of human limitations."

"Of course I can guess," J.D. said to him in the same manner, carefully keeping the annoyance out of her voice. "So what? I want to know what Orchestra thinks."

Stephen Thomas did not reply.

"It's easier to demonstrate than to tell you why we had an advantage while you gave yourselves calamities," Orchestra said. "I will show you."

Orchestra's constant, slow pulsing quickened and intensified.

J.D. wished, irritably, that Stephen Thomas would remember her job: to ask the obvious questions. She was tired of telling him the obvious questions might not have obvious answers. He was so smart in some ways and so damned oblivious in others.

If only Feral hadn't taken notes on everything, she thought. And if only Stephen Thomas hadn't read Feral's journal after Feral died. If I'd known Feral was taking notes, I never would have admitted to him how attractive Stephen Thomas is to me. I think he's almost as attractive as Feral thought he was.

Feral had teased her gently when she told him she would not pursue the attraction. Feral, on the other hand, had planned on pursuing Stephen Thomas as soon as possible. He had never had the chance.

Stephen Thomas was right, J.D. thought. I knew Feral was a journalist. I shouldn't have told him anything I didn't want to see in print. Still, I wish he'd warned me.

The only thing I don't understand is why Stephen Thomas was so angry when he found out . . .

He had not said anything directly, which was also unusual for Stephen Thomas. All too often he said exactly what he thought without filtering it first. But he had told her, snapping, that he planned to publish Feral's journals. He had, in effect, warned her that the journals would make her look pathetic and ridiculous.

J.D. sighed. Amusement I would have understood, she thought. Or bored resignation to something that must happen all the time.

Why do I care how I look to Stephen Thomas?

Orchestra gathered herself to swim. Her sides expanded as she took in a great gulp of water and pulsed it through her body. She set the island of her body into motion, and the mist coiled into eddies.

The breeze freshened as Orchestra's speed increased. The mist drifted backwards in long streamers.

Orchestra pulsed beneath them, taking in water and

spewing it out, surging forward through the sea. Her mouth and snout parted a way for her; the ridge of her head protected the dorsal pool from the rushing bow wave. The wind of her speed cleared the fog and revealed the crystalline black sky.

J.D. thought the boat into motion behind them; it followed silently.

"Rest," Orchestra said. "Rest, and look upward."

J.D. did as the whale-eel asked, floating in the warm pond among the flowers. The cool breeze touched her face and her throat above her bathing suit. Her nipples hardened, goosefleshed. She let her body sink beneath the surface.

I can't stand it, she thought. I don't care if everybody on *Starfarer* is watching me, I particularly don't care if I knock off the LTMs. She took off her mask, eased the artificial lung from her back, and let it sink to the bottom of the pool beside her. Then she grabbed the straps of her bathing suit and stripped the suit off underwater. She wadded it up and balanced it on the lung.

The LTMs clambered to the top of the pile, perched on the material, and settled.

Warm alien water covered J.D.'s body, tingling and caressing.

Suddenly, nearby, the water bubbled and gushed. Startled, J.D. pushed herself upright. Even nearer the geyser, Stephen Thomas plunged backward through the flowers.

"What the hell!"

Zev watched, laughing with delight.

In a splashing fountain of spray, one of Orchestra's eyes bulged through the flowers. Like the head of a sea serpent, the socket scanned one way, then the other. The eyeball appeared, rotating forward. It looked dull and dry. The eye blinked, once, twice, disappearing backwards. Each time it appeared it was wetter and shinier. Flakes of skin or dry mucus or caked salt sifted onto the water, dissolving or sinking. The actions reminded J.D. of waking up, rubbing the sleep from her eyes.

When she realized what was happening, she relaxed back into the pond. Zev had barely moved, even when the eye eruption splashed him. He had placed his trust in Orchestra, and Zev's trust was unbreakable. Embarrassed, Stephen Thomas breast-stroked forward. A broken flower hung over his shoulder. Angrily, he flicked it away.

"I thought we'd discovered Nessie," J.D. said sympathetically to him, out loud. He grimaced.

"I haven't used this eye for a while," Orchestra said. "I forgot where I put it at first. But now I can see you."

Zev swam over, breast-stroking through the flowers like a lithe gilt frog. He reached Orchestra's eye and looked straight into the vertical pupil.

"Hello, young Zev," Orchestra said.

"Hello, old Orchestra," Zev said. "Can you move your eyes around?"

"Yes, though that is rather slow. It's easier to resorb one and grow another." The eye socket tilted. "It's good to be able to see straight up." Down the length of Orchestra's back, as far as J.D. could see, random bulges of the whale-eel's eyes stretched upward. Bemused, J.D. followed Orchestra's gaze into the sky.

Smallernearer loomed overhead, a dull silver-gray disk surrounded by stars. Its inhabitant so far had remained silent. J.D. would never meet it face to face. It would never meet anyone, face to face, unless someone figured out how to fall like gossamer through an airless sky, how to hover without blasting exhaust and fire into the aerogel.

Just for a moment, too tempted to resist, J.D. touched *Nautilus* with her link. Its control surface sought her, welcomed her. She moved along one curving face, trying out one path, another, like a gymnast imagining an airborne twist and turn. She asked her question by

NAUTILUS

imagining *Nautilus* on course for Smallernearer. The knowledge surface showed her the answer: Yes, Nemo's starship could make a close approach to Smallernearer, if she asked it to. But the gravitational stresses would be violent and destructive if she brought the singularity that provided its mass so near another world.

While her link was diverted, she sent a private message to Esther and Kolya, a few words of appreciation and concern.

"We're fine, boss," Esther replied directly to her mind. "Want your car keys back?" Esther's matter-of-fact humor came through the link plainly.

"Not yet," J.D. said. "You can drive it Saturday night." Esther chuckled.

J.D. shut down the distant link and returned to Largernearer. She had to think herself back into her body; the enhanced link cut her off from all other sensations when she opened it fully to touch the knowledge surface.

Her vision returned. A wave of light passed across Smallernearer's surface. J.D. gasped in surprise.

"Holy shit!" Stephen Thomas said.

"What was that?" J.D. said through her link.

"Light was our introduction to another intelligence."

"What—?" Stephen Thomas said aloud.

"Shh!" J.D. recognized a symbolic statement, a metaphor, the beginning of a tribal tale, a myth. Nearby, Zev settled in the pool and prepared to listen. Flowers popped up around him, between his body and his arms, between his bent knees. Watching him, J.D. smiled. She might lust silently after Stephen Thomas, but she loved Zev.

"We evolved beneath this sky," Orchestra said. "Look farther."

Guided by Orchestra's gaze and by the link to her mind, J.D. looked deeper into space.

A huge star shone steadily. A binary star, its double

243

bulge visible to the naked eye. But it could not be a star. It shone too clearly, it was too close and too distinct. And if it *were* a binary star, it would be as easily visible from Earth as from 61 Cygni.

"These are the Farther worlds," Orchestra said. "For all of time, my people could see them circling each other, as we see Smallernearer rotating above us and revolving around Largernearer."

J.D. wondered how Smallernearer had avoided becoming tidally locked, with one face always to Largernearer, like Earth's moon. She thought, the being who lives there is a construct. Artificially created. Maybe the planet's motion is, too.

"We always knew of worlds beyond ours. Our cosmology required no fictional explanations. Our music of the spheres was the song of Smallernearer. Millennia ago, our neighbor tried to explain to itself the dynamic equilibrium that existed on our world. It imagined the organic chemicals and made them come together in its mind. When they reached a certain complexity, it understood that intelligence might be the result.

"Smallernearer conceived the idea of organic life, life that could exist in this inhospitable atmosphere, this wild water. Its imagination leaped. Could another intelligent being exist somehow?

"Five thousand years ago, it signaled to us.

"It thought a single being covered Largernearer. It still thinks of us that way. And why not think of the elements of an ecosystem as a single organism? It's a matter of point of view."

J.D. had always found the Gaia hypothesis aesthetically pleasing, though some people back home took it too far. They tried to force a hypothesis about the activities of life into explaining the origin of life. They tried to think of Earth itself as sentient.

"Smallernearer was persistent. At first my people had no way of signaling back. As the years passed, we tamed the phosphorescent plankton, we strengthened it . . ."

Orchestra's pulsing slackened to her normal breathing rate. She slowed, stopped, and settled. Waves splashed against her seaward side, over her dorsal fins. Cold water flowed over her snout into the warm pool, and the flowers on her forehead folded into buds.

"Look," Orchestra said.

J.D. looked out over Orchestra's head, across the ocean.

The surface glowed with bands and spots of violent blue-green light. The brightness intensified. Overhead, puffy clouds lit up with reflections, like a lightning storm without the thunder. A strange odor scented the air, a mixture like ozone and chlorophyll, new-cut grass during a lightning storm, a fragrance that rose from the glowing plankton.

Overhead, Smallernearer replied with a wash of light across its pearl-gray surface.

J.D. gasped.

"We learned to converse, and we turned our attention to worlds beyond our own.

"That is the end of the story, and the beginning of the Four Worlds."

Orchestra fell silent.

"It's a beautiful story," J.D. said. "Thank you for telling it to us."

"You're welcome. I have enjoyed Europa's tales for many years. Your cosmologies are so imaginative!" The whale-eel added, with humor, "Earth's account has increased from the sum of the royalties I've offered."

An interstellar audience, J.D. thought, every writer's wildest fantasy. Wonder what they'd think of my novels . . .

She brought herself back to the conversation.

"It took more effort and ingenuity to begin communicating with the Farther worlds," Orchestra said. "We can only see their lights when one Farther world casts its shadow across the other. But their eclipses are frequent. Once we established contact, it was easy."

J.D. laughed aloud. Easy! Human beings had taken an order of magnitude more time to develop starfaring technology. The Four Worlds had first communicated with each other five thousand years ago, when the first civilizations of Earth had barely begun. Their ships had rescued Europa and Androgeos little more than a thousand years later, during Earth's second millennium B.C.E.

"That *is* quite an advantage," J.D. said. "To *know* about other beings, to communicate with other intelligences . . ."

"Yes," Orchestra said. "Now our communication spectrum no longer requires darkness, and we use visible light only on ceremonial occasions."

"Do you fight?" Stephen Thomas asked.

"Fight?"

"Do you have wars?"

"What would we war about?"

"Territory. Resources. Xenophobia. Difference of opinion. We've always found some damned thing."

"Your wars made us wait for you even longer! We have no wars. We all have our own territory. If we want more, an ecosystems analyst can bring a barren world to life more quickly—and more coherently, and *much* less wastefully—than alien life could overwhelm a naturally evolved ecosystem. We can mine the outer worlds for resources, if we need more than we have. We treat our differences in philosophy as a sport."

"Sounds Utopian," Stephen Thomas said.

J.D. hoped the skepticism in his tone was not as obvious to Orchestra, to all the people listening throughout the Four Worlds, as it was to her and probably to all the human beings from *Starfarer*. It *did* sound Utopian. J.D. suspected Orchestra of smoothing out the rough spots. But she also believed the whale-eel's tale was true in broad outline.

"Have you colonized other worlds?" J.D. asked.

"We have not, from Largernearer. You understand that you're allowed to claim only barren worlds, to make of them what you will? You may not trouble worlds that might evolve."

"Yes," J.D. said. "We understand that."

"The Largerfarthings have found one world to their taste, but it will not be finished for another generation. The Smallerfarthings are aggressive in their exploration—"

"Aggressive?" J.D. almost laughed, then reconsidered, and not only because of politeness. Representative's representative Late was the least likely example of aggression she could think of . . . but his boss, the Representative of Smallerfarther, had intimidated her thoroughly. J.D. could well imagine him sailing into a star system, waking long enough to look at the projection and indicate a barren world to be changed and seeded and brought to life, then falling asleep for fifty years—or a thousand—until the work was finished and he could reap its benefits.

"And we all collaborated in creating Tau Ceti III for humans," Orchestra said. "It's a shame you couldn't visit it."

"We saw it," J.D. said. "It's extraordinarily beautiful. We were rushed when we left Tau Ceti. We wanted to explain to Europa why we'd behaved so rudely."

And a good thing, too, she said to herself. Orchestra isn't mentioning the built-in booby trap. But if we'd landed after the cosmic string started to withdraw, Tau Ceti III's whole biosphere would have collapsed as completely as the alien museum. The string didn't accept us, so the planet wouldn't, either.

Now, she hoped, they would have a second chance.

"Maybe we'll get to go back soon," J.D. said. "And appreciate your handiwork."

"I hope so," Orchestra said. "The ocean design would amuse you all, I think."

"Can you send Smallernearer a greeting from us?" Zev asked.

"Of course . . . but you may speak directly, as you do to me."

"I know . . ." Zev grinned. "But I'd like to see it in lights. I'd like to see the ceremony."

A sense of amusement radiated through Orchestra's connection with J.D., with them all.

Centered around her immense body, circles of blue-green light expanded, moving across the water like ripples. The circles wavered where they crossed the ocean's swells, and disappeared over the horizon. Streaks of light, straight golden lines, radiated through the circles. The cut-grass storm scent intensified.

Overhead, a similar pattern replied from the surface of Smallernearer.

J.D. gazed around her, watching two worlds resonate with welcome. Stephen Thomas knelt nearby in the shallow warm water, staring upward, the colored light washing over his pelt. All down his neck and back, the fine pale hair stood on end.

Zev stood knee-deep in Orchestra's pond, his arms raised to the sky, his face wild with joy and amazement.

The glass boat moved silently away from Orchestra. The whale-eel rode low in the water, flooded and then revealed by the long slow swells that piled up against her side and broke into surf over the waveward dorsal fin.

At the stern of the boat, J.D. and Zev waved farewell. Stephen Thomas stood on the fantail, gazing at the huge alien.

"We'll come back soon!" Zev called to Orchestra, using his link and his voice as well. He put his arm around J.D.'s shoulders.

"I will wait," Orchestra replied.

"I'd be all right, if I stayed," Zev said, gazing wistfully back at Orchestra.

"I know you would," J.D. said. "But I'd miss you."

He grinned, tightened his arm around her, and leaned his head on her shoulder. "Me, too."

As the boat drew away, the LTM they had left behind transmitted an image of the whale-eel closing her frontal eyes and sinking deeper into the water.

The flowers garlanding her back floated in calm water. When she had sunk so they lay at sea level, with new water eddying into the central pond, a school of large four-fins swam and wriggled their way into the meadow, mowing paths through the blossoms as they grazed. When they had all entered the pond, she raised herself a few meters, cutting the pond off from the sea.

"Orchestra's hunting!" Zev said.

"She entertained us in her pantry," Stephen Thomas said in a matter-of-fact tone.

"I wonder if she has an extra mouth up there on top of her back," Zev said, "like she has eyes."

"You guys," J.D. said. "We're not sitting around a campfire telling scary stories!"

"It was only an observation," Stephen Thomas said. "Zev said she must hunt from concealment—I can't think of a better disguise. Predator as living room."

"I didn't mean she'd eat *us*," Zev said, and grinned.

Suddenly Orchestra tilted forward. The water rushed from her back over her head, carrying the school of four-fins with it. Like a huge vacuum cleaner, she sucked up the four-fins. They swirled into her mouth. Her teeth snicked closed.

"Holy shit," Stephen Thomas said.

"She must be hungry," Zev said. "She's so big, she must eat a lot, but she's been talking to us all day and all night."

The stealthy hunter settled into the sea again, disguised within her garden and her encrustations, waiting for more prey to come within her reach.

J.D. shivered. Her metabolic enhancer pumped out its last energy and faded into recovery.

Zev was warm against her side, but the wind touched her. Though her skin was nearly dry, her hair was damp, and she was still naked. Out of the water, in plain sight of the LTMs and Stephen Thomas, she felt body-conscious as well as cold.

"I'm freezing," she said. "I've got to go in."

She put the artificial lung into its tank and hurried into the deckhouse, grateful that the interior bulkheads had been built of translucent rather than transparent glass. In the privacy of the glass boat's cramped head, J.D. stepped into the shower and soaped off the alien salt. She rinsed herself quickly. The warmth felt good, but she was sick of being wet. Her fingers and toes were wrinkled.

The boat's hydrophone picked up the ambient music of the sea harp. The music swooped and shivered, stopped abruptly and burst out even louder, moved and halted, as Orchestra experimented with the controls of her gift.

Damp but warm, J.D. slipped across the hall and went into one of the glass boat's tiny cabins.

"Shower's free!" she called.

"Thanks." Stephen Thomas's voice carried through the translucent corridor of the boat's superstructure.

J.D. left the cabin illumination off. The boat's running lights shone through the wall, blinking rhythmically, forming strange shadows. J.D. picked up her shirt. It slipped from her fingers. The sea had wrinkled her skin so badly that touching anything sent shivers up her spine. She wished she had brought some hand lotion. She had meant to, but in the excitement of meeting Orchestra, she had forgotten.

She stared stupidly at the floor, at her crumpled shirt. Still naked, she sank down exhausted on the edge of the narrow bunk.

Zev opened the door and came in. He sat beside her and without a word put his arm around her shoulders. Grateful, J.D. leaned against him, then held him.

He stroked her short damp hair, speaking calmness in soothing soft whistles of true speech. His warmth soaked into her and surrounded her.

Easing her to the bunk, Zev pulled the soft blanket up around her and tucked it in, but drew her hand from beneath the covers. He reached into the pocket of his shorts and brought out her tube of hand lotion.

"I like pockets," he said. "Pockets are the only good thing about clothes." He warmed some of the lotion between his palms and rubbed the soothing ointment into her puckered fingers.

Comforted by Zev's touch, by his voice, J.D. fell asleep.

The Representative made a decision. Waking fully for the first time in many years, he vibrated his leg tendons. The organic connections tore, freeing his leg-tips from the tender growing points against the chamber walls. Fibers of precious stone, not yet crystallized solidly into the tips of his leg-spikes, sparked with light and floated free. His nutrition and elimination channels snapped. The openings clotted and sealed with the organic crystals of his growing enzymes.

He flexed again. The long amethyst and emerald and ruby, turquoise and ebony and diamond spines of his walking legs touched the wall of his chamber, moving his inner body a short length this way, a short length that. As he exerted himself, damage occurred in his muscles, in his joints. He would always carry the damage with him, and his life would be shorter for the strain.

He initiated a metamorphosis.

Victoria waited anxiously for the glass boat to return. She sat in the observers' circle of the *Chi*, her couch turned outward. Starlight shimmered on the quiet harbor. Smallernearer loomed overhead, a shadowed ghost.

LTM transmissions floated at either side of Victoria's

chair. The sea harp sang softly, now and again changing its harmonics as Orchestra played with its vanes, its depth, its position. On Orchestra's brow, the eye in the pond flash-blinked and continued to gaze at the LTM the whale-eel had invited J.D. to leave.

A wave splashed over the LTM. It quivered on small clutching feet. Water washed around it, over it.

Orchestra submerged into the dark sea.

The signal from the LTM on Orchestra's back vanished when it sank beneath the surface, but the floating LTM continued to transmit. The holographic image changed; the LTM picked up ambient sound and created its surroundings from the reflections. In the water below, shapes turned transparent, translucent. A school of four-fins miraged past, squirting water jets as visible as their bodies. Sea flowers swayed and twisted.

In the distance, a wide flat shape pulsed forward, stopped, pulsed again.

Orchestra lay very still. The sea flowers drifted easily. The distant creature pulsed nearer. It possessed the same basic four-finned, jet-propelled anatomy as so many of Largernearer's creatures, but the dorsal fins had shrunk to delicate crests; the ventral fins had widened and stiffened and angled outward. The creature sailed through the water like a flying saucer.

The UFO creature sidled closer to Orchestra, then paused, opening its mouth and taking in water.

Smelling the flowers? Victoria wondered.

The creature pulsed the water behind itself. The propulsion brought it to the edge of Orchestra's flower garden. It sank, and delicately nipped off one of the scarlet blossoms.

The UFO creature vanished, swept with a rush of water into Orchestra's mouth.

On the surface, the sea roiled. The LTM crouched and clutched its moorings.

Orchestra chewed, slowly, luxuriously.

Victoria whistled softly.

I wonder, Victoria thought, which of the floating islands we saw were whale-eels, and which were really islands?

Satoshi strode into the observers' chamber and flung himself into his couch, spinning it around so it faced outward.

"Did you see that?" he said. "Did you see it?"

"Pretty amazing, eh?"

Satoshi chuckled. "You know what Orchestra reminds me of? The ideal philosopher of the Greeks. A creature who can figure things out just by thinking about them."

Victoria smiled back. "I expect Orchestra's people did some experimenting, alongside their mythology-creation."

"I wish I could visit the Smallernearer," Satoshi said. His eyelids flickered as he touched his link and sent a message out into space. "Do you hear me, Smallernearer? I wish we could visit you. Do you ever get lonely?"

A moment later, light spattered across the surface of Smallernearer. Victoria opened her link and listened.

"I hear," the Smallernearer said. "I wish. My thoughts are more complex than my form. I offer you my complexity."

"Thank you," Satoshi said, in awe. "We offer you our friendship."

"You have found my creators," the Smallernearer said. "If you find their home, you might discover others like me."

"Your creators——? Oh," Satoshi said. He glanced ruefully at Victoria. "You mean the other ones. Smallernearer, truly, the fossils are a performance. An art form. They can't lead us to more people like you. I'm afraid you're unique."

"I am unique in Civilization," the Smallernearer said. "So far. But soon I won't be alone. On another world, in another system, another structure like me has the potential to become aware."

"Maybe it will have some idea where the creators came from," Satoshi said.

"It will know its creator," the Smallernearer said. "*I am its creator.*"

As the Representative moved, as he prepared himself to enter a gravity field for the first time in half his life, he sealed his chamber and floated it free of its dock in the hull of the Four Worlds ship.

He steadied himself, using his jewel-spine legs as springs against the slow acceleration. His space boat shuddered; its disused steering rockets channeled fuel, gentling him away from the huge spaceship. When it had moved a safe distance from the Four Worlds ship, the Representative applied power to the thrusting rockets.

His space boat moved toward *Nautilus*.

J.D. stood at the stern of the glass boat, gazing out over the high, long swells of Largernearer's ocean. She thought she could see Orchestra's bright flower topknot, but she could not be certain. She felt refreshed after her nap. Zev still dozed in the bunk, and Stephen Thomas must be asleep in his cabin.

The low thunder of breakers on the far side of the island rolled across the silent morning sea. The boat approached the lagoon. This evening, J.D. could take Victoria and Satoshi to meet Orchestra.

She closed her eyes and touched the knowledge surface of *Nautilus*. As her link took over her perceptions, her knees went weak. She willed her distant body to sit on the deck, not fall, an offhand thought. She had already become part of *Nautilus*.

The star Sirius expanded brilliant and blue-white in her vision. Astonished, she gazed at it in wonder, able to look directly at its white-hot surface.

I did it! she thought. I reached something in Nemo's memory that isn't autonomic reactions!

The Sirius memory was enormous. It stretched around her to the limit of her vision, in more directions than she knew how to name. Nemo must have lived in the system for many years, for centuries. But as she widened her vision, she perceived echoes of other stars, other planets.

Now your shell is here, Nemo, she thought. Did you ever see this system before? Did you think one of your children might become a youth at 61 Cygni, among the Four Worlds?

She stretched, opening her sight to the whole system.

And she saw the Four Worlds space boat powering toward her starship.

Arachne's alarm propelled Griffith out of sleep.

He woke with a great gasp and a shudder, wet with sudden sweat. His room was hot and stuffy and bright with the light of the projected image.

Staring at the image, he wiped his sweaty face on the sheet.

As he had feared, feared and expected, the Four Worlds ship was staging an assault on *Nautilus*. A tiny, awkward space boat floated from the alien ship's ornate flank. The engines powered on gently, pushing the boat into a curving path. Arachne projected the boat's path, the path of *Nautilus:* In a few hours, they intersected.

Keeping his gaze on the image, Griffith got out of bed and opened the window. Everyone else on board slept with their windows wide open, but Griffith thought the habit stupid and dangerous. The night breeze skimmed his body. The air was cool and heavy with midnight rain.

He sent an emergency message through Arachne to General Cherenkov, to Petrovich. Griffith still thought of the cosmonaut as General Cherenkov. Griffith had trouble with familiarity.

The pause lengthened.

Maybe they sent another boat—maybe I didn't see the first one, and *Nautilus* is already taken over, Griffith thought. Maybe this boat is just reinforcements. Maybe the aliens have already overwhelmed Petrovich, taken him prisoner . . . killed him.

Griffith's pulse raced.

I should have *made* them let me go along! he thought. J.D. Sauvage is a naive fool. I could have . . .

He wondered what he could have done, weaponless against Civilization. They said they had no weapons, they said carrying weapons through transition was enough to get a whole world banished. They said they did not make war on each other. But Griffith was not prepared to take everything they said at face value. The alien humans had proven themselves untrustworthy and the quartet struck Griffith as far too good to be true. The Representative of Smallerfarther, on the other hand, Griffith thought he understood.

He wondered whether a single group had sent the invading spacecraft, or whether they had all conspired.

Petrovich's image faded into existence in Griffith's room. The government agent blew out his breath with relief.

Kolya jerked his attention away from the universe and back to 61 Cygni, to *Nautilus*. Both Arachne and Griffith poured emergency messages into his link. His helmet projected an image of Griffith in front of his eyes. The effect put Griffith at the edge of a crater, protected from vacuum by nothing more than a sleeveless t-shirt and a pair of baggy sweatpants.

A glowing red bar hovered above his head: Arachne's indication that the transmission was scrambled. The Four Worlds people could not listen in.

Unless, of course, their code-breaking abilities exceeded those of Arachne. But if that were true, they could have gone into Arachne first thing and taken Victoria's algorithm, instead of asking for it.

"They've started the invasion!" Griffith said. "I'm coming over there—"

"Calm down," Kolya said.

Griffith raked his fingers through his sleep-tangled brown hair, trying ineffectually to comb it.

"This is a nightmare!"

"I see the report." The secondary image, projected between Kolya and Griffith as if the two of them were sitting on opposite sides of it, showed a tiny space boat edging away from the Four Worlds ship and accelerating into a curving path that would bring it to *Nautilus*.

"I'll have to take the transport," Griffith said, half to himself. He glared at the image of the Four Worlds boat. "If I had to, I could ram that sucker. No matter what it's made of, I'll do some damage."

"You'll do—" Kolya cut short the brusque command. "Consider your decision carefully, Petrovich."

"Dammit, Petrovich, they're *coming* for you! I *told* you—"

Kolya drew back from the conversation with Griffith and sent a message, uncoded, toward the tiny alien boat.

"I observe a citizen of the Four Worlds approaching on a visit."

Kolya kept his voice neutral, though his heart was pounding. Perhaps Griffith was right all along. Perhaps Civilization could not be trusted.

The pause lengthened.

"Petrovich—"

"Shh!"

Griffith shut up. He also stormed out of the field of Arachne's transmissions. The red bar faded away.

"Call J.D.!" Kolya shouted after him, but he had no way of knowing if Griffith heard him.

VONDA N. MCINTYRE

• • •

J.D.'s link connected with Kolya's.

"I see what's happening," she said. "I'll come to *Nautilus* as fast as I can."

"I think that's wise," he said.

A powerful transmission cut off his voice.

Kolya's suit radio received a powerful transmission of a voice so heavy that it buzzed painfully in the receiver.

"My representative sends intriguing reports. I find I have the desire to visit your species in its own environment. Intriguing reports."

"Forgive my ignorance, but . . . who are you?"

"I am the Representative from Smallerfarther."

"We're flattered."

Kolya considered telling the Representative that *Nautilus* was not the natural environment of human beings. But that might send him to *Starfarer,* and if he was capable of doing damage . . .

Don't be foolish, old man, Kolya told himself. The Representative has no interest in *Starfarer.* Civilization knows how to build starships like *Starfarer.* He wants *Nautilus.* If he lands, if he goes to the center of *Nautilus* . . . he could take it over.

Kolya flashed a call at *Starfarer,* toward Gerald, toward Miensaem Thanthavong. He tried not to sound panicky. He aimed a copy toward J.D. down on Largernearer.

Longestlooker entered the conversation. Her image appeared in Kolya's field of vision. The Largerfarthing had a smear of dirt on her shoulder, muddy brown against sleek black, from the fossil dig.

"Representative," she said, "the planetoid is barren. Come visit the human people's starship. You will find it much more interesting."

"That is impossible, I fear," the Representative said. "The gravity would damage me. Impossible."

"But you're *from* Smallerfarther!" Kolya said.

258

"Not for many years," the Representative said. "I am old, and frail."

Kolya snorted in skeptical sympathy. He found it hard to believe that the interstellar Civilization suffered from diseases like arthritis.

"I'm old, too," he said. "Exercise is good for you."

"Speak for yourself," the Representative said.

"Representative," Longestlooker said, "permit me to escort some other humans out to meet you. Then you wouldn't have to endure the difficulties of travel."

"The human people have already paid their respects," the Representative said, his heavy voice smooth behind the buzz. "It would be arrogant to expect them to come to me twice."

Kolya's spacesuit twiddled the radio settings, but the buzz remained. It gave him a blazing headache.

Gerald Hemminge joined in. "Representative, I know the perfect compromise. Let us send our transport ship to meet you. It will bring you to the axis of *Starfarer*, where we can meet in zero g."

"I would not fit inside your transport," the Representative said.

"Then you may attach your boat to our airlock, as Europa does."

The Representative paused.

Is it possible? Kolya thought. Has Gerald succeeded? Did he push the Representative so far that one more step would be rudeness?

"Most kind, most kind," the Representative said, "but I fear my boat is not sufficiently maneuverable. I must land. Most kind."

"If you're in danger—"

"No, no, you go to far too much trouble over me."

Esther loped over the horizon, coming closer fast.

"We have no structure here that you'd fit inside," Kolya said.

"I do not need a structure," the Representative said.

"The gravity of your starship will trouble me somewhat, but I will submit to it in order to greet you."

Kolya muttered a low curse.

Esther's canter slowed. She came to a stop beside Kolya. He leaned his helmet against hers so he could speak to her without the radio, without anyone else hearing.

"I am running out of suggestions," he said.

"How about, 'If you land here we'll rip off your pretty legs and make necklaces out of them'?"

"Not very diplomatic," Kolya said. "But an idea to consider."

He switched to an outgoing transmission.

"Representative," he said politely, "your craft might be damaged by the rough terrain."

Esther glanced at Kolya. He shrugged sheepishly at the ridiculous warning.

"We've had no chance," Petrovich said, "to prepare a proper landing field for space boats."

"My craft is very versatile," the Representative said, his tone condescending.

"I thought you said it wasn't very maneuverable," Esther said.

The Representative hesitated longer than the transmission lag.

"My ship," he said, "is more versatile than human people's spacecraft, and you have landed safely."

"Look," Esther whispered.

The image of the space boat sailed into a small tight orbit around the image of *Nautilus*.

Overhead, in reality, the space boat traveled across *Nautilus*'s sky.

"We've got company," Esther said.

They hurried over the horizon and returned to the expedition tent.

Griffith slammed out of the guest house, still buttoning his shirt. He ran along the winding path toward the slope of the main cylinder's end.

He had been right all along. The Four Worlds planned to take over *Nautilus*. Probably they would kill General Cherenkov. If he was lucky they would only keep him hostage and trade him for MacKenzie's algorithm. Then they would have everything they wanted from *Starfarer*. They would have no reason to let the EarthSpace ship keep flying.

Everyone on board except Griffith thought Civilization was peaceful. They believed that Civilization bore no arms because the cosmic string reacted if a ship brought weapons of war through transition.

The faculty had overlooked a loophole. No one had mentioned any prohibition against owning weapons within a star system.

If you weren't allowed to do that, Griffith thought, the string would never have come near Earth in the first place. We have plenty of ordnance back home. The string would have avoided us.

He raced up the hillside. As he neared the axis the radial acceleration dropped, till he could leap along nearly weightless. This close to the sun tube, the light was bright and hot. Griffith had to be careful to look away from the glare.

He propelled himself over the border between the rotating cylinder and the stationary axis, into zero g.

The waiting rooms and control chambers were deserted. No one else was trying to rescue Petrovich. Maybe no one else had the nerve to fly the transport. Griffith figured he and the computer could land it. After that it would be up to Klein to get the thing off *Nautilus*. Or Sauvage could speed up the rotation of the alien starship. Fling the transport right off it.

Might not land at all, he thought. Might just ram the Four Worlds boat and be done with it.

He wondered if the transport would survive the impact, but his curiosity was purely intellectual. If he thought he needed to ram the Four Worlds boat, he would.

He tapped into Arachne's message traffic. Useful information: The Representative from Smallerfarther was acting alone.

Or pretending to.

Everyone was trying, more or less ineffectually, not to panic. J.D. asked for calm and understanding—and an explanation. Petrovich tried to persuade the alien not to land. Crimson Ng, at the fake archaeological dig, was trying to get some information out of the Representative's representative, who had progressed from his usual lethargy to a deep sleep. The quartet from Largerfarther claimed ignorance of the Representative's motives.

That's all real convenient, Griffith said to himself, sarcastically.

Griffith opened the transport's hatch and sealed it behind him. Arachne's projections followed him through the door. The systems checked the pressure while he checked the position of the alien space boat. It orbited *Nautilus*, spiraling closer. Soon it would prepare to land.

In the glass bubble at the front of the transport, Griffith strapped himself into the pilot's acceleration couch. He could have been in the observation cabin of a fancy sightseeing ship. The chamber contained nothing but several couches and the wide glass wall, now obscured by the bulk of *Starfarer*.

He connected to Arachne through his link and requested a departure sequence.

The lax security of *Starfarer* struck him all over again. These people assumed anyone cleared by EarthSpace to join the expedition—or to visit—would be trustworthy. Information flowed freely, and the barriers to change existed for safety, not secrecy. Most of the faculty and staff could not, for example, make changes in the level of light the sun tubes transmitted. But when Infinity Mendez—or Alzena Dadkhah, before she fled—made adjustments, they worked completely in the open.

Griffith snorted. It would be all too easy to plant

a double agent, someone from the Mideast Sweep . . .

But . . . no agent of the Mideast Sweep had come on board—not, at any rate, one who had become known. Instead, there were at least two spies from EarthSpace allies or EarthSpace itself, from the people responsible for *Starfarer*'s security. Griffith was one. Whoever had crashed Arachne was the other. Griffith believed Chancellor Blades was the second spy.

He wished he knew the truth for certain; he wished he knew if the second spy was his ally or his enemy. He wondered if anyone on board knew for certain. The senators? He dismissed the idea. Orazio would not know, because she supported the deep space expedition. Derjaguin opposed the expedition in particular and EarthSpace in general, but he was far too radical in his politics to be trusted with top secret information.

"Griffith! Hey!"

Arachne created an image before him. A voice burst out of the shadowy ghost shape of Infinity Mendez. Griffith tensed, on alert. The image could do nothing to him, but the man behind the image might be able to stop him. Griffith severed the transport's flight controls from Arachne's influence.

"What are you doing?" Infinity's image solidified. He floated in front of Griffith: He was in the waiting room of the transport dock.

"Same as you, probably," Griffith said. "I'm going to help General Cherenkov."

"Then let me in," Infinity said.

"Not likely."

Infinity's image vanished. If he had turned his attention toward getting reinforcements, toward gaining control of the transport ship, he was too late.

I have to do this, Griffith thought. I bound myself to the expedition back home, when I tried to stop the military carrier.

But Petrovich had stopped him. Griffith had done

nothing public that would prove his loyalties had changed.

Which means I could probably get away with pretending I was an innocent victim of the hijacking. Like the senators, like Gerald Hemminge.

If I do nothing now.

If he took the transport, if he defended J.D. Sauvage's starship from the Four Worlds, he would be declaring his loyalties. The trouble was, he did not know where his loyalties lay. He was confused. Before he had come to *Starfarer*, he had never been confused in his life.

If I pretended, I could go back to the way things were. Back to not being confused, to knowing whose orders I should obey.

That was the trouble. Petrovich would not tell him what to do.

Griffith had spent his adult life pretending to be something other than what he was. No, not something *other*. Something *less*. He was good at pretending, good at being invisible, good at telling lies. He was so good that his superiors need never know he had strayed. When they debriefed him, he could beat the lie detectors.

It would be a risk, but a risk that might save his career, if not his life.

And Griffith knew he could not do it. Not even to save himself. Particularly not to save himself. He did not know why he did not want to lie anymore. But he would not pretend he had worked ceaselessly against the expedition.

With a soft curse, he snapped an order at the onboard computer to free the transport from *Starfarer*'s dock.

The glass boat streaked through the mouth of the lagoon. J.D. sat against the stern rail, slipping in and out of a communications fugue, anxious to be ready as soon as the boat reached the *Chi*, equally anxious to stay in touch with *Starfarer* and *Nautilus*. Zev hovered beside her, and Stephen Thomas fidgeted.

"The tide's still out," Victoria said in the background of J.D.'s mind.

"I know it, I can see it," Stephen Thomas said. "What is it, two hours till it's in again?"

"At least that, till we have enough water to load the boat," Satoshi said.

"Can you bring the *Chi* to us?"

"We could," Victoria said, "but I'm worried about fuel. J.D. will want speed . . ."

"We'll leave the damned boat," Stephen Thomas said. "Come back for it later."

"If we can," Satoshi said.

Victoria hesitated. "Yes," she said finally. "That's a good idea. We'll be ready to lift off when you get here."

Infinity's presence appeared in her link.

"Bad news," J.D. said, anticipating what he was about to say.

"On all counts. The space boat's fast. Real fast, according to Longestlooker. If you move *Nautilus* fast enough to get out of his way . . ."

"The stress would be hard on *Starfarer*."

"Yeah."

"I was afraid of that."

"Maybe it would be worth the risk," he said desperately. "Esther and Kolya—"

Esther was listening in. "Lover, it'll do us no damned good at all if you get us out of range by busting up *Starfarer*."

"I won't leave you to—"

"To what? The Representative says he wants to pay us a visit. Maybe that's really all he wants to do."

Infinity snorted with disbelief.

J.D. appreciated Esther's bravery, even her bravado.

"What do you think, Kolya?"

"When I agreed to stay on *Nautilus*, I knew something

like this might happen. I hope the Four Worlds are listening in, because I want them to know how much contempt I have for duplicity."

"There's something else," Infinity said. "Griffith is on his way over there."

"What!" Esther exclaimed. "What for?"

"To help," Infinity said dryly.

Esther went into a communications fugue and came out a moment later.

"It never occurred to me to lock up the transport," she said with disgust. "And even if it had, I wouldn't have done it. In case something happened to me. In case somebody needed it. Not *Griffith*."

For the first time, J.D. felt real fear that the encounter would end in disaster.

She felt herself being pulled away from the link.

"I have to go," she said.

As she opened her eyes, the bottom of the glass boat scraped gently on the floor of the lagoon. The boat's twin hulls crushed the flowers beneath them, but left them upright beneath the transparent central deck. A kilometer away across sandbars and tide pools, the *Chi* waited.

"We're here, J.D." Zev's voice was urgent, his expression apprehensive. "Let's go."

Ten

Still soaking wet from the dash across the slippery mat of sea flowers and through the fingers of sea between the sandbars, J.D. hurriedly strapped herself into her acceleration couch.

"Everybody set?"

"Ready," Victoria said.

"Me too," Satoshi said.

"Let's get our asses out of here," Stephen Thomas said.

Zev stroked his fingertips from J.D.'s wrist to her fingertips, signaling, Let's go.

The *Chi* powered up. It shuddered beneath them. The noise enclosed them. The little ship rose from the island. Below, in the lagoon, the glass boat floated free of the sand. It would wait for them; it would survive, if they could return for it before the next worldwide storm.

The *Chi* rose above the peak of the volcano. The spume of a wave breaking against the cliff spattered the glass of the observers' chamber.

Blue sky turned purple, indigo, black. The *Chi* burst out of the atmosphere into space and headed for *Nautilus*, in high orbit.

An image of Orchestra sparked into existence before J.D.—not the whale-eel's sleek, independent AI, but an image of Orchestra herself, striated with life-forms, trailing seaweed.

"Goodbye, human people. Goodbye, diver people. Visit me again soon."

J.D. was nonplussed by Orchestra's calm.

"Do you have any advice, when I speak to the Representative? Do you know what he wants?"

J.D. knew what he wanted. If Orchestra gave her a different explanation, she would find it hard to believe.

"The Smallerfarthings are willful," Orchestra said. "They are not known for violence, but they will go . . . as far as you allow. He wants you to give him your starship, what else? Oh, and the algorithm, of course. You know that . . . don't you?"

J.D. smiled ruefully, appreciating Orchestra's direct response.

"Yes," she said. "I know that. I was hoping this was just a friendly visit."

"It is that, too," Orchestra said. "But the Smallerfarthings like to be rewarded for their friendship. He hopes you will reward him richly. Excuse me, I am going to go listen to Beethoven."

Her image faded out.

Stephen Thomas laughed sharply. "Big fucking help," he said.

Orchestra's AI swam in from space, passing through the glass to enter the observers' circle. It startled J.D.; she had not seen it since they left *Starfarer*.

"May I listen to Beethoven, too?" it asked.

"I'll put it on a separate channel for you," Satoshi said, "because the rest of us have to talk."

Through her link, J.D. listened as Satoshi directed Beethoven's Sixth into the AI's transmission.

"This one's different!" the AI exclaimed with delight. "Do not worry, I will pay!" It fell silent and still, drifting with all its eyes closed.

J.D. turned down the music channel till she could barely hear it in her head.

"Now what are we going to do?" she said.

"Tell the damned thing to fuck off and die," Stephen Thomas said.

Victoria glanced at him, annoyed.

"Orchestra *said* he's willful." Stephen Thomas shrugged. "Let's be more willful."

"Might work," J.D. said. "Anything's worth a try."

"We'd better decide quick," Satoshi said. "Look."

The *Chi* approached the complex constellation of *Starfarer* orbiting *Nautilus*, the Four Worlds ship orbiting Europa's starship, the two massive little starships revolving near each other around a common center of gravity. The transport moved from *Starfarer* toward *Nautilus*.

The sixth mass in the equation, the Four Worlds space boat, a tiny speck compared to the other bodies, circled ever closer to *Nautilus*. It prepared to land.

J.D. shot a transmission through space.

"Representative," she said. "My colleagues are anxious to meet you. Please . . . wait for us to prepare an appropriate welcome. It wouldn't be proper otherwise."

After a moment's transmission lag, the reply arrived.

"I never stand on ceremony," the Representative said airily.

"Shit," Stephen Thomas muttered.

J.D. sighed.

Griffith tried again to communicate with Petrovich, but the cosmonaut would not reply. Petrovich exchanged messages with the *Chi*—with J.D., Griffith supposed—and with *Starfarer*, but they were coded and Griffith could not receive them.

The Representative's boat curved gently into orbit around *Nautilus*.

The transport followed.

Intent on the boat, Griffith accepted an incoming communication before he realized it was not from Petrovich.

J.D. Sauvage's image formed nearby, a red coding streak overhead.

"Mr. Griffith," she said, "please don't . . ."

He glared at her, angry and disappointed, and snapped a code onto his own transmission.

"Don't do anything *stupid*?" he snarled, when she did not continue.

"If you want to put it that way."

"What do you plan to do? Let that—thing—take over your starship?"

"No." She sounded grim. She was ordinarily so mild that her tone surprised him. "But I hope we can reason with him. I don't want anyone injured!"

"Move the damned ship out of his way!" He did not know for sure whether she could control it when she was not on it. Maybe the Four Worlds could scramble her commands. But it was worth a try, and to his mind she should have tried it already.

"*Starfarer*'s under enough strain already," J.D. said. "Infinity's worried about the stresses. I'd have to move so slowly—it wouldn't make any difference."

"Mendez is a *gardener*," Griffith said.

"Mendez," J.D. said coldly, "helped build *Starfarer*."

"Somebody's got to do something! Spin the ship, keep that boat from landing. It's got to be armed! If you won't—"

"Please be patient," J.D. said. "If I spin *Nautilus* fast enough to make landing hard for the boat, I'd spin Kolya and Esther right off the surface! There's not much holding them down. I know you're concerned about them, about him, but—"

Taken aback, Griffith cut off J.D.'s message and stopped transmitting his own.

Am I *that* obvious? he wondered. He hated the idea that anyone could guess his changed allegiances so accurately.

He tried once more to communicate with Petrovich,

but his message bounced off *Nautilus* and vanished into space.

"Petrovich, dammit!" Griffith shouted. "Why won't you tell me what to do?"

The Representative's boat puffed a plasma cloud, a gentle glowing touch that lowered its orbit and sent it downward.

"Please prepare to receive me," the Representative said. His powerful transmission carried his heavy commanding voice and the strange buzz behind it.

Griffith went cold. His attention narrowed to a tunnel with the alien boat at its end.

I have to do something *now*, he thought. I *have* to.

He slowed the transport, letting it sink toward the surface of *Nautilus.* J.D. and the *Chi* were still a half hour away. The transport received another message; he accepted it without acknowledging it or replying. His lifelong habit was to collect as much information as he could and to admit that he knew as little of it as possible.

"Please, Mr. Griffith," J.D. said. "Please, we've got to try to solve this without any violence."

What about Petrovich? Griffith shouted silently.

J.D. strained against the safety straps of her couch, gazing intently at *Nautilus,* staring at it through the diagram the Chi's computer projected for her: *Nautilus,* the Representative's boat, the transport. Victoria spoke urgently to Jenny Dupre and Infinity Mendez, while Satoshi stayed in contact with Gerald Hemminge, and Stephen Thomas coordinated with Avvaiyar and Miensaem Thanthavong.

But none of it matters! J.D. cried quietly to itself. Nothing we can do can keep the Representative from landing on *Nautilus,* not without endangering either *Starfarer* or Kolya and Esther.

The only way we can stop him is by letting Griffith loose.

She enlarged the images of Kolya and Esther.

"You're the ones in the most danger—"

"No," Kolya replied. "Griffith is in the most danger. He's willing to throw his life away to stop the Representative."

"I don't want anyone hurt!" J.D. said.

"Civilization brags about being peaceful," Kolya said. "I think we should take them at their word. As a challenge."

"I can't let you endanger yourselves," she said. "If Griffith really can land the transport—" J.D. glanced a question at Esther. "Can you lift it off again?"

"It can land here," Esther said. "If you call it landing, to flop down like a big rock. I *might* be able to take off, but . . ." She shrugged. "It wasn't designed to land, anyplace, anytime. It'll be a mess . . ."

Crimson Ng squatted on the ledge above the fossil bed. Before her, the Representative's representative spread out over the rock, gold and green in the shadows. His coat looked soft and smooth, but his emerald spines thrust out through it, fully extended, fully erect and defensive. He looked like a cross between a crystal garden and a porcupine.

One of Europa's meerkats stood on Late's back, where his shoulder blades would have been, if he had had shoulder blades. Rising on its hind legs, the meerkat gripped two of the spines with its front paws and stared around, keeping watch for the rest of the tribe. The other meerkats pattered and snuffled around the edges of the dig. Every so often Quickercatcher or Sharphearer would shoo them away from the fossil bed so they would not dig in it and disturb the site.

Crimson wished she had thought of that, and brought in a marmot or an otter from the wild cylinder to mix up the fossils' strata. More confusion in the provenance would have been a good twist of the plot. Too late now for these fossils, the fossils of the Fighters. And if she ever found the fossils of the other ones, the river would have jumbled them more than enough.

Sharphearer let one of the meerkats climb onto her back. The meerkat, peering over Sharphearer's head, was about the only comical thing around right now.

"Why won't he wake up?" Crimson asked Longest-looker. "Hey, Late, come *on!* "

"Exhaustion," Longestlooker said.

"Or embarrassment," Quickercatcher said, his voice edgy.

"It isn't Late's fault, what the Representative does!" Sharphearer exclaimed. "Be fair."

Quickercatcher sat with his tail curved primly around his front paws.

"He could have warned us what might happen," he said.

"How could he know? The Representative hasn't ever come out of his nest the entire time we've known him!"

"He came out during the Thirteenth Whole Community," Longestlooker said.

"When was that?" Crimson asked.

"We—we Largerfarthings—gather to reaffirm our community. Every five years we gather in small communities, every twenty-five in medium communities. And every hundred-twenty-five we gather in a Whole Community."

"Not Earth years, of course," Quickercatcher said.

"I mean, how long ago was that?"

"About . . ." Longestlooker paused, figuring. "About eight hundred years—"

"—Everyone was surprised and pleased that the Representative would make such a gesture," Sharphearer said.

"She means eight hundred Earth years," Quickercatcher said.

"But he only came out of his nest," Fasterdigger said. "He didn't come all the way to Largerfarther."

"It was the gesture that counted," Sharphearer said. "The token."

"I *know* that," Fasterdigger said.

"And I suppose," Sharphearer said, "this is an even greater honor. For him to travel to you."

"He wants gratitude for his honor." Androgeos sat on the bank of the river, his elbows on his bare knees, oblivious to the effect of rocks and mud on his pleated silken kilt. "And if you give it to him, you'll spoil everything."

"J.D.," Crimson said aloud and through her link, "Kolya, Esther, I'm sorry, the Representative's representative isn't talking."

The Representative's ship vanished over the horizon.

"What d'you think he's planning to do?" Esther said.

"Maybe just what he claims."

"And maybe try to take J.D.'s starship! Where's Europa, where's Quickercatcher—can't they *do* something?"

Her eyelids flickered as she linked with Arachne.

Europa and Quickercatcher appeared so quickly they must have been waiting, watching.

"Make him go away," Esther demanded.

"Esther, my dear, please—don't panic," Europa said.

"I'm not panicked," Esther said with annoyance. "I'm pissed off!"

"This is a very unusual event. The Representative honors you with his visit."

"There's nothing we can do," Quickercatcher said. "We have no way to stop him—even if we wanted to," the Largerfarthing added quickly.

"He's an elder," said Longestlooker. "His judgment carries great weight."

"And what," Kolya said calmly, "if his judgment says he should possess *Nautilus?*"

"Haven't you learned we're not violent?" Androgeos's image appeared in the far curve of the expedition tent.

"Please, Nikolai Petrovich," Quickercatcher said. "We're your hosts, your sponsors. You're our guests, our clients. It's to all our benefit to weave a community."

As *Starfarer* rose above *Nautilus*'s horizon, the transport separated from it, a small spark moving away from the spinning gray cylinder.

"Will he behave savagely?" Quickercatcher's voice was quiet, apprehensive.

"Who knows what Griffith will do?" Esther said. "Griffith doesn't even know what Griffith will do."

"He'll do what Kolya tells him," Infinity said. "Kolya—?"

"Our guerrilla accountant is not that predictable," Kolya said, still staring out the window. Another of Arachne's images appeared nearby: the constellation of *Nautilus* and *Starfarer*, the transport, the Four Worlds ship, and the Representative's space boat.

The space boat's orbit tightened.

"The Representative is going to land," Kolya said.

As the transport separated from *Starfarer*, Griffith listened to the communications between *Starfarer* and *Nautilus*. He expected, at any moment, Petrovich's image. He expected the cosmonaut to tell him to stay where he was, but he hoped Petrovich would ask for his help. Griffith would do whatever the cosmonaut asked.

Kolya Cherenkov maintained his silence.

Griffith, tense, edged the transport into a curve toward *Nautilus*. As the engines whispered, the Representative's space boat spiraled in toward the surface of the starship.

If he poured on the power, recalculated his course, he could catch the boat and ram it before it landed.

The transport outmassed the boat by a couple of orders of magnitude. Griffith would probably survive the encounter. The Representative probably would not. Whether Griffith would survive the aftermath, he could not know. He tried to put that consideration aside from his decision.

But he did not know what Petrovich wanted, and he did not know what was right.

He had spent his life obeying orders, committed to the structure from which the orders came. Now he was cut off from the structure, and he had lost his faith in it as well. Nikolai Petrovich had made him consider his loyalties.

I have to do something! he thought.

He had always believed that for any situation, some action existed that was a proper response.

For the first time in his life, he considered the possibility that the proper response might be inaction.

Petrovich would not tell him what to do, and he would not blindly follow J.D. Sauvage's plea, for she would never accept force as a necessity.

He only had a few moments to decide. The transport loomed behind and above the Representative's boat, in perfect position. Griffith engaged the transport's computer.

He took the most difficult action he had ever taken in his life.

Griffith accelerated the transport, pushing it into a higher orbit around *Nautilus* as the Representative's boat sank toward the surface.

In that moment he gave up any chance of interposing himself between the Four Worlds and Petrovich.

He started to close his connection with the transport's computer, to shut off the radio. He did not want to know what would happen next.

Then he changed his mind. He oriented himself toward the glass wall that looked out into space and down toward the planetoid, and he accepted all the transmissions from *Nautilus*.

He floated in zero gravity, in silence and confusion and despair, torturing himself by watching everything that happened.

The Four Worlds boat settled slowly to the surface of *Nautilus*, blowing aside the ancient dust, leaving a starburst of dark stone beneath it. The gravity of *Nautilus* was so low that dust blew off the worldlet entirely, streaking upward, dissipating, spewing sideways and over the horizon.

Esther jumped when the dust struck the window of the expedition tent. She grabbed for her helmet, ready to seal herself into her suit. When no hiss of escaping air followed the blast, she relaxed.

"Look," she said to Kolya. "You can see where it hit."

Kolya, too, wore his spacesuit, and held his helmet in one hand. He bent down to inspect the pockmarks on the outer surface of the window: tiny pits and scratches.

"The Representative should have landed at a greater distance," he said. He knit his stripy eyebrows. "I suppose we should be grateful he didn't land on top of us."

"Would have solved some of his problems," Esther said. "I'll be real glad when the cavalry gets here. J.D., I mean."

"In the meantime," Kolya said, "we had better go out and . . . hold the fort."

She glanced at him quizzically.

"American culture is all over," Kolya said. "Even in guerrilla outposts."

Esther plopped her helmet on.

They loped toward the strange, organic-looking spacecraft. As they approached, it settled, an oblate, three-legged sphere.

"Baba Yaga," Kolya said.

"What's that?"

"A fairy tale. Baba Yaga had a house that stood on legs like chicken feet. It crouched to let you in. It was a popular story, when I was a child."

"I never heard it."

"I doubt it's told much anymore. Even back home. It isn't the same if you can't tell it in Russian."

They were only twenty meters from the Baba Yaga boat when a cloud of gas and vapor spit suddenly from a tiny orifice.

J.D. was astonished when Griffith moved the transport from its threatening position. She sent him a message of thanks, but he did not reply, he did not acknowledge. She had no time or attention to spend wondering about his motives.

Nautilus grew from a point to a tiny disk as the *Chi* powered toward it. J.D. urged the explorer craft onward, willing it to outstrip the limitations of its fuel and its orbit.

Zev fidgeted in his acceleration couch, and frowned at the transmission from the surface of *Nautilus*.

"Where's the Representative going to go?" Zev asked. "He can't fit in the tent, and underground isn't beautiful the way it was when Nemo was alive."

"He wants to retrofit the starship," J.D. said. The center of *Nautilus* held captive a quantum black hole, the source of the starship's gravity and power. "Change its controls. Remember what Europa said? She was going to pith it."

J.D. could not get the image out of her mind: a long, sharp needle, probing into a brain, scrambling the complex planes and angles of Nemo's ghost. If Europa could replace Nemo's controls, the Representative could do it, too.

"I'm sure the Representative can't take over your starship," Victoria said. "If he could, Androgeos probably could have, eh?"

Unhappily, J.D. shrugged her shoulders within the safety straps of her couch. "Gerald says I have to turn it over to EarthSpace, and Senator Derjaguin says I have to give it to the United States. Maybe Civilization will say I have to turn it over to the Four Worlds." The one material thing I ever really wanted, J.D. thought, and everybody else wants it, too.

"It's yours fair and square," Stephen Thomas said. "Even if Nemo hadn't willed it to you, you were there to salvage it. The same as anybody in Civilization would have."

"But we aren't members of Civilization yet," Satoshi said. "They might have different rules to apply to their clients."

"I don't want the Representative anywhere near the core," J.D. said. "The knowledge surface is all that's left of Nemo."

"Have you figured out a way inside it?" Satoshi asked.

"There isn't a way. I mean," she said quickly, "the way is a progression. I get a little farther every time. I'm like a baby, taking first steps. Or maybe just babbling and kicking, who knows?"

"You took *Nautilus* through transition!" Zev said. "When Andro threatened you, you made it spin."

"Pretty good babbling and kicking," Satoshi said.

"But that's what the starship was built to do," J.D. said. "Moving the starship is like breathing." She sighed. "What I can make it do is rudimentary. And I don't doubt that Civilization's controls for it are easier and more efficient than Nemo's. But I can't bear to give up the knowledge surface. Even if I never figure out how to get inside it." Her response to the knowledge surface was emotional, not rational. She knew it; she had made a conscious decision to keep an old-fashioned interface with the starship so she could also keep her final connection with the squidmoth.

"It'd be a big mistake to lose everything Nemo had

collected for a million years," Victoria said. "You have plenty of time to figure out how to gain access to the information."

"Maybe the squidmoth baby will tell you," Zev said.

"I'm afraid to go anywhere near the squidmoth baby. It's so *different* from Nemo."

"It's different from the sides of Nemo you saw," Stephen Thomas said. "The sides I saw were rougher."

"Yes." J.D. had watched the LTM recordings of what Nemo had shown to Stephen Thomas, an acidic pond of attendants ripping each other to shreds. But that had been during the last few days of Nemo's life, when the deterioration of impending death had begun.

"There's something weird about squidmoths," Stephen Thomas said.

Satoshi laughed, and after a moment everyone else joined in.

"Weird, huh?" Satoshi said. "Unlike anybody else we've met?"

"Not to mention what *they* think about *us*," J.D. added. "I mean it—"

"You're only annoyed because you haven't figured out how their molecular genetics work yet," Victoria said.

"You don't have any idea why I'm annoyed," Stephen Thomas said.

Victoria tensed and Satoshi frowned at the tone of Stephen Thomas's voice. He startled J.D., too.

"I can imagine ways for the dendritic molecules to code for enzymes and structural molecules and that kind of crap." Stephen Thomas continued the discussion as if he had not just snapped at his partner. "What I *can't* figure out . . . is how the molecules can evolve."

During an awkward pause, no one said anything. J.D. decided the only thing she could do was pretend she had not noticed the interchange.

"It evolves the way everything does," J.D. said. "By mistakes. By sloppy goopy imprecise biological processes."

"Nope. Not with squidmoths. No mutations. No variation. They've got different types of dendritic molecules, but within each type, all the molecules are identical."

"That *is* strange."

"Fucking right. So if you do figure out how to get into the knowledge surface, do me a favor and look up 'mutation rate' in whatever Nemo used as an index. Look up 'squidmoth evolution.' "

"I hope there *is* an index."

"There'd have to be!" Victoria said.

"Would there?" J.D. asked. "I don't know why Nemo collected observations and information. Maybe squidmoths are packrats. Maybe they pick up stuff indiscriminately—obsessively—and store it away. Maybe the knowledge surface is Nemo's equivalent of a dusty attic."

"J.D.'s got a point," Satoshi said. "Everybody in Civilization agrees the squidmoths never do anything with what they learn. They don't apply it to their environment. They just float around and watch."

"I can see myself," J.D. said, "wandering through Nemo's collection. I'd be fascinated and I'd probably never come out. But the attic could be stuffed with mouldering newspapers and the last millennium's math books."

"Nemo lived for a million years," Victoria said. "Hard to imagine, in that long time, not picking up a few diamonds."

"Hidden," Stephen Thomas said, "under the mattress."

Outside, the disk of *Nautilus* had grown large enough to reveal its craters and irregularities.

J.D. glanced anxiously at the *Chi*'s holographic display of speed, orbit, acceleration.

"We'll be there soon," Victoria said to J.D. "But we don't want to land and run out of fuel."

"Beats the hell out of running out of fuel and *then* landing," Stephen Thomas said.

J.D. wished he would leave the edge out of his voice, or shut up, even if he was right.

"I just don't know how far the Representative will go," she said. "He's risking a lot to move around so much. Years of his life."

"If worse comes to worst," Satoshi said, "if he tries to force his way past them, Kolya and Esther can probably pick him up and carry him back to his starship."

"Or tie his legs in knots," Stephen Thomas said. "That would be some sculpture. I bet Crimson would appreciate it."

"What if he has weapons?" Victoria asked J.D.

"You sound like Griffith!"

"Mr. Griffith has a tendency toward paranoia," Victoria said. "That doesn't mean he's always wrong."

"He must have decided he was this time," J.D. said.

They heard nothing from the transport. It orbited *Nautilus* at a distance. Griffith still could choose to act.

"Civilization wants a lot from us," Satoshi said. "They want *Nautilus*, they want Victoria's algorithm, they even want Crimson's fossils."

"I'd be willing to give them the algorithm," Victoria said. "Or trade it. I'd like something in return. Some answers."

"I think Europa was right," J.D. said. "We'll find examples to follow. But we have to choose our own answers."

"The point is," Satoshi said, "they haven't offered to take any of it by force."

"Maybe they've kept the big guns in reserve," Stephen Thomas said. "Until now."

"Or they've created a society in which force isn't an acceptable choice," J.D. said. "I wonder if that's as strange to them as it is to us?"

The Representative braced his leg-tips against the walls. Their softness cushioned him from fractures, but the acceleration of landing pulled at him terribly.

You had better get used to the gravity, the Representative told himself. If you succeed, you will stay here and earn your line's future life.

He would earn their life, but spend his own.

Worth it, he said to himself. Worth it.

The boat sank toward the surface of the starship. The starship.

Worth even the risk of failure, he thought.

The acceleration of the engines eased, then ceased, dropping him abruptly into the faint gravity of *Nautilus*. The Representative waited for the boat to ground itself. Outside, the two humans left their shelter and approached him. He wondered how far they would go to stop him. The Representative cared little if the humans had to be taught lessons, but he did not want to be the martyred reason.

He felt out his new metamorphosis, admiring himself. A flawless opaline shell protected his vital organs and his several clusters of compound eyes. The hair had dropped from his legs, which projected from joints in the opaline shell. He was even more beautiful than before, all jewels and semiprecious stones.

The Representative walked himself down the interior walls of the boat, till he perched, stilt-legged, on his leg-tips. The tips had not had time to solidify; he balanced on bundles of sharp bright fibers, half-formed jewels held together by nerve tissue and organic matrix. When he stepped, the fibers fractured and split.

He ordered the boat to pierce itself. A tiny opening appeared.

The air whined out; the whine receded to silence. The vacuum's coldness touched the raw nerve endings of the Representative's legs. He gave another command; the boat split open. For the first time in centuries, he faced the surface of a world. He touched the ancient dust gingerly with the tip of one leg.

The Representative tottered outside.

• • •

Esther waited for the Representative, amazed and entranced and apprehensive. He emerged from the space boat like a spider from an egg case, stood still and watchful, then unfolded his legs to their full length.

J.D.'s encounter with him, in the cave, had not given Esther any impression of his great size. His body, no longer hairy but iridescent, translucent, was rather small, but his crystalline legs were several meters long. He probably did not mass more than a human being, yet he stood much taller than Esther, taller even than Kolya.

Like a giant spider, the Representative picked his way across the tumbled plain.

Besides the jointed legs of ebony and amethyst and turquoise that had been visible to J.D. and her LTMs, he strode on legs of emerald, ruby, and diamond. His legs were solid near his body, only partly fused near their tips.

He hesitated before each step, as if he were footsore.

Behind him he left footprints of precious stones, a shining trail of uncut jewels and broken crystalline fibers.

As he walked, his leg tips cracked and shattered.

"Representative!" Esther ran toward him. "Stop, you're breaking!"

"Esther!"

She bounded past Kolya toward the Representative. He loomed over her; she had to lean back and look up to see him. He tilted his body, orienting himself toward her. She thought she could see eyes beyond the opalescent shell. He poised spraddle-legged and frozen above her.

Slowly he bent the joints in his legs, lowering his body to her level.

Kolya bounded to her side. They stood together, facing an alien representative of the interstellar civilization.

284

Esther trembled, so deeply and so hard that the steadiness of her own voice shocked her.

"Pieces of you are falling off!" she said. She glanced sidelong at Kolya. He set his jaw so hard his mustache bristled. He caught her gaze and looked away fast.

He isn't angry, Esther thought—he's trying not to laugh. Oh—oh, *shit!* That's probably exactly what the Representative is doing, taking a dump, and I just called the whole star system's attention to it.

Esther almost burst out laughing, too.

If I'm careful not to look at Kolya, she thought, both of us might pull off this meeting with a shred of dignity left. On the other hand, if the Representative pulls out the particle-beam guns . . .

"Is your shedding a normal function—er, activity?" Kolya asked.

Esther let her eyelids flicker just long enough to send code to the *Chi* and to *Starfarer*: What's going on, J.D.? Europa, help me out, would you?

A silent reply flashed before her.

You're doing fine, J.D. said.

I can't help, Esther, I'm sorry, Europa told her. No elder of the Representative's stature has walked free since I've known the Smallerfarthings.

"Great," Esther muttered to herself, and thought, He doesn't take a walk for four thousand years, and he has to pick *Nautilus*—!

She said to herself, He wants J.D.'s starship *bad*.

"It is a natural result of my venturing into gravity," the Representative said to Kolya. "But not, precisely, normal."

"Does it hurt?" Esther asked.

The opalescent sphere bounced a handsbreadth up, then sank again.

"Of course it hurts," the Representative said. "Can *you* lose parts of *your* legs without causing pain?"

"Only my toenail clippings," Esther said.

"We'll help you back to your boat," Kolya said. The quaver of amusement in his voice nearly pushed Esther over the edge.

"But I've just arrived," the Representative said. "The pain is not as unbearable as the rudeness of leaving so soon."

"Then we'll wait here with you," Kolya said firmly. "Until J.D. arrives and can greet you properly."

"But J.D. already greeted me."

"I thought you were returning her house call," Esther said.

"I came for that reason, and to give you a gift."

"The Farther worlds already gave J.D. guest water," Kolya said. "And the Nearer worlds gave her rainbow-fins. We couldn't take anything else, it would be greedy."

The Representative bent his jointed amethyst leg, held it a handsbreadth above the ground, placed it gingerly down.

"Mine is a rare and valuable gift," the Representative said. "Given at great cost. My own substance, which to you is precious jewels. Precious and rare."

His emerald leg gestured toward the trail of broken precious stones.

"We cannot possibly accept your toenail clippings," Kolya said.

"You mustn't injure yourself to give us presents," Esther said, controlling herself with more will power than she knew she had. "Besides, we don't have anything for you."

"My pain isn't important," the Representative said. "Only a free exchange of gifts and friendship and knowledge. Haven't I offered you a rich enough gift?"

He raised his emerald leg, let it hover, tapped it hard on a stone. Emerald segments fell away and bounced, glittering. The Representative jerked his leg-tip from the ground.

Esther's laughter vanished. She hated to see anyone

hurt that much. It must be in my damned *genes*, she thought dryly. Next I'll be trying to feed him chicken soup.

She found herself craning her neck to see him, and she took a backwards step.

Wait a minute, she thought.

Instead of letting herself be distracted by sympathy, Esther watched carefully. As the Representative put his leg down, he stretched forward. He shifted, balancing himself. When he stilled, his body hung closer to Esther.

He was edging toward her, entering her social distance till she backed away from him. He was herding her and Kolya toward one of the craters.

What? she thought. Does he think he can push us in?

Even if they fell, in the gravity of *Nautilus* they could scramble out again. They could probably jump out again. They would have to be tremendously unlucky to fall badly enough to get hurt.

She flashed a message to J.D., to Kolya.

I see what you mean. J.D.'s code appeared in Esther's visual field. Esther, Kolya, if you can, please don't let the Representative into the center of *Nautilus!* Don't endanger yourselves . . . but I'm afraid he'll destroy the knowledge surface. I'll be there soon.

"Still not sufficient?" the Representative said.

The Representative limped onto his emerald leg, but this time, Esther did not move out of his way. Kolya, too, held his ground.

The Representative had broken away all the thin fibers; now he walked on clusters of fist-sized jewels. Another handsbreadth higher on his legs, the clusters had fused into a single crystal.

He raised his ruby leg, and smashed it against a chunk of rock. The rock exploded. He struck loose segments of blood-red stone. Nerves and matrix hung loose. His joints convulsed, contracted, jerking his leg into a sharp, painful angle. Rubies lay amidst sharp gravel.

"Stop, please!" Esther said. "Why won't you stop?"

"My gift is insufficient."

"Will you stop if we take your gift?"

"No!" Kolya said. "Take *nothing* from him!"

The Representative raised his diamond leg. Shakily, his ruby leg still clenched, he balanced on only four supports. He positioned his diamond leg above the large sharp chunk of ruby.

Esther plunged forward and grabbed the diamond fibers as they struck toward the ruby cutting surface. The diamond edges ripped against her gloves. Air burst out. Water vapor froze instantly into ice crystals. The air dissipated, exploding the cloud of ice against Esther's faceplate. Her suit pressure dropped, then stabilized as the self-sealing function kicked in. The Representative's first leg joint struck her fingers, numbing them with the shock. The Representative struggled. He tried to jerk his leg free. Despite the pain in her hands, Esther held the cold diamond spike.

"Let me go! Let go! Do you—" The Representative's loud voice caught and faltered for the first time. "Do you want my whole leg?" A stream of pale yellow fluid oozed from the upper joint of his diamond leg.

He tapped Esther's shoulder with the sharp edge of his broken ruby leg-tip. The outer layer of fabric ripped with a sharp scream. The Representative raised his leg again.

Kolya lunged for the ruby leg, grabbing it, immobilizing the Representative.

"We want nothing from you!" Kolya said. "But if you hurt my friend you will *not* survive!"

The numbness in Esther's hands gave way to tingling, to sharp pain. Her gloves sealed against the surface of the diamond, pressing the sharp surfaces into the cuts. A warm trickle of blood ran down her fingers, into her palms, down her wrists.

The air pressure in her suit increased slowly.

"We want you to stop trying to give us gifts," Esther said. "We won't trade *Nautilus* for twenty-four dollars' worth of beads!"

The Representative grew very still. Esther looked up at Kolya. Ghostly behind his gilded faceplate, his face was pale, his expression grim.

"Your hands?" he asked.

"I don't know," she said. "I think I'm stuck to this guy."

"Now what?"

"Beats the hell out of me."

She was afraid to let the Representative go, afraid he would continue to crack himself to bits, afraid the sealant on her gloves would rupture again. The Representative remained preternaturally still.

Esther did not know what to do. She looked out into space, wishing J.D. would hurry. Largernearer loomed overhead. Esther felt cold and distant.

She picked out the *Chi*'s glint against the cloud-streaked blue surface of the planet. On Largernearer's dark limb, in the night, luminous patterns flickered across the sea. They wound through the clear spots, beneath breaks in the clouds. The distant, obscure disk of Smallernearer answered in kind: Electric blue sparks flowed over it.

Her bloody hands full of diamond, Esther wondered what the two worlds were saying to each other.

She wished they would give her a hint what to do.

J.D. felt helpless. The struggle between Esther and Kolya and the Representative went on, in miniature, in the center of the observers' circle. It reached an impasse.

"Oh, Christ in a canoe," Stephen Thomas said. "Look."

A second space boat floated free of the Four Worlds ship.

"Quickercatcher!" J.D. cried. "*What* is going on now? You've got to stop this!"

The Largerfarthing took a very long time to respond. In the transmission from *Starfarer*, the quartet huddled together, peering anxiously at a cluster of holographic images.

Behind them, Late lay so still he was almost invisible; his spines had flattened beneath his pelt. Two meerkats scampered around him. A third stood on a rock ledge above them, keeping watch.

A pattern of beach pebbles, grass blades, and glimmering beads lay on the ledge beside the meerkat.

"It's the Eldest," Quickercatcher said.

"The Eldest, of Smallerfarther," Longestlooker said.

"No one ever sees her," Fasterdigger said.

"No one but Smallernearer has ever seen her!" Sharphearer exclaimed.

They all spoke together; J.D. had trouble separating the information from their excitement and apprehension.

J.D. groaned.

The *Chi* entered orbit around *Nautilus* and prepared to descend.

But the second space boat was already landing.

The Eldest's boat fell toward *Nautilus*.

"Petrovich!" Kolya shouted.

Griffith saw everything that happened, heard everything that happened. Kolya cried out for his help, but it was too late.

Griffith groaned, in misery and confusion, folded up and held his knees against his chest, and hid his face. He cut off communication with the outside world.

Weightless, he tumbled slowly.

The desperation in Kolya's voice, when he cried out to Griffith, chilled Esther even through her shock.

Griffith did not respond.

The second boat landed.

The spatter of dust particles against Esther's helmet, against her suit, felt like a million tiny blows; it sounded like a sandstorm at hurricane force. She ducked her head, protecting her faceplate. She dreaded hearing a puncture of her suit. She could not protect herself. What she could do was keep herself from being blinded. A few dust grains scraped the faceplate, leaving bright-edged scars. But Esther could still see. She heard no hiss of escaping air, felt no drop in pressure.

She raised her head.

The bright pinpoint of the *Chi* streaked past, far above.

And the Eldest's ship had landed.

Kolya, too, had made it safely through the storm of the Eldest's exhaust.

"Now what?" Esther said, more to be sure her suit radio was working than because she hoped for an answer. "Representative! What's happening?"

In the shadow of his gilded faceplate, Kolya was tense and pale, his expression drawn into a grimace. He clutched the Representative's leg with a death grip.

"Kolya?"

"I don't know," he said. "I *don't know.*"

"I fear . . ." the Representative said, speaking for the first time in long minutes, " . . . you have bested me. So the Eldest has come."

The second boat puffed vapor, then split open. Inside, an adamantine glitter shifted.

Maybe Kolya can keep hold of the Representative. Esther's thoughts ran wildly forward. Maybe I can stop the Eldest. Are they going to send one person after another, till one of them gets past us and wrecks what J.D. wants most to keep?

"You have failed."

The new voice was a rusty monotone.

"Not yet, we haven't!" Esther said belligerently. "Do you call this civilized behavior?"

"I have failed," the Representative said, ignoring Esther. "I have failed, I have broken myself, I have spent my life."

Esther looked up, stunned.

The Eldest used English, she thought. I thought she meant me and Kolya. Doesn't she?

"A noble failure," the Eldest said.

The hard glitter within her ship shifted, then stilled.

"Join me," the Eldest said.

The Representative's legs jerked feebly.

"Let me go, youngests," the Representative said. "You've nothing to fear from me. Let me go."

"I can't," Esther said. Her palms stung violently, and her fingers cramped. She wanted to flex her hands, but she was afraid of breaking the sealant. At the same time she thought, How do we know we have nothing to fear anymore?

"I must join the Eldest," the Representative said.

"Don't move!" Kolya snapped. "Esther's suit might seal again, it might not. It's too dangerous."

He sounded himself; he had lost the desperate uncertainty of the last few minutes.

The Representative strained against Esther's hands. She gasped; the sharp, shattered fibers cut deeper into her wounded palms.

"I told you not to move!" Kolya shouted at the Representative. He jabbed upward with the ruby leg, as if it were a spear.

"Please, youngests, let me go," the Representative pleaded.

"I'm going to let your leg loose," Kolya said. "And then I'm going to pick up your body and carry you to our tent. When we're close enough for Esther to get inside safely, we'll let you loose."

The Representative quivered, but did not struggle.

292

"Do you understand me?" Kolya said.

"I understand. Please hurry."

Across the plain, the side of the Eldest's boat began slowly to knit.

"If you resist, I *will* break you."

"I understand."

Kolya slowly let loose of the long shank. The Representative stood stock-still.

Kolya lifted the Smallerfarthing elder from the ground. Esther followed the motion with her stuck hands. She clenched her teeth. Her knees felt shaky, and she saw everything at a distance. She moved along with Kolya as best she could. The tent stood only a hundred meters away, but the distance felt enormous.

"Please hurry," the Representative said.

"Shut *up*," Kolya snarled.

They reached the entryway of the expedition tent. Kolya lowered the Representative, who stood shakily on five legs.

"We'll free your hands and dive into the airlock," Kolya said to Esther. "When you're loose, push your hands together. Even if it doesn't seal, you ought to be all right. Understand me?"

"Uh huh."

He eased her fingers from the long shattered jewel of the Representative's leg. The sealant pulled away. Her hands came free. The air rushed out, deathly cold on her blood-wet wrists. She clamped her hands together, slowing the leak. The pressure on her palms was excruciating.

The Representative sprang away from them and limped toward the Eldest's boat, stumbling and awkward on his uneven legs.

With her last energy, Esther plunged into the tent's entryway. Kolya followed. The airlock closed and the small chamber repressurized.

"Damn that hurts!" Esther muttered. "Damn." She staggered. Kolya grabbed her.

"Just a minute more. A minute more, we'll be safe."

Air, warm, thick air, filled the entry tunnel. The inner door opened. Esther's knees gave out.

"It's all right," Kolya said. "*Slava bogu, boje moi, spasiba . . .*"

On the surface of *Nautilus,* the Representative spidered unevenly across the pitted ground. The Eldest's boat gaped, half closed—half open! The Representative probed with two front legs, found the aperture, slid two leg-tips inside. At his caress, the aperture eased. The Representative pulled the rest of his body inside.

The Eldest held herself across the width of the boat's interior. A geometric pattern of diamond spikes and threads nearly obscured her body, and her eyes. She stared at him steadily.

"I did not tell you why I called you to me," she said.

"No," the Representative said.

"What do you expect? What do you hope?"

"I've always hoped for your favor. I'm prepared to pay the price of your disappointment."

The boat quivered around him. He pressed his leg-tips against the spongy walls, bracing himself. His legs hurt, they hurt so much, they would hurt him forever.

Esther gasped when Kolya drew her mangled gloves from her hands. Blood and sealant and needles of diamond stuck them to her skin. They pulled free reluctantly.

You're lucky, she kept telling herself. Lucky. You could have lost your hands. You could have lost pressure entirely. You could be dead.

When she freed her arms from the suit, she almost fainted. She was covered with blood from the elbows down.

"What a mess," she said. Her voice felt far away. "That will take some cleaning up." She meant her space-suit.

Kolya slapped pressure bandages against her palms. They oozed into the cuts, stopped the bleeding, secreted a topical anesthetic, encapsulated dirt particles and small faceted diamonds and pulled them from the wounds.

Kolya helped her the rest of the way out of her suit and made her lie down. The blood did not faze him; he washed it from her arms.

He's probably seen a lot worse, Esther thought. A *lot* worse.

"Glad I wasn't wearing my jacket," she said. Her ugly fluorescent lime-green jacket hung on its hook in her cubicle.

What a dumb thing to say, she thought, I never wear my jacket inside a spacesuit.

Kolya blinked, his eyelids flickering for a long moment as he went into a communications fugue. Through her own link, Esther heard him reassuring their colleagues, then asking for a few moments of quiet and privacy.

"Lie still, be quiet," Kolya said. "You're in shock. You'll be all right." He covered her with a blanket. The warmth felt good.

"Thanks," she said.

"Little enough that I did," he said. "I panicked, like a raw recruit."

"Could have fooled me," she said. "We're okay, we still have *Nautilus.*"

Outside, a blast of dust scoured the tent wall: The Eldest's ship had taken off.

"And the Rep has given up."

A lower, more distant rumble swept beneath her. She bolted upright, afraid the Four Worlds ship had sent more invaders.

"What—?"

"It's just the *Chi*. J.D. will be here soon. Lie down."

"Kolya . . . what *happened* out there?"

"I *told* you," he said angrily. "I panicked!"

"No," she said. His distress broke her heart.

"I wanted Petrovich—Griffith—to behave in character, to blast in and destroy the invaders. To save us—" He laughed bitterly. "No matter what it would have meant to the future of Earth and Civilization." He fell silent.

Esther tried to think what to say.

"The one time I asked him to act, and he didn't," Kolya said, bemused. "There's hope for him yet."

He gave Esther a painkiller to augment the bandages' mild anesthetic. The drugs made her even dizzier.

"Everything's okay now," Esther said. "It worked out." She cast around for something else to say, some way to reassure him. "I'd hug you, only my arms feel kind of numb."

"What?" he said.

"I don't know. Forget it. I'm drunk. Don't you know better than to give drugs to a sick person? I don't care what you think, *I* think you were great out there."

He bent over her cut hands. His shoulders shook.

"Kolya?"

He glanced up. He was chuckling.

"It has been," he said, "longer than I care to think, since anyone called me 'youngest.' "

Esther grinned at him.

Kolya grew serious again.

"You're easy on me, my friend," he said. "Easy on me for what happened today, and hard on yourself for what happened back home. I think you should equalize the standards."

"I . . . I don't know. Maybe. I'll see how I feel when I'm not so drunk."

Kolya smiled. He hesitated. He leaned over and kissed her on the forehead.

• • •

The transport returned to *Starfarer*, returned its controls to Arachne.

The slow slide of the opening hatch vibrated softly. Griffith stiffened, his body ready for attack or defense. He kicked the bulkhead, by mistake. In free-fall, his abrupt motion sent him tumbling out of control. Adrenaline propelled his mind from deep, oblivious misery to alertness. He cartwheeled in the center of the observation chamber, out of reach of anything he could grab to stop his spin.

Infinity Mendez floated in the entryway, watching Griffith tumble and flail. Mendez kept his expression carefully neutral. Gerald Hemminge and Avvaiyar Prakesh hovered behind him.

Infinity launched himself easily from the doorway, sailed past Griffith, pushed him in a way that counteracted his spin, and brought himself to rest against the far wall.

Griffith glared. Instead of backing down, Infinity gazed at him with mild amusement that was worse than open contempt.

"You did right," Infinity Mendez said.

"I—What?" He knew better than to shake his head to clear it; the motion would make him even dizzier than he already was.

"Everything's all right. The Representative—" Infinity stopped, then shrugged and spread his hands. "I don't know exactly what the Representative did, or what the Four Worlds did, but they've left *Nautilus*."

"General Cherenkov?"

"He's okay." Infinity added, pointedly, "So's Esther."

Griffith used all his training to keep himself from showing any reaction.

"Listen." Infinity's voice held uncharacteristic anger. "You could have got my friends killed, and you didn't. I'm trying to thank you. Kolya's been trying to tell you

297

the same thing. Maybe you don't want to hear it, I don't give a damn. Thank you anyway."

Griffith hesitated. Strangely enough, he felt good.

"But I—" he said. He stopped. "I mean—you're, er, you're welcome."

In the expedition tent, J.D. waited patiently while Esther slept. The pilot's breathing was strong, her pulse steady, and her hands showed no sign of infection, poisoning, or allergic reaction.

Esther shifted beneath the fabric of the sleeping bag.

"J.D.," she said, abruptly wide awake. "Hi."

"Hi. How are you feeling?"

"Strange but okay. Drugged."

"An accurate perception."

Esther grinned.

"You were magnificent," J.D. said.

"Was I? What happened? I remember it all—but I don't know what it *meant*."

"I'm tempted to stomp Late like a rug till he tells me, but that wouldn't stand me in good stead with the alien contact guild."

"So maybe we'll never know?"

"Maybe."

"Damn."

Esther looked at her hands, at the transparent bandages cleaning and healing the wounds. A smear of dissolving blood lay just above the cuts. Above the bloody haze a constellation of bright irregular shards worked their way upward.

"Look," Esther said. "The Representative left me something to remember him by."

J.D. looked. "What—? Diamonds—!"

"Industrial grade, I bet," Esther said with a laugh. "Good souvenirs, though."

"I don't know . . ."

"What?"

J.D. shook off her unease. "I was thinking about gifts. The rituals we went through. I think they were benign— reciprocal. But I bet if you'd accepted the Representative's jewels, he would have made a claim on *Nautilus*."

"I wasn't even tempted," Esther said. "Isn't that strange? Because I'm going to have a hell of a time finding a job when—if—we go home. I could use a stake."

"I know," J.D. said sadly.

"Shall I collect these crystals and send them back to him?"

J.D. considered. "No," she said. She gestured toward Esther's diamond-scattered palms. "Those are no gift. You earned them. Keep them."

"I might have to give them to EarthSpace—or the U.S. government."

"Don't remind me."

"You aren't going to turn *Nautilus* over to them! Are you?"

J.D. hesitated.

"No."

"Good." Esther sat up. "J.D., I found water!"

"What, *here?*"

"Yes. Ice, I mean. Where Nemo's lungs were."

"That's—" Joy caught in her throat like champagne bubbles. "That's wonderful! That'll make it possible to start terraforming . . ."

I should have realized *Nautilus* must have water somewhere, J.D. thought. But I just haven't had time to *think* about it.

"Thanks for telling me."

"Didn't have a chance before."

Voices, their words muffled, rumbled through the fabric wall of the expedition tent.

"Who's here?" Esther asked.

Kolya tapped at the fabric door.

"Come in."

299

He leaned into the room. "Petrovich will—ah, you're awake, how are you?"

He came in, light on his feet in the negligible gravity. He sat on his heels beside Esther.

"I'll be fine," she said. "What about Griffith?"

"He'll be here soon."

"What's he coming here for?"

"I asked him to," J.D. said. "I have to go back to *Starfarer* for a little while longer—to stand on our friend Late, among other things. And I didn't want to leave Kolya here all alone."

"You aren't alone," Esther said to Kolya. "I'm here."

"You have to spend some time in the health center."

Esther looked at her hands.

J.D. thought, If she were a character in an adventure novel, she'd object. She'd insist on staying behind, heroically, to guard the starship, no matter what the risk to her health. And she *is* heroic.

J.D. prepared to argue.

"Oh, hell," Esther said. "I guess I'd better." She grimaced with disgust. "Griffith! Can you trust him?"

"I trust him . . . to do as Kolya asks," J.D. said.

"I may have broken him of that habit," Kolya said ruefully. "On the other hand, I believe he has decided—decided of his own will—to throw in with us."

Kolya gazed down at Esther. "Perhaps I'll let *him* stay here alone. And I'll come back to *Starfarer* with you."

"I wish you could."

"I won't be gone long," J.D. said, hoping it was true.

Victoria's image appeared in the tent. J.D. accepted the message and projected her own image back to the *Chi*, which perched on *Nautilus*'s surface a few hundred meters from the expedition tent.

"Griffith's here," Victoria said. "J.D., it's time to go home."

Eleven

J.D. and Satoshi helped Esther out of the transport. With her hands covered in bandage compound, she moved awkwardly in zero g.

As usual, half the people on board *Starfarer* were waiting to greet them.

I ought to be getting used to this by now, J.D. thought. I'd probably be right here with everybody else, wanting to hear firsthand what happened, even if I'd watched every minute of it while it was happening. If I weren't lucky enough to be in the vanguard.

Infinity Mendez moved through the crowd with uncharacteristic abruptness. He even pushed off against a couple of people when his forward momentum slowed.

He dragged his hand across the bulkhead and stopped in front of Esther. He took her gently by the shoulders and gazed into her eyes.

"You're all right," he said, part assertion, part question.

"Sure," she said.

He hugged her, being careful of her hands.

"Let's go home."

"Health center first," J.D. said. "Then home."

"Okay."

They made their way through the waiting room.

Florrie Brown joined them and went with them toward the exit.

J.D. let out her breath in a long, relieved sigh. She felt as if she had been holding her breath since leaving Largernearer, as if she had spent the last few hours struggling for air. The fear and the worry and the confusion lifted from her.

The Largerfarther quartet hurtled into the waiting room, a riot of bright fur and shining eyes and arms and legs. They grabbed for the walls and the doorway to scramble to a stop, and clustered solicitously around Esther. Infinity extricated his friend from their concern and vanished through the doorway with her and Florrie Brown.

Quickercatcher and the others turned their attention toward J.D. To her surprise, Late clung to Sharphearer's back as if nothing had happened. Europa and Androgeos followed them in. Europa was her usual elegant self, but another morning of excavating had left Andro grubby. His pleated white kilt showed the dirt much worse than Europa's homespun skirt, especially around the knees.

"J.D., it was so exciting!" Quickercatcher said, nudging her with his nose and taking her hand in his two-thumbed grip.

"It's good that Esther is all right," Fasterdigger said, his low voice rumbling.

"The Smallerfarthing Eldest—" Longestlooker said.

"Her visit is a great occasion!" Late's voice poured through J.D.'s link like warm honey. "A great occurrence, a great honor!"

"Did you have a nice nap?" J.D. asked Late, her tone prickly.

"A nap? Oh, no, I wasn't sleeping! I was in communication with the Representative and I had no attention left to spare. *You* know, you understand."

J.D. regarded him suspiciously. But it was true that when she involved herself fully in her expanded link, she perceived nothing through her other senses.

"I needed your advice," she said, unwilling to forgive Late so easily. "Yours, too, Quickercatcher. You're supposed to be *helping* us, I thought—"

"*I* am supposed to be helping you," Europa said. "And I was of no use either."

"That's sure true," Satoshi said.

"None of us had any advice to give," Longestlooker told them. "But now we have an invitation." She glanced at Quickercatcher.

"The Four Worlds invite Earth to join Civilization," Quickercatcher said. He made a thoughtful jut of his chin, and bristled his soft mauve whiskers.

J.D. exhaled with a "Huh!" of surprise. She started to accept, to agree, to shout in triumph. But she had no air left to speak with. She drew in a breath.

"Will you visit the Farther Worlds," Longestlooker said, "and participate in the ceremony?"

"We'll have to discuss it with our colleagues," Satoshi said.

"You can't reject the invitation!" Androgeos cried. "Don't you understand what this means?"

For once, J.D. agreed with the brusque younger Minoan. Satoshi was right . . . but J.D. longed for *Starfarer* to accept the invitation instantly, by acclamation.

"Please, Satoshi," Europa said. "Our friends are showing great confidence in us."

"I know it," Satoshi said.

"We aren't in charge," Victoria said. "However much we want to accept, however sure we are about accepting—we have to discuss it with everyone."

"Satoshi's quite right," Gerald said smoothly. "No single person, no single group, can make a decision of such importance."

"You must understand that, Longestlooker," J.D. said. "You and your siblings, you agree before you act."

"Usually." She gazed fondly at Europa, at Androgeos. "But we don't necessarily expect Earth human people to behave that way." The Largerfarthing blinked her eyelids from outer corners to inner, amused.

"Human people spawn unique situations," Quickercatcher said.

"Every one of them awkward," Androgeos said, with no humor at all.

"Andro—" J.D. was out of patience with him. She understood better why he was so aggravating, but the knowledge did not make him much easier to take. "You've given us a few awkward moments, too, you know."

"If we're so awkward," Stephen Thomas said, "why are we being invited to join Civilization?"

Both Gerald and Androgeos glared at him, but J.D. thought, I should have asked that question. We all should have.

"Because you are unique," Quickercatcher said.

"And that's enough?" J.D. asked. "You've told me each evolutionary system is unique. There's no hierarchy of uniqueness."

Longestlooker raised her chin, then ducked her head, thoughtfully.

"Our colleague from Smallerfarther gave us a good example to follow," she said. "We're risking ourselves for you."

"Why?" Stephen Thomas said again.

"Without risk," Longestlooker said, "there can be no achievement."

"Will you justify our risk?" Quickercatcher asked.

"I hope so," J.D. said. "But we all have to agree."

"Then let's go discuss it with everyone," Androgeos said.

"Not tonight," Satoshi said firmly. "Too much has happened. We're all tired and overwrought."

J.D. touched Arachne through her link. "I've proposed a meeting," she said. "For tomorrow." Seconds to the meeting had already begun to gather.

"Good," Satoshi said. "We'll sort things out then."

"Unless the Smallerfarthings have more surprises planned for us tonight," Stephen Thomas said, his humor badly timed.

Victoria walked down the long slope between *Starfarer*'s axis and the living surface. The crowd from the waiting room had dispersed, as everyone headed home to regroup. Victoria and Satoshi and Stephen Thomas straggled down the trail, apart from each other, the distance more than physical. Victoria wished she knew how to close it.

She lengthened her stride and caught up to Satoshi.

They reached the bottom of the hill. The trail was wide enough to walk three abreast. Victoria glanced at Satoshi; they closed the distance between them and Stephen Thomas. With Stephen Thomas on one side and Satoshi on the other, Victoria felt normal, as normal as she ever had since Merry died.

"The invitation surprised me," she said by way of making conversation.

"Is it sincere?" Satoshi said.

"I hope so!"

"It's another damned plan for them to get your work!" Stephen Thomas said.

Victoria grinned. "They could charge us dues. One algorithm's worth, for membership."

"But that's exactly what they do," Satoshi said, "if I understood Europa correctly."

"If it's in return for a full place in Civilization, they can have the algorithm with my blessings. And I'll say that at the meeting."

They reached the turnoff to their house. Stephen Thomas stopped, suddenly awkward. He stared down the main path. It led to the guest house.

"I guess . . ." he said, "I guess I'll see you at the meeting."

Victoria grabbed his hand, and Satoshi's.

"I think we should sort ourselves out before we try to help sort out *Starfarer*," she said. "Will you come home? Can we try?"

"Yeah," Stephen Thomas said.

Satoshi said nothing, which scared Victoria. She knew what he was thinking, and not saying: Sort ourselves out . . . if we can.

Victoria kissed him, and brushed her lips against Stephen Thomas's. The warmth of his skin startled and pleased her. She drew her hand down his cheek, along the side of his neck. The thin cool chain of his necklace was missing. She could not remember when she had seen him wear it last. That was strange.

"What happened to your necklace?" she asked Stephen Thomas. She stroked the gold pelt, smoothing it against his shoulder. "Did it chafe you?" Still, she was surprised he had taken it off. Merry had given Stephen Thomas the crystal of watermelon tourmaline. Stephen Thomas always wore it. It would look pretty against his dark skin and gold fur.

Stephen Thomas absently touched the hollow of his throat, where the crystal usually lay.

"I left it on Feral's grave," he said.

Shocked, Victoria let her hand fall. The distance between her and Stephen Thomas stretched to the horizon. Stunned, she started to tremble.

"Victoria? Are you okay?"

"Merry's necklace is gone?" Her voice quivered and her vision blurred.

"It isn't gone," Stephen Thomas said. "I left it—"

"Somewhere in the wild side, lying in the dirt!" Victoria's eyes stung and her throat burned with the effort of holding back tears. "The last thing Merry ever gave you—ever gave any of us!"

"If you wanted it," Stephen Thomas said, "I'd've given it to you."

"I didn't want it! I liked seeing you wear it. I wanted you—"

"Victoria," Satoshi said softly, "Victoria, stop, please."

"I don't understand—" Her voice broke.

"Jesus Christ," Stephen Thomas said. "I can't do anything right anymore, can I?"

He looked at her for a moment, his teeth clenched. Victoria tried to speak, but she was too hurt and angry. And she was afraid to cry in front of him again.

Stephen Thomas walked away from his partners, rigid with fury.

"Stephen Thomas!" Satoshi said. Stephen Thomas kept walking. Satoshi gripped Victoria by the shoulders. "Say something to him!"

"I can't," Victoria said. "I don't know what to say anymore."

Stephen Thomas flung his shorts onto the sand, plunged into the shallow sea, and swam away from shore. He flailed desperately through the water until his breath burned his throat and his muscles ached with exhaustion.

He stopped. He breathed in great sobs of air, dazzled by the light on the water all around him.

When he had caught his breath, he turned over and floated facedown, light from the sun tubes pouring hot on his back. He withdrew himself from the land, from everything that had happened beyond the soft boundary of surf.

On the sandy sea floor his shadow glimmered, broken into a mosaic by the motion of wind and wave and the long tendrils of seaweed that tickled his arms, his legs, his body.

He spread his fingers and let his hands drift beneath him. The swimming webs caught every small current. When he spread his arms, his hands moved from his shadow into sunlight—what *Starfarer* used for sunlight— and glowed a deep red-gold. He caught the light in his hand, cupped it, released it.

Starfarer's shallow ocean sound-sparkled around him, drawing a picture in his mind. The waves ran up the beach in a long crescendo. Artificial lungs, growing in an underwater pen, breathed steadily, stolidly. The pulsing wave generators throbbed within the end of the campus cylinder. Plus-spin, one of *Starfarer's* rivers gushed out into the sea, warm and brackish and silty, a soft whisper in the distance. The long strands of kelp hummed and sighed, like silk ribbons caressing each other in the wind.

He wished he could stay in the ocean forever, even in *Starfarer's* tiny, shallow, artificial sea. It gave him little comfort, but at least he would be alone. He could stop fighting, stop hiding his grief and his fear, stop inflicting his confusion on his partners. He thought he must be going crazy, and driving Victoria and Satoshi crazy with his descent.

Stephen Thomas raised his head to breathe. He combed the silver worm out of his hair and let the creature coil around his wrist. His hair drifted across his eyes. A breeze cooled his wet skin, but tears ran hot down his face. He ducked underwater again. The tears dissolved and vanished into the salt water of the sea. His hair fanned out across his shoulders.

A splash and slide from the direction of the beach revealed another swimmer. Stephen Thomas lay very still, moving only to breathe. He did not want to talk to anyone; he had chosen the deserted, weedy shore because so few people ever visited it.

He considered diving, disappearing, swimming away.

A sleek brown shape slid between the whisper of the kelp, quick and streamlined. A glitter of fish fled the shadow. Zev streaked beneath him, spinning, blowing bubbles that tickled him from knee to throat.

Zev broke the surface fast with barely a sound or a ripple, then slapped back into the water with an enormous splash. Stephen Thomas lifted his head just in time to get the wave across his face. He snorted and coughed and pushed his hair out of his eyes.

The young diver faced him, floating easily.

"What's wrong?" Zev asked.

Stephen Thomas took a deep breath, let it out, and sank. Underwater, in the kelp forest, the light blued. Small fish darted away, arrowing between the stems. Tiny snail shells clustered on the fronds.

Zev kick-dove and followed him underwater. He spoke: a long trill of clicks and squeals. Stephen Thomas understood the tone of concern, but the words were too fast for him to understand.

"Go away," Stephen Thomas tried to say in true speech, but his mouth filled with water and the water distorted his words.

Zev hovered before him, watching and waiting patiently till Stephen Thomas needed air.

They rose together. Stephen Thomas drew a long, deep breath. Salt and iodine, the smell of sea and kelp, tinged the cool air.

"What did you say to me?"

"I can taste your sadness." Zev hesitated. "You were crying. I can taste your tears."

Stephen Thomas felt himself blushing. The blush would not be obvious against his darkened skin.

"I didn't mean to embarrass you," Zev said.

"Don't divers have any sense of privacy?" Stephen Thomas snarled the words, infuriated by his own transparency.

"Not much," Zev said. "We don't have much to be private about . . . If I felt sad, I'd want someone to notice."

There was no point in challenging Zev's perceptions. Zev could see the heat of the flush of blood to his face. Stephen Thomas knew it, because Stephen Thomas could do the same thing.

"Why did you come here in the first place?" Stephen Thomas asked.

"To find out what's wrong."

"Not here. Not now. Why did you come on board *Starfarer*? Because of J.D.?"

"Partly," Zev said. "Mostly. But . . ."

"What?"

"I was bored."

"Bored!"

"Uh-huh."

"How could you be bored? J.D. talks about the wilderness like it's idyllic."

"It is."

Stephen Thomas waited. Zev remained silent.

He's already answered my question, Stephen Thomas thought. Idyllic . . . and boring.

"What do divers do all day?"

"We swim, we play, we take care of the kids, we catch fish."

"And at night you sleep the sound sleep of the righteous," Stephen Thomas said.

Zev ignored, or did not understand, the sarcasm. "No, divers don't sleep soundly at all. Not when we're in the water. You have to wake up and breathe every few minutes. So we drowse, and tell stories."

"When do you dream?"

"We don't."

"People have to dream, Zev. Otherwise they go crazy."

"We aren't crazy! There are a lot more crazy people here than back home!"

"Hey, take it easy. I just meant you must've dreamed so quickly you never noticed it. Something like that."

Zev's anger vanished as suddenly as it had come. He closed his copper-brown eyes, his long fair lashes brushing his smooth mahogany skin.

"I never dreamed, before I came on board *Starfarer*."

"But you drowsed . . . and told stories." Stephen Thomas wondered if the stories took the place of dreams. "Just the divers? Or the divers and the orcas?"

"Both. Our cousins tell more, they've been there longer. Millions of years longer."

"Telling million-year-old stories?"

"Yes."

"Hmm." Stephen Thomas restrained his skepticism. "Can't you tell stories from when you were still . . ." He did not want to say, "still human." The divers were human, but changed. He used Zev's way of describing the difference. "From when you were still ordinary?"

"I guess we could, but we never do." He considered. "That's funny, isn't it?"

"Maybe the stories are too painful. Estranged families—"

"But most of us know our land families. I know my grandparents, my mother's parents, they visit all the time. They're nice. I have an uncle and aunt and cousins. Who live on land, I mean." He sighed. "I hope they're all right, I hope they didn't get into trouble when the family went to Canada."

"They probably got a visit from the Feds," Stephen Thomas said. The divers had fled their wilderness home for asylum in Canada, rather than act as spies.

"I wish I knew if everybody got away all right." He hesitated. "I'm sure they did."

"You don't need to reassure *me*."

"I bet things weren't boring on the way to Canada. I wish I'd been there . . . but I'm glad I'm here."

"So's J.D.," Stephen Thomas said.

"Why are we talking about me?" Zev asked. "Everybody's worried about you."

Stephen Thomas eased back in the water, ducked his head beneath the surface, and straightened again. His hair slicked back from his face. He slipped the silver worm from his wrist and onto his hair.

Zev waited patiently.

"I have some things to think about," Stephen Thomas said.

"All by yourself?"

"Yes."

"You're still a lot like an ordinary human," Zev said. He did not mean it as a compliment.

"What would a diver do?"

"Talk about it. With your mother—"

"That isn't a choice I've got."

"I *know*," Zev said. "Nobody came to *Starfarer* with their parents. Nobody brought their children. It's weird."

That was not what Stephen Thomas had meant. He did not know his mother. He did not say so to Zev; that would have struck the young diver as the strangest thing Stephen Thomas had ever said.

"You should talk to your family, Stephen Thomas."

"I tried! You wouldn't understand."

"I thought I spoke English pretty well," Zev said. "You'll have to practice true speech more, so we can talk. Do you want to try French in the meantime?"

"I don't speak French. You speak English fine."

"We're talking about me again!" Zev said, exasperated. "Why won't you tell me what's wrong? Are you mad? Because I didn't know everything that would happen when you changed?"

"I'm not mad at you."

"Are you mad at J.D.?"

"That's . . . a complicated question." Stephen Thomas did not want to lie, flat out, to Zev—for one thing, Zev probably could tell he was lying, if he lied hard enough to make himself uncomfortable.

The trouble was, Stephen Thomas himself was not certain of the truth.

"No, it isn't," Zev said. "You're mad, or you're not. She thinks you are."

"It isn't that I'm mad," Stephen Thomas said.

"Then what?"

"I'm jealous of her!" Stephen Thomas shouted. He passed beyond embarrassment to humiliation. "Of her and Feral," he said. "I've never been jealous of anyone in my life, but I'm jealous of J.D. and Feral."

Zev frowned, startled and shocked.

"I told you you wouldn't understand," Stephen Thomas said. "Shit, *I* don't understand. I should be glad for them . . . For what they had."

"How can you be jealous of someone's friend?" Zev asked, baffled. "Besides, you were friends with Feral, too."

"I'm jealous because they were lovers!"

"No they weren't," Zev said.

Stephen Thomas made an inarticulate sound of frustration.

"She would have told me, if they were."

"Why?"

"Why not? Because she would. We talk about everything. Did she tell you?"

"She might as well have." It was the only explanation for the way she had reacted to his plan to read and edit and publish Feral's *Starfarer* journals.

"What if they *were* lovers?" Zev's voice was uncharacteristically sharp. "Why should *you* be jealous?"

Stephen Thomas regarded J.D.'s lover. Like every young man, Zev possessed his own unique combination of sophistication and naivete.

"For the same reason you are, Zev," Stephen Thomas said. "Only Feral's gone. You still have J.D."

Shocked, Zev kicked hard, arched his body, and dove backwards out of sight.

Stephen Thomas did not see him again, and when he stopped treading water and let himself sink into the sea, Zev's sound signature vanished in the distance.

"Shit," Stephen Thomas muttered. He had hurt Zev. He had done it deliberately, out of his own pain. But all he could feel was relief that Zev was gone, that he was alone again.

He floated on his back. He let all the air out of his lungs and sank just beneath the surface. The light of 61 Cygni glittered on the low waves, dazzling him.

J.D. sprawled in the squishy fabric chair in her office. She had so much work to do, but she was too drained to begin.

She should find Quickercatcher and have another long talk. She should try again to persuade the Largerfarthing that the fossils were props for a performance, pieces of art in their own right. The Four Worlds were going to be massively disappointed when they finally learned—finally accepted—the truth. J.D. wondered what members of the interstellar civilization did when they were massively disappointed . . . or massively angry.

And she should clear everything up so she could go to *Nautilus*.

A flicker of motion caught her eye.

Zev stood uncertainly in the doorway.

J.D.'s mood lightened.

That's what it felt like the first time I saw the quartet, she said to herself, with surprise. It felt like seeing Zev. Like seeing someone I love.

"I thought we talked about everything," Zev said.

His voice held an unnatural note. She had never before heard suspicion in the voice of any diver. Everything was so open, between people in the sea. They had given up privacy in exchange for trust.

"I thought we did, too," she said mildly.

"Then why didn't you tell me about Feral?"

"Tell you what?" she asked, confused. They had talked about Feral several times.

"That you were lovers."

"Who told you that?"

"What difference does it make?" Zev exclaimed.

"Who on *Starfarer* makes up silly rumors and spreads them around?"

His stiff stance eased. He looked sleeker, calmer: The hair on his arms and shoulders smoothed from its bristly tension.

"Makes up rumors?" he said. "Makes them up!"

"I liked Feral," J.D. said. "And he was very attractive. I probably would have slept with him—made love with him—if the subject had come up. It didn't. If it had, I probably would have told you about it—if the subject had come up. Would it have made a difference to you?"

She pushed herself from the chair, wishing again for time to replace it with something less engulfing, less awkward. She wished, too, for the grace and ease of being in the water. In the sea, the subject never *would* come up, because there would never be any mystery to begin with. Everyone would know if she and Feral had made love, and no one would think another thing about it, except to be happy for them.

"Would it have made a difference to you?" she asked again.

"I don't know," he said.

He put his arms around her and hugged her very tightly.

"I don't know!"

He kissed her fiercely. She could feel his arousal against her, through his shorts and the genital pouch.

She kissed him back, but she felt uneasy.

She was used to gentleness from Zev, not frantic intensity. He fumbled at the hem of her shirt, pulling it free and reaching beneath it, straining to reach her breast, awkward, ripping the material at the base of one of the buttons.

"Hey, stop it."

"I want—"

"I *don't.*"

She pushed his hand down.

He was strong, but it was not in Zev to use his strength against her. He stepped away from her, hurt and confused.

"I can't just run down to the corner and get a new shirt," she said, annoyed. She straightened her clothes, fingering the torn fabric as if the damage might heal.

"Sure you can. There's lots, some anyway, I saw them when I went looking for something that didn't rub my fur off."

"Not a new *old* shirt," J.D. said, ignoring inconsistency. "Who told you Feral and I slept together?"

"Stephen Thomas," he said.

"What!"

The confusion and embarrassment she had been feeling transmuted in a blaze to anger.

"J.D., it's all right," Zev said quickly. "I believe you."

"It isn't all right!" J.D. said tightly. "He lied about me, he hurt you—"

It hurt even worse for Zev to affirm his trust in her than for him to be suspicious of her in the first place.

"Where is he? When did you see him last?"

"Swimming. In the bay with the pen for the artificial lungs."

She dragged a mask and flippers from a box of equipment and headed for the door.

"Where are you going?"

"To talk to Stephen Thomas." Maybe I'll drown him, too, she thought.

"I'll come with you."

"That isn't a good idea."

"When will you come home?"

"I don't know."

She plunged out of the house, untidily tucking in her shirt-tail, fingering the rough edge of fabric where the button hung loose.

• • •

J.D. pulled an artificial lung out of the enclosure, arranged it on her back, and swam straight out from the beach. She made no effort to approach Stephen Thomas silently, no effort to surprise him. She wanted him to know she was here.

He lay in a dead-man's float.

"Stephen Thomas!" When he did not respond, she ducked her head and said his name in true speech.

She surfaced beside him.

He jerked his head up and gasped a long deep breath as he flung himself backwards and around and flailed into motion.

Did I scare him? J.D. wondered. Good. I hope I did.

She swam after him, catching up easily, her strong smooth stroke cutting through the water with barely a splash.

"Stop, dammit!"

He kept swimming. "Why? Pace too much for you?"

She stayed beside him, even when he dove deep.

J.D. swam easily underwater. Eventually, *Starfarer's* best natural athlete would realize he could not outdistance a practiced long-distance swimmer.

He flailed away from her. J.D. was mad enough to let him drive himself to exhaustion. He surfaced; she stayed underwater. She turned over; when he dove again he came face to face with her.

Bubbles burst from his mouth, obscuring and muffling his exclamation.

Whatever he said, it was not true speech.

Stephen Thomas stopped, hovered, then let himself rise.

J.D. followed.

They surfaced together, J.D. smoothly, Stephen Thomas with an angry splash. Out of habit he raked his hands back through his hair, but the silver mutualist had held his ponytail in place. He was breathing hard

J.D. pushed her mask to the top of her head.

"Why did you tell Zev I slept with Feral?" J.D. asked. "You upset him terribly. And you're making Victoria and Satoshi so unhappy. Fox is moping like a lovesick schoolgirl—"

"A spoiled rich kid is more like it, somebody ought to tell her to grow up—"

"And so is Florrie."

"Why is everybody blaming *me?*" Stephen Thomas yelled.

"I'd like an explanation."

"I want some fucking privacy," Stephen Thomas snarled. "First Zev, now you—"

"Come to shore," J.D. said. "I want to talk to you."

"We can talk out here."

"No, we can't."

"Why not?"

"Because you don't know enough true speech to understand how angry I am."

She pulled down her mask, back-stroked into a turn, flipped over, and settled into a strong freestyle stroke.

She swam ten meters before Stephen Thomas followed. He swam as if he were slapping and punching the water.

J.D. reached the shore well ahead of him. She threw the lung back into its pen, then crossed the hard wet beach. Above the high water line, rough beach grass grew in clumps in hot dry sand. The grass tangled around the twisted roots of one of Crimson's monumental pieces of artificial driftwood. She let herself dry in the warm sunshine, in no hurry to cover herself. What did it matter what Stephen Thomas thought of her stocky body? She already knew he could not stand the idea that she found him attractive.

He strode out of the ocean, flinging water from his mahogany body like silver rain. He was unusually tall for a diver, and his sapphire eyes gave him a wild look. He swiped at his pelt with the edge of his hand, currying the water from his chest, his belly, the thicker hair over his genitals.

Turning away, J.D. sat on the gnarled root of the drift-wood stump. The warmth of the splintery wood soaked into the backs of her thighs, and the scent of weathered cedar surrounded her.

Stephen Thomas let himself slump in the natural chair of another twisted root.

"So talk," he said, his tone hard.

J.D. pretended calm, but when she spoke her voice shook.

"We've got to work out our difficulties directly."

He remained silent, not making what she wanted to say any easier, piercing her with the blue knife of his gaze.

She took a deep breath. "Don't spread any more stories about me. You hurt Zev, you made him think I didn't trust him. It isn't his fault—"

"Sure it is," Stephen Thomas said.

"But he didn't mean to make you into a diver!" J.D. said, "He'd never hurt anyone deliberately. I'm sure you didn't mean to hurt him but—"

Stephen Thomas looked away. "I did mean to."

"You—" His admission shocked her. "How *could* you—?"

Stephen Thomas shrugged. "I was pissed off."

"Why do you hate me so much? I'm sorry I—stop taking it out on Zev! We've *got* to stop making everybody miserable."

"Just make each other miserable, huh?" Stephen Thomas laughed harshly, sarcastically. "Jesus Christ, what a bunch of primates. We sneak around behind each others' backs, lying to each other, pretending we're so honest and civilized!"

"Sneak around! I don't know—" Her anger dissolved in an abrupt, embarrassing blush. "Oh, no, Stephen

Thomas, I thought you knew about . . . about me and Zev and Victoria. It was . . ." She stopped. She had been about to say it was not serious, it was all in fun, for play.

But for her it was serious, and she longed to spend time with Victoria again.

"I'm sorry!" she said. "We didn't keep it from you on purpose. And it's still no excuse for you to lie about me!"

He left her completely confused. He had seen her and Victoria embrace, he could not be so oblivious—

Stephen Thomas stared at her, his pale eyebrows drawn together, his eyes narrowed.

"I *did* know, what does that have to do with anything? And what the fuck do you mean, I lied about you?"

"You told Zev that Feral and I slept together!"

"Why not? You want everybody to tell the truth—"

"It isn't true."

"But I—you—"

"I didn't sleep with Feral."

"Oh." Stephen Thomas sounded uncertain. "I thought you did."

"Why?" she asked, astonished.

"Because you were so embarrassed when I found his notes. What other reason—Why *were* you so embarrassed?" He let his eyelids flicker.

"Come back!" J.D. said. "Don't go wandering off into Arachne now! *Didn't* you read his notes?" Relief surged over her.

She would be sorry if Feral's work was lost, locked irretrievably in Arachne. But she was glad at the same time, glad Stephen Thomas could not read Feral's description of her schoolgirl crush.

"Sure I did," Stephen Thomas said. "Most of them. When you acted so embarrassed, I didn't—" His webbed hands clenched, and his toes dug into the tree root, claws shredding bits of wood. "I couldn't face reading the file about you. About you and him. I thought. I . . ."

Downcast, he leaned forward, wrapped his arms around his legs, and hid his face against his knees. "Shit, J.D. . . . I'm sorry. I am so sorry." His voice was muffled.

J.D. tried to remember any other time when he had looked uncertain, when he had admitted he was wrong— or when he had been wrong. Or when he had apologized.

"Even so," J.D. whispered. "Why did you try to hurt Zev?"

"Because I thought you got to love Feral and I never had the chance. I couldn't stand—I wanted . . ." His voice fell to a whisper. "Oh, god, I wanted somebody else to be as unhappy as I am, and Zev was in the way . . ."

Angry and humiliated, she could barely hear him. Her eyes stung. She wiped away tears with the heel of her hand.

"It was you Feral loved," she said softly. "It was you he wanted."

He raised his head and looked at her. The mistrust in his expression broke her heart.

"Read what he wrote," she said dully. "I think it's important for you to read that file."

As he lowered his head again, his eyelids flickered. The taut muscles across his shoulders relaxed and he went into a communications fugue.

J.D. rose, brushed the sand off her skin, and climbed into her clothes. Her worn cotton shirt lay soft against her skin, but the new canvas pants from *Starfarer's* stores were still stiff and scratchy.

She walked to the water's edge, folded her arms across her breasts, and stared out across the starship's small ocean. On the slope of the seaward end cap, fog rolled down the side of the glacier that helped power the weather systems. Tiny waves, artificially generated, stroked her toes. Her feet pressed into the hard wet sand. Full of life and potential, the sand vibrated against her soles.

A larger wave washed in, swirling around her ankles, soaking her pants cuffs. The wind freshened. J.D. shivered and let the metabolic enhancer cut in.

I wonder what Feral wrote, J.D. thought. I wonder . . . what he said about me.

Feral had a sweet nature, but he did not soft-pedal what he wrote. He would not go out of his way to make fun of her, of anyone, but if someone made a fool of herself, he would not hesitate to describe the incident.

Feral had teased her, when they talked about Stephen Thomas. It was gentle teasing, teasing without malice.

I could just as well have teased him back, J.D. thought. Why didn't I?

She answered her own question: because he wasn't embarrassed about being attracted to Stephen Thomas, and I was. Feral went along with what he felt, and I . . . I didn't want to admit to being so predictable. I didn't want Stephen Thomas to think I was just like everybody else, overwhelmed by his beauty and blind to any other quality he has.

Stephen Thomas had been silent for ten or fifteen minutes, surely enough time to read Feral's last file.

She walked up the beach, crossing cold wet sand to the high water mark, then scuffing her feet in the hot dry sand. She was glad of the warmth.

Stephen Thomas remained as she had left him, sitting on the cedar root, leaning forward, staring at the sand. But now his eyes were open. His long dark fingers moved, delicately picking out tiny shells, placing them in a precise pattern, the outline of a maze. His hair had dried in stiff salty curls. The silver worm adjusted, tightened, kinked around the tangled strands.

Stephen Thomas dashed the pattern away, scooping up the shells in the amber webs and flinging them into the roots of the downed cedar. They clicked against the wood, rattled as they fell, caught in cracks and rootlets, and scattered on the sand.

J.D. sat on her heels beside him. He raised his head. She steeled herself. Now he knew how she felt about him. She would have to go through all the embarrassment, all over again.

But his expression held no amusement, no pity, not even the resignation of an attractive person faced with turning away one more unwelcome advance.

Sadness filled his face.

"I've fucked up so bad. I didn't take time for Feral, I thought we'd always have time. I embarrassed you, I hurt Zev, Dr. Thanthavong's scared to let me in the lab, and Victoria and Satoshi . . ." He did not even try to explain what was going on among the partners. "God, J.D., I must be nuts." He scrubbed his hands across his face. "I miss Merry so much . . ."

"Tell me," she said. "About Merry."

He glanced at her with a mix of grief and confusion. "Merry? Merry wanted me as a partner—not just a lover, a partner—before we ever met. Without knowing . . . what I look like." Stephen Thomas smiled, and his grief lifted for a moment as he remembered. "That never happened to me before. Merry was interested in everything. Not many people read genetics journals, and fewer people outside the field write you about them. We corresponded. Real letters. Merry used an antique fountain pen, isn't that weird? Then I was up in the northwest, for a seminar, and Merry asked me out, and we met . . ."

His voice shook. He paused, gathering himself again. He whistled softly through his teeth.

"I never felt like that about anybody before. Or since, till Feral. We rode around on that fucking motorcycle—have you ever ridden a motorcycle?"

"No."

"It's fun. Jesus, it's exhilarating. It's dangerous, but, god, you think it's worth it. Until it catches up with you . . ." He stared at nothing, at something invisible, his gaze unfocused, then squeezed his eyes shut and returned from wherever he had been. "We rode around till dawn, we stopped at Merry's favorite view spots. We looked at the city and the mountains and the sound. Every time we stopped, we made out."

He shifted his body, quickly, jerkily, as if to throw off energy and feelings he was not prepared to face. As he crossed his legs, the pink tip of his penis appeared from within his genital pouch, and vanished again. J.D. pretended not to notice.

"In the morning, we went home, and I met Victoria and Satoshi."

J.D. smiled fondly, recalling the affection among them before their current—and, she thought, she hoped, temporary—differences and difficulties.

"I bet you fit right in," she said. "When I first saw the three of you—"

He laughed, the first time J.D. had heard him laugh with real humor since Feral died.

"Fit in!" He laughed so hard he gasped on the words. "I guess not?"

He wiped the tears of laughter away with the back of his hand. His eyes were bright, the pupils dilated.

"Victoria and Satoshi thought I was . . . a one-shot. One of Merry's fancies, we used to call them. Merry had a taste for a beautiful body or a pretty face. Preferably both in the same package. Not necessarily much up here." He tapped his temple with his forefinger. "So I was kind of unusual. I mean, I didn't know this at first, but the reason Merry wrote to me was because I fit the plan for the partnership. The fireworks were a surprise." He grinned. "To both of us."

"What about Victoria and Satoshi?"

"I wanted to join the partnership. I wanted to be in Merry's life, permanently. And I liked Victoria and Satoshi. So I had to . . ." He opened his hands, palm up, and spread his fingers wide. Light poured between them. The capillaries formed a delicate tracing. "I had to seduce them, if you want to know the truth." He added, wondering, "It was fucking hard work."

J.D. held back the urge to suggest he intended the pun, but she had to smile. She wondered if Stephen Thomas had ever had to go out of his way to seduce anyone else in his life.

"And I fell in love with both of them," he said sadly. "But now I've fucked things up so good, I doubt they even want to talk to me, much less let me try to seduce them again."

"Maybe you should let them seduce you," J.D. said.

"After what happened, they wouldn't want to."

"Did you fight?"

"Yes. No. I don't know. It all started when I mentioned Merry, and Victoria started to cry, and I . . . It's like there was somebody else inside my skin. I panicked." He raked his hands through his hair, making the tangles tighter rather than unsnarling them, and knocking loose the silver worm. It curled around the end of his thumb, just above the edge of the swimming web. "All she needed was for me to hold her, and I ran out like . . ."

At a loss, he shrugged. He slipped the silver worm off his thumb and straightened it before it could curl up into a tight spring. He held its ends delicately between his fingertips. Light sparkled off the worm's silver segments as it twisted and writhed. Stephen Thomas put it in his hair. It struggled, trying to find its proper place, coiling into the unkempt strands.

"Maybe if you talked to her, if you apologized—"

"I've tried to talk to her! Dammit, give me *some* credit. I behaved like an idiot, but I tried to work out . . . whatever it is that's wrong. Every time we try again things get worse!"

"What about Satoshi?"

"We haven't fought, not exactly. But . . . I don't think he can stand to touch me anymore."

"Oh—!" J.D. made a sound of protest and disbelief.

Stephen Thomas ran his hand down his thigh, smoothing his short pelt, letting his fingers rest just above his knee.

"The last time he touched me . . . he froze."

"And—?"

"And nothing. I felt like shit anyway. I said I wanted to sleep alone and he went away and . . ." He shrugged, and said again, "And nothing. That was back at Tau Ceti."

"Maybe he was just surprised. You've gone through a lot of changes. Maybe he needs some time to get used to them. Not to mention," J.D. said dryly, "the opportunity."

"Maybe . . ." A hopeful note crept into his voice.

"Why don't you go home—"

"They might not even want me home."

"I can't believe that's true!" Her annoyance and frustration snapped out. "I think they aren't sure you want to come back!"

Without making a physical move, Stephen Thomas abruptly withdrew from the subject.

"It isn't your problem." His tone was so offhand and careless that J.D. sat back, startled and confused. "I don't know why I'm dumping it on you. And Zev. I'll apologize to Zev." His eyelids flickered briefly. "There. I sent him a message, I'll talk to him as soon as—and Victoria and Satoshi and I—we'll work things out."

He smiled at her.

Any other time, J.D. would probably have fallen for his charm. She probably would have agreed that everything was all right, everything was going to be all right.

That's how he uses his charm, she thought. That's how he's developed it. For smoothing things over, for making them come out right. And usually it works.

His attempt to dismiss a difficult conversation offended her. She knew, though, that if she snapped at him again he would withdraw even farther.

"You told me because I asked," she said. "And because I didn't just ask to hear you say, 'Things are fine, J.D., everything will work out fine.' You hardly ever talk about your other partner—"

"It's been a year! I should be over Merry's death by now!" he said angrily. "Why'd you ask me, anyway, why didn't you mind your own business?"

"Because you said, 'I miss Merry so much.' "

"I did not."

"I'm sorry, Stephen Thomas, you did. We were talking about Feral, and you said—"

"Oh, god." His voice was a groan. "I did." The look in his eyes was that of a fighter punched in the head. "Victoria thinks I don't even care that Merry died," Stephen Thomas whispered. "She thinks I cared more about Feral. I did care about Feral, but—"

Stephen Thomas collapsed. He fell forward on his knees, his head down, his hands clenched till his fingernails dug into his skin. He shuddered, violently, silently.

J.D. flung her arms around him and held him. He folded in on himself as if he had to hold his heart inside. His breath came in ragged gulps.

After a long time, the shuddering exhausted him. His body quieted. Every few minutes, without a sound, he quivered in her arms like a wounded animal, like a racehorse with a shattered leg.

Slowly, gradually, he relaxed. He put his arms around her and rested his head on her shoulder. She stroked the back of his neck. She teased the silver worm till it wrapped around her finger. She smoothed his tangled hair, then let the worm curl back into place.

Stephen Thomas leaned against her, his body hot against hers.

He buried his face in the curve between her neck and shoulder.

At this moment, she could have him. She knew he felt as she had felt before Zev came on board *Starfarer*: as if he were starving to death through his skin. But his desperate hunger and loneliness had nothing to do with her, and she was too proud and too stubborn to respond to it. To take him.

Too proud and too stubborn, she thought. And too dumb.

"Stephen Thomas," she said softly. "Stephen Thomas, let's go home. I'm sure Victoria and Satoshi want to see you."

He sat back, letting her go. She dropped her arms to her sides. Her shirt stayed warm from his body.

"I can't fix it anymore," he whispered. "I can't."

"Of course you can't!" she said, without thinking, her response purely visceral.

"But I *did*," he said. "I always did before. When Merry died . . . I *could* help. I listened, I held them when they cried—" His voice rose and his eyes burned blue in his dark face.

"I believe you," J.D. said. "You got your partners through a tragedy. Victoria told me she never would have made it without you. But . . . who helped you?"

"I don't need—"

"You kept your partnership from collapsing!" J.D. said angrily. "Are you going to wreck it now because you *don't need*? My god, no wonder Victoria thinks you didn't care!"

He opened his mouth to retort, then closed it.

A moment later he said shakily, "I don't know what to do."

"I can't tell you," J.D. said. "But I think going home would be a good start."

J.D. waited at the gateway of the partnership's garden until the arched door of the house closed behind

Stephen Thomas. She picked a fragrant carnation and carried it with her.

As she approached home, Zev hurried onto the porch. The front door banged. Uncertain, Zev stopped.

"I heard from Stephen Thomas. He said he's sorry, he wants to talk."

"He didn't mean to lie to you," J.D. said. "He misunderstood something."

J.D. walked straight to Zev and put her arms around him.

"I love you so much."

"I love you, too." He hugged her. "I don't understand the way I felt. Stephen Thomas said I was jealous, but I don't think—" He drew back to look in her eyes.

"It doesn't matter," J.D. said. "It's all right now."

Stephen Thomas stopped just inside the door.

Victoria and Satoshi sat at the kitchen table. Neither had eaten much, though dinner was a rice and tuna and vegetable casserole that Victoria made, not for special occasions—it was too plain, she said, so plain that people teased her about the mythical blandness of Canadians—but for family times. It *was* plain, but it never had any leftovers.

Victoria and Satoshi had set a place for Stephen Thomas at the table.

"Stefan-Tomas." Satoshi was the only person ever to make up a pet name that Stephen Thomas liked.

He suddenly felt hopeful, and even more scared. He felt the beginning of the terrifying shudder that had taken over his body back on the beach.

Victoria hurried to his side. "What's wrong?" She took his hand and drew him toward a chair. "Come sit down, eh? Then you'll be all right, you'll feel better—"

He tightened his hand around hers.

"No!" he said fiercely. "I'm *not* all right. Don't tell me what I feel, Victoria, not any more. I love you. I believe you love me, if I haven't screwed that up—"

"No!" she said, as fiercely as he. "You haven't, of course you haven't—"

"—but you don't know how I feel!"

"Neither of us does," Satoshi said. "You have to tell us."

Stephen Thomas loosened his death-grip on Victoria's hand. He must have hurt her, yet she left her hand in his, still and trusting. Satoshi put his hand on Stephen Thomas's arm, slid his fingertips down the soft pelt, and entwined his fingers tentatively in Stephen Thomas's webbed hand.

"I miss Merry," Stephen Thomas said to his partners, for the first time since their eldest partner died.

His body shook. The trembling had never stopped, he had only managed to suppress it. It rose and expanded from his core, taking his body out of his control, scaring him breathless. He wrapped his arms around himself, bending forward, struggling for air. He receded from his perceptions: Victoria froze in shock and surprise, then held him and whispered to him, soothing nonsense words. Satoshi drew away and Stephen Thomas groaned, at the edge of panic and despair. Satoshi returned to him, embraced him, completing the partnership's small broken circle.

"We're here," Satoshi said. "I'm here."

Victoria and Satoshi led Stephen Thomas to the couch and sat on either side of him, cuddling him. Their warmth and love soaked into him like sunlight, like cosmic rays, illuminating and warming the chill that shook him, softening and melting the cracked glass wall. Stephen Thomas felt free, and vulnerable, and terrified, and hopeful.

The terrible shuddering finally eased.

"I miss Merry," Stephen Thomas said again. "I miss Merry so much . . ."

Stephen Thomas talked about Merry for an hour. He told his partners what he had told J.D., and more, as he had not been able to tell them while they too were grieving. And he talked about Feral. Meeting Feral was the first experience to get through his glass wall since Merry died.

"Then when Feral died, too . . ." Stephen Thomas tried to explain the glass wall. He had never told his partners, or anyone else, about the glass wall. "It was like I was closed in all over again, squeezed—"

The words spilled out of him as if he could not even stop to take a breath. Victoria listened. Sometimes she cried, but when the tears streamed down her face they were in response to his pain instead of drawing her desperately away to face her own. She gripped Stephen Thomas's left hand. Satoshi, more tentatively, held his right. Stephen Thomas remembered the wonderful times and the terrifying times of his courtship of the family, when he had feared he would never persuade Victoria and Satoshi to consider him.

"I never was sure," Stephen Thomas said, "why you finally decided I had more than two neurons to rub together."

"We never thought that!" Victoria said.

"You *still* think I don't—?"

"You know what I mean."

He grinned. Victoria smiled back.

"We were pretty impressed," Satoshi said, "the first time Professor Thanthavong called you."

"Miensaem's not immune to a pretty face and a beautiful body," Victoria said. "Not any more than Merry was."

"Probably not, but that isn't how she talked to him."

"She's never made a pass at me," Stephen Thomas said. "She's the only boss I've ever had who didn't."

"It's quite a shock, to come home and find a Nobel laureate virtually sitting in your living room. After you introduced us . . ." Satoshi shrugged. "Pretty shallow of me, but that's when I started to realize what Merry saw in you."

Stephen Thomas gazed at Satoshi for a long moment. "Can you, still? Is there any chance?"

Satoshi hesitated. "I've felt so weird. About the changes in you. If you can give me some time . . ."

"I'll change back," Stephen Thomas said abruptly.

"Would you? Do you want to?"

"Yes. No." He spread his right hand in Satoshi's fingers, stretching the swimming webs, pressing them against Satoshi's skin. "I don't want to. At first I was afraid to try. Shit, my medical records are squashed to mush."

"Miensaem said she could do a reduction comparison. She could just take out the diver genes."

"She could get close. But she can't swear I'd change back exactly! Nobody can, not till we go back to Earth."

"I don't understand why you want to *be* this way," Satoshi said.

"I like it," Stephen Thomas admitted. "It's interesting. It's a challenge."

He released his hold on Satoshi. Like Victoria, Satoshi left his hand resting against Stephen Thomas's fingers.

"But it isn't worth losing you," Stephen Thomas said. "Fuck, yes, I'd change back, I'd risk it. In a hot wet second."

"That's a big step to take before Satoshi's sure!" Victoria stroked his forearm, the delicate pelt, and reached across him to touch Satoshi's knee. Her nipples hardened beneath her cotton shirt. Any other time—any time before Stephen Thomas had begun to change—the partnership would already be halfway to one of the bedrooms. If they made it even that far.

Satoshi stared at the floor, rubbing the ball of his bare foot back and forth against the rock-foam tiles, flexing his toes. Stephen Thomas unconsciously flexed his foot as well, felt his claws extend, relaxed and retracted them just as they tapped the floor, before they scraped against it.

His pulse quickened, with arousal in the presence of Victoria's excitement, with fear in the face of Satoshi's apprehension.

I'm afraid Satoshi will stand up, bolt—but that isn't Satoshi's style, Stephen Thomas thought. That's more like something *I* would do.

This time, he would not bolt.

"I love you," he said. "Tell me what you want."

Satoshi raised his head. Concern shadowed his dark eyes.

"Victoria's right," he said. "Changing back is too much to ask this soon." He took a deep breath. "We could try . . ."

Eager, apprehensive, Victoria rose and led her partners down the hall, and into the comfortable clutter of Stephen Thomas's room.

The faint smell of sandalwood hovered in the air. Victoria let her hand slide through his; she left his side long enough to light a new stick of incense. The heavy scent flowed around them like a cloak.

Victoria pulled her shirt off, unzipped her jeans, and pushed them down over her hips till they lay in a tangle on the floor with her sandals. Stephen Thomas knew every line of her intense body, every curve and hollow. He was trembling; he wanted to fall on his knees before her and spend the rest of his life giving her pleasure.

"Now you," she said, challenging him with her voice, her stance.

He took off his blue silk t-shirt, as self-conscious, as nervous, as the first time he had made love with all three of the partners together. Merry had been there, Merry had led, and guided, cried out in ecstasy and moaned with effort and joy. Now Stephen Thomas felt alone. He was all too aware of Satoshi, very near but holding back.

VONDA N. MCINTYRE

He pulled off his shorts and let his partners see his diver's body naked, at close range, for the first time.

"You're just as beautiful," Victoria said. "But . . . it's like you're not even naked."

Stephen Thomas glanced at Satoshi, who stared at the thick gold hair covering the genital pouch.

"I'm all there, partner," Stephen Thomas said. "It just needs . . . a little coaxing to come out." He smiled, showing more bravery than he felt. "Talk dirty to me."

Victoria went to Satoshi and slid her fingers up his muscular chest, dragging his black t-shirt off over his head. The hem of the shirt ruffled Satoshi's dark hair. Stephen Thomas joined them. Looking into Satoshi's eyes, he put one hand on his belly, fingertips beneath the waistband of his pants. Satoshi said nothing. Stephen Thomas thumbed open the top button, and slid his hand downward.

"Not yet," Satoshi whispered.

Stephen Thomas drew his hand away, backed off, but Satoshi grabbed his wrist, drew him closer, and slid his palm up Stephen Thomas's arm to the back of his neck.

When he tangled his fingers in Stephen Thomas's hair, the silver mutualist clenched and wriggled, trying to hold fast to the strands. Satoshi flinched.

"Are you going to wear that thing?"

"I'll take it off to love you," Stephen Thomas said. His voice was tight. "Wait. You do it. Tickle it."

He took Satoshi's left hand, Victoria's right hand, and showed them how to loosen the mutualist. His hair fell free. He grabbed the silver worm. It twisted; he let it coil itself around the earring rack on his desk.

Satoshi tangled his hand in Stephen Thomas's hair and drew his taller partner down to kiss him.

Stephen Thomas responded, as chastely as he could. His penis throbbed within his genital pouch; it probed for the opening.

Satoshi's lips felt cool. Satoshi drew back.

"Your lips are so warm, your skin . . ." He kissed Stephen Thomas again, gently, tentatively.

Stephen Thomas turned to Victoria and kissed her, too. There was nothing chaste about their kiss. She opened her mouth and took his tongue between her lips, between her teeth. She slid her knee up his thigh, to his hip. Then she drew away from him and kissed Satoshi. She opened the lower buttons of his cargo pants, then pushed them down his hips and stripped him. She pulled Stephen Thomas closer into the circle.

He kissed Satoshi again, gently, carefully.

"Lips the same," he said.

"Almost," Satoshi said. "Except for the heat."

Satoshi stroked Stephen Thomas's arm, from shoulder to wrist, his back, from shoulder to waist, smoothing his fine gold hair, seeking the familiar lines of his muscles.

Victoria held Satoshi's penis. Stephen Thomas cradled Victoria's breast with one hand, and slid his other hand between Satoshi's legs. Satoshi liked it when one partner caressed his penis, the other his scrotum.

"Hands almost the same," Stephen Thomas said. "A little different."

When Satoshi felt the warm amber swimming webs enclosing him, he tensed.

"Should I—?"

"It's all right," Satoshi said. "It's all right."

He caressed Victoria, petting her clitoris. He slid his left hand down Stephen Thomas's stomach, exploring the genital pouch.

"A lot of difference, there."

"Are you . . ." Satoshi hesitated. "Are you furry?"

Stephen Thomas laughed. "Not *all* over."

Victoria moved her hand up his inner thigh, pressing her fingers against the opening, slipping inside, seeking the weight of his hidden penis. It pressed outward, the pink tip probing forward, already slick with his excitement.

Stephen Thomas gasped, and his breath quickened. Victoria was right, he thought, it *is* my first time.

Twelve

Silence enclosed the house; dawn silvered the world.

Sitting in the windowseat, J.D. relaxed. She was grateful for the solitude, for the quiet, and weary from her center to her skin.

Zev was still asleep, but J.D. had not slept well. She was too keyed up over the meeting later on this morning.

We *have* to accept the invitation, she thought. We *have* to. What else could we do?

But she feared that on the brink of triumph, something would obstruct the path the Four Worlds had opened.

J.D. fidgeted, tired of waiting, anxious to act, to improve alien contact's chances of going to the Farther worlds.

The baby squidmoth, J.D. thought.

If it damages the wild cylinder, we might not have any choice but to go home.

I've got to keep that from happening, she thought. It's three hours till the meeting. If I get up right now, and hurry, I can visit the squidmoth baby before the meeting.

Another squidmoth tantrum was the last thing she wanted to experience. But it was worth the risk, if she could persuade the being to leave *Starfarer* willingly. If it would not, she feared the consequences. For *Starfarer* and for the larval squidmoth. During the meeting, someone was bound to bring up the problem of Nemo's offspring. J.D. wanted to present a solution.

In early morning's rising light, her front yard glowed yellow with daffodils. The spring flowers erupted through mud washed in by the snowmelt. After everything that had happened, J.D. could hardly believe time had not passed to summer, to winter, to another year.

The flowers and leaves brushed against each other, swaying. The warm breeze carried with it the moist, green scent of spring.

The breeze ruffled the daffodils like a silk scarf. Here and there a cluster of stiffer tulips formed eddies in the motion of the daffodils.

J.D. wondered if she would be here when the hard green eggs of the tulip flowers burst into bloom.

She had to get back to *Nautilus*. She had to dive into the knowledge surface as if it were the ocean, and stay there until it permeated her like the salt of the primordial sea.

If she could navigate it, descend into it, she would possess all the knowledge of Nemo and Nemo's ancestors.

Right after the meeting, I can go, she thought. *Right* after.

She jumped up, left the house, and hurried across her yard, heading for the end of *Starfarer*'s cylinder and the wild side ferry.

Over by the river, where the light cast dappled shadows through a grove of young trees, the path moved.

J.D. stopped short. *The path moved?*

The rippling continued.

At the grove of trees, the Representative's representative inch-wormed from dappled shade to sunlight.

"Late!" J.D. exclaimed. "What are you doing? Are you all right?"

"I am . . . for now," he said.

"You're unusually active today. Won't you hurt yourself?"

"It doesn't matter anymore," he said lugubriously.

"What's wrong? Why are you so unhappy?"

"I've heard nothing from the Representative."

All sorts of possibilities occurred to J.D., about what might be happening to the Representative, cooped up with the Smallerfarthing Eldest in the strange little space boat. Half the possibilities were bawdy and the other half sinister. She kept her speculations to herself.

"What does that mean?"

"I . . . I had hoped . . . that he gained a reward for his line. But I fear . . ."

He fell silent and stretched himself flat against the path.

"Please forgive my ignorance," J.D. said, "but why would he expect a reward? If he was trying to possess *Nautilus*—"

"He risked himself, J.D.! His risk was brilliant, audacious."

Late raised his forward third from the path, revealing shiny suckers, agitated radula. The radula combs appeared, swiped themselves across the sharp teeth, and disappeared again.

"He *deserved* . . ." Late's fur bristled, and his spines rose from the dapples. "But it has been so long. I fear for us."

"What might happen?"

"If the Eldest did not countenance his risk, his line will end."

"His line. You're part of his line. Right?"

"Yes."

"And—?"

"I will have no place. I'll be cut off from my society . . ."

"Banished?"

"I served well, I acted in the Representative's place so he did not have to spend himself," Late said. "I don't want to die."

"Is there something I can do to help?" J.D. said with sympathy. "Were you looking for me?"

The Representative's representative shrugged his whole body, bristling out his fur and extending his spines. He fluttered forward. He could move with surprising rapidity, when he chose.

"I am looking for an adventure," Late said. "I have never had an adventure, and I might not have much time left. You have adventures, so I came to you."

"An adventure? I don't—I guess I *do* have adventures. But—I'm awfully sorry, I have to go over to the wild side. Maybe we could think of an adventure after I get back? After the meeting?"

"The wild side," Late said. "The wild side, yes, that would be an adventure. I will come with you. To the wild side."

J.D. moved gingerly across the inspection web toward the squidmoth baby. Her safety line would catch her if she fell again, but the fall a couple of days ago had scared her.

"Be careful," the Representative's representative said to her.

"I'm trying," she said.

Late rode her shoulders, overbalancing her and making her feel even less secure on the open web. She regretted bringing him. Here on the outside of *Starfarer*, he was a heavy burden, and a reluctant adventurer. He had taken an interminable time to enter the *Chi*, find his spacesuit—J.D. had pulled it from the bundle of spacesuits the Farthings brought with them—and ripple into it. The suit looked like a high-tech plastic shopping bag, translucent and covered with sensors and grippers. He put it on by edging himself inside, one ripple at a time.

After that, he followed her so slowly that J.D. finally got the hint and offered to carry him, as Sharphearer so often did. He accepted instantly, gratefully eager, and climbed up her back to fasten his forward pincers to the shoulders of J.D.'s pressure suit.

She had not taken into account that Sharphearer had four legs to her two, or that Sharphearer usually carried Late through zero gravity. The inspection web had the highest gravity on campus.

Lugging a medium-sized Chinese carpet, plus carpet pad, J.D. walked a tightrope.

Where are all the silver slugs? she wondered. Maybe I could get one of them to help.

She put out a query. Arachne asked if her request was essential.

J.D.'s back hurt and her shoulders ached. She was only halfway to Nemo's offspring, and she felt as if she had been on a strenuous hike. Replying to Arachne in the affirmative, J.D. stopped to rest.

"Are we there?" Late asked.

"No. I can show you an image if you like."

"I will . . . savor the anticipation of viewing squidmoth spawn," Late said.

The silver slug humped around the curve of *Starfarer*'s cylinder. It clutched the ship's skin, upside down.

"Here's your new ride," J.D. said.

"My . . . ride?"

"The artificial. The silver slug. Over there."

Late clamped against her back, all the pincers scrabbling for a hold on the irregularities of her pressure suit and its support pack.

"Hey, be careful—you'll tear something!"

"My suit is quite sturdy. I am all right where I am, truly."

"You'll be better on the slug," J.D. said, thinking, I didn't mean you'd tear *your* suit. "Come on, I'm in a hurry."

Late's body rippled against J.D.'s back, pressing the support pack uncomfortably between her shoulders.

"You want me to ride . . . on a synthetic creature?"

"Sure."

"How do human people *think* of such things?" Late asked, marveling. "Such bizarre things."

"We do it all the time. You ride in spaceships, what's the difference?" It occurred to her that she had never seen anyone ride a silver slug; maybe they disliked being ridden as much as orcas did. But the orcas had strong tastes and a quick and alien intelligence; it had never occurred to J.D. to wonder if silver slugs could be said to like or dislike anything.

"I cannot, I'll be upside down!" Late protested.

"You're often upside down. You were *eating* upside down on the lichen shelf."

"I wasn't upside down, *you* were upside down. There was no gravity there! I'll fall off. There's nothing to hold to!"

"Okay, the slug can crawl down on the web and turn over and you can flatten on its back. You've got a line, you'll be perfectly safe." She hoped the slug could crawl on the web. She assumed it could; the slugs had been designed with versatility in mind.

"I'm sorry, I had no idea I was being such a trouble, you go ahead, I'll catch up to you." Very, very slowly, he loosened one edge from its death grip on her suit.

J.D. knew when she was licked. Late would take half an hour to disengage himself, and heaven only knew how long to reach the squidmoth nest.

And here I was going to challenge him to walk it, she thought.

"All right, never mind. Stay where you are, it's only a little farther." J.D. sighed, then thought hopefully, Maybe he's being careful because he isn't getting ready to die after all.

342

She trudged on, grabbing the edge of the silver slug and letting it move above and ahead of her to pull her along. She was anxious to try to speak to Nemo's offspring again. She had some ideas about communicating with it without frightening or upsetting it.

You were expecting it to be like Nemo, she told herself, but that's a silly expectation. It hasn't even metamorphosed into its juvenile form yet.

Nemo had lived, as a juvenile, for a million years.

She missed the calm intelligence of the old, wise, juvenile squidmoth, who gained information effectively by making statements, testing hypotheses, changing each hypothesis in response to results.

The iridescent sheen of the egg nest appeared over *Starfarer*'s horizon. J.D. hurried toward it.

The squidmoth nest was larger than when she visited it before, its edges reaching wider, the central bulge larger.

Approaching the squidmoth, she fell silent. The translucent, iridescent nest was so delicate that for a handsbreadth its border lay transparent and nearly invisible against the stone.

The egg nest grew past and around the inspection web supports. It loomed and bulged, threatening to lose its hold on the cylinder and fall, to slide down the supports and engulf J.D. like a sticky, slimy blanket. Its edge crept around the curve of the cylinder.

J.D. moved cautiously onward, till she stood beneath the nest's central mass.

"Why didn't you bring your little machines?" Late asked. "You aren't transmitting, I thought human people transmitted *everything*."

J.D. gestured upward, where an LTM clung like a mechanical lizard to one of the inspection web supports.

"That LTM's making a record. I'm about the only person who's interested in Nemo's offspring. Everyone is very busy."

J.D. gazed up at the squidmoth egg. Egg? Larva? She needed a whole new set of terms, or a conversation about taxonomy with Arachne, or with the squidmoth.

"What a strange thing," Late said. "Every bit as ugly as everyone—"

"Hush!" J.D. said, annoyed. "It can hear you and it can understand you."

"I beg your pardon," Late said, both chastened and offended.

"And it isn't ugly, either!" J.D. said. "It has the beautiful shimmer of its adult parent, who was my friend."

The baby squidmoth made no response.

She wished again that 61 Cygni's resident squidmoth had remained in the system. Why had it left, after being here so long, at the same time *Starfarer* arrived? She worried; she wondered if the two events were connected in a causal way, rather than coincidentally.

Right now it just matters that it's gone, she thought. I would have liked to ask it about young squidmoths.

She sat on the inspection web. Late clambered down from her back and secured himself grimly around several web strands. J.D. leaned back against one of the supports, gazing upward at the shimmering, slowly pulsing mass.

Arachne replied to her request, sending a message to Infinity Mendez, returning with a reply.

J.D. accepted. Infinity appeared. His image floated between the inspection web and the surface of *Starfarer*.

"I'm in the tunnels," he said. He widened the view so she could see. Silver slugs congregated behind him, spewing rock foam into the rough stone corridor.

Arachne showed a small schematic of the wild side cylinder, pinpointing Infinity's position. He was above her, above the egg nest, several levels higher in *Starfarer*'s skin. Thin tendrils extended from the egg nest up almost to the tunnel. Silver slugs sparkled here and there, bunched above the squidmoth. Another cluster of slugs congregated on the far side of the cylinder, directly opposite the squidmoth's nest. Balancing out the mass change, J.D. thought.

"It's a lot farther inside than I expected." J.D. cleared her throat before she spoke again, hoping to smooth the consternation from her voice. "Are you repairing damage?"

"It hasn't done much damage," Infinity said. "But just in case, I'm giving it more stuff to dig through. I figured if it does dig in, if it has to go through rock instead of corridors, it might stop before it got to the inner surface."

"Thank you, Infinity," J.D. said. "I never would have thought of that. What about the water?"

"It's using some. Not enough to worry about." He shrugged. "All things considered, it's pretty benign. If it keeps on behaving like this, it can stay right there as long as it wants."

J.D. blew out her breath with relief.

"Can you find out," Infinity added, "if it's going to grow much more?"

"I'll try," J.D. said.

"No doubt it is excreting into your water supply," Late said. "Typical squidmoth behavior."

"You don't know anything *about* typical squidmoth behavior!" J.D. said, furious. "*I* know more about squidmoths than everybody in Civilization combined!"

"I know it," Late said mildly. "But I think you should turn your intellect to matters of importance."

J.D. muttered something.

"What?"

"I thought you wanted an adventure." J.D. did not repeat what she had muttered. She thought, I've been hanging around Stephen Thomas too much.

"Adventures are hard work," Late said.

"I can't see any contamination," Infinity said. "Arachne's keeping up an analysis. If there's a change, we'll know it."

345

"Thanks," J.D. said, relieved. "Again."

Infinity gestured an acknowledgment; his image vanished.

J.D. opened her link, offering communication to the young squidmoth, but protecting the knowledge surface.

The wild cylinder spun, propelling J.D. and Late and the young squidmoth through several cycles of starlight and shadow.

J.D. thought she saw a pattern in the nest's growth, a slow progression. Arachne gave her a speeded-up image, superimposing the LTM's record over the real egg nest.

The image crept outward while the light of 61 Cygni fell upon it; in the darkness, it slowed and stopped. When the image reached the edge of the real nest, the recording ended.

It's photosynthesizing, J.D. thought, like Nemo did. Powering its growth with starlight. No wonder Nemo chose Sirius as the place to reproduce, within the blue-white light, where the energy flux is high.

If I hadn't taken *Nautilus* out of the system, if I hadn't pulled this young one along with me, it would be back with its siblings. Growing faster, and probably healthier.

She wondered, again, about the egg case that had escaped, the egg case she had lost while *Nautilus* passed through transition.

J.D. widened her link.

"I'd like to speak with you," she said. "I promise not to touch you again. I've been worried about you."

She expected tentative curiosity.

"I don't care if you touch me," the young squidmoth said abruptly, arrogantly.

"Hello," J.D. said, surprised. "I'm glad you're speaking to me. Are you all right?"

"You didn't hurt me."

"I'm glad to hear it."

"You *couldn't* hurt me!" The voice swaggered like a buccaneer's, articulate and self-possessed.

"You sound a lot different than the last time we talked."

"I was an *embryo!*"

"What are you now?"

"Second instar—you would say."

"A juvenile?"

"Soon!"

The squidmoth was only a few days old, and about to become a juvenile. Nemo and J.D. had met when Nemo was still a juvenile, toward the end of Nemo's million-year lifespan. After metamorphosing, after adult reproduction, the squidmoth died. So members of the species must live virtually all their long lives as juveniles.

"Will you grow deeper into the rock?" she asked.

"My life is growth!"

Infinity Mendez's reassurance began to erode.

"When you become a juvenile, won't you need your own starship?"

"I am *on* a starship."

J.D.'s heart followed the pull of centrifugal force and ended up below the inspection net, reeling as the wild cylinder spun past the stars.

I'm going to *have* to persuade it to leave, she thought.

"But this starship is smaller than your parent's."

"I am adaptable."

"This starship belongs to human people," J.D. said.

"Human people are mobile."

"We have no place to be mobile *to.*"

"I don't care."

"Even if we left, you can't control *Starfarer*, you wouldn't be able to go where you wanted."

"I don't care."

I think I've made a terrible mistake, J.D. thought. I should have taken Andro's advice to try to move it when it was smaller, when we might have moved it without hurting it. Without any damage to the wild cylinder.

"Won't you let us help you?" J.D. asked. "If you tell us where to take you, to get the kind of starship your people usually—"

"It isn't me you want to help."

"I want to help human people, it's true," J.D. said. "If our starship is destroyed, we'll be stranded here. Some of us might die. But I want to help you, too."

"That's what all the Civilized people said while they were chasing my juvenile parent."

J.D. sighed with frustration. She could not blame the being for its suspicions. Nemo, the baby squidmoth's adult parent, had never mentioned being pursued. But Europa had referred to piratical predators, members of Civilization trying to steal the ships of squidmoths.

Nemo and other juvenile squidmoths had exchanged unfertilized eggs, becoming juvenile parents to each other's offspring. The juvenile parents had bequeathed memories to their offspring, just as the adult parents did.

Apparently the baby squidmoth remembered its juvenile parent's experience as an intended victim of the predators. J.D. wondered if the memories of the chase would be terror, of the hunt and the escape? Or memories of amusement, excitement, and triumph?

In Europa's story, the pirates had followed a squidmoth into transition, intent on stealing a single ship or finding the graveyard of the other ones' starships.

The pirates had not been seen thereafter.

The reclusive squidmoths, the oldest existing species, had scavenged the small massive starships of the vanished and mysterious other ones. The starships gave them tremendous power, which as far as J.D. knew they never employed except in self-defense. Androgeos complained that they never put the ships to good use, using them only as orbiting homes.

But how would Andro know? J.D. wondered. Nemo was a million years old. Civilization is—how old? A few tens of millennia? To a member of Civilization, a squidmoth might be immobile. To the squidmoth, a rest of only ten thousand years might be hyperactivity.

J.D. decided to give the immature squidmoth some straight talk.

"We have to come to an accommodation," she said. "I've persuaded my colleagues to let you stay, but you must be careful not to damage the cylinder—not to go deeper into the rock."

"I crush your threats with my tentacles!"

The fulmination startled her. Nemo had been mild and friendly. Except for one moment of fright, J.D. had always felt comfortable and respected in the squidmoth's presence, despite her own relative youth and inexperience.

"You don't *have* tentacles," J.D. said. The LTM transmissions revealed a pool of cells metamorphosing around a central neural mass.

"You'll be sorry when I do!"

This isn't Nemo, J.D. reminded herself. No matter how much you miss your friend, Nemo's gone. The young one is different. Different age, different personality—

"What are you going to do?" Late asked.

"I don't know," J.D. said. "Nothing, yet."

The inspection web vibrated violently beneath her. Late's pincers clamped tighter on the cables; the metal transmitted the shriek straight through J.D.'s suit. The sound made her flinch.

"Be careful!" Late cried to the squidmoth. "Intelligent beings are beneath you!"

J.D. laid one hand gently on the dorsal surface of Late's spacesuit. The Representative's representative fell silent, still agitated, quivering.

Above her, the squidmoth quaked. Its surface rippled and plunged. The web supports, projecting down through the substance of the squidmoth, tore holes in the protoplasm. J.D. grabbed at the cables, convinced all over again that the creature was going to fall out of its crater and crush her.

"Scared you!" the squidmoth said.

Its presence crowded her link, pushing and taunting her.

J.D. heard a note of panic in the bravado of the voice.

"That must have hurt," she said.

I may be asking it for something it can't do, she thought. It can't help growing, maybe it can't help digging. I might as well tell a child to decide not to go through puberty.

Above her, the rips closed slowly, healing around the web supports. Livid scars marred the smooth surface.

"Nothing hurts me."

J.D. opened her link wide. Her senses blanked out, erasing perception of her body, of the weight on her shoulders, of the stars spinning beneath her. She searched, thoughtfully, for another way to reach the youngster. She slid toward *Nautilus* and onto the knowledge surface, seeking information about the development of squidmoth. But the species did not raise its children after the adult parent freed the egg cases.

Nemo's memories of youth were a million years old. J.D. could not gain access to them, though she was able to penetrate the surface a little deeper than last time. Tantalizing images of distant stars and of transition tempted her.

During J.D.'s distraction, the immature squidmoth poured its presence through her link and scrambled toward Victoria's algorithm.

"Dammit!" J.D. cut her connection to *Nautilus*, evicting the squidmoth at the same time. The world flashed into reality; she regained her perception of her body. Only the smallest thread of communication remained between her and the invader.

"I told you before," she said sternly, "you may not have that."

"Fuck you!" the squidmoth cried. "Bitch! Shit! Damn! Poop! Fooey!" Through the attenuated link, its voice was the faint echo of an infuriated scream.

Prepared for the anger, J.D. maintained her balance on the inspection web. Late hunkered down on his cables, all four edges curled around strands, the pincers clamped.

Maybe the squidmoth has been hanging around Stephen Thomas too long, too, J.D. thought. Though for all the offhand profanity Stephen Thomas uses, he hardly ever directs it at anybody in particular.

J.D. projected her image through Arachne to speak to Infinity Mendez. His image appeared before her in return.

"Have you been listening?"

"Yeah, unfortunately."

"What age am I dealing with?"

"Sounds like an adolescent to me ... Relative to a human kid? About thirteen. The profanity stage." He chuckled. " 'Poop.' "

"Don't laugh at me!" the squidmoth screamed. "I'll squash you!"

J.D. damped down the squidmoth's transmission frequency.

"What do I do?" she asked Infinity. "How do I get through to it?"

"You wait for it to outgrow the phase," Infinity said.

J.D. hesitated, wanting a better answer.

"Look at it this way," Infinity said. He was standing on an extra layer of dense rock foam, while behind him the silver slugs continued to laminate the space with a deeper and deeper barrier. "You won't have to wait till it's eighteen. At the rate it's changing, you'll probably only have to wait a couple of days."

Ruth Orazio sat in the warm sand of the beach, folded her arms on her knees, and gazed across the sea.

"Hi."

Ruth turned. Standing on the dune behind her, Zev looked fondly down at her.

"How are you feeling?" he asked.

"I'm just fine," she said. "And how are you?"

She wondered if Zev had kept his promise to her. He was open, guileless; keeping a secret would not be easy for him. He was the only person besides Europa who knew she was pregnant.

If he talked to her in public in this solicitous tone, no one would be fooled for long. Besides, being spoken to like that nauseated her worse than morning sickness.

"I'm glad you—"

"Zev," she said sternly, "I'd rather not discuss—"

"We have to. You have to release me from my promise."

"No."

She was glad she was sitting down; her knees felt shaky. He slid down the dune and sat anxiously beside her.

"I didn't think it would matter if I didn't tell J.D.," he said in a rush. "I thought I could pretend I didn't know, I thought it was just a little thing—I thought—I don't know what I thought. I'm happy for you—"

"And I'm grateful to you. Don't spoil it now."

"But I can't keep secrets from J.D. I thought she had kept one from me—she didn't, but I thought she did, and I felt awful—and if she finds out—" He spread his webbed hands.

"Zev," Ruth said gently.

"—she'll feel the same way!"

"Do you tell J.D. everything? Every conversation you have, everything you do?"

"I would if we were back home," he said. "But here there isn't time. Everybody's so busy . . ."

"Then—"

"But I tell her everything important."

NAUTILUS

"Then consider our conversation unimportant."

He looked at the ground, digging his claws into the sand.

"But it was important. It *is* important."

"Telling her will just make things harder for her. Don't you think she has enough on her mind?"

"The more good things you have on your mind, the easier it is."

"Everyone on the deep space expedition agreed not to have children during the trip," she said. "Why get them upset about me?" She was afraid to reveal Civilization's rules; bad enough that she was breaking *Starfarer*'s.

"But you aren't a member of the expedition," Zev explained sincerely. "Not officially. It isn't your fault you're here."

Ruth flopped back in the sand, aggravated, and gazed obliquely past the sun tube, at the far-overhead ocean. Light glittered from the waves.

"Ruth—?" Zev said, worried, but relentless. "I *have* to tell J.D. Please don't make me break my word to you."

She sighed, sat up, and rose. The dry soft sand squeaked beneath her feet.

"Come on," she said. "We'll talk to J.D. together."

J.D. reached the amphitheater while it was still deserted.

The terraced bowl opened out before her. Still shaken by the adolescent squidmoth's tantrum, she was grateful for the silence and the open space. She had spent too much time beneath the looming presence of the egg nest. Needing light and air, she had thrown off her spacesuit and fled the airlock, leaving the Representative's representative still releasing his seals.

How strange, she thought, to feel claustrophobic when all of space lay beneath my feet.

She walked down the path; she liked to sit midway down the hillside. The grass of the terraced seats was

353

bright green and slightly damp, new blades thickly covering desiccated brown wisps. The grass had recovered from the heat wave and from the snowstorm.

So far we've muddled through, J.D. thought. We reached consensus to leave the solar system. We defied it, when Gerald blocked, to leave Tau Ceti and go to Sirius.

So far, almost all of us have agreed. Maybe we will again.

Gold and mahogany in the sun, Zev strode through the entryway. Senator Orazio accompanied him.

Zev hugged J.D. and sat down beside her, uncharacteristically solemn. Ruth Orazio sat next to him.

"I have something to tell you," Zev said.

When he, and the senator, had finished, J.D. bent forward and hid her face in her hands.

"J.D.—" Ruth said.

"I'm happy for you," J.D. said, her voice muffled. "I am. Honestly."

"What will you do?"

J.D. took her hands from her face. "Why did you tell me?"

"I didn't want to keep secrets from you," Zev said.

"Oh, Zev—!" she said, appreciating his motives but, for once, wishing his candor were not so complete. "I won't do anything," she said to Ruth. "I hope you'll do the same."

"Within reason," Ruth said.

They smiled at each other, sealing a fragile agreement.

The rest of *Starfarer*'s people began to gather around them. Ruth patted J.D.'s hand in reassurance and went to sit a few terraces away.

J.D. sighed.

"I knew what was right back home," Zev said. "I wasn't so sure about here."

"You did right," J.D. said. Now she understood better why he had been so upset. She squeezed his hand.

Victoria and Stephen Thomas and Satoshi arrived together. Whatever Stephen Thomas had said to them when he got home, it had worked. J.D. smiled to see them. They looked happier than they had since Stephen Thomas started to change. Victoria glowed with transcendent joy. Satoshi, content and bemused, touched Stephen Thomas's back, letting his hand linger on the blue silk of his loose shirt. Stephen Thomas's exuberant arrogance amused and delighted J.D. Even the pang she felt at having let him go when she could have had him stood apart from her pleasure in the reconciliation of her friends.

"They're going to be okay now, aren't they?" Zev said softly.

"Yes," J.D. said. "I think they are. Maybe it won't be easy. But I think they are."

She grinned at Zev. He leaned forward and gave her a quick, hot-tongued kiss. J.D. wondered, with a flash of anticipatory pleasure radiating from her center, if Stephen Thomas was anywhere near as good a lover as Zev. Being a male diver conferred benefits that had nothing to do with being concealed from sharks.

Midway up the opposite slope of the amphitheater, next to Fox, Gerald Hemminge stood up to speak.

His colleagues settled into silence.

Damn! J.D. thought. I let myself get distracted, now Gerald will get in the first word . . .

"Gerald Hemminge." Following tradition, Gerald spoke his name and paused. No one challenged his right to speak.

"Our guests," he said, "our sponsors from the Four Worlds, have honored us. Before we accept their invitation, we should ask them to make it clear how joining Civilization will benefit us. So far, they've given us little and asked for a great deal: Victoria's algorithm and Crimson's fossils."

"But I want them to have the fossils," Crimson said,

breaking the rules of the meeting with cross-talk. "The whole point of excavating them is to study them."

"They want our coffee and our chocolate, too." Florrie Brown sat with Infinity and Esther, who looked rested and energetic.

Though it was rude to interrupt whoever was standing to speak, a ripple of laughter passed across the amphitheater. J.D. wondered if Florrie had made a deliberate joke, or if she was thinking, as J.D. was, of the times on Earth when delicacies or drugs created flash-points for war.

"Indeed they do," Gerald said, his words polite, his tone sharp. "And they claim rights in the alien starship."

J.D. noticed, as she was sure she was meant to, that Gerald did not refer to *Nautilus* as belonging to her.

"I believe," Gerald said, "that we should return to Earth."

J.D. held back her protest, but she perched on the edge of the grassy terrace, ready to leap to her feet the instant Gerald gave her an opening.

He noticed her agitation and smiled at her with a hint of condescension. He spread his hands, taking in the amphitheater. "It's because of J.D. that we *can* go home now. We have the alien spaceship. We have an *alien!* It may not grow into sentience during our lifetimes. It may not *hatch* during our lifetimes! But it *is* alien life. By definition, the deep space expedition has succeeded."

He paused, glanced around the amphitheater, turned to include the people behind him.

"Back on Earth, they think of us as fools and fantasists. Our families fear we're dead! Don't you think we should go home and validate ourselves?"

J.D. leaped to her feet before Gerald could take another breath to continue.

"J.D. Sauvage," she said, and barely paused. "If we go home now we'll be stranded!"

"I was not quite finished, J.D.," Gerald said mildly.

"I'm—" J.D. collected herself, took a lesson from Stephen Thomas, and did not apologize. "I thought you were, Gerald. Please, tell us your solutions."

"The cosmic string isn't predictable any more. It left our system, yes—and it could come back as abruptly."

Victoria made a skeptical sound. She glanced over at Avvaiyar Prakesh, the astronomer, who grimaced with equal doubt.

"On the other hand, we could wait out here for several lifetimes—for five hundred years of banishment—and the string still might not return!" Gerald said. "Is anyone here prepared to risk that?"

"Sure," Stephen Thomas said.

"Yes," J.D. said.

Gerald replied to Stephen Thomas. "I'm not at all surprised. You'll no doubt be arrested the moment you land."

In the United States, changing into a diver was illegal.

J.D. protested. "No court—"

"I did not say he would be convicted, I said he would be *arrested*."

"Along with everybody else on campus," Stephen Thomas said.

That earned him a rueful laugh. They were all likely to be prosecuted for stealing the starship.

Senator Derjaguin rose out of turn, but Gerald ceded time to him with a welcoming gesture.

"I have influence back on Earth," he said. "If you return, I'll use it as best I can to support you."

"Like the United States," Stephen Thomas said sarcastically, "supported the deep space expedition?"

"The longer you delay," the senator said, "the harder it will be."

"I'd rather take my chances out here," J.D. said. "I think we should—"

"Why do you people adopt meeting rules you're not willing to follow?" Gerald said indignantly. "I still have not finished."

"Why not?" Stephen Thomas asked, ignoring Gerald's complaint. "Give J.D. a turn."

"In a minute," J.D. said. "Gerald, what do you plan to do about the supercharged bacteria?"

"Pretend our young genius never discovered them."

"Fuck, no!" Stephen Thomas said.

"I absolutely reject that suggestion!" Professor Thanthavong said. "I'll have no part in transmitting these bacteria in secret. However beneficial—however essential!—they might be."

"Professor Thanthavong," Gerald said with careful courtesy, "can you cure our entire ecosystem?"

"No," she admitted. "Not without destroying it."

"Then we have no choice," Gerald said. "If Stephen Thomas weren't so accomplished, we wouldn't know about it."

"But we *do* know about it," Thanthavong said.

"Earth can't join Civilization without the protection of the bacteria. We might as well—"

"Take them to Earth? In secret?"

"Yes."

"What you're suggesting is profoundly immoral."

"And it's the way Civilization has always proceeded! What's the alternative?"

"Tell. Tell everything."

"Professor, forgive me, we'd be shot out of the sky."

"I disagree."

"At the very least, we'd never be allowed home."

"No one will be trapped on *Starfarer*. We can cure individuals. The cure isn't enjoyable, but it isn't difficult, either."

"The public outcry against letting us back home—even cured—will be worse."

"You may do as you like," Thanthavong said coldly.

"Lie about the bacteria, as you've chosen to lie about Crimson's performance. Whoever you persuade—I won't participate."

Shock, embarrassment, and fascination combined into a heavy silence.

J.D. rose. Her motion broke the tension between Gerald and Professor Thanthavong. Gerald reluctantly sat down.

"Gerald has proved my point," J.D. said. "The Four Worlds are taking a tremendous risk by welcoming us."

She looked around the amphitheater, trying to gauge the response. Victoria gave her a small smile of confidence, a supportive nod; Satoshi gave her a thumbs-up. But Gerald looked bored. Senator Derjaguin shifted irritably. Senator Orazio frowned and stared at her feet. *Will she keep our bargain?* J.D. wondered. J.D. disliked secrets, but she feared what might happen if Ruth's became common knowledge.

"The Four Worlds are offering us confidence that we haven't necessarily earned," J.D. said. "They're giving us another chance. How *can't* we take it?"

"Why?" Ruth Orazio asked.

J.D. looked at her sharply. Ruth gazed back calmly, as if they shared no secrets.

"As a guest, I may be speaking out of turn," Ruth said, "but you *did* ask a question. Why are they offering their confidence to a bunch of violent barbarians? Are they taking a risk for risk's sake?"

She is trusting me, J.D. thought. *It's a good question, one I wish I could answer. Ruth would have said the same thing even if we hadn't talked, even if she weren't pregnant. Maybe even if she was a member of the expedition.*

"They're taking a risk because J.D. proved to them that we *aren't* violent barbarians," Stephen Thomas said.

A deep blush, as much of pleasure as of embarrassment, heated J.D.'s face.

"The senator's correct to ask the question!" Gerald said. "I believe they'd do anything to keep us here. They want the algorithm. They want the source of the fossils."

"The sculptures," J.D. said automatically. She brushed her short hair back from her forehead, a nervous gesture. "But you're right," she said. "I agree with you."

"Remarkable," Gerald said cheerfully. "Then you agree that we should protect the algorithm—use it solely for Earth's benefit. It will give us quite an advantage."

"No," J.D. said, troubled by the comment, but unwilling to be distracted from her point again. "And it isn't me you should be asking about the algorithm, it's Victoria. I do agree with Ruth that the Four Worlds have their own reasons. Which probably have nothing to do with me, flattered as I am by what Stephen Thomas said."

Victoria had reacted to Gerald's remark, too. Distracted, she stared at nothing. A representation of her algorithm, swirls and wisps of color, drifted into half-intensity before her. She started, pulling her attention back to the meeting. The holographic image faded.

"It doesn't matter what the Four Worlds' reasons are!" J.D. said. "Look at what happens if we go home now. *Starfarer* pops into existence in the solar system. Everybody says, Hey, where have you guys been? And what do we say?"

She glanced around the amphitheater again, letting her colleagues imagine answers.

Professor Thanthavong chuckled ruefully.

J.D. grinned at her. "Right. We say, We met five different kinds of alien people! Six if you count the Minoans. But none of them could come back with us. Except, of course, this infant alien that we abducted."

"And," Victoria said, "we saved Victoria's algorithm for Earth's use . . . except, of course, we can't use it because the cosmic string has withdrawn from the solar system."

"And Earth got an invitation to join Civilization." Satoshi extended the imaginary dialog. "But we turned it down and came home instead, but, of course, maybe they'll invite us again in five hundred years."

"Oh, and by the way," Stephen Thomas said, "the aliens infected us with a new bacterium, and it's fucking tough to eradicate—but of course you won't mind if we bring it back to Earth, will you?"

"You sound like the Largerfarthings," Gerald said caustically. "Next you'll all be braiding feathers in your hair."

"It's a perfectly good fashion!" Florrie Brown said. She flicked her braids forward over her shoulders; some of Sharphearer's polished beads decorated them.

"I agree," Ruth Orazio said, brushing her fingertips against the bit of scarlet fluff tied into her hair.

Gerald ignored the rustle of laughter. "And we never abducted the squidmoth. Rather it was left in our nest like a cuckoo's egg!"

"We've come this far," J.D. said. "If we go home now, we've got nothing. If we go home as members of Civilization, we have a chance. I urge us to accept the invitation and visit the Farther worlds."

She sat down. Her armpits were clammily wet; a drop of nervous sweat rolled down her spine. She leaned back against the riser of the next terrace, feigning calm.

The whisper and buzz of earnest conversation crept through the quiet. For a long time no one rose to speak.

Professor Thanthavong stood up.

"I think J.D. is right," she said. "I urge all my colleagues to stand with her."

J.D. sprang up, Zev beside her. The partnership rose as one.

Griffith, projecting his presence from *Nautilus* to his usual spot alone on the top terrace, stood up almost as quickly. He had to be physically present to join consensus, that was one of *Starfarer*'s rules. But J.D. appreciated his virtual support nevertheless.

The members of the physics department and the genetics department, astronomy and biochem, the staff, the art department, *Starfarer*'s only resident member of Grandparents in Space, and the people who had no official place, like Zev, like Esther, like Kolya in projected image, all joined the decision.

Sitting beside Gerald, Fox hesitated, fidgeted, and finally jumped to her feet.

To J.D.'s surprise, to her gratitude, even Ruth Orazio rose to back her up.

Soon only a few people remained sitting.

"You must return to Earth," Senator Derjaguin said sadly, knowing they would not.

"I'm sorry, Senator," J.D. said. "Gerald, please, don't break consensus. Won't you join us?"

"Come *on*, Gerald," Fox said.

"I cannot," the acting chancellor replied. He did not look at Fox.

"Are you blocking?"

"I have no wish," he said, "to repeat the humiliation of being ignored. I abstain."

All she could think of to say was, "Thank you."

"Shall we sail to the Farther worlds?" sailmaster Jenny Dupre asked. "Or is *Nautilus* going too, with us in orbit?"

"Wait—!"

J.D. turned toward Infinity Mendez, startled by his outburst.

"I keep *telling* you," he said. He paused for a moment, uncomfortable as always when he was the center of attention. When he spoke again he had forced his voice to a tense calm. "We *can't* move *Starfarer* anymore. Not this soon. The ecosystem's got to have some stability."

"The sun mirrors—" Avvaiyar said.

She let her eyelids flicker, touching Arachne for a moment. J.D. did the same, and saw the same pattern.

Distressed, J.D. sank to the terrace.

"I see," Avvaiyar said. "You're right."

"Yes," J.D. said. "I'm sorry, Infinity, you did tell us, and we didn't pay you enough attention."

"It isn't something I'm happy to point out," he said.

At the Farther worlds' distance from 61 Cygni, the mirrors should have been sufficient to maintain the stability of the weather. First, though, the weather had to recover its equilibrium. Arachne could not predict exactly what would happen if Starfarer moved farther from 61 Cygni. A dangerous number of possibilities involved the same destructive extremes that the starship had barely survived.

Esther Klein made an exasperated noise.

"We don't have to take Starfarer," she said. "Did the invitation say we had to take Starfarer? Leave it in orbit around Largernearer!"

"Can you fly us to Largerfarther in the transport?" J.D. asked. "Are you up to it?"

"I am," Esther said. "The transport's not—not enough range. But you have Nautilus. There's Europa's starship. We could even send a delegation on the Four Worlds ship if they'd take us, or put our stuff in the transport and dock it with the Four Worlds ship and camp out in it."

"Any of that would work," J.D. said. "Sure it would!" A tendril of worry twisted around the idea of splitting up the expedition. She pushed it away.

Esther faced J.D. squarely. "If we go on Nautilus—I could be your relief pilot."

J.D. had not gotten as far as considering a backup pilot for Nautilus, but Esther's idea was sound. J.D.'s control through the knowledge surface was nothing preternatural.

But it could be risky, too, J.D. thought. If Esther knows how to fly it, would she take it? Could they force her to take Nautilus from me?

Esther gazed at her, all blunt courage and hope.

"It isn't straightforward," J.D. said. "There are changes . . . But, if you want, we'll talk about it."

"That's all I ask." Esther's voice was a little uneven. "Thanks."

"J.D.," Professor Thanthavong said, "would you invite our Four Worlds guests to join the meeting?"

J.D. closed her eyes and flowed through her link to Quickercatcher, to Late, to Orchestra's AI, to the Minoans. She reached beyond them to Orchestra herself, to the Smallernearer.

Quickercatcher's presence mirrored his physical being, allure surrounding a straightforward, sturdy core. Late had shrugged off his usual lethargic attitude; he bubbled with excitement.

"I have news, J.D.!" he said. "Good news!"

Quite a change, J.D. thought, after just one adventure.

"I do, too," she said. "Will you and the quartet please join the meeting, so we can accept your invitation?"

A second later, Orchestra's response returned from the surface of Largernearer. She gave J.D. the gift of a slow, powerful tide of approval.

The Smallernearer said nothing, but only watched and waited, time-lagged by the distance.

"This is wonderful." Quickercatcher's pleasure glowed around J.D.

"Please come into the amphitheater," she said. "We'll share our good news."

Sharphearer's fluorescent fur glowed at the mouth of the tunnel. J.D. could make out the pure white of Andro's kilt. An incongruous thought floated through J.D.'s mind: I wonder how he keeps the pleats so sharp.

Quickercatcher led the group from the entry tunnel, his fur changing from grayed purple in the darkness to soft mauve in the light. Fasterdigger was harder to see, his brown and orange spots camouflaging him in the dark; Europa's homespun skirt and vest had the same effect. Longestlooker's black-on-black pelt kept her invisible until she strode fully into the light. Orchestra's

AI accompanied them, appearing, disappearing, expanding, then contracting to miniature size.

The representatives of Civilization walked down the ramp into the amphitheater. Late rode Sharphearer, holding on with his back half, waving his forward edge, ratcheting his teeth; two of Europa's meerkats clutched the fur of Fasterdigger's forward shoulders.

J.D. rose to greet them.

"We accept your kind invitation," J.D. said. "We'll visit the Farther worlds. We accept the responsibility of being members of the interstellar Civilization."

Europa came to her and embraced her, and Quickercatcher nudged her arm with his nose. A trill of happiness began. The sound expanded; it became music. The Largerfarthings trilled their pleasure, each a different note. The harmonics beat and blended. Short of breath from joy, J.D. laughed.

"We all have news," Longestlooker said.

"You next, Late," Sharphearer said, "yours is next most important."

Late twisted his wide, flat body, orienting himself toward J.D.

"I have been promoted," he said.

"Congratulations," J.D. said. "What happened?"

"The Representative has proven himself!" Late exclaimed. "Did I tell you that he would? I did! The Eldest has given him leave to start his own line."

J.D. glanced at Europa, uncertain how to react. What Late had told her was that the Representative had failed.

The Minoan smiled quizzically.

"Think of it as bestowing a title of nobility," Europa said. "The Eldest gave the Representative's line more territory, resources . . . and breeding rights. Late will metamorphose."

"I'll succeed the Representative," Late said. He arched his back, exposing his spines.

"So the Representative's risk paid off," J.D. said. "Even though he failed."

"Risk has many results," Late said. "The result you didn't foresee might be the most valuable. There is no failure, just different outcomes."

It was a viewpoint J.D. had not considered before. She would have to think about it later, when she had time and quiet. When she was on board *Nautilus*.

"I'm glad for you," J.D. said. "Though it's a pity this couldn't have happened before the Representative injured Esther."

The pilot sat with Infinity and Florrie, watching the encounter in silence. Though she acted neither frightened nor angry, Esther kept her distance.

"It wouldn't have happened otherwise!" Late said. "Not hurting her, I don't mean hurting her." He twisted the other way, opening his edges toward Esther. "We regret your damage, and we'll compensate you." He turned back to J.D. "But of course, J.D.," he said earnestly, "human beings heal, so it isn't as if the damage had happened to a Smallerfarthing."

J.D. made a sound of disbelief, a sound that even she could not distinguish between a laugh and a sob.

"I don't understand you at all," she said. "And I know this means a lot to you, but to me it would mean being trapped in a tiny room for the rest of my life."

"Yes. Yes! Bliss." He added quickly, "Though I did enjoy my adventure."

J.D. expected more explanation, but Late hunkered down on Sharphearer's back, rippling contentedly. Sharphearer patted Late's dappled fur, smoothing it around the spines.

"We have news as well," Longestlooker said. "News for Crimson."

The Largerfarthing moved sinuously to look across the terraces at the sculptor. Near the bottom of the amphitheater's bowl, Crimson sat crosslegged next to Avvaiyar.

"What is it?" Crimson asked.

"The Farther worlds want to help you. We have experience, exploring alien sites. We've equipped an expedition with modern excavation equipment. It's coming to join the dig."

As Gerald opened his mouth to speak, Crimson jumped up and spread her arms in exultation.

"That's wonderful!" she said. "An official joint interstellar excavation!"

"Longestlooker," Gerald said, "this is very generous of the Farthings, but it's hardly fair to take over Crimson's project—"

"But, Chancellor," Quickercatcher said politely, "she's already welcomed us."

Fasterdigger said, "We can learn from each other."

Sharphearer added, "She will want to come on one of our excavations, I know."

J.D. felt sorry for Gerald, caught in Crimson's performance. She admired Crimson for throwing herself into it so fully, for having the self-confidence to expose her sculptures to the floodlight of the Four Worlds' technology and experience.

She wondered what it would be like to go on an archaeological excavation to a true alien site.

"Longestlooker," J.D. said, "who's coming to visit us from the Farther worlds? Are they paleontologists? Or artists?"

Longestlooker bared her teeth at J.D., as if trying to smile like a human being.

"Why, J.D., they are paleontologists, to Crimson, but if you like, to you, they will be artists." She lightened the effect of her bared teeth by closing her eyes, outer corners to inner.

"It's a good idea, Chancellor Hemminge," Europa said. "We mustn't take the risk of missing anything—no offense to Crimson, but she's never excavated an alien site before."

"I'm not taking offense," Crimson said. "But I will if

you don't accept what I've been saying: I welcome the Farther worlds' archaeologists."

"Is everything settled?" Androgeos asked. "*Starfarer* will proceed—?"

Someone started to explain to him why *Starfarer* had to stay behind. J.D. retired from the discussion; she and Zev joined Victoria, Satoshi, and Stephen Thomas. Victoria gave J.D. a quick, warm hug, and Stephen Thomas patted her fondly on the shoulder.

"We did it," J.D. said. "Somehow, we did it."

"We sure did," Satoshi said. "*You* did."

"I'm going over to *Nautilus*," J.D. said. She touched Arachne and sent a message through space to Kolya. A moment later his image appeared. Griffith hovered, ghostly, behind him.

"Are you ready to escape from my rock?" J.D. said to Kolya, with an apologetic smile. "I'm truly sorry to have left you there so long."

"I don't mind," Kolya said. "But if you begin classes in *Nautilus*-flying, I'd like to attend."

"I'll keep that in mind, Kolya, thank you."

His gaze shifted: Esther climbed the terraces toward them.

"Hi, Kolya," Esther said.

J.D. heard a note in Esther's voice that she had never perceived before, even when the pilot was talking to Infinity Mendez. Her voice carried tension, anticipation, potential.

Kolya replied with a fond smile. His stripy eyebrows arched, and the smile-lines crinkled around his eyes.

Esther grinned. "Look, I have another diamond."

The emerging diamond shard caught the light and refracted it across her opalescent palm. Moving her hands gingerly, Esther plucked it out of the bandage compound, showed it around, and put the diamond in her pocket.

"I'd be glad to run you over to *Nautilus*, any time," she said.

"I'd like to go now," J.D. said.

"Okay," Esther said without hesitation. "I'll check out the *Chi*. Are you guys ready to come home?" She spoke to Kolya, but included Griffith in her glance.

The *Chi* could fly itself to *Nautilus* and back, but if Esther wanted to return to *Nautilus*, that was fine with J.D. Traveling alone on the *Chi* made her uncomfortable.

Satoshi was gazing at the appealing group of Largerfarthings. Longestlooker reared, rising above all the humans. With serpentine grace, she dropped to all fours again.

"I wonder if she knows," Satoshi said.

"Knows what?" Stephen Thomas said.

"That Crimson's an artist. That the fossils are a performance."

"If she knows," J.D. said, "she's an awfully good actor."

"The Farther worlds wouldn't send a ship all the way across the system," Victoria said, "for an art performance." She hesitated. "Would they?"

"I don't know," J.D. said. "But . . . that would be wonderful, wouldn't it?"

"J.D., J.D.!" The voice came through J.D.'s link, and at the same time something twitched the cuff of her pants.

Late reared up beside her, a third of his body rising from the ground.

J.D. started, then collected herself.

"I must go with you—to pick up the Representative's boat," Late said. "*My* boat. It will be my home. Will you take me along?"

"Yes, I suppose," she said. "But I'm leaving *now*. Sharphearer will have to take you to the dock. I won't wait!"

"J.D., this is most unlike you," Late said, taken aback. "But I will do my best."

Late ruffled away, making a path for himself, pushing people aside with discreet pressure from his spines.

"How long are you going to stay?" Victoria asked. "I want you along on the trip to the Farther worlds."

"I'll be with you," J.D. said. "But I'll be on *Nautilus*." The final decision had not yet been made about how the delegation from *Starfarer* would get to the Farther twin worlds. No matter what they decided, J.D. would accompany them. However fond she was of the Largerfarthings, however much she had come to respect Europa, she would neither let her friends split off from *Starfarer* alone, nor leave *Nautilus* behind.

"All right," Victoria said.

J.D. hugged Victoria, and when they parted both Satoshi and Stephen Thomas embraced J.D. Satoshi kissed her cheek, then held her shoulders wordlessly. J.D. smiled. Stephen Thomas enfolded her and rested his forehead against her shoulder, as he had on the beach the day before.

"Thank you," he said softly.

She drew back from him, as shy about him as ever. "I'm not going away forever," she said.

Her vision sparkling with happiness and sadness and anticipation, J.D. hurried out of the amphitheater.

Thirteen

J.D. headed for the *Chi*. Zev strode along beside her, a bounce in his step.

"How long are we going to be gone?" he said. "What should I bring? Can I leave my suit in the closet?"

They left the amphitheater's access tunnel, moving from cool shade to warm sun. Grass sprouted on the washed-out mud. In a warm and protected place a clump of scarlet tulips nodded softly in the breeze.

"J.D.?" Zev said uncertainly.

"Love, will you stay on *Starfarer* while I go?"

"No! Why?" He stopped. "J.D.!"

She kept going.

He caught up to her. "I'd like to go along."

"You can join me soon. We might all go to the Farther worlds on *Nautilus,* together. But I want some time alone."

He silently, stubbornly, accompanied her up the hill.

"There's nothing *there* yet," she said. "No place to swim, no air—"

"I *know* that," he said stiffly.

She stopped trying to cajole him, stopped trying to make up reasons why he would not want to go.

"When you're with me," J.D. said, "my attention is always partly on you. No matter what else I'm doing, no matter what else I'm thinking about."

Zev grinned, pleased but not yet mollified.

"When I go to *Nautilus*, I won't have any attention to spare. I'll be focused on the knowledge surface. I'll hardly even be in my body. I'll be . . ." She shrugged. "Somewhere else."

"Then you shouldn't be there all alone." Zev's voice was troubled. "What if something happens?"

"Nothing will happen. I was all alone before, and I was farther away."

"A *lot* farther."

On *Nautilus*, after Nemo died, she had been the only aware being in the Sirius system.

"And I was okay."

"I can't change your mind about this, can I?" Zev said.

She held his hand. They climbed the slope, their steps growing longer and more buoyant.

"No."

"I'll miss you," he said, resigned. "Every minute."

"I'll miss you, too. I won't be gone long." She appreciated his maturity, his respect for what she asked of him.

They passed the border between the rotating cylinder and the starship's stationary axis. The last trace of gravity vanished. They pushed off into free-fall.

"Do you think wings would work?" Zev said, as they eeled along from handhold to handhold.

"Hmm?" J.D.'s mind was on *Nautilus*, her attention distracted by a brief narrow touch to the knowledge surface.

"Just small ones." Drifting down the corridor, he drew his right forefinger down the radial side of his left forearm. "Enough to pull you through the air. A few courses of feathers, or maybe another web . . ."

"You could build—"

"I didn't mean build," he said. "I meant grow."

They reached the *Chi*'s dock.

Esther hovered in the hatchway. She turned herself right side up in relation to J.D. and Zev.

"Ready to go?"

"I'm not waiting for—" J.D. did not know what to call Late any more. Was a nickname, however appropriate, proper for a Representative?

"The other passenger's here already. Spacesuit and all. Came up in the elevator."

J.D. laughed. "I said I was in a hurry, but I didn't even think of the elevator." She turned. "Zev . . ."

Esther ducked into the *Chi,* leaving them alone.

J.D. and Zev kissed, long and slow. J.D. broke away reluctantly.

"Goodbye," Zev said. "Swim with sharks, J.D."

J.D. grinned at Zev's use of the divers' blessing for good fortune and excitement. She touched off, leaping toward the *Chi*'s hatch.

After the meeting, Satoshi started putting together a committee to organize the delegation to the Farther worlds. He invited Europa to join them; the alien human accepted.

It would sure make things easier, Stephen Thomas thought, if the Minoans took us to Largerfarther on their ship.

Neither the transport nor the *Chi* had that much range. J.D. could take them on *Nautilus,* but a trip across a star system while living in an expedition tent did not sound like much fun. On the other hand, traveling on the Four Worlds spaceship, with its contingent of Largerfarthings and Smallerfarthings, would be quite an experience.

Crimson pleased Androgeos by inviting him to help prepare for the arrival of the Farther worlds' archae-ologists.

Victoria conferred with Infinity and Jenny Dupre about the stability of *Starfarer*'s ecosystem with relation to its orbit.

"Stephen Thomas."

Professor Thanthavong sat beside him on the terrace.

"You were right," she said.

"What?"

"The dendritic molecules. They're extremely stable."

"My preparations were okay." He retreated from flowering relief, then gave up trying to keep control and laughed with pleasure.

"They were indeed. Mind you, I'm not entirely convinced the molecules carry genetic information—" She held up one hand to stop his protest. "But I am leaning in that direction."

"I have some ideas about what's going on," Stephen Thomas said all in a rush. "What if the squidmoths use stable genetic molecules on purpose?"

She frowned, considering. "That would eliminate their potential for evolution. Would *you* do that?"

"Sure," he said. "I can evolve any way I want." He spread his fingers, stretching the new swimming webs. "And squidmoths have been around a lot longer than we have."

"Of course," Thanthavong said. "Of course! I don't think of them as being technological creatures, but they are. More than we are. They're just so *different*."

"Maybe they don't want to change," he said.

"It is possible."

"Can I come back to the lab now?" he asked. He waited, fighting his nerves, for her to answer. When she hesitated, he defended himself. "I wasn't nuts to think the dendritic molecules might be genetic—"

"That's got nothing to do with it."

"And I didn't screw up the preparations."

"I'm worried about *you*," she said. "Not squidmoth genetics and not the preparations. *You*."

She peered at him closely, narrowing her eyes. Thanthavong was not short-sighted. Stephen Thomas felt like she was trying to see through his skin.

374

"You are more composed than last time we spoke."

"Some things . . . changed," he said. "It's complicated." He made himself go over their last conversation. "I sounded pretty crazy, didn't I?" he said. "I guess I was. It's better now."

"Hmm," Professor Thanthavong said.

A few terraces above, Stephen Thomas's graduate students watched the conversation anxiously. Lehua decided it was safe—or decided to take the risk that it was not—and climbed down the grassy steps. Mitch and Bay trailed in the wake of her energy and her long, fine red hair.

A few paces away, Lehua hesitated.

"Come sit," Professor Thanthavong said.

The students joined them, Lehua crosslegged, intent, Bay lying on his stomach and pillowing his chin on his fists, Mitch sprawling and fidgety, gazing across the amphitheater where Gerald and Fox spoke together, he intensely, she with agitation.

I wonder, Stephen Thomas thought, if Fox knows Gerald's got no biocontrol. He'd tell her, wouldn't he? Someone should warn her, but she'd never believe me.

"Stephen Thomas has some thoughts about squidmoths," Professor Thanthavong said. "About stable genetic molecules."

"It makes sense," Stephen Thomas said, forgetting Fox and the acting chancellor. "If the squidmoths decided not to change, it'd explain why the molecule's so complex. The hypothesis predicts heavy-duty repair enzymes. It predicts that if the molecule *does* change, it won't work at all. Intentional stasis."

"The squidmoths are constructs?" Lehua asked. "Like the Smallernearer?"

"I hadn't thought of that," Stephen Thomas said. "But it's sure possible. Or they engineered themselves. Decided they liked the way they are. Maybe even changed the nature of their own genes."

375

"I wonder how long they've been the same?" Mitch said. "Nemo was a million years old."

"In a few generations, that turns into real time," Bay said, straight-faced.

Stephen Thomas chuckled. They all burst into laughter.

Lehua jumped up. "Let's go to the lab—" She stopped, remembering that Stephen Thomas had been banished. "I'm so sorry," she said. Then she remembered no one was supposed to know he had been banished. "I'll just go try to pull my foot out of my mouth—"

Stephen Thomas turned toward Professor Thanthavong.

"Let's all go to the lab." Thanthavong smiled at him. "Welcome home."

The *Chi* touched the cratered surface of *Nautilus*. The exhaust spread silver-gray dust. As soon as the *Chi* powered down, J.D. jumped out of her couch. Beyond the transparent wall of the observers' circle, a hundred meters across the barren plain, Kolya and Griffith left the expedition tent and loped toward them. J.D. and Esther went to the airlock. Late fluttered behind them, walking on his pincers and the corners of his suit.

While she was putting on her spacesuit, J.D. thought, I've got to find out how to build connectors like Civilization's. Build, or is it grow? It would be much more convenient if the tent could attach its door to the *Chi*'s hatch, like Nemo's webbing did.

Late rippled and slid into the airlock.

"You could let me out while you dress," he said. "I could be on my way to the boat. I needn't bother you any more."

"Could you give me a hand?" Esther asked J.D. "No pun intended." Her bandaged hands were awkward with the fastenings.

"Sure," J.D. said.

"I've been wanting to ask you something," J.D. said to Late, ignoring his suggestion. "Back on the Four Worlds ship, when you introduced me to the Representative . . ."

"That's long past," Late said nervously.

"I heard my voice, and I heard your voice. But I didn't hear his voice."

"You heard . . . my voice."

She waited for more explanation. Late lay like an overlarge rug in the small airlock, his edges lapped up against the walls, fluttering anxiously.

"You heard *me*," he said. "I knew what the Representative wanted. He did not need to expend effort."

"Weird hospitality!" Esther exclaimed.

"Not weird," Late said with dignity, "to us."

"Thanks for telling me the truth," J.D. said.

She fastened Esther's helmet, then put on her own. Late rumpled against one wall to give J.D. and Esther floor space. When they had wedged into the airlock, its cycle began. Kolya and Griffith waited outside the *Chi*.

"Are you all right?" Kolya spoke through the suit radios.

"We're fine, we're on our way," J.D. said. Why didn't he use the link? she wondered, then startled herself by realizing how comfortable she had become with direct communication.

The airlock opened. She stepped onto the ground of her home. *Nautilus* greeted her. She had expected the knowledge surface to feel the same. Instead, proximity gave her an impression of satisfaction, of welcome.

She fell toward her expanded link, stumbled slightly as she forgot about her body, caught herself, and backed off.

Just a little while longer, she thought. A little while longer and I'll be alone, I'll have some peace and quiet.

Late galumphed across the dusty plain toward the Representative's boat. Esther and Kolya embraced, awkward in their spacesuits. Griffith waited at a distance.

"Thank you for your help, Mr. Griffith," J.D. said. "Joining us must have been difficult for you. I'm grateful."

"Yeah," he said uncomfortably. "Well." He shrugged, clenched his fingers, relaxed them. "I mean, thanks."

"Look," Esther said.

Across the plain, Late dove headfirst into the Representative's space boat. Broken bits of precious stone, the remnants of the Representative's shattered leg-tips, tumbled out onto *Nautilus*'s surface. The rear of Late's suit fluttered and flexed.

"Don't do that," J.D. called to him. She loped across the ancient dust. Her curious colleagues followed.

J.D. picked up one of the diamond shards and tossed it into the Representative's boat.

Late threw it out again. J.D. picked it up. Late reared above her, blocking the boat's opening.

"The pieces," he said, "will bounce around and cut me. The edges are very sharp."

"They're valuable. The Representative might want them back."

"He will not," Late said, "want them back. I promise you. Don't make me take them with me, please."

He took the huge diamond. He rotated it, flashing rainbow starlight from its broken edge. "The value," he said, twisting his forward edge toward Esther. "Of the stones. Would the value approach a fair compensation for the hurt we did to you?"

Kolya grasped her arm before she could reply.

"It would *begin* to approach," he said. "But she could not accept it as a complete settlement. She would have to discuss the situation with a lawyer. Her lawyer would have to discuss the situation with . . . whatever your equivalent of a lawyer is."

"A lawyer," Late said, and, at J.D.'s surprised yelp of laughter, added, "We aren't so different after all, I think."

"What do you say?" J.D. stretched her link toward Europa, asking the Minoan's advice. Europa replied with reassurance . . . and amusement.

"It's a beginning," Esther said. "As long as it doesn't obligate *Starfarer* to anything."

"Very well. Late, you may leave the rocks for Esther. In return, I'll transmit your promise." She indicated one of the LTMs clinging to her suit. "Esther's claim against Smallerfarther isn't settled yet."

"I agree." The edges of his spacesuit ruffled as he placed the fist-sized chunk of diamond at Esther's feet. "I am the new elder of my line, and I regret the injury we caused. Please accept all these stones as a token—only a token—of our restitution."

"Thank you," Esther said.

"I must go," Late said.

With no more ceremony, Late inch-wormed into the open boat, flipped the rest of the jewels out of the chamber, and let the boat close around him.

Esther stood, bemused, in the midst of a scatter of precious stones.

Kolya, being practical, pulled a sample bag from the thigh pocket of his spacesuit.

"They'll be easier to pick up now than after the boat's exhaust covers them with dust."

They collected the uncut jewels while the space boat knit its opening. A few spurts of gas, a shower of ice crystals, leaked from it, then it sealed around its developing atmosphere. J.D. imagined Late inside—had he flattened himself to the floor, or was he already metamorphosing into a new and different being, his spines extending to the walls, his body contracting into a ball of brindled fur, eyes appearing—? And what had happened to the Representative, what did he look like now?

379

Esther and Kolya and Griffith boarded the *Chi;* J.D. entered the expedition tent. As soon as everyone was safe, the Smallerfarthing space boat powered up, spurted exhaust, and rose into the sky.

As J.D. took off her spacesuit, Esther projected her image into the tent.

"We'll be off and leave you in peace," she said. "Just give a shout when you want to come home."

"Thanks," J.D. said. She grinned. "I want to see the necklace you make with those stones."

Esther held a chunk of raw diamond against her throat.

"Ugly, huh? But when EarthSpace tells me they've fired my ass, I won't care too much. And if I get arrested, I can hire a lawyer." She grinned ruefully. "Two lawyers. I've never hired a lawyer before, and now I need one in each star system. Is anybody on board a lawyer?"

"I don't think so," J.D. said. "Remember? Gerald said no one was qualified to defend Chancellor Blades."

Victoria, back on *Starfarer,* joined the conversation. Her image constructed itself like a pointillist painting in the expedition tent. "That was a barrister," she said. "What Esther needs here is a solicitor."

"You guys aren't serious, are you?" Esther said. "I mean, I'm not going to *sue* the Four Worlds."

"You don't have to if you don't want to," Infinity Mendez said, projecting his image near Victoria's.

Satoshi joined the conversation. "You could let them sweat about it for a while."

Esther laughed.

"We're on our way," she said. "Bye, J.D. Remember what I said about the starship-flying classes."

Her image faded. Victoria waved, and disappeared; Satoshi did the same. Infinity's image turned translucent.

"Infinity," J.D. said. "How are things—?"

"Still stable." His image steadied. "There's a good

cushion of rock foam above the nest now. I rerouted most of the plumbing—left some water for the kid. We should be okay."

"Thanks."

He disappeared.

Outside, the *Chi* lifted off.

J.D. was alone.

She drank some water, used the bathroom, and settled herself comfortably into one of the two air-foam chairs. Like the furniture in her office, it was too soft and too low for her tastes.

I wonder, she thought, if *Starfarer* could spare one of the silver slugs for a while—No, two of them, a lithoblast and a lithoclast—to build a little rock-foam house and some furniture frames. I'll have to ask Infinity . . . he's been testy, lately, about people borrowing them . . . Can't blame him, they're guarding the chancellor, and the squidmoth, and doing all their regular work, too . . . Maybe when we go home I could buy a pair of silver slugs from EarthSpace.

When we go home. She was assuming that the cosmic string would soon return to the solar system. She was assuming *Starfarer*, and *Nautilus*, would gain complete freedom. She had no proof for the assumptions, yet she believed them.

Everything's going to be all right, J.D. thought, with wonder. It's going to be all right. We'll be able to go home. We'll be able to take the senators back. Ruth will be all right. We can hand Blades over to EarthSpace, and when it comes out what happened, he'll come to justice. With whoever sent him. Whoever caused Feral's death.

J.D. touched the knowledge surface. Its arcs and volumes rose around her like the cliffs and crevasses of an ancient glacier. Victoria's algorithm had integrated itself into the fabric of Nemo's ghost mind. The surface selected transition points, pinpointing the most complex kinks and knots of 61 Cygni's resident cosmic string, solving their equations, seeking destinations farther and farther away.

The pattern of the destinations formed a tear-drop shape. The point aimed toward the center of the Milky Way, as if the knowledge surface sought a deliberate path.

Is it purposeful, J.D. wondered? Or chance, or an artifact of the string? Why would anyone want to go to the center of the Milky Way, where *Nautilus* could never survive?

Nemo had tried to explain where squidmoths came from: the far side of the galaxy, beyond the center, beyond the concealing clouds of dust and star-stuff.

Is the knowledge surface looking for a way to its home? she wondered. The way we always look first for a way back to Earth?

The surface did not answer her question. The pattern could be a coincidence. Besides, the path as yet traversed only a tiny fraction of the distance to the center of the galaxy. At this rate, J.D. would be long dead, *Nautilus* passed on to someone else, through several generations, before the starship could trace a route beyond this arm of the Milky Way.

She turned her attention inward, where the core of *Nautilus* existed as a heavy scent of energy. She found the echoes of Nemo's tunnels, the vessels of Nemo's web: too easy to equate them with the blood vessels of a human being. They were *different*. She found the chamber where Stephen Thomas had watched the attendants struggle and dismember each other in a pool of acid. All that was left now was a crust of crystals, a miasma of sublimating, corrosive oxides, a perception that prickled uncomfortably in her mind.

The chamber where the oxygen-producing creatures grew, where they breathed out gases tinged with hydrocarbons, lay empty and silent.

The air in the tent is clean, J.D. thought, recycled to purity, as flat as the guest water.

She missed the bite of Nemo's atmosphere.

She found Esther's reservoir of water ice spreading frozen tendrils through the starship's body. It contained enough water for a passable small sea. But surface water, without an atmosphere, would boil away into space.

That's going to be my problem, J.D. thought. Keeping enough air for a habitable environment. What does it take to terraform a starship? How much does it cost?

She could not use Earth's credit, built up over the centuries by Europa's efforts. Then both EarthSpace *and* the United States would have a real claim on *Nautilus*.

What about my own work? J.D. thought. I do wonder what the Four Worlds would think of my novel.

On a whim, she sent a copy of the novel's text through her link toward Europa's planetoid.

J.D. widened her perceptions to include *Starfarer*, in orbit around *Nautilus*. She could sense their tenuous bonds of gravity. She expanded her perceptions again to encompass the tiny local constellation of *Starfarer*, *Nautilus*, Europa's starship, the Four Worlds ship. She extended again, taking in the Nearer worlds, once more to include the Farther worlds.

The ship carrying the archaeological party proceeded at a stately pace from Largerfarther toward *Starfarer*.

J.D. opened her perception as far as she could.

A yellow point marked the position of Earth's sun. An ordinary star, it was bright because it was so close.

J.D. could see—could perceive—its planets. Pluto was a dark shadow. The Jovian planets looked like gaudy Christmas tree ornaments, decorated with colored stripes and bright rings and baubles. Mars was cold, silent. Earth, a riot of green and blue and swirling weather patterns, circled grandly by the Moon. Venus twirled, mysterious beneath its veil of clouds, and Mercury hid at the edge of the brightness of the Sun.

J.D. wondered if she was seeing the solar system, or seeing Nemo's memories of it.

If only I'd had more time with Nemo, she thought. If only I'd met 61 Cygni's squidmoth . . .

But Nemo's offspring possessed all Nemo's memories.

Has it calmed down from its tantrum? J.D. thought. If Infinity is right, if it's an adolescent, it's probably got its temper back. Maybe it's even outgrown the rebellion phase.

J.D. tapped into the LTM transmission from the surface of the wild side. The blue-white egg nest lay quiet and still, like a splash of spilled milk. Iridescent veins quivered just beneath the skin of the central bulge.

J.D. extended a tentative greeting.

Instead of backing off or erecting a barrier, the squidmoth larva responded with quiet curiosity.

This is more like it, J.D. thought. More like Nemo . . .

"I'm sorry I upset you before," J.D. said.

"That was my previous instar," the squidmoth said.

"Have you metamorphosed into a juvenile?"

"I have metamorphosed *not* into a juvenile."

"Will you talk to me?"

"Tell me what you want to talk about."

"I was looking at the solar system." She pointed it out. "I can see the planets—or I can see Nemo's memories of them. I don't know which. Can I see so far? Can you see them?"

"I see them as you see them."

"But do you *see* them as they are now, or do you see your memories of them? Did Nemo ever visit Earth's system?"

"I understand the motion of the spheres, so there is no difference between seeing them and remembering them."

"Sure there is," J.D. said. "A human being would need a powerful telescope to see the Sun's planets. Do you?"

"If I wished to see the planets as they are, not as they were, I would travel to the system."

"I *know* I'd be seeing them as they were when their light left the system," she said. "But am I seeing them or seeing your adult parent's memories?"

"Yes."

J.D. sighed, frustrated. As an experiment, she turned her attention to another star, one distant and dim. There, too, she detected the reflected light of planets. Her question remained, for Nemo or one of the ancestors whose memories Nemo possessed might have visited that star system as well.

But it was wonderful to look at distant stars, and see the signs of other worlds.

"You will go to your home system to see your planets," the young squidmoth said.

"No," she said. "I wish we could, but our solar system's still empty of cosmic string. Once we go home, we have to stay. We don't want to leave Civilization." She wished she knew what had happened after *Starfarer* fled. Once *Starfarer* no longer loomed over the Mideast Sweep, had political tensions eased? Or had they tightened, had they broken?

"I'm so worried," she admitted. "About Earth. About my home."

The young squidmoth quaked suddenly in J.D.'s mind.

"Home!" it wailed. "Home!"

It flung her away, wrenching loose their connection. The LTM transmission shuddered. The milk-blue splash of the squidmoth nest darkened against the wild side's skin as its protoplasm rushed to the central bulge. The membrane dried and cracked.

Iridescent veins solidified into cables. The surface thickened and contracted, forcing the protoplasm into the crater, toward the wild side's interior. Hydrostatic pressure surged, smashing stone.

J.D. cried out.

In pure silence, huge cracks opened. Chunks of moon rock shattered. Rock-foam matrix twisted and deformed. The spin flung shards against the inspection web. They bounced from the cables and vanished into space.

"Don't!" J.D. shouted. "Don't, you'll destroy *Starfarer*, you'll destroy yourself!"

"Home!" the squidmoth wailed. "I want to go home!"

Nemo had reproduced in the Sirius system, now empty of cosmic string. *Starfarer* could enter transition and return the squidmoth to Sirius.

But it could never leave, and its ecosystem would not survive.

"I'm sorry!" J.D. said. "We didn't mean to isolate your siblings! We can't take you home, *Starfarer* would die. Please, don't—"

The larval squidmoth wrenched itself in its crater. Broken stone cascaded toward the campus cylinder.

J.D. made a precipitous decision.

"Will you trade your place for a home on *Nautilus?*"

"No!" Europa flared into sudden, intense presence. "If you don't want the ship, give it to me—to us—to the Four Worlds!"

"You want me to live—in my parent's shell!" A wave of agitation and disgust poured from the squidmoth to J.D.'s link. "You want me to live in a grave!"

"You'll live in a grave anyway, if you breach the cylinder!"

"I don't care about *your* grave."

The squidmoth nest passed into darkness. Cut off from the light, the immature being clenched violently, then fell quiet.

Messages poured through Arachne and out to J.D., from J.D. to Arachne and *Starfarer*.

"Victoria! Are you all right? Infinity! Where are you?" She was afraid he might be in the wild side, directly in danger.

"I'm here," Victoria said. "I'm right in my office, I'm all right—but what about you? What happened?"

"I'm with Esther," Infinity said from his house. "The barrier's holding so far. Can you get that guy to hold still?"

"I'm afraid—I'm afraid it's reacting to something I said."

Gerald projected his image into her tent. "Perhaps you'd best stop provoking it!" he said. "This happens each time you approach the creature!"

"You're right," J.D. said, chagrined. "I thought I'd made peace—"

Avvaiyar Prakesh projected her image from the astronomy department.

"Something else has happened," she said, her expression grim. "Something as bad. Worse."

"What?"

J.D. extended herself through the knowledge surface. Before Avvaiyar spoke again, she knew what had happened.

"Oh, no," J.D. whispered.

"The string," Avvaiyar said. "The cosmic string is receding from 61 Cygni."

J.D.'s link fell silent. Gerald remained, his image reflecting his shock.

J.D. struggled with numb disbelief.

Quickercatcher projected his image into her tent. He cuddled with the rest of the quartet in the VIP suite of the U.S. Embassy, startled awake from his midday sleep.

"Why is this happening?" J.D. cried.

"I don't know," Quickercatcher said. Longestlooker's sleek head emerged from the tangle of blankets and pillows.

The Largerfarthing scrambled out of the resting nest. Fasterdigger and Sharphearer stretched languorously. Fasterdigger arched his neck and whispered to Ruth Orazio, who snuggled against his side. As she woke, she pushed her hair back from her face. The bit of red fluff in her hair brushed her cheek.

"The question may be," Longestlooker said, "why it didn't happen before."

Maybe she's right, J.D. thought. Maybe we just outpaced the reaction of the string. And now . . . it's caught up with us.

Longestlooker reared on her hind legs and scanned the room.

"What will you do?" she asked, moving her gaze from J.D., to Gerald, to Ruth. She dropped to all fours again.

"I don't know." J.D.'s voice was uneven with confusion and despair. Zev projected a tendril of his presence to her, sharing her distress, offering comfort.

"J.D.," Gerald said gently. "Victoria. Please believe I feel no satisfaction in saying this . . ."

Maybe he truly did not, but this vindicated him. He had been right all along. If they had turned back as soon as they reached Tau Ceti, as soon as the alien museum self-destructed, no one would have died and the cosmic string would not have cut itself off from any system. J.D. would never have met Nemo, but Nemo's offspring would all be free, instead of trapped in the Sirius system, lost in transition, or ensnared in a psychotic episode on an alien starship.

"We have no choice, now," Gerald said. "For our own good, for the Four Worlds, for Civilization . . . we must go home."

"There must be something else we can do—some other choice—!" J.D. appealed to Quickercatcher. "Tell us the truth, tell us the truth, Civilization *must* know how to control the string, tell us what we have to do!"

"I can't," Quickercatcher said, raising his chin, exposing his throat with regret. "I tell you as I would tell my siblings, no one knows how to change what's happening."

Infinity appeared again, looking grim.

"J.D., we're in bad trouble on the wild side."

J.D. opened her link completely—the physical world vanished—and gathered all the information she could grasp straight into her mind. Arachne's neural traffic. The young squidmoth's angry mutterings. Avvaiyar's report on the string. The cracks in the wild side's skin hurt like wounds in her own body.

Transmissions—perceptible but not comprehensible—flashed among the Four Worlds spaceships, the Four Worlds themselves.

J.D. called to Orchestra, to the Smallernearer, but neither had any comfort. Orchestra offered sympathy, and a calm disinterest in the workings of the string. The Smallernearer feared the loss of interstellar communication, the loss of contact with the distant sibling it had created.

The Smallerfarthings and the Largerfarthings were part of Civilization. When they imagined being cut off from it, they fell toward panic. Even Late, metamorphosing, climbed blearily above his fugue to react to the crisis.

"Can *you* help?" J.D. asked. "Don't your people know these secrets?"

"We know what the Largerfarthings know," he replied.

"That's an ambiguous reply, at best," J.D. said. "I'd like to talk to the Eldest."

"That's impossible!"

Even Longestlooker reacted with shock to that proposal.

"We aren't lying to you, J.D.," she said. "I wish you'd believe that."

"You won't believe me when I tell you the truth!" J.D. said. "Maybe your superiors know something you don't. Maybe Late's superior knows. I want to talk to him—direct!"

"That's impossible," Late said again.

"Why do you keep saying that?"

"We do not know our achievements," Late said. "He's gone."

"Gone? *Dead?*"

"Gone into rapture, with the Eldest."

J.D. opened her eyes. Instead of clearing, her vision blurred. Tears filled her eyes and rolled down her face. She wiped them away on her sleeve.

"Victoria," J.D. whispered.

Victoria touched J.D.'s link. Satoshi and Stephen Thomas joined the conversation.

"If we stay, we'll be stranded, and the Four Worlds with us," Victoria said. "We *can* risk another system. We'd be putting off the inevitable, but at least we'd be putting it off."

"And maybe destroying our ecosystem," Infinity said.

Satoshi spoke grimly. "*Starfarer* depends on both cylinders. If the wild side disintegrates, it'll tear up the sail. The spin on this side will go wonky. We'll have to evacuate. Unless we're back home, we haven't got anyplace to evacuate *to.*"

"How can you do this to us?" J.D. said to the immature squidmoth. "Your parent was my friend."

The being responded with an incoherent shriek and another shudder that quaked the wild side.

"J.D.—!" Infinity protested.

She drew back, rejected and hurt.

Nemo's *gone*, she said to herself. If you keep denying that, you're going to destroy your other friends.

"We have to go home," Victoria said.

"I know," J.D. replied softly.

It was simple; it was obvious. Gerald was right. They had no choice.

"You could stay," Stephen Thomas said.

"What?"

"On *Nautilus. You* could stay. You could be part of Civilization. Like Europa and Andro."

"No!" Zev said, distressed. "Stay here all by herself?"

J.D. hesitated. *Nautilus* gave her freedom. If the string was reacting to *Starfarer* itself, she could safely stay behind.

If she wanted this freedom, she could go anywhere she wanted, except back to Earth. Except home.

"I . . ." She was tired of saying, I don't know.

"J.D.?" Zev said, quiet and intense.

"I have to think for a while, Zev," she said. "I love you."

J.D. drew away from Zev, as gently but as quickly as she could, a whirlpool of grief annihilating her elation. Rudely, desperately, she cut off everyone who was trying to talk to her. Gerald's image disappeared, and Infinity's, and the colorful group of Largerfarthings.

What difference does it make what I think, or what I want? J.D. thought. It doesn't matter anymore, we have no choice.

She could not understand how everything that had been going so well had reversed so suddenly and so completely.

She burst into tears. All alone, she cried.

Chandra was a little drunk. She sipped at a crystal snifter, then took a deep swallow, drinking far too quickly for good brandy. She would have a hell of a hangover in the morning. At least being drunk helped her forget the surge of pleasure and joy she had felt when Sharphearer touched her. She had nearly drowned in it, nearly surrendered to it.

She never surrendered to pleasure. The price was too high. There was always a price, always hidden, always too high.

"I'll drink me a drunk worth recording," she said to her empty living room. "There's nothing else worth my time on this damned rock." *Starfarer* was boring. They would not let her join the alien contact department. They let Zev, and he was not even a member of the expedition. "Maybe I should sleep with somebody in alien contact," she muttered. "Maybe that would work."

Arachne signaled her and displayed an image a handsbreadth above the thick wool carpet. The image whirled around her without moving, she was that drunk. Chandra almost sent it away. Arachne was supposed to signal to her if anything anomalous happened, but so far the computer had sent her nothing but weird tangled twists of its mind. Nothing she could record or use.

"Stupid damned computer." She looked at the image to prove it was useless.

The wild side spun from shadow into the bright light of 61 Cygni. The immature squidmoth soaked in the brightness, moved in response to it, clenched and shuddered. The wild side quaked under the being's convulsions.

Chandra brought the violent image closer, enlarged it, wrapped it around herself. Sober—feeling sober—she pushed through the woven light and out the carved wooden door, leaving it open behind her.

A bright spot burned in the back of J.D.'s mind with the pressure of her waiting messages. She let them form, voices and moving images floating around her: her colleagues in alien contact, Zev more and more agitated as her silence lengthened, the quartet bidding Crimson farewell, accepting her gift of a block of stone full of alien sculptures.

A new message arrived: Jenny Dupre, floating in the transparent zero-g chamber of the sailhouse. J.D. accepted it in real-time.

Easier to talk to an acquaintance, just now, she thought. Easier than talking to a friend. Or a lover.

She thought better of her decision as soon as Jenny spoke.

"We have a bad problem," Jenny said.

"Just one?" J.D.'s voice was high and tense.

The schematic told the story. The string was receding fast. Too fast for *Starfarer*'s sail to take the starship to it.

"They want us gone very badly," Jenny said.

Or, J.D. thought, someone wants us stuck here.

"You're going to have to be careful," Jenny said. She traced a line across the schematic, showing J.D. where the stresses on the starship would be least.

She assumed J.D. would use *Nautilus*, and its gravity, to tow *Starfarer* into transition.

It's a fair assumption, J.D. thought. What else would I do, what else *could* I do? Another decision taken out of my hands.

She urged *Nautilus* toward the transition point, changing the starship's path gradually so gravity would pull *Starfarer* with it. So *Nautilus* would not rip itself away to freedom.

The Nearer worlds fell behind.

Europa took Victoria's hand. "Goodbye," she said. "I am so sorry." She pressed her smooth cheek to Victoria's, held her for a moment, then drew away. Her motion, in the zero-g docking room, made them drift apart. "Perhaps—"

"Don't—!"

"Don't say we'll see you again," Stephen Thomas said. "We all know that isn't going to happen." He stretched out his hand to Victoria; she grasped it and brought herself to a stop.

"Very well," Europa said.

"Come home with us," Victoria said suddenly. "Come back to Earth."

"That's absurd," Androgeos said, holding the slab of alien sculptures to his chest. The plaster that protected it made dull white smears on his silk-smooth skin.

"I've thought of it," Europa said. "It tempts me."

"Europa!" Andro said.

"My dear," she said, "you were so young when we left.

393

You don't remember what it's like to be with your own kind. It's all right, I envy you your ease with our hosts. But . . . I don't entirely share it."

"Will they . . . let you keep your home now?"

"Oh yes," Europa said sadly. "They are very kind to their clients. But I had hoped . . . to become a full citizen."

"It almost happened," Victoria said. "Next time, we'll know more. We'll be accepted."

"In a hundred years," Stephen Thomas said.

"We'd better go," Androgeos said.

"You won't come with us, eh?" Victoria said to Europa.

"No. I have my place here, my job. I've done well for my home world in the past, I'll do well in the future." She smiled slightly. "I may even modify my opinion of symphonic music."

"We could do even better—" Andro said.

"—with my algorithm. I know. It's too bad, Andro, but that's something Civilization is going to have to come and get."

"You are admirably consistent," he said. He glanced impatiently around. "Where's Quickercatcher, where's the quartet? We must leave soon." His eyes went out of focus for a moment as he spoke through his link to the Largerfarthings.

"And where are my meerkats?" Europa said.

Infinity Mendez's image appeared.

"They're forming a commune in my closet," he said. "I don't think they'll let you move the new kits."

"You will have to take care of them for me," Europa said.

Infinity let his image fade out.

"Here we come, we're coming!" Quickercatcher's musical voice trilled from the hall. He and his siblings burst into the waiting room, a tangle of legs, arms, tails, colorful fur. Fasterdigger floated with his arms stretched straight up, holding Ruth Orazio's hands, drawing her through free-fall with him.

"We must go," Europa said.

"We have decided," Longestlooker said, "to stay."

"Stay?" Androgeos said, baffled.

"On *Starfarer*," Longestlooker said.

"With the human people," Quickercatcher said.

"No!" Androgeos released the block of fossils. It drifted and tumbled as he kicked off from the wall and sailed toward the quartet. "No, if you go, I'll never see you again, you'll die in exile!"

Stephen Thomas caught the block and wrestled with its inertia, bringing the stone and plaster block to a halt before it did any damage.

Andro bumped into Sharphearer, grasped her around the neck, pushed her and her siblings into a spin. The quartet snuffled with amusement and fondness.

"Hey, be careful!" Ruth Orazio released Fasterdigger's hands and drifted toward the wall, out of Andro's way.

"Androgeos, sweet friend, you and Europa wish to stay in Civilization, as Earth's representatives," Sharphearer said.

"And that is admirable," Longestlooker said.

"But someone—someone from Civilization—must represent us to Earth," Quickercatcher said.

Androgeos buried his face against Sharphearer's fur. The Largerfarthing stroked his glossy hair and gently nuzzled his neck.

"It will be all right," Sharphearer said. "You'll be all right."

"Of course I'll be all right!" Andro said angrily. He drew back from Sharphearer, his face wet with tears, a few strands of Sharphearer's fur stuck to his cheeks. "It's you I'm worried about. *You!* It's too dangerous! The squidmoth spawn is going to destroy the whole place!"

"Even a squidmoth," Longestlooker said, "wouldn't be so foolish as to destroy its own habitat."

"What will you eat?" Androgeos said. "And—"

"Cotton candy," Fasterdigger said, and trilled.

Androgeos glared at him, resenting the joke. "—Where will you sleep, who will you *talk* to?"

"Shh, shh," Sharphearer said.

"May we bring our resting nest to your dock?" Longestlooker asked Victoria. "It will sustain us, until we change to accommodate your food."

"May we go with you?" Quickercatcher asked. "We are willing—but you must welcome us."

"I welcome you," Victoria said, overwhelmed. "Of course I welcome you!"

All around, the images of other people formed, echoing Victoria's welcome.

"I think I can promise," Ruth said, "that you'll be welcomed back on Earth, too. Welcomed with gratitude."

The gravity of *Nautilus* held *Starfarer* in a stately array that approached the cosmic string. J.D. extended herself through the knowledge surface, trying to observe from such a distance that the anomalies and dangers disappeared. She failed. She was constantly aware of the frantic cries and struggles of the young squidmoth. It broke her heart. She should be able to calm it, but she knew she would only agitate it again.

The silver slugs congregated above it, filling in the cracks of its thrashing. At Infinity Mendez's instruction, they also cut around the squidmoth nest. They left it attached to a lozenge of stone, as if isolating a tumor. As a last resort, Infinity would break the egg nest free and let it tumble into space.

"I don't want to do this," he said to J.D. "I don't want to hurt the dumb kid. And we could end up with just as much damage. But it might turn out to be our only hope."

"How did this happen?" J.D. said. "Our choices were unlimited . . . and now we don't have any left."

"I don't know," Infinity said sadly. "J.D. . . . can you accelerate faster?"

She touched the knowledge surface. *Nautilus* already was accelerating toward a knot of cosmic string—toward the place in space where its motion, and *Starfarer*'s, intersected. Then J.D. would have to do some careful and stressful maneuvering to suit Victoria's algorithm.

"I can," she said. "A little more." It surprised her to discover that *Nautilus* did have limits. "But . . ." She showed him the schematic, the vectors, the numbers, for the maneuvers they would have to make at transition point.

"No," he said. "Forget it. That's too much stress."

Infinity sat in his garden, deep in a communications fugue. Esther paced on the porch, feeling useless. Whenever she went inside, Europa's meerkats chittered at her, warning her away from the naked, squirming kits.

She was tempted to take the ferry over to the wild side and try to talk some sense into the squidmoth, but if J.D. could not make it listen, how could she? Besides, Infinity had asked everyone to stay on campus. The wild side was too dangerous.

She looked at her hands. The bandage compound continued to work the diamond fibers out of her palms. One bit glittered at the surface of the organic bandage. She picked the shard out, put the diamond in a little hinged box, and slipped the box back into her pocket.

Her hands no longer hurt. She clenched her fingers. The job of diamond fibers into flesh had faded.

That's a relief, she thought. I'll be of more use if we have to evacuate, if we all have to cram on board the transport and the *Chi*—and the Largerfarthings' resting nest?—to survive. But if that happens in transition, and we separate from *Starfarer* . . . we'll never get out.

Chandra made her way across the inspection web, stepping gingerly on the lines. She moved from one support strut to the next, pausing at each to recover from dizziness. She held tight to her lifeline, sliding it along its overhead track.

Near the squidmoth, she spotted all the LTMs. They focused closely on the egg nest. She stayed out of view. No one cared if she got any good stuff out of this stupid expedition. If they thought she was in danger—as if she had not put herself in danger a hundred times before, so they could have their cheap safe thrills—they would probably come out and get her.

She needed the danger; she needed to wipe away the temptation to return to the Largerfarthings and fling herself into their midst.

The web shuddered beneath her feet. All her nerves throbbing, she clenched her hands around the web supports and opened herself to the quake, to the terror.

Victoria wondered if she and Stephen Thomas should leave, to give the Minoans and the quartet privacy for their goodbyes. Only a few moments remained, or the alien humans would be stranded.

Androgeos embraced each member of the quartet. They trilled and nuzzled him. As Europa hugged Longestlooker and stroked her deep black fur, Andro broke away from Sharphearer, bolted for the hatch, and disappeared.

He did not even stop for the fossils.

Stephen Thomas watched him go, shrugged, grinned, and took the fossil block through the hatchway and into the boat's tunnel.

"Can't let Crimson lose her exhibition," he said.

As Stephen Thomas vanished, Gerald arrived.

"Europa . . ." Gerald said.

"I can't stay any longer," Europa said.

"But you *will* work for our reinstatement," Gerald said.

"I've been working on Earth's behalf for four millennia!" Europa cried. "That's a hard habit to break, Gerald, even if I wished to. But I swear to you, there isn't any person, any establishment, with the ability to judge Earth's case."

"Tell them," Gerald said, "tell everyone, about the algorithm. And remind them that the longer we work on it—the better it becomes—the more power we'll have when we're finally let out of exile."

Europa narrowed her eyes, startled by his vehemence.

"Don't use my work to threaten Civilization!" Victoria said, equally shocked.

"There's no threat, only observation. Your algorithm means wealth and power to Earth, as soon as we can use it freely. When we return, we'll have considerable effect on the structure of Civilization."

Distressed, Europa pushed off toward her boat. Victoria touched her briefly as she floated by.

"I wish . . ." she said.

"Yes," Europa said, as she disappeared. "I wish, too."

Stephen Thomas returned from stowing the fossils. The hatch closed.

"That was inexcusable," Victoria said to Gerald. "Now they'll be certain we're violent barbarians!"

"I made no threat," Gerald said again, as calm as a well-fed shark.

The Largerfarthings huddled together. Longestlooker opened her mouth and closed her jaws with a sharp *snap*. Sharphearer ducked her chin, and raised it again thoughtfully.

Are they having second thoughts? Victoria wondered. I'm having some second thoughts of my own.

"Look," Stephen Thomas said.

Arachne created a puddle of light in the center of the room. Europa's boat fell away from *Starfarer*'s axis and accelerated toward the miniature world of her starship.

The Four Worlds ship emitted a space boat, larger,

more convoluted, more mechanical, than the boat of the Representative.

"That is ours," Longestlooker said.

"Our support while we visit you," said Quickercatcher. They both sounded quite calm.

Victoria gave Stephen Thomas a grateful glance. He had defused the tension, without even knowing its source.

The Largerfarthings' boat scudded to the axis of *Starfarer,* entered a dock, and fastened its umbilical tunnel to the hatch.

"You're welcome to stay in the embassy as long as you like," Ruth Orazio said to the quartet. "I enjoy having you as my guests."

Fasterdigger clasped her hand gently. "We enjoy being your guests."

Starfarer plunged toward transition.

Are we going to make it? J.D. wondered. The cosmic string was only a few minutes away, but it was accelerating. *Nautilus* still closed in on it, but even *Nautilus* had limits, and *Starfarer* had limits to its strength.

The young squidmoth cried incoherently in J.D.'s mind. She gasped, huddled deeper into the soft chair, and shivered.

Zev projected his image into the tent.

"I want to be with you," he said. "This way, if not for real. Don't send me away, J.D., please, not again."

"I won't," she said. "I'm sorry if I hurt you, love. I wish I'd let you stay."

He grinned. "Maybe I shouldn't have said, 'Swim with sharks.' "

J.D. laughed.

"Can I help?" he asked.

"Yes. Just by being here."

He moved closer. J.D. imagined that the warmth of his body emanated from the cool image at her side.

Gerald had gone—probably to tell Chancellor Blades everything that had happened, Victoria thought angrily. Not that Blades could do anything about it. Still . . .

The quartet took Ruth Orazio into their resting nest to show her around. Victoria and Stephen Thomas remained alone in quiet zero g.

They drifted closer, touched, embraced.

"You've got a right to be pissed off," Stephen Thomas said when she told him what had happened.

"He's got a bloody nerve," she said.

"But we knew that already," Stephen Thomas said. "Eh?"

Victoria laughed, shakily.

"Hey." Stephen Thomas hugged her, opened his hand, stroked his webbed fingers across her short curly hair. "Longestlooker's right. Everything's going to be okay."

"I wish I could *do* something," she said. "I feel so damned helpless."

In the sailhouse, Satoshi felt less helpless but more frustrated. He had spent the last hours working with Jenny Dupre. They struggled futilely with some arrangement of sail and starship that would keep the young squidmoth shaded and lethargic.

Every possibility they projected put far too much tension on the starship's abused structure.

"It's useless," Jenny said to Satoshi.

They had no more time. Transition approached. The sail had to be furled before *Starfarer* reached the cosmic string.

Deep in a communications fugue, Jenny stretched herself far out into the sail lines and contracted them, as easily as she would draw her hands to her chest.

The sail shimmered, folded, spiraled into a slender silver rope.

Satoshi detached himself from Arachne and followed Jenny out of the fugue.

"We might as well have taken a sail patch to the wild side," she said in disgust, "and covered the squidmoth over like a blanket."

"Hmm," Satoshi said thoughtfully. "Not over, under."

"Ah. I've never been on the outside of the cylinder, I always forget that the stone isn't the ground. It's the sky."

"Everybody forgets, when they haven't been out for a while." Satoshi knit his eyebrows, imagining the mechanics of her suggestion. "Your idea could have worked, if the kid weren't throwing rocks."

Each time the young squidmoth wrenched itself in its crater, more chunks of *Starfarer*'s skin exploded downward, ricocheting from the inspection web, flying off into space or toward the campus cylinder.

What's going to happen, Satoshi thought, if it starts throwing bigger pieces?

J.D. gazed fondly at Zev's image as *Nautilus* plunged toward transition point. The gravity of *Nautilus* drew *Starfarer* along.

She was tempted to stay behind. She faced the reasons against it: few supplies, no assurance that Europa would help her if she remained. No assurance that the Four Worlds would keep their connection to the cosmic string—and if they did not, she would feel responsible.

If she stayed, she would be cut off from her friends until and unless the cosmic string returned to Earth, or until the isolation defeated her and she joined *Starfarer* in its exile.

And the reasons for returning: If *Nautilus* accompanied *Starfarer*, her starship would be one more thing of value sequestered in the solar system.

If someone in Civilization does have control over the string, J.D. thought, would this be enough to make them rescind our exile? *Nautilus*, and Victoria's algorithm, and the lure of the fossils they think are so old?

If I go home, she thought, I'll be stranded. In an empty star system, *Nautilus* is like a racehorse attached to a farm wagon.

She had no illusions that EarthSpace would provision her or help her terraform *Nautilus*, unless she ceded them her rights.

What difference does it make? she said to herself. I'll probably be dead before the string returns. In a hundred years, nothing will matter to me anymore.

It seemed to J.D. that the drawbacks and the advantages—too many of one, too few of the other—of either course balanced each other out. The only unbalanced factor in the equation was Zev.

She could lead *Starfarer* to the transition point, overshoot the point with *Nautilus*, and leave *Starfarer* in position to return home.

But she could not have the perfect freedom of *Nautilus*, and Zev as well.

Crimson poked through the gravel on the riverbank, upstream from the Fighters' fossil site.

She was glad the quartet had decided to stay. She thought at least one of their reasons was her fossils, her performance. She liked digging with the Largerfarthings, and she wished she had been able to go on the real alien excavation.

"Some other century, maybe," she said aloud.

Arachne's observations of the young squidmoth whispered in the back of her mind. She ignored them, refusing to spend the next few hours in fruitless worry.

A pale, jagged, anomalous shard of rock stood out stark against the dark rounded pebbles. Crimson pounced on it, grabbed it, and shouted with pleasure.

A strangely articulated appendage lay perfectly preserved in the stone.

Once she had found the first bit of sandstone, the rest visually jumped out at her. This was the ruin of her second fossil bed, the site that had been wrecked in the flood. She thought of this site as the final resting place of the other ones, the creatures she had created by de-evolving Nemo.

She found the remains of the slab, tumbled up against the cliff, out of context, its provenance damaged, but the fossils nearly complete.

She wondered what Quickercatcher would say when he saw this dig.

A tangle glowed in J.D.'s mind, traced out by the knowledge surface and Victoria's algorithm.

The algorithm filled a chasm in the knowledge surface with its bright sharp peaks and spirals, blending its edges in multiple dimensions. It pointed the way home.

Starfarer dragged behind her, tethered to *Nautilus* by the tenuous bonds of gravity. The young squidmoth had fallen quiet, gathering itself for another tantrum. The lithoblasts struggled to repair the damage it had done; the lithoclasts ate away beneath its nest, preparing to cut it free.

But if Nemo's offspring were cast loose in transition, it would die.

If it was not cast loose, *Starfarer* might be lost.

Europa's planetoid fell behind, spinning slowly.

"Stay, J.D.," Europa said through her link. "You can—"

The transition point blossomed before J.D. She opened her eyes. She pulled away from the knowledge surface just long enough to feel the stiffness of her body, long enough to see Zev, gazing at her, wondering, waiting.

She squeezed her eyes shut. *Nautilus* surrounded her again, and together they plunged through space.

She still had time to change her course, to pass around the eye of transition.

• • •

Victoria and Stephen Thomas floated through the transparent tunnel leading to the sailhouse.

Victoria had been anxious to view transition as intimately as she could. But she was distracted, worried. Gerald Hemminge's words weighed on her mind. She hated to think that their farewell to Civilization was a threat.

Stephen Thomas squeezed her hand. Her fingertips rested against the warm silk of his swimming webs. They entered the sailhouse, where Satoshi and Jenny drifted among the stars.

"There's nothing more to do," Satoshi said. "Only wait, and hope."

"There's one thing . . ." Victoria said.

"Goodbye, Europa," J.D. said. "Goodbye, Androgeos. Take care of Alzena. I'm . . ."

She let her message trail off. Her eyes stung and she was tired of apologizing.

Nautilus brushed through the knot of cosmic string and plunged out of existence.

All J.D.'s perceptions of the Four Worlds vanished, cut off by the boundary between normal space and transition.

The knowledge surface resonated. J.D. was all alone, more alone than she had ever been before. She listened, she watched.

The buzz and hum of energy echoed in her ears. Energy and gravity sparked and cried and spun.

Other starships pass, she said to herself. Other ships from Civilization, coming from other destinations. Will I see them?

Victoria finished explaining.

Stephen Thomas laughed. "Gerald will have a heart attack."

Victoria protested. "This is serious!"

"Sure it is. Gerald will still have a heart attack."

"That shouldn't affect my decision." Then she giggled. "And it won't. Not much, anyway."

"It's right," Satoshi said.

"It is," Stephen Thomas said.

Victoria let her eyelids flutter, sending a message through Arachne toward J.D.

J.D. did not respond.

"Look," Satoshi said.

A great gentle glow of rainbow light washed over them: the transition spectrum.

Nautilus had vanished.

Victoria caught her breath. It scared her to think of J.D. all alone in a place that Victoria could not fully explain or describe.

"That's us, in a few more minutes," Jenny said. "If you're going to make a decision, you're going to have to make it soon."

"What do you think?" Victoria asked. She wanted the opinion of someone outside her family.

"I agree," Jenny said. "I agree with Satoshi and Stephen Thomas. Otherwise your work will end up with people like Blades, like the people who tried to kill us, who killed Feral."

Victoria made her decision. She *had* already made it, but she was glad to have support and confirmation.

She touched Arachne. Opening Arachne to the Four Worlds, Victoria released her transition algorithm to Europa and Androgeos, to the Farther worlds and the Nearer ones, to Civilization.

"No!" Gerald shouted, his disembodied voice echoing through Arachne's transmissions.

Victoria winced. At the same time, joy rushed toward her from Quickercatcher and his siblings. They dove, entranced, into the complexity of Arachne.

"How could you?" Gerald cried. "All your work, gone!

You're a traitor to Earth, a traitor to your own kind!"

Europa's voice whispered beneath Gerald's anger.

"Thank you, Victoria," she said softly. "Oh, my dear, thank you."

Victoria had no time to answer.

Starfarer plunged into transition.

At the moment of change, the young squidmoth erupted into a frenzy.

Rock pelted Chandra. A chunk ripped away, carrying her lifeline attachment. The lifeline dropped past her feet and hung beneath her, useless. Chandra clung tight to the web supports. If she fell, she would be flung out into transition forever and no one would ever find her.

Her enhanced nerves throbbed and pulsed; blood engorged the veins that nourished them. She wished she could take off her spacesuit and expose herself to transition raw, naked.

More stones pelted her, clanking and bouncing from her helmet and her suit.

Above her, the young squidmoth thrashed and groaned, transmitting exultation and pain. The milk-white cover of its nest, dried in a pattern like frost on a window, cracked and flaked and fell away. Chips of glass and shards of stone showered down. The broken crust revealed a ropy, leathery brown hide, twisting, pulsing, nothing at all like Nemo's delicate iridescent scales.

Beyond the edge of the egg nest, a silver slug pressed itself down from a deep crack in the skin. Chandra expected it to spew rock foam into the crack to fill and stabilize it. Instead, it pressed its snout into the end of the crack, spewed thick solvent onto the broken rock, and slurped up the remains before they boiled away into the vacuum. The crack widened.

The slug was not a smooth-coated silver lithoblast, but a silver-moiré lithoclast.

Chandra watched, enchanted by terror.

The lithoclast was cutting the squidmoth loose.

And Chandra along with it.

"J.D. is going to kill me," Infinity said, "if I send Nemo's kid off into transition."

"If you don't," Esther said grimly, "*Starfarer* will come out of transition in pieces."

"Yeah." He tried to see better what was going on, but several of the LTMs had been knocked loose and lost. He had only an incomplete picture of the squidmoth nest.

Overcoming the lithoclasts' resistance, Infinity urged the silver slugs to cut *Starfarer*'s skin faster than the lithoblasts could repair it.

Starfarer appeared in transition, chasing *Nautilus* through the strange multidimensional space. J.D. observed it through the knowledge surface, but could not reach *Starfarer* directly through her link to Arachne.

She brought herself closer, anxious about her friends. The starship was whole, its cylinders spinning evenly.

The squidmoth nest rotated into view.

It had created a crater worse, more damaging, than the crash of the nuclear missile. Silver slugs ringed it, eating at the stone, undercutting the nest, struggling to eject the squidmoth youth from the wild side.

"Oh, no," J.D. whispered. "Oh, no, please . . ."

But *Starfarer* had no choice.

The young squidmoth struggled in its nest, flinging itself back and forth in a panic. The egg nest had peeled away, revealing the being itself. Its ropy skin clenched and spasmed. A long and multiply articulated appendage stretched down from its center.

All Nemo's incarnations, from juvenile through chrysalis to winged adult, had been beautiful. The offspring, to J.D.'s eyes, was ugly. As it spun out of sight, she tried to make herself see it as beautiful. She failed.

As it spun out of view, she noticed the spacesuited figure standing beneath it.

Stephen Thomas floated in the sailhouse, his body as relaxed as if he had been in the sea. Victoria and Satoshi and Jenny Dupre drifted nearby.

While they were distracted by transition, he let himself settle into Arachne. He had tried to persuade himself that his partners were safe, that the computer could not be hunting them.

But he was frightened by their vulnerability, terrified by the danger.

He opened himself to Arachne.

Chandra stretched herself upward, trying to reach the squidmoth. Its leg, its antenna, whatever it was, flailed wildly. She ducked. It knocked against her, scraping the fabric of her suit, leaving a deep scuff.

She flattened herself against one of the web supports, holding tight, drawing in every sensation, savoring the terror . . .

"Infinity, look!" Esther said, incredulous.

A person stood beneath the writhing alien being as it humped its back and struggled in its crater. Another articulated limb unfolded from the convolutions of the body, caught itself into a tense arch, and whipped against the inspection web. The cable snapped. The thick wire sprang apart, coiling and twisting.

"Get out of there!" Infinity shouted, out loud and into Arachne. "Who the hell is it?"

"It's Chandra, of course," Esther said. "Who else would it be?"

"What's she *doing*?"

"Showing up J.D.?" Esther said. "Trying to get the critter to leave, when J.D. couldn't?"

"Trying to get herself killed, is more like it."

"Or collecting something unique?"

"There's nothing we can *do*," Infinity said. "There's no time to get out there and drag her off—" His eyelids flickered and he vanished into a communications fugue. Esther joined him. Arachne was slow and sluggish, all its capacity focussed on transition. Esther saw what Infinity was doing. She took control of a second lithoblast and urged it over the crevasse.

The squidmoth crater spun into J.D.'s view. The being had twisted more of its body into sight.

Its back humped again. One gnarled end slowly pulled free. It reached through the broken cable, probing blindly, purposefully, with the articulated antenna. It stretched and arched, drawn outward, downward, by the force of the cylinder's spin. Two upside-down silver slugs crawled toward it, toward the person clinging below it.

J.D. did not know what to hope for. That the squidmoth would free itself before Infinity Mendez had to cut dangerously deep into the cylinder to expel it, or that it would stay where it was, hang on, and come out of transition safely with *Starfarer*. But she could not see the end of their course yet, the spot that would lead the starships back into the solar system.

Maybe I could catch it, she thought. Wait for it to come free, and offer it sanctuary on *Nautilus*. Maybe it would spend some time in a grave . . . to save its own life.

Arachne focussed intently on *Starfarer*, on keeping it stable through transition, working to compensate for the struggles of the squidmoth.

Stephen Thomas waited, and watched.

A malevolent presence rewarded his patience.

• • •

The squidmoth wrenched itself a final time, cracking rock and web supports, knocking Chandra against the cables. She held desperately to the wires. Transition blossomed around her. The squidmoth screamed and cried. Chandra could not tell what sensations came to her through vibration, what came through her link, what came through the suit radio; she could not even distinguish those sensations from what she saw. The nerve clusters covering her body took it all in, gulping the experience like water.

The squidmoth arched its body, whipped its head and antennae back and forth, and exploded free of the wild side.

The squidmoth flung itself free. It tumbled away from *Starfarer*, twisting and spinning, a cross between a giant leech and a grasshopper, a horrible creature.

J.D. slowed *Nautilus*, determined to do her best to save the being no matter how she felt about it.

The squidmoth stretched itself, engaged itself with the fabric of transition, and slowed its rapid tumble.

It sailed toward her, immense and terrifying, the most alien presence she had ever experienced.

It carried Victoria's transition algorithm like a newborn child.

J.D. gasped.

And then the other squidmoths streamed toward her.

Many were juveniles, like Nemo, riding the starships they had inherited from the other ones. Others were larval, like those J.D. had left behind in the system of their birth—she touched the knowledge surface and found that the cosmic string had returned to Sirius. Perhaps some of the larvae *were* Nemo's offspring.

They collected around the wild side squidmoth like a swarm, one after another freeing itself from its starship and clustering together. J.D. lost count as the hundreds passed to the thousands. The mass grew until it exceeded the length of *Starfarer*. The wild side squidmoth, and Victoria's algorithm, vanished into the center of the roiling melee.

Nautilus fell abruptly out of transition.

Stephen Thomas watched in awe as a malignant presence reassembled from Arachne's fabric. It patterned itself on a carcinogenic blueprint that similarly self-assembled from individually banal subsections. It fascinated Stephen Thomas even as it repelled him. It was an extraordinary creation, twisted toward the service of evil, no longer under the control of any intelligence.

It forayed past the connected nodes of Victoria and Satoshi, blindly seeking the connections Stephen Thomas had severed. Lost, it wandered toward Satoshi's node.

Stephen Thomas shouted at it, distracted it with a probe of anger, prepared himself to fight it.

Without turning, without even moving, it reoriented itself.

It snatched him by the throat.

Infinity pushed the slug to its limits, crawled it down the shuddering web struts, slid it around and beneath the web itself, and slipped under Chandra where she lay clutching the wires. Esther's slug approached from the minus-spin side, giving the artist a surface to lean against. Chandra's breath labored against Infinity's slug. The lithoblast curled its edges around the cables, securing itself. If it lost its grip, it would fall away into space. It might take Chandra with it.

"It's all right," Infinity said to Chandra. "It's all right, let's move back to solid ground." The squidmoth nest hung suspended from the wild side cylinder by a few arches of rock foam. He freed the other lithoblasts from their inhibitions. They moved toward the crevasse to fill it in.

• • •

J.D. gasped at the abrupt change.

Nautilus moved peacefully into the solar system, a system empty of any connection to Civilization.

J.D. started to cry.

She huddled in the soft chair. In her home system, she was more alone than she had ever been before.

The last thing she wanted to do was send a message to Earth. But she sought the planet out. She had subconsciously feared that *Starfarer*'s departure might have precipitated war, though *Starfarer*'s presence in orbit had been a major point of contention.

She found Earth spinning as peacefully as *Nautilus*, no storms of nuclear dust streaking its white swirls of cloud, no patches of biochemical warfare blighting its surface.

She wiped her eyes. If no one had been watching for her transition spectrum, it would be a while before anyone would notice she had returned. She would wait, wait for *Starfarer*, and all together they would try to explain what had happened. She was desperately grateful for the quartet's decision to return with them. Now that the young squidmoth had fled, the quartet was *Starfarer*'s only physical proof that alien beings existed.

A wash of rainbow light burst over her.

Starfarer dropped out of transition and into normal space.

Zev threw his image instantly into the expedition tent.

"Are you all right?" he asked. "Did you see what happened?"

"Yes," she said. "But I don't understand it."

Victoria followed Zev, her image forming nearby. "We made it," she said.

"Not by much," Satoshi said. "A close call."

"What about Chandra?"

The artist's voice expanded around her. "I'm right

here," she said, aggressive and self-confident. "I got stuff no one else could ever get!"

J.D. laughed with relief, with disbelief.

Simultaneously relieved by their safe transition and depressed by their forced return to Earth, Victoria touched Satoshi's wrist, and stroked her hand down Stephen Thomas's arm.

His whole body was rigid.

"Stephen Thomas!"

She cried out to him, directly through her link.

Victoria's distress drew J.D. into Arachne. Zev rushed in behind her. J.D. followed her link to the gnarled and poisonous clump that immobilized Stephen Thomas. He struggled vainly, trapped, his strength nearly exhausted. Victoria and Satoshi rushed to help him—they did not look like themselves, but their neural nodes concentrated their personalities; they were unmistakable. Victoria glowed with energy and anger; Satoshi was calmer, a burnished presence of strength.

Tendrils of the computer tumor stretched toward Victoria's node, toward Satoshi's.

"He's protecting us," Satoshi said. "He was right . . ."

"Who asked him to protect us—to risk himself—all alone—!"

J.D. struggled to approach him, but the carcinoma whipped out savagely with sticky, burning tentacles.

J.D. felt a curious and unfamiliar presence. The quartet appeared, trailing knowledge from their first exploration of Arachne.

Quickercatcher laid his chin on J.D.'s shoulder and gazed at the malignancy.

"We don't know our way around yet," Quickercatcher said softly, "but that does not look right."

"Stephen Thomas is in trouble," J.D. said. She lunged forward and grabbed one of the twisting tentacles of the carcinoma. It slashed at her fingers. A rush of pain jolted up her arm. She held on desperately. Victoria plunged down beside her and thrust both hands deep into the grotesque mass.

She gasped. Satoshi was right beside her, pushing into the entrapping medusa. Zev jumped in, letting the medusa grab him, then kicking at it with his clawed feet, using its own strength against it.

Quickercatcher bounded forward, snapping at the medusa with sharp teeth, stabbing with his clawed front feet. His siblings leaped into the fray, teasing and misdirecting the attention of the medusa. J.D. ripped tendrils away from Stephen Thomas's arms. Victoria dragged desperately at one that encircled his chest and squeezed the air from his lungs. Satoshi wrestled with twisted whips of fiber, yanking them away from his partner's throat. Stephen Thomas gasped for breath; he struggled to escape tendrils that tried to penetrate his flesh.

Longestlooker snapped one free, and Fasterdigger crunched one between sharp teeth. Sharphearer dove to the center of the medusa and bit at a bright bit of light. J.D. followed, and ripped the connecting nerve free.

The medusa contracted, protecting itself, pumping energy to repair its damage. It shrieked with rage, trying to frighten them away.

It relinquished its hold on Stephen Thomas and scuttled toward J.D., toward Quickercatcher, seeking escape.

"We've got to stop it," J.D. said. "Otherwise it'll spread—"

"Do what Infinity did with the chancellor's house," Zev said. "Only prettier. Turn it into a pearl."

Infinity's slugs had laid rock foam over the house in which Chancellor Blades had taken refuge.

J.D. set Arachne to covering over the medusa and its blueprint, enclosing them before they could disassemble into harmless, invisible parts. In her mind, J.D. imagined a layer like mother-of-pearl covering the malignancy, encapsulating it, another layer—not outside, but inside—putting more pressure on it, squeezing its life.

The medusa moaned.

"That is very clever," Quickercatcher said.

"Very pretty," said Sharphearer.

"It is more fun," Fasterdigger said, his usual diffidence replaced by bright excitement, "to rip it into tiny pieces."

"They'd all grow into new ones."

"Oh, good!" Sharphearer said.

"There's not much interesting prey," Longestlooker explained, "on board the Four Worlds ship."

The surface of the pearl increased in depth, intensified in luster, as Arachne created layer after layer, moving inward.

Arachne squeezed the tumor to nothingness.

In the sailhouse, Stephen Thomas shuddered and gasped for breath, opened his eyes, and clutched at Victoria and Satoshi.

"Jesus," he whispered when he could speak again, "Jesus god, I've never been so scared in my life. Are you all right, did you—"

"We're fine," Satoshi said. "You're okay. It's going to be okay."

Exhausted, J.D. embraced Zev, embraced the quartet. Within Arachne, she could hug all five people at the same time.

J.D. twined her link with Zev's.

"Even better than a shark," Zev said.

J.D. laughed shakily.

Back in the expedition tent, J.D. trembled with exhaustion. She pushed herself to her feet. Even in the low gravity her knees felt weak. She touched the knowledge surface, comforted by its solidity.

At that moment, the swarm of squidmoths fell out of transition.

The mass roiled and quaked as larval squidmoths like

leeches with long spindly legs, and juvenile squidmoths like hermit crabs dragged from their shells, their abdomens naked and ugly, crawled over and under each other, each seeking to reach the center.

Victoria's transition algorithm reflected through the mass, the only thing of beauty about it.

"Human people have helped us," the squidmoths said.

The squidmoths' collective voice reminded J.D. of Nemo. Her perception of their ugliness receded.

J.D. drew a deep breath. "How did we help you?"

The composite being displayed a map of the Milky Way. No dust clouds obscured any part of the beautiful, massive spiral.

"We have explored for a long time," the being said, "watching and learning and knowing until the time approached for us to return home. But we had come too far. We did not have enough time to span the distance."

"You needed Victoria's algorithm," J.D. said.

"It had to exist," the metasquidmoth said, "but it was necessary for us to wait for someone to imagine it."

"Welcome to our solar system," J.D. said. "I'm sorry you'll have to wait so long before you can continue on your journey—but maybe a hundred years—even five hundred—isn't very long for you." The squidmoths were so old, and they had been effectively exiled too; perhaps they would not mind waiting for the string to return.

"It's time, now, for us to return home, to evolve once more."

"Damn!" Stephen Thomas said in triumph. "I was right, you don't evolve—unless you choose to!"

"We choose to evolve," the metasquidmoth agreed.

"Why did you follow us?" Victoria asked. "You're stranded now!"

"We were stranded before—before you—on this side of the galaxy. Thanks to human people, thanks to you, we are free."

A transition spectrum, a brilliant, powerful rainbow flux, illuminated the knowledge surface, flared from the solar mirrors of *Starfarer*, scintillated through the wavery plastic window of the expedition tent.

A single being fell out of transition, glowing with light and energy; the new squidmoth plunged into the swarm and disappeared, drawing with it a great tangled skein of cosmic string.

Quivering within the knots of string, poised on the edge of transition, the metasquidmoth turned its attention to J.D.

"Will you come with us?"

Nemo's friendship echoed in its voice.

"I . . . How far are you going? How long is your journey?"

"We must travel . . . perhaps a thousand years, perhaps ten thousand. A short trip."

J.D. laughed. A short trip—only in relation to a million millennia!

"I'm sorry," she said. "I can't, I don't live that long, thank you, but I couldn't leave my friends for that long."

"Goodbye."

The metasquidmoth vanished.

Speechless, J.D. stared into the transition rainbow.

The cosmic string remained.

The solar system, J.D. thought, is full of cosmic string!

"J.D.!" Quickercatcher exclaimed. The quartet trilled with surprise and happiness.

"Fuck it, we're free!" Stephen Thomas shouted.

The exile's lifted, J.D. thought. Or . . . is it? Was there any exile, or did the squidmoths—the other ones—plan it all this way?

"Now what?" Victoria said, a little shaky.

"We have a lot to face," Satoshi said, "now that we've come home."

Victoria chuckled wryly.

"A lot of things I don't want to face," J.D. said.

Like giving up *Nautilus* to EarthSpace, she thought.

She thought back to the gathering of squidmoths, each leaving a starship behind to spin off into transition, like jewels washing out of a riverbank.

She wondered if she could find the starships again.

"Now we know where the other ones leave their starships," J.D. said.

She spoke to Zev, to Victoria and Stephen Thomas and Satoshi; she included Esther and Infinity and Kolya.

"What would you say to a prospecting expedition?"

About the Author

VONDA N. MCINTYRE has been writing and publishing science fiction since she was 20. Her novels include **Dreamsnake** (winner of the Hugo Award, presented at the World Science Fiction Convention, and the Nebula Award, presented by the Science Fiction Writers of America), **The Exile Waiting**, and **Superluminal**. She has written one children's book, **Barbary**. Her books and short stories have been translated into more than a dozen languages. The *Starfarers* series includes the national bestsellers **Starfarers, Transition, Metaphase** and **Nautilus**, a series that has the distinction of having had a fan club before the first novel was even written. She is also the author of Bantam's next *Star Wars* novel, **The Crystal Star**.